THE BOYS

A Novel by
PARMAN REYNOLDS

Black Rose Writing | Texas

ISBN: 978-1-68513-176-0
PUBLISHED BY BLACK ROSE WRITING
www.blackrosewriting.com

Printed in the United States of America
Suggested Retail Price (SRP) $21.95

The Boys is printed in Byington

*As a planet-friendly publisher, Black Rose Writing does its best to eliminate unnecessary waste to reduce paper usage and energy costs, while never compromising the reading experience. As a result, the final word count vs. page count may not meet common expectations.

OTHER TITLES FROM
PARMAN REYNOLDS

In 1980s East Texas, Luther Holman, a local janitor, awaits trial for the murder of a prominent local, the same man potentially responsible for the murder of Luther's young daughter, Summer.

Unexpected help arrives with a new legal aid attorney, who replaces the pliable local defender. As the trial opens, the certainty of Luther's conviction crumbles as the capable defense attorney exposes the state's falsified and contrived evidence. Determined that Luther will be convicted, the sheriff uses intimidation, physical abuse and threats directed at Luther's mother and wife to try and force a confession.

In the midst of the trial, the sheriff's worried secretary becomes aware that an earlier murder conviction rested on similar shady dealings. To find out what really happened to her dead friend, she dives into her own investigation of the earlier case, but soon realizes she must rely on a newcomer with a murky past to uncover the truth.

As the sheriff ratchets up the pressure on Luther, other citizens in the county are confronted by law enforcement's continued endemic corruption. With the trial's expected outcome constantly shifting, the conflicting aims of all of the parties combine to produce an unexpected climax.

THE BOYS

1

James and Finch hugged the far corner of David's living room, letting the walls close in against them and provide space from the rest of the sorrowful souls. Each mourner offered sighs and shakes of the head while professing an ardent desire to provide vague but potentially valuable sustenance to the grieving widow, who clung to her now-fatherless child as if any momentary lapse of contact would signal his own imminent loss. Despite her efforts, the namesake son maneuvered out of his mother's grasp and headed down the hall, away from the grieving adults. Along the way, he motioned to an older girl to join him. The two children disappeared into the boy's bedroom and remained there.

Finch's eyes roved the ordinary room fitted into an ordinary house set in an ordinary suburban neighborhood. For most people, this place would have been a stepping stone for greater things, a short-term stop for building equity while planning for something better. David had loved the house, including all of its shortcomings. He told Finch once that it was the only place he had ever lived that made him, if only temporarily, feel normal.

This somber day marked the two men's formal goodbye to their long-time friend. James and Finch had each known David since middle school, and both had worked to save him from a terrible life at the hands of his dissolute father. James assumed, as did everyone else, that David had died a hero's death, a sacrifice proclaimed on the local news as a singularly brave, selfless act. Finch, who knew David more intimately than anyone, entertained a more complicated version of this public fable. But Finch protected the legacy of his dead friend, letting everyone else believe the official version of David's demise, if for no other reason than to bring comfort to his family. It would also let Finch put some needed emotional distance between himself and the grieving widow and left-behind son.

The two men looked impossibly different. James, the tall, successful investment advisor, sported his usual expensive dark suit, white shirt and discrete tie, all worn with an easy confidence that expressed a serene acceptance of his place in the hierarchy of local society. Finch's garb included his worn, and only, sport coat. Respected and loved by his clients for his gentle manner and attention to their needs, James retained a stable of loyal clients. He came today with Jeanette, his pretty blonde wife, flanked by their two overachiever kids. Finch, alone as always, lived a bohemian yet unartistic and solitary life, stripped of family constraints, steady female companionship, or likely much in the way of assets. At this point in his life, James secretly envied Finch's freedom and lack of worry about paying for everything that James' family needed to maintain their lifestyle. But there was little point in James revealing his feelings to his childhood friend. Finch was indifferent, if not impervious, to almost all forms of praise or condemnation, so the opinions of others regarding his own personal value, or lack thereof, were meaningless.

As the low conversations rumbled through the room, producing a background noise that was both unintelligible and annoying in its own way, James and Finch balanced their punch cups and plastic dishes containing the remnants of Finch's mother's celebrated chocolate coconut cake, and plotted their revenge. Across from them, David's wastrel shit of a father slouched on the couch, alone, looking bored and uneasy. Few of the visitors even knew who he was. The old man was a drunk and furious chain smoker, unrepentant of his enormous sins. So far, he had escaped the endpoint of his destructive life. He was, James had surmised before, too fucking mean to die. The two of them watched the old man, each of them subsumed with their own thoughts of the bastard's demise.

After gulping punch from his cup, the old man coughed up some of the red liquid as it ran down the valleys of his stubbled chin and stained his shirt. He then gagged. A few nearby mourners glanced in his direction while silently pleading, please, God, let someone else take care of this. Most, hoping that the situation would resolve itself, ignored the distressing noises. With some effort, the old man flung his head back to clear his airway, coughed a few more times with descending ferocity, then settled back as his face returned to its familiar grimace. Secretly relieved, the audience returned to their interrupted conversations. After attempting to use the tiny napkin to sop up the punch on his chin and shirt, the old man soon abandoned the effort.

"After this is over," James whispered, "let's go by his house, ask to talk to him, offer to reminisce about David. Once inside, one of us will hold him down while the other puts a pillow over his face until he suffocates. We'll arrange him on the sofa, like he died in his sleep, maybe drop a lit cigarette on the couch for effect. I figure a state-funded autopsy for cause of death is unlikely. By the time the smell alerts the neighbors, I doubt they'll be able to tell what actually happened."

Mentally rehearsing the option, Finch raised the small plastic plate and forked the last bit of cake into his mouth. He chewed for a bit before swallowing. A slow shake of his head revealed his decision. "I can see you've given this some thought. But that's too quick. He needs to suffer. How 'bout we gag him, blow his fucking nuts off, and watch him bleed out?"

James took his own time considering Finch's alternative. It didn't occur to him to ask if Finch had the stated means to kill the old man. He assumed it was a given.

"Well," he eventually said, "we'd need to be careful about being seen and heard, make it look like maybe a robbery gone bad. We could take a few things, mess up the house like we were looking for something."

"Yeah," said Finch, "No problem. Let's do that."

"I wasn't kidding, Finchie," James said.

"Neither was I."

James glared at the old man. "We'll give it a week, maybe two, let this all simmer down. Then we'll kill him."

Finch took a sip of the punch cup reclaimed from the edge of the plate. "Looking forward to it, buddy."

2

David lingered at the perimeter of the cluster of men, only partially listening to the escalating conversation. He had grown quite tired of the heated debate now reaching the pinnacle of macho bullshit. Each of them, except David, were spinning tales of increasing confidence about their work successes and rising importance to their various companies. Steely, unblinking stares with narrowed eyes comprised unspoken offers for further verbal battle. Aggressive looks were met with either eye rolls or, alternately, sideways glances if the recipient was successfully intimidated. David preferred they just get it over with—take out their dicks and wag them around and agree on who had the biggest one. When eventually questioned about his own contribution to his company's welfare, he begged off, saying he needed to take a leak.

Leaving the puffed-out chests behind, David headed for the hall bathroom. The locked door stopped him, so he waited, feet out, his back flat against the opposite wall, figuring this solitary option was demonstrably superior to rejoining the party. Eventually, a woman emerged, looking sheepish for occupying the place for so long. She ducked her head as a quick smile crossed her face. The whispered apology faded into the air as she headed back to the living room and the party. David entered and locked the door, feeling for the first time this evening like he was comfortable, happily alone and away from the tumult. The bathroom, like the rest of the apartment, was both striking and familiar. His hosts both had well-paying jobs and loved their new three-bedroom condo near the top of a recently constructed downtown high-rise. This place was immense compared to David's cramped one-bedroom apartment several blocks away. Still, he loved living near the vibrant nightlife, great restaurants, and public transportation. The extra cost, compared to something larger and further out from the city center, was well worth it to him.

After finishing peeing, David washed his hands and surveyed his face in the mirror. Early thirties, nice enough looking, a good job, but so far unattached. That's the only reason he kept getting invited to this type of affair. Once certain people figured out that, no, he wasn't gay, they were determined to find him a woman to settle down with. So far, that had produced no favorable results. All of those previous deadends suited David just fine. After wiping his hands on the towel, he considered slipping out the front door and into the elevator, then disappearing into the dark night. But that would be rude. He loved and admired his hosts and wouldn't offend them, ever. The appropriate thing was to stay and thank Max and Ja'Neel. He owed them that much, and more.

David headed back into the fray, angling for the owners of the apartment. Max was in an animated conversation with some financial guy who pretended to know, absolutely, which direction the stock market would head next. All he needed was investors to prove his system a success. Ja'Neel, immersed in a frowning conversation with a clutch of women, was likewise engaged. David expected the talk concerned the spilling of infidelity secrets, at least based on the facial expressions. Neither host seemed immediately approachable, so David stopped by the bar for another drink, then approached the hors d'oeuvres table, where he grabbed a dessert plate and loaded on a few petit fours. Settling on one end of a loveseat, the only vacant place left in the living room, he took his time, consuming the drink and food, surveying the crowd and waiting patiently for a break in the action so he could make his apologies and leave.

A woman flinging herself down next to him interrupted David's reverie. Clad in a tight red dress, she looked about his age. After crossing her thin legs and adjusting her hem, she sat silently and stared straight ahead, either unaware of his presence or, alternately, completely disinterested in him. An odd attitude, he thought, considering how physically close we are. But good news, too. He wasn't in any mood to strike up a vapid, pointless conversation so close to heading out. Perhaps her feet hurt because of those tall heels and she simply needed a break from standing, and thus had no interest in starting up a conversation. Attractive but distracted, he concluded after a surreptitious second glance to his side. Continuing on with his drink and appetizers, he patiently waited to see what would happen next. The woman carried her own drink with a cocktail napkin thrust under it, which she settled into the recess of her lap, then crossed her arms over her chest.

After a bit, while still looking out into the room and not at him, she said, "Why are all men such worthless fucks?"

Maybe the remark was rhetorical. Maybe she was skipping the preliminaries, getting right to the point. Regardless of what prompted the complete denunciation of males, he felt obliged to reply. "Maybe men aren't all fucks. Just the ones you pick."

She turned to him, a scowl furrowing her forehead. "You saying I make shitty choices?"

"I'm only offering a potential answer to your query."

Leaning forward, almost toppling the drink, she grasped her exposed knee with the intertwined fingers of both hands before she spoke again. The woman had dark hair, cut square at her shoulders, and dark eyes, too, all prominent against her pale skin. She turned again to address him.

"I'd expect a comment like that from a man," she said. "It's always the woman's fault, never yours."

David considered her professed certainty about male turpitude. "What I'm saying is lots of couples somehow find each other and seem to be reasonably happy. I refuse to believe that most women are satisfied with being married to, or companions with, worthless fucks."

"Says you," she said, scanning the room once more. "Maybe all women are unhappy and you're too ignorant to know any better."

"Perhaps," he said, while formulating a reason to leave the sofa.

"So, which one is yours?" she said.

"Which one?"

She nodded toward the crowded room. "Which one of these women, or men, belongs with you?"

"None, I'm happy to say."

"Then why're you here?"

"You'll have to ask the hosts." He stood up. "Maybe they made a poor choice as well." He glanced down at the woman. "Well, this worthless fuck is ready to go home. I hope you can someday find a man that measures up to your standards."

She glared at him. "I'm in a bad mood."

"No doubt. Enjoy the rest of the evening." With that comment, he headed for the party's hostess, as her group's gossip session appeared to wane. Ja'Neel spied him angling for a word and broke away.

"Hey, David, are you having a good time?"

"Sure," he lied, smiling back at her.

Ja'Neel was a real sweetheart, nothing like the ballbuster he had just talked to. He remembered the first time he saw her. He and Max were sitting in the university library, working on a history project presentation due the next day. Immersed in a discussion about how to present their research, Max looked up and spied Ja'Neel, sitting there with her friends, across the room. His startled expression betrayed the instant attraction. Max, by nature shy if he didn't know you well, immediately went over to talk with her, telling her how beautiful he thought she was, and asked if it would be possible to have her phone number. To the surprise of her friends, Ja'Neel agreed. After Max returned to his table, he called her to make sure the number was good, and asked would it be alright if maybe they could talk later, and if not, please let him know. She said, yes, of course she'd given him her real number, and that she'd be available, say, after seven that evening. For the rest of their planning session, Max was worthless, drinking in his new obsession from afar. Ja'Neel would catch his eye, from time to time, and give him a demur smile. David had to finish the project by himself.

David hooked his arm around Ja'Neel's waist, giving her an affectionate squeeze and a quick kiss on the cheek. He whispered, "You ever get tired of that weird guy you're married to, you give me a call."

She laughed, showing a perfect row of white teeth that contrasted with her dark skin, and hugged him back. "When he throws me out, you'll be the first one I call." Her tone turned serious, her dark brown eyes shading to black as she turned to scan his face. "Did you meet anyone tonight, David? Anyone you liked?"

"Stop trying to set me up."

"Someone needs to."

Max disentangled himself from the hustler and appeared at Ja'Neel's shoulder. "Trying to steal my wife again, I see. Hands off, buddy boy."

"Not that you deserve her," David said, grinning.

"You're so right." Max bent down and kissed Ja'Neel, then beamed at her as his arm also wound around her waist. "Hey," he said, "you've got another man's arm around you."

She smiled. "Easy, boys. There's room enough for two."

Max, tall and resplendent with auburn hair and a hint of freckles, appeared to be the opposite of his petite Black wife, but whatever the chemistry was between them, it was long lasting. Even after two years of living together as a prelude to ten years of marriage, they were still crazy about each other, a fact obvious to everyone who knew them.

David winked at Max. Time to start their routine. When they had her between them, their mock battle goal was to make her laugh, despite her repeated refusal to do so. The effort only ended when she inadvertently gave in, even if it meant whispering salacious things in her ears.

"Let go," David said. "I was here first."

"Not like you'd know what to do with her."

"Whatever I'd do, it would be better than she gets from you."

As the exchange continued on, Ja'Neel tried without success to stifle a laugh. Having finally lost, she stamped her foot. "You two!"

David and Max exchanged a palm smack.

Ja'Neel turned to Max, genuine concern showing in her voice. "I asked David if he met anyone he liked. He won't tell me anything. Make him talk to me."

"Well?" Max said. "You heard the lady. Spill it."

"You know me, not in the market. Thanks for the invite, though." He gestured toward the sofa woman, who was getting up. "Who's that?"

"Iris," Ja'Neel said. "Did you meet her?"

"Not really. She sat down beside me and asked why all men are worthless fucks."

Ja'Neel scowled, and Max raised an eyebrow. Neither one seemed surprised by the revelation.

"She's had a difficult breakup recently," Ja'Neel said. "I asked her to come tonight, see if maybe that would help get her out of her funk. You should cut her a little slack."

"Guess that explains it," David said, giving Ja'Neel a final squeeze, then grabbed Max's outstretched hand. "Thanks for the invite, guys. Nice party. Really."

Ja'Neel's eyes followed him with that worried-mother look, as if tonight's unfinished business could be a confirmation of future failure. "I'm going to find someone for you, David. I mean it."

"Night." David waved back at them over his shoulder as he left to collect his coat.

In the guest bedroom, he selected his own from the pile of coats and started putting it on. Iris entered the room, ignoring him again, then pawed through the stack until she found hers. He stood there for a moment, turning down his collar and pulling at his shirt cuffs, watching her, curious about the upcoming actions of such an unhappy woman. She was trying to fit herself into the coat, but in her hurry, she was poking her arms in all the wrong places, repeatedly missing the openings.

"Damn, shit, fuck." She held up the coat in frustration. "Could you at least help me on with this?"

He took her coat without comment and spread it out behind her. She turned and dropped her arms into the sleeve pockets. He set the coat onto her thin shoulders as she went about working up the front buttons.

Finished, she turned to face him. "Thanks."

"See," he said, "maybe we aren't all as bad as you think." Something about her grouchy attitude made him want to pull her to him and give her a big kiss, then see if she slapped his face. He resisted. "Walk you out?"

A suppressed glare crossed her face, but she relented. "Okay."

They rode down the elevator in silence until Iris broke the quiet, turning to him, another petulant look on her face. "And why is it that when men say things to hurt a woman, they use the most demeaning, sexually perverted language?"

He considered not replying, but said, "I wouldn't do that."

"Really?" she said, looking completely skeptical. "Even if you were totally pissed?"

David shrugged. "All I can say is I don't treat women like that."

She turned back to face the doors and didn't reply.

Out on the sidewalk, David said, "I didn't bring a car tonight. I live a few blocks from here, so I walked instead. Sorry, but I can't give you a lift home."

"I don't own a car," she said. "I always use ride share."

He pulled out his phone while she put on her gloves. "Give me your address, and I'll call you a ride."

Smirking, she said, "Oh, so you can find out where I live?"

He sighed, ready for this uncomfortable association to end. "I thought you could use a break, is all. Never mind. Well, goodnight."

As he turned to walk away, she grabbed for his coat sleeve. "Look, I'm sorry for being such a bitch. You're David, right? I'm Iris. Could we maybe go someplace quiet and have some coffee?"

3

Iris looked up, under her eyebrows, at David across from her. He slowly stirred his coffee, marking time. Bored, likely, but nice enough to not make excuses, then leave her there by herself.

"You must think I'm a miserable person," she said, restarting the conversation.

His head popped up, a suppressed acknowledgment conveyed by the slight tug of a smile. "Well, based on what you've said to me so far, that seems to fit."

"I'm having trouble getting over a terrible relationship."

"That's what Ja'Neel told me," he said, glancing down at his coffee. "Those can be difficult."

"It was abusive. I should have left before I did, but I stayed. I keep blaming myself—"

"*Stop it!*" he said, his intensity startling her. "The *victim* doesn't need to blame themself. *Listen* to me..." He reached out and unexpectedly grabbed her hand. "It's very, very important that you forgive yourself. Do you *understand* me?"

She stared down at his hand, shocked by his reaction. Lifting her eyes again, she saw an intense, raw look on his face. Then, without further comment, he withdrew his hand as his countenance settled back to its former impassiveness, as if the reproach had never happened.

"Okay," she said. "I'll try."

"Good."

She watched him stir some more. Picking up her own spoon, Iris started the same routine with her own coffee. The black liquid, paler now from the cream she'd added, moved in a slow revolve within the white porcelain. She wondered why all restaurant coffee cups looked the same. There must be a giant factory somewhere spitting out billions of these things. She should try to think of something funny, maybe inspirational, to say back at him, but nothing came to her.

"It takes time," he finally said.

"A century or so should be enough."

His quiet chuckle made her smile, despite her reservations.

"I was thinking before. . ." he began.

"About what?"

"When you were putting on your coat back at the apartment, I thought about kissing you."

"Why didn't you?'

Her answer surprised him. "I thought you'd slap my face."

She assessed his answer. "Maybe I would've. I don't know. It could have gone the other way."

"You mean that you might have liked it?"

"Yes."

"Well, you know, there's the problem with a man taking advantage of a vulnerable woman. A rebound thing she'd likely regret."

"You think I'm vulnerable?" she said.

"I'd say so."

As the halting conversation continued, both of them trying to feel out the other, unsure of where this was all headed, they eventually fell into an easy dialogue. Likely, she decided, David simply felt sorry for her and didn't want to seem callous by refusing her invitation for coffee.

Propping her chin on an upturned palm, she said, "Thanks for coming to coffee with me. You didn't have to do that. I. . .I needed to get out of there."

"Why?"

"It tires me out, the pressure to socialize. It's like if you don't go through the motions, you aren't wanted."

"I don't feel that way. Pressure, that is," David said. "Sometimes I like to sit by myself and see what other people are up to. Watch them work the room, you know? I was doing that when you sat down next to me. There's a certain satisfaction in knowing you aren't expected to be the star of the evening."

"It's different for women. If we aren't smiling and laughing, being pleasant, we must be a cold bitch, undesirable."

"You think so?"

"Most people do."

"You sure?"

"No. But that's how I see it."

The server arrived to refill their cups, but Iris waved her off, having already had enough coffee for the night. David did likewise. Iris felt at loose ends, the Saturday evening winding down like a deflated balloon, her helpless to stop the leak.

"I guess we should go," she said. "But I need to use the restroom first."

"Sure," he said, reaching for the check.

"I'll get that," she said, grabbing for the slip. "I asked you, remember?"

He let go and watched as she dropped her debit card on top of the table.

"Be back in a minute." Iris headed for the rear of the restaurant.

When she returned, the receipt was lying on the countertop. David slid out of the booth. Iris scooped up her card and put it in the purse already slung over her shoulder. They walked out together, his hand maybe on her back, a gentle touch that she imagined more than felt.

Standing on the sidewalk, they scanned the street for a taxi. Despite the constant pedestrian traffic, nothing looked promising. He pulled out his phone and opened an app.

"Okay if I get you a ride this time? What's your address?" he said.

She gave it to him. After entering the information, the app said a car would be by in a few minutes.

"Well," David said, "Guess this is it. Thanks for the coffee."

"You're welcome. Thanks for coming with me. I'm. . .I'm glad you did."

"I'll wait," he said, looking down at her, directly in her face. "Make sure the car shows up. I don't want you out here alone this late at night."

She felt something move inside of her. "I could use that kiss," she blurted out.

Standing there on the sidewalk adjacent to the busy street, they pressed their mouths together, oblivious to the people snaking around them. When they broke free, she realized she was grasping his coat lapels with both hands. She let go and pressed the fabric down.

"Hope I didn't wrinkle your coat," she said, trying to control her breathing, working hard to smooth it out.

"It's fine," he said, still looking at her. "We could maybe share the ride. Go somewhere else together. If you wanted."

She looked up at him, her mouth open, but no sound came out.

"What does the 'E' stand for? Your middle name?" He added, "I saw it on your card. Iris E. Duncan."

"Emily."

"Iris Emily. Nice."

"My parents liked the classic names," she added, not knowing what else to say.

After a pause, he said, "How about my place?"

She needed to hesitate giving her answer, thinking how it might sound if she immediately agreed. Instead, she rushed out, "Yes, I'd like that very much."

• • • • • • •

Partway through the sex, as his hands pushed into her waist, he said, "Hey, hey, slow down, Iris. Easy."

She was on top, straddling him, churning away, and found the remark particularly insulting. She stopped moving and glared at him. "You don't like how I do this?"

"All I'm saying is why don't you take your time? This isn't a contest."

She leaned forward, feeling his cock pop out of her, then rolled over onto her back next to him. If they hadn't been in the middle of his double bed, she would scoot over to the farthest edge; instead, forced to lie next to him, she felt trapped. Fixing her eyes on the ceiling, she concluded that this embarrassing disaster would be a fitting end to the evening. Not entirely unexpected, now that she thought about it.

"Sorry I don't fuck the way you like," she said.

He moved closer. "I didn't say that. I mean, what's the hurry?"

Turning his remark over in her head, Iris felt pissed and hurt at the same time. Sure, she had eagerly agreed to have sex with him and assumed she was giving him what he expected and wanted. After all, that's how Curtis insisted on things, fast and hard, shoving his big cock inside her with a fierce determination to prove his manhood. Curtis, that complete piece of shit. They always fucked like mad and fell apart, spent, when finished. Invariably, she was glad when it was over. Parts of it she really hated, the way he went on and on like a piston, measuring his prowess by how long he could keep at it. One time she caught him, eyes closed, lips moving, counting the fervent strokes. The worst of it was when he was in one of his sadistic moods, squeezing her tits until she wanted to cry out, or grabbing her by the throat and choking her. She went along, mostly without complaint, because she wanted to please him, make him like her, but even that effort wasn't enough in the end.

The last time, she was down on all fours while he delivered his machine gun style of sex. That was bearable until he wound his fingers into her hair and pulled her head way back, hurting her neck. She asked him to let go, please stop. Instead, he started slapping her ass with his free hand until it stung so much that she cried out for him to quit. With that, he wrenched one of her hands behind her back and pushed her face into the bed. When he finally finished, she collapsed into the crumpled sheets with a gush of sobs. The fuck's the matter with you, he yelled, you know you like it rough? Not receiving a coherent string of words trying to bubble out through her choking, halting reply, he cursed her, slapped her butt hard one more time, then pulled on his clothes and stalked off to the bar down the street, but not before haranguing her again for her bad behavior.

Iris knew that when Curtis returned, he would be even angrier, plus being drunk. If he wasn't too far gone, he would force her to have sex again; otherwise, he would end up falling down in the hall and pissing himself after he passed out. That was when she realized it had to be over. After gingerly pulling on her underwear, the pain of her bottom too raw to avoid, she gathered up her things from his apartment, using grocery bags and anything else that was handy. There wasn't that much to salvage. Waiting on the steps outside for her ride, she considered sitting down, but the cold, hard steps would be a poor choice.

Curtis called her all the next day, and the next. Receiving no reply, he showed up at her apartment on the third day, yelling and pounding on the flimsy door, demanding to be let in. She told him to please leave, that their relationship was over with, and put her back to the door, hoping this would give the thin slab of wood enough support, though she expected at any moment he would try to break it down. Eventually, worn out, he stopped yelling, but not before calling her a stupid whore who couldn't satisfy a man. The next day, the super stopped by, saying the neighbors didn't like the disturbance, not one bit, and if she couldn't control her boyfriends, she'd have to move out. Two weeks after that, Curtis left a profanity-fueled message on her phone that he had found someone else who was twice the woman she was, one who was more than happy to satisfy his needs. Perhaps that was why she hated Curtis so much and was so angry about everything right now, not just because of how their relationship ended, but the self-loathing she felt for succumbing to his demands.

Three days later, she was in David's bed, getting criticized by another man.

"What do you want me to do, asshole?" she said, pulling the sheet over her, determined to impress on David how much his comments had deeply hurt and insulted her. "Perhaps I need a lesson in proper sex technique."

"Please, don't get mad at me. All I meant was we could take our time, not get in a big rush."

She turned over, her back toward him. "This was all a mistake. I should have known better."

He pressed against her in response. She could feel the wet condom against her butt, the cock inside already softening. Well, that hadn't lasted very long. David wasn't nearly as well-endowed as Curtis. If he said anything more about the sex, she would let him know that his masculinity was sorely lacking, an assessment that, based on experience, was the easiest way to hurt a man.

His hand caressed her stomach as he kissed the outside corner of her shoulder. "I didn't mean I don't like you, or I'm not enjoying having sex with you. I want a little more romance, is all."

"You sound like a girl," she said without looking at him. Perhaps that would hurt his feelings, let him know how his rejection had likewise injured her.

"Maybe. But I think your kisses are pretty special. And I love touching you."

Iris rotated her head back toward him. "Nice save."

"I meant what I said. Come on, turn over. Please?"

She reluctantly turned to face him. "What do you want me to say?"

"You don't have to *say* anything." With that, he started kissing her again, his tongue probing her mouth as he rubbed her back. She settled against him, at first hesitant, but soon overcame her self-imposed resistance and eagerly sought his mouth as well.

"Now, tell me what's wrong," he said.

"Nothing." The expected reply.

"You've been hurt, Iris. I'm thinking pretty badly. How about you tell me what happened? I'm here to listen."

She looked into his eyes, not believing his profession of concern at first, but now seeing instead a sad, understanding look that mirrored her own grief. So she talked about all of it while he rubbed her back and periodically delivering those soft kisses of his. When she finished, he grabbed a tissue from the nightstand, wiped her eyes, and had her blow her nose. For once, she found herself happy and content in a man's arms.

"Make love to me," she said, feeling his warmth, her eyes closed.

"Maybe we should wait. In case you're not ready." He worked his fingers through her hair, soothing her.

"Please. I want to. I mean it."

"If you change your mind, anytime, let me know. Then I'll stop and we'll talk about it, okay?"

"Alright." All she wanted now was to feel his mouth and hands on her.

The rest of their lovemaking was a sensual blur, a comfortable, sustained passion she had never felt before. He took his time with her, making sure she was fine with what he did, seeming to kiss her incessantly. He had this special way of caressing her nipples while sucking on her clit, which sent shivers through her body. When it was finally over, she lay pressed against his side, her leg across him while his arm encircled her back.

"I need to go to the bathroom," she said in a low voice, almost a whisper. "Clean up and go home."

"You could spend the night," David said. "I'd like you to stay. If you wanted." He kept rubbing her back, the easy caresses so satisfying to her.

"I should go. Really."

"Okay," he said, kissing the top of her head. "Whatever you want."

She closed her eyes and exhaled soft, murmuring noises as her free hand strayed to the side of his neck. She would remain in his arms for another minute, maybe two, then get going.

After she didn't get up, he started stroking her again, the tips of his fingers gliding over her skin. His touch felt so reassuring, so pleasant, so loving. The minutes extended. Soon, she slept like the dead.

• • • • •

The next morning, they made love again, then showered and got dressed. David had the advantage of being able to put on clean clothes while she was stuck with the dress from last night. Her outfit was too fancy for the morning, she said, so he offered to put on a sport coat to make them look more like a couple. That accommodation was unnecessary, since no one seemed to pay any attention when they sat down for brunch at the small restaurant. They talked and held hands straight through before their meal arrived. Iris knew their situation was obvious to anyone bothering to look—sex, then food—but she didn't care. By early afternoon, it was finally time for her to go, but not before they had made detailed plans for the next weekend.

"I'll call you on Wednesday," she said. "Make sure you haven't changed your mind about Friday night."

He chuckled. "Not a chance. Sure you wouldn't like me to drive you home?"

"Thanks, but no. It's the other way, and, well, if we went to my house, we might not get out of bed until Monday." It was killing her to say this, since she wanted nothing more than to spend the rest of the weekend with him.

He laughed at her frankness and reached for her hand, enclosing it in a soft but secure grip. Taking a deep breath, Iris smiled back at him while the thought of them, together, smoldered in her chest.

The Uber driver pulled up to the curb. He kissed her goodbye before opening the backdoor. She got in and watched him stand back and close the door. He waved as the car drove off. She turned around and looked back through the rear window. He was sticking his hands into his coat pockets, needing relief from the frosty morning air. He would have on his winter coat and be warm if not for trying to keep her from looking awkward. She wanted to still be there, standing beside him, her hand, along with his, in the same pocket.

Once home, Iris lay on the bed and contemplated what had happened. She should get up, change clothes, and do something constructive for the rest of the day. But she lingered, her hand moving between her legs, touching the places where his fingers, his mouth, his cock had been. Come on, wise up, she told herself. This was nothing but a weekend fling. Misplaced lust, a rebound thing that would dissipate like morning mist on a hot summer day. Next weekend they would, for certain, struggle through an awkward reunion. With little or nothing more to say, the magic of the past two days, which had glued them temporarily together, would be gone forever. She should be honest and say as much when they talked on

Wednesday. Yes, that's it. Be proactive and head off the impending disaster. This was the correct, logical course of action.

Then she forced herself to admit what she really felt. She was unexpectedly, ridiculously, undeniably in love with David Perry. No doubt at all.

A man like that who was so sensitive, so loving, but didn't have a permanent woman. How was that possible? What was his story? She now wanted desperately to know. Regardless of the answers, she realized that he was the only man she had ever truly, deeply wanted. What she needed was for him to love her as much as she did him. If only she could keep from screwing it all up.

4

Finch despised his name. Not the Finch part so much, despite it referring to a small, flighty bird, but the rest of it wore on him. When he was born, his parents were still unsure about a first name. Outside of Mrs. Finch's room, a Spanish-speaking family engaged in an intense, loud discussion about something. Finch's dad stuck his head out and heard them referring to "el derecho." He liked the sound of that word, derecho, and his wife agreed. Unfortunately, on Finch's birth certificate, his name was misspelled as Derecto Bartholomew Finch. Only later, in middle school, did Finch discover that "De Recto" would translate from Spanish as "Of the rectum."

Growing up, he grudgingly learned to live with a stupid name. The Latino kids laughed at him in every class when the new teachers called his name on the first day. Those students used the split moniker "De-Recto" every chance they got, since most of the teaching staff didn't get the joke. After that, he pleaded to be referred to as D.B., or Bart, which sometimes worked. By the time he reached high school, he only went by his last name. Finch to everyone. Everyone except his two closest friends, James and David, the only ones allowed to call him by the more affectionate Finchie.

Perhaps his constant distress from defending his given name kept him from going to college and working through the same problem repeatedly. It certainly wasn't because of his intelligence, since he was the brightest of the three. Perhaps instead it was his intent to cut himself loose from expected behavior. Finch wanted to see and do as much as possible, a desire that he could never satisfy by living a conventional life. That decision resulted in him skipping further education and drifting across the country, working temporary jobs. Along the way, he became proficient in construction, working as a ranch hand, plus taking turns at commercial cooking and other disparate endeavors. For a time, he repaired computers and enrolled in advanced IT courses. He took to most things with an eagerness to learn and an innate flexibility in applying his knowledge. Seldom did his employers not beg him to stay when he said it was time to move on. He always refused because he hated becoming bored with things and people and places, and grew desperate for something new. Along the way, there were a few scrapes with the law, but nothing serious. Mostly, he kept out of everyone's way and worked hard. Never expecting much out of life had a way of forging pleasant experiences when you set your sights so low. Once the internet and smartphones took over, the organization of his life got a lot easier.

In some places he made his temporary home, he would find female companionship. Some were single, others divorced and needing a lover and help with the kids. He was good to the women he slept with, and, like his employers, most didn't want him to leave when it was time to move on. The repeated, tearful farewells came as he loaded the small trailer connected to the end of his old Subaru. Promises and offers were extended, accompanied by whispered goodbyes and requests for a return visit anytime he was in the mood. But he kept going, pulled along by an insatiable desire to see more, know more, do more. He never expected to settle down, instead intending to work until he fell over dead. Not that he dreaded death. He could see himself dying alone in some run-down hotel room, but that was okay, too. Such an event would only truncate further adventures.

To outsiders, Finch appeared to be the weakest link in the trio. A ne're-do-well, a rambler, a vagabond, a man without direction or a permanent job, whose only concern was himself. Finch didn't disabuse that appraisal, as he didn't much care about what people thought of him. Only his two genuine friends knew better. Finch was the rock, the glue that held the three together, the most dependable, the most generous, the best friend one could find.

It was Finch, at age twelve, who had talked James' parents into taking David in, revealing only enough to impress on them how critical saving the boy's life was. Yes, he could go to a foster home, but you know how those things often work out, the unfortunates often being ruined by the experience. Finch's family might take him in if James' didn't. Finch told them he bunked in a tiny bedroom with his younger brother, and there were the two girls in the other room. If James' family couldn't help, Finch said he would give up his own bed for David and sleep on the couch from now on. He would get a job, do anything it took, to help his family handle the extra cost of another person to feed and clothe. James' parents, wealthy and spread thin in their vast house, were at first leery of the temporary arrangement. I'm not asking you to adopt him, Finch said. Just give him a place to stay for now. After Finch skillfully parried each of their arguments in succession, the parents looked at each other and realized they had no real excuse to refuse. James knew then that Finch would someday become a brilliant lawyer, but he had overlooked another, stronger characteristic of his friend—the wanderlust that subsumed all else.

The thing most important to Finch was keeping in contact with the other two men who still formed his nuclear bond. If they needed him, he was there. It didn't matter if he had to quit a job, catch a last-minute flight, or drive all day and all night and all the next day to get there. He provided whatever support they needed, guaranteed. Their friendship, their unquestioning trust in him, was the one anchor in his life, accompanied by his own certainty that their lives mattered more than his. Over the years, he had been called multiple times by each of the two, maybe only offering a willing ear for an anxious question, or seeing them for a day or two when they needed his help to straighten things out, or providing a fresh perspective and a clear path forward. It didn't matter if the conversations took place at night in a bar, hidden from their unsuspecting families, or if instead he dropped by officially at their houses for a few days. The spouses often wondered what hold this rough man had on their husbands, but his loyalty to them was complete, absolute, never-ending.

Finch was framing a spec apartment building when James called and told him that David had been murdered. The news shocked him, made him sick. David, the best of them, spent years working to overcome his past so he could build a new life for himself and his family. David, the one who had deserved to be the happiest and live the longest, was gone.

As soon as he received the call, Finch put down his tools and walked off the job, the foreman yelling at his back not to expect a re-hire, goddammit, *you hear me?*

By that afternoon, provisioned and packed, Finch was on the road. Only one thing mattered, and that was getting to David.

5

Life for James Randolph had always been easy. He grew up in the big house on Searcy Circle, the one fronted by four enormous fluted Corinthian columns and planted in the ideal part of the cul-de-sac. His father ran a factory and dabbled in investing on the side. James and his sister had the run of the house, the product of an over-indulgent mother and an often-absent father. James' friendship with David and Finch puzzled his mother, seeing as these boys weren't "really his kind," as she used to say, but James persisted because he saw things in each of the other two that he admired and needed in his own life. His mother eventually agreed to host the other two boys in her house from time to time, and grew to have genuine affection for both of them.

That comfort and familiarity helped tip the balance when Finch pleaded David's case to them, and so David came to live in the house at the end of the street. The temporary stay stretched out through the end of high school as the fruits of an upper middle-class lifestyle enveloped David, giving him succor. Not that David wasn't always grateful. He made sure he was always respectful and kind, never giving his foster family a bit of trouble, something James' dad always remarked on when James periodically got into difficulty. Once David moved in, his grades steadily improved, a feat that James often struggled to emulate.

By the time David graduated from high school in the top ten percent of his class, James' sister, Jackie, two years younger, was deeply in love with David. This can't happen, David told James one night, you know what I've been through. Besides, no way I'm ruining my relationship with this family. Once David left for state college, naturally on scholarship, he stayed away, only coming back for a few of the major holidays. He worked through the summers, too, telling his second family that he needed the better-paying jobs he could get elsewhere, but he and James and Jackie all knew it was David's deliberate attempt to distance himself from a situation that he felt was impossible to acknowledge. Jackie wrote David long, tearful letters the first year he left, though the frequency of the correspondence stretched out as time went on. She was, despite her longing for David, only a junior in high school back then. David promptly answered each missive with courtesy and friendship, but nothing more. Eventually, as her own college life bloomed, Jackie found another man to be enthralled with, and so the David problem seemed to disappear. She laughed about it later on, when they were all together, saying how silly she had been at that age, but all three of them knew that her affection was real, and that, except for David's reservations, he would have ended up a son-in-law to the Randolphs. James remembered, at David's wedding, the intense look in Jackie's eyes as she watched him and his new bride out on the floor for their first dance.

James took any demeaning comparisons of himself to David in stride. He knew both too much and too little about what motivated his friend to succeed. James' school marks were solidly in the middle, his results more like Finch's. The difference was, despite being smart as hell, Finch didn't much care for the discipline of school, while James often struggled to do as well on purpose. With David's tutelage and Finch's clear understanding of the facts, James made it through high school with a solid set of grades. James went to a quality college, not the best one his father had hoped for, but set on a track that amplified his father's interest in finance. Though he wasn't an outstanding student there, either, his friendly, straightforward manner and innate charm often proved irresistible to the people he met.

Upon graduation, James secured multiple job offers from investment management firms. He took the one back in the city, which leveraged his acquaintances with old family friends and offered good, long-term prospects. His reward was rising rapidly into management. James knew you didn't need to be the smartest person, or the best prognosticator, to succeed in his chosen profession. You only needed to make people feel comfortable with you, want them to be your friend, trust you with their finances, and then he would find a portfolio manager to handle the actual investments and allocations. At this, he excelled.

By now, James had gained a wife and a couple of kids. Like his mother, he indulged them all, creating ever-rising expenses that had now grown to what he once thought to be an enormous amount of money. Alone at night in his study, he often worried about how he was going to pay for it all. Early on, he swore to only live off his earnings and not invade his generous trust fund. He wanted to leave it all to his own children, he proclaimed, a resolve that had never seemed to bother his sister, Jackie, about her own funds. Contrary to his stated resolve, almost every month now there was some new and unexpected expense that James' trust fund financed. A new kitchen appliance, ballet costumes for his daughter's program, outfits for his son's Little League team—all of it needed paying for, and his salary from the firm never seemed to be quite enough. Before now, things had a way of always working out, as if the universe had designated him deserving of its benevolence. That prior certainty, lurking in the back of his mind since he was young, now seemed like a phantom contract about to be ripped in two.

James was the first one David's wife called when her husband died. She couldn't find Finch's number, she said, must have misplaced it, but James knew she contacted him instead because she didn't much want to talk to Finch, especially about such a traumatic and emotional matter. A cold bastard, she called him once before, only interested in himself. She found him self-absorbed and uncaring. This wasn't Finch at all, at least around his close friends, James had told her. But Finch seemed content for her to feel that way about him as long as it did not poison David's feelings. The time when David had what amounted to a breakdown, it was Finch he reached out to, and Finch who got David re-directed and centered again. Not that David's wife refused to recognize the help. But she said, later on, after the crisis was over, maybe all they did was go somewhere and talk it out for a couple of days. That meant David's problems weren't all that severe in the first place, probably only a temporary funk. Finch left as soon as his curative powers had done their work. James, who spent most of that crisis taking care of David' wife, emerged as the true savior. Now, she clung to him and not to Finch. James felt this was unfair and said so, but Finch was ambivalent. Let her think what she wants, he said. I don't care.

The present difficulty that James faced was that his upward career trajectory had stalled out. For the last two years, he had received only modest raises, and the size of his yearly bonuses, the real reward in financial markets for doing well, had plateaued and was now declining. At this rate, he worried that he might have to dip into the trust fund even more, or raid his retirement to ensure their lifestyle. An alternative, never seriously considered so far, was to cut back on expenses.

Today, as the after-funeral reception broke up, James comforted the taciturn, angry widow while Finch, standing beside him, looked out of place as usual. James assured her they would assess the family's finances right away and find them a path forward, one thing he could offer because he already had their financial assets under management. Without checking, though, he knew that even with the small term life insurance payout the family didn't have sufficient funds to get them through for very long, possibly only enough for a couple of years, maybe three, even considering their modest rate of expenditures.

David, despite trusting James, would have done better if he had invested his savings in index mutual funds instead of with James' active management recommendations. But David was already way behind by this time in his life, so they had agreed on a riskier course, with potentially much higher future rewards. Despite James' best research efforts, the small-cap growth companies he selected for David's portfolio often ran up against insurmountable problems and blew up. A few succeeded remarkably well, but the rest, well, there were always issues. Some ran out of cash before the big breakthrough was ready, some experienced problems with commercializing their ideas, while others stagnated in industries no longer at the vanguard of the latest investment trends. Hell, one CEO absconded with all the corporate cash and headed for South America, at least last they heard. Why couldn't he find the next Amazon, the next Tesla, singled out of the huge mix of story stocks? James knew, deep down, that the chances of a score like that, spread over the enormous universe of up and comers, were miniscule, but that hadn't stopped them from trying. A cache of significant new investment cash, promised several years ago, would have balanced out the portfolio when invested in more conservative offerings, but the new money never materialized. Unexpected expenses, David had said, sorry, let's leave it at that.

David's widow called James a few days after the funeral, grateful but frustrated, and wanted to talk about her present guest. Despite her acquiescence to Finch's offer of fixing up the place, she was already looking forward to him being gone. For now, he hung on like the itinerant uncle, the odd accessory, concerned about the family but simultaneously serving as a vaguely unwelcome presence. At least he was conscientious, she said, busying himself doing the repair work around the house that for years David had either avoided or could not accomplish. Finch told James that he understood the impression she had of him, and so he stayed out of her way as best he could. Still, a reminder of the foreign presence occurred every time she looked out of her kitchen window at the dirty Subaru and attached trailer blocking part of her driveway.

Housed temporarily in the spare bedroom, Finch kept to himself. He seldom seemed interested in interacting much with his adopted family, except for his obvious fondness for the son, and instead stayed busy with the repair work. At the evening meals he would sit there, quiet and uncomfortable, while David's wife made a few attempts at conversation. After a few days of this, she gave up on Finch and retired as soon as possible to the living room to watch TV, silently signaling Finch to go to his room or take a long walk. Already, she was regretting her offer of asking him to stay. Jesus, she thought, it'd been only a week since he arrived, but seemed like a month, maybe two. Would he leave voluntarily, or would she have to throw him out?

Davie was back in school, as his mother wanted to reestablish some normality to her son's life. Finch offered to help Davie with his homework, she told James one night when he called to check up on the family. Perhaps he would do minimal damage, she said, and at least that left her alone with her own troubled thoughts. James said something she hadn't expected. You can never go wrong trusting in Finchie, he had said. He's the best there is. When she protested James' lavish praise, James enigmatically added that if she only knew what Finch had already done for your family, you would have a different view.

After she hung up, she sat there in the darkness of her bedroom, thinking over James' comment, wondering if maybe she had missed something. Or if maybe she had missed a lot.

6

Nine weeks after David and Iris first made love, they moved in together. It was a difficult adjustment for David, having a woman's things, so much *stuff,* all about his apartment. Not that Iris was messy or disorganized, just that they had duplicates of things they *didn't* need, and a shortage of others that they really *did* need, yet all the closets and cubbyholes were now filled. They had talked and talked before about who would move in with whom, never doubting the eventual action, but the question of which apartment to consolidate their lives into was difficult to answer. Each option had its pros and cons. His one-bedroom was nicer but smaller, hers more spacious but a bit run-down and needing a refresh. Since his apartment won out, that made the accommodation of her added items more difficult. After leaving what she felt she could do without for the charity pickup, they bundled her belongings into multiple car trips, and, for the furniture, a day of back and forth with a borrowed truck completed the move. Now, at least, they were situated. Mostly. Several more boxes of donations, stacked on top of each other, settled against the wall in the narrow hallway and begged for a decluttering trip.

David enjoyed waking up next to Iris and listening to her steady breathing. She told him that, for the first time, she now slept well, all of it because of him. His fingertips brushed her side, a soft enough caress that she wouldn't stir from. It was almost time for the alarm, so he did not want to spoil any precious remaining minutes of her rest. He was like that, always thinking of others, what they might need or want, even if they didn't say. It was what had originally attracted him to Iris, the knowledge that he could understand her mental anguish and support her as she healed. That certainty of purpose made him feel good. Fortunate, he knew, because he badly needed an anchor in his life to hang onto.

After getting up, he headed for the small bathroom to get a head start on their joint need for the tight facilities. With his usual efficiency, he would be out of the shower about the time the alarm went off. Iris briefly awakened, hit the snooze, and was out for another five. Enough time for him to towel off, brush his teeth, shave, and slide on some deodorant. He pushed a small amount of gel through his hair, combing through the short strands, letting the air do most of the drying. Needing little more to get ready for the day, other than dressing, he sat on the edge of the bed, pulling on his socks, when the second insistent alarm went off. Iris stretched, reluctantly arose, and kissed him good morning as she stumbled toward the bathroom. The assembly line, after dropping him off, attached itself to the second resident of the house and began to speed up.

Iris came out with a towel wrapped around her, hair up and safely secured from getting wet. Of course, since today was a Tuesday. He knew her schedule by now. She would not wash her hair for two more days, saying shampooing every day was bad for it, you have to keep the natural oils working. Funny how their domestic cycle automatically slipped into his subconscious, he thought, a subtle reckoning with changing times. She started searching the closet for today's preferred outfit without meaningful success. Finished dressing himself, he moved up behind her.

"Morning, beautiful," he said, kissing her shoulder. She turned, a smile crossing her face. Iris loved it when he was affectionate in the morning. She always said it reminded her of their first weekend together.

She turned and laced her arms around his neck, her mouth searching for his. David's hands slid down the back of the towel, raising up the lower edge, and caressed her bottom.

"You keep that up, you're going to make me late, handsome," she said when their lips parted.

"You could call in sick," he said.

Closing her eyes, she looked as if she was seriously considering his suggestion. Then she said, "Better not. I've got a lot going on today." But she made no move to disentangle herself from him, instead remaining there, soaking up his attention.

"In that case, you better get a move on," he said, pushing her slightly away from him with a pat on her butt.

"I know what this really is," she said. "You're already tired of me."

"Don't want to get you fired is all."

"Sure?" she said, but she kissed him and then turned back to the crowded closet.

"I am so, so sure. We need the money."

She stuck out her lower lip in false agitation. "Now I know what you really need me for." She shed her towel. "See what your short-sighted capitalistic focus is missing out on?"

Admiring her naked form, he gave her a visual caress, then a tactile one. He loved touching her, her smooth skin sliding past his fingers. Grinning, he said, "I'll get us some coffee."

With that, he headed to the kitchen and poured them both cups, thinking this morning, like he often did in these early days, of the night they had awkwardly bonded over the same beverage. What an unexpected outcome, he thought. The confirmed bachelor was now committed to his new girlfriend. And it all felt right.

David returned with the coffees and watched her getting ready. Iris was like an engine with barely enough energy to start up, sputtering and sluggish at first, cylinders misfiring, coughing out the telltale smoke of unburned fuel, then gaining speed as it warmed and the seconds ticked by. By now, she laid out her clothes and was finishing putting on her underwear. Taking the cup from him, she set it on the small credenza and took a quick sip. Dressing, including adding the simple jewelry she wore, took less than a minute. The coffee cup and Iris headed for the bathroom for final makeup and hair, all to be completed in a whirlwind of motion and purpose.

After washing out his cup, he stepped into the hallway to retrieve their coats from the front closet.

Iris headed out of the bathroom and rinsed out her own cup in the kitchen sink. Entering the hallway a few seconds later, she slipped her arms into the coat he always held up for her. It was a silent acknowledgement of how this simple action had brought them together.

"Alright, what's on your schedule today?" she said as she flipped her hair out of the coat and rapidly fastened the buttons. Snick, snack, one, two, three. Down her busy hands went.

"Meetings in the mornings. I've got a report due this afternoon." He shoved his hands in his coat pockets. "Not all that exciting, I'm afraid. How about you?"

"Some new clients are coming in. They asked me to sit on the session."

"That's good news," David said, then added, "Right?"

"Yes, I think so."

Iris was now in full business mode, an abrupt change he had learned to expect. "See you back here at the regular time?"

She nodded as she gathered up her phone and purse. "Let's get to it."

7

At the breakfast table that morning, utensils clanging against plates provided the only initial sounds. Finch broke the monotony.

"I'll be leaving tomorrow," he said. "Time for me to move on."

David's wife looked across at her temporary tenant and attempted to suppress her reaction. Oddly, she was now used to Finch and his unique ways. As far as him leaving, was that a disappointment or a joy? She wasn't sure. Maybe a bit of both.

"You know, you can stay as long as you like. There's no hurry for you to go," she said.

But the relief in her voice was palpable. He had given her a date certain, something that a personality like hers needed. Finch had a fleeting thought about when he was a little kid and first realized that most adults had this annoying habit of never really saying what they actually meant. It had confused him as a child, but, as almost everyone did, he caught on soon enough, the social understanding now innate and certain. David's widow, though, always got to the point.

"I've stayed long enough." He glanced around the room, playing for time. "The exterior painting's done, and I think I've fixed about everything inside the house that needed repairs. You've still got a few loose shingles on the roof. I'll take care of that today. You think of anything else, let me know."

"You've been a big help, Finch," she said, the gratitude in her voice obvious. "I really appreciate it."

"I was happy to do it, help you out," he said, returning to his eggs. "I know David would want that. You've been real nice, letting me stay on after the funeral and all. I know I've been an imposition."

Without looking at him or refuting his statement, she said, "I think that's what David would've wanted me to do."

She put her hands in her lap and sat motionless. She would be glad to enjoy a simple existence, one with only herself and her son. Still, she had grown accustomed to Finch and his solitary habits. There was something else, not yet acknowledged, behind her reticence. He waited for her to say more.

"I'm glad you came. For the funeral." She said, brushing away sudden tears, her emotions still raw under the façade of getting on with their lives. "David thought so highly of you. I know he would've been glad that you made the effort."

"No way I wouldn't have come. I'll get my things packed up tomorrow morning. After that, James and I are going over to see David's dad, see if he needs anything, before I leave town. It's the courteous thing to do."

"Yes, I suppose so," she said, thinking over what he had said. "David never got along well with his father. I don't know why. He never wanted to talk about it." She took a sip of her coffee and glanced at her son, David Jr., whom they had always called Davie, getting close to finishing his breakfast. "I thought, you know, it would be good for Grandad Perry to be part of Davie's life, but that hasn't worked out. David was such a sweet man, but he was fine with his father not being involved, so I always wondered. . ." Her voice trailed off, the thought incomplete, forming a failed attempt at explaining the confusion of events now outside of her grasp.

"Hard to know what happens in families," Finch said, taking a drink. He didn't need to tell her that David had told the old man that if he ever touched Davie, he would kill him.

"But Mr. Finch," Davie said, "You promised to help me again with my homework."

"I will. Tonight. Whatever you need."

"Davie says you're a wonder," she said, glancing at her son with a mother's look of complete adoration. "He says you make the concepts so clear." There was conviction in her voice, the dispelling of an earlier certainty that someone like Finch could never possibly be good at such things.

"I can stumble through a problem here and there. You've got a real smart boy here. He just needed a few things explained a different way." He reached over to give Davie's head a pat.

Finished, Finch left the table and headed for the sink, plate and cup in hand. "I need to get on the roof before it gets too cold. Weatherman said it might snow a bit later on today. I'll go over and say goodbye to my parents after lunch."

With that, he moved on to the garage and got out the extension ladder. He would finish with the shingles in a short while, but he relished the idea of staying longer on the roof, away from people, sitting there above the ground, alone with his thoughts, feeling nature's slight, cold breeze as he watched the world wake up.

The noise the garage motor made telegraphed its tired struggle to hoist the sectional door. He would check it out, see if it needed replacing or only the rollers greased, when everyone was gone. Finch heard the SUV start and watched it back out as the two of them headed for Davie's school. Turned around in her seat, she was gauging the distance between her vehicle and Finch's rig strung out alongside the driveway. Davie rewarded Finch with an excited wave and Finch returned the goodbye gesture. The images of the boy and his mother blurred, partially obscured by the reflections of the morning clouds off the tinted glass. It was like they were there, but also not. Often, he thought to himself, things in life were never quite clear.

8

Soon after they moved in together, David and Iris had their first real argument. Not over whether to get married, but if they ever wanted children. Iris was full of enthusiasm at the prospect of a gaggle of perfect little Davids running around their house, each a carbon copy of the man she adored. David refused to commit to having a child at all, let alone two, knowing that sparing the world some potentially awful genetic characteristics might be more important than progeny. At first amused by his reluctance, Iris grew agitated, and eventually, angry and hurt. Was this a blanket repudiation of his interest in having a baby with her? Did he find her so unacceptable that he couldn't imagine her as a mother of his children?

The conflict led to a shouting match one evening as they were about to go out for a planned dinner. Iris started it, remarking that if they had kids, they would need to get a babysitter for nights like this. David grew sullen and told her he knew what she was doing and to quit pressing him. After an escalating mishmash of recrimination and accusations, Iris ended up infuriated by his comments. Rather than have dinner out, their last meal of the day became mac and cheese instead of steak tartare. After that, she retreated behind a slammed bedroom door, and David spent an uncomfortable night on the couch.

The thaw didn't come until the next morning, when David knocked quietly on the door and asked if he could come in and discuss things with her. Iris initially ignored his entreaties, but gave in quickly because the thought of not reconciling with him was impossible. They ended up having makeup sex and avowing never to hurt each other like that ever again. David said he would consider children, and if she wanted to get married that was fine, too, let him know after she thought it over. That exchange was at odds with Iris' expectations, seeing as she always wanted a very public marriage proposal, complete with dramatic knee-bending and the offered ring, followed by her unbelieving thrill at the offer and the hands-to-face pretend shock. Her gushing agreement, their perfect kiss, the enthusiastic clapping of bystanders, the snapping of photos, the rush of subsequent smiles, hugs and kisses, and the exuberant postings on social media would merge to provide the perfect commemoration.

Instead of a movie moment, though, the actual occasion was classic David, him avoiding springing anything major on her without prior authorization, so she said she would think it over and let him know, despite the reality that she didn't need any time at all to arrive at a decision. Iris delayed it, anyway, for a few weeks, hoping he would mention it again, maybe in a still-thrilling way, leaving a family lore story to tell their children. But for David, the marriage offer was hers to respond to when she got around to it, so Iris said, one night when they were out, that she wanted to marry him and have his babies and would love him forever. He gave her his trademark smile, held her hand, and said that made him a happy man.

Having now sealed the deal, Iris settled for a trip to the jewelry store to pick out her wedding ring, which was ultimately fine with her, being as his taste was unlikely on a parallel course with her own. They announced their engagement with a small mailing of save-the-date cards proclaiming a vague window of time about a year in the future. They would provide another mailing after the venue and time became official.

In the meantime, work kept them both busy. Iris' job at a boutique event planning service meant she was usually rushing around, solving one crisis after another. That aspect left David alone on most weekends, unless he agreed to dress up and tail along as the unwanted spouse, meaning sitting at the back table with the social misfits. Instead, he chose those nights to binge-watch his favorite streaming titles, but was smart enough to not indulge in those that Iris also wanted to see. If he watched them ahead of time, he pretended otherwise when she was ready to see the show, offering to make runs for food and drinks during the action, professing that she could catch him up when he returned. This arrangement worked well enough for both parties. Iris often suspected he had watched ahead of time, but she didn't want to challenge him and confront the misdirection.

During the same period, David focused on building his career at a mid-sized business consulting firm. His grades in college landed him a nice position back in his hometown, providing him with an opportunity to build an upwardly mobile life for them both. He figured that once Iris, being Iris, had a baby, this new, wonderful little person would enthrall her and likely result in her working only part time. That meant he needed to advance as quickly as possible and start putting aside additional money as soon, and as much, as possible. For this, he relied on James for investing advice, and, for a time, things seemed on track.

With the wedding date set, Iris went into full planning mode, working overtime to detail every romantic display, table decoration, sequence of events, party favor, keepsake, and menu item. David, bemused by all of this activity, saw getting married as more about the "yes" and less about the event itself. Still, he indulged her and accompanied her on all the trips, including tasting wedding cakes and picking out the few household items they still needed. Once that was all confirmed, they worked on the registry and guest list and agreed on the dance music. Despite getting a cut rate, the cost of the festivities continued to climb, and he seriously offered her the option of an elopement as their best choice. No, of course not, she said. She wanted a real wedding. Besides, she said her mother's heart would break if they skipped the event, seeing as Gayle was an integral plotter in the festivities. They finally agreed to split the cost with her parents. It wasn't like David's father, if he were even to be invited, was going to contribute to the event. Iris' mother, shocked at the idea of the senior Mr. Perry not even showing up, eventually accepted her daughter's insistence that there was too much water under that bridge.

David spent a lot of time during the pre-wedding days attacking their budget, working through differing scenarios to determine how soon they could afford to have a child. He knew that Iris badly wanted one, and would be unhappy until there was a plan in place to make it happen. Adding a third member would require a larger apartment in pricey downtown, a location he still preferred despite the higher cost. The alternative was to move further out, to the 'burbs, a relocation that, due to lack of public transportation, would require the purchase of another car to accommodate the long commutes and differing job schedules. He was conservative with his estimates of baby costs, from car seats to clothes to doctor's visits, but it looked to him like they needed to delay having a child for at least three years, maybe more, to prevent a financial meltdown, and that was assuming Iris would continue to work, at least part time, after having the baby. Maybe if he was a better provider, looking forward to having a child would be more enjoyable, like what James had pulled off. But David was not James, and he saw no way to make this work right now. He and Iris would just have to wait to start a family. By then, she might be in her mid to late thirties, but women had babies in their forties these days, he rationalized, so everything should work out. Yes, he told himself, with a little persuasion, things would all fall into place.

One night, while they were cuddling and watching a movie, he told her his major concern, that they needed to wait before having a baby. After a long discussion, and some hurt feelings, she finally agreed, but said she'd like to start a family as soon as they could afford it.

Two weeks before the wedding, Iris told him she'd missed her period and was already pregnant.

9

David's widow brought her bowl of oatmeal to the table and sat down without saying a word. Finch was already there, finishing up, alone in his thoughts. It was Saturday, a quiet day in the house, and Davie was still asleep in his bedroom. Finch was up before the sun appeared and already dressed. Today he was leaving town, but first he and James were going to kill David's father.

She stared into her bowl and said, "I know. . ." Then she stopped.

"What?" Finch said, seeing the obvious concern on her face.

"You don't know me that well, but I believe in saying what I think and not hiding things. We haven't always gotten along so well, Finch, in the past, but I wanted to say, before you left, how much I appreciate the work you've done around the house. David never seemed to have time for it."

Finch shrugged. "He was busy working and had other things to do. I don't. 'Least not right now."

"Still, it was very kind of you." She began nibbling at her breakfast.

"I wanted to do it," he said. "Not just because of David, but because of you."

She stopped eating and gave him an odd look. "Because of me?"

"Yes, I, uh, think you're a very special woman. You made David's life very meaningful. And you gave him a son that he adored."

Surprise showed on her face, followed by grudging acknowledgement. "Thanks for saying that. We had our issues, like all married couples do, but I loved him. . ." She stopped to dab at her eyes. "Damn, I hate this."

"Look," he said, "when I'm gone, you'll have some time to yourself, alone, time to grieve without having to put on a brave face for me. It's important you get that."

Brushing back the tears, she said, "You see a lot, Finch." After a few more bites, she added, "I need to know some things. About David."

"Such as?"

"Why did he go live with James? What happened between him and his father? He wouldn't talk about it. Ever. Now that he's gone, I want to know. Will you please tell me?"

Finch sat back in his chair, wondering how much to say, how much to conceal. "I guess it doesn't matter that much now. That you know. I can give you the outline of what happened, but only David knew all the details. If you're sure you want to hear this."

She nodded. "I do."

"His mother left when he was about six. Packed up her things when David was at school and was gone by the time he got home. Couldn't stand the old bastard she was living with, I suppose, but was a bad enough mother that she didn't care about leaving her son there. That knowledge always haunted him." Finch took a sip of coffee, thinking about how much to censor. "David's father was abusive. Emotionally. Physically. Sexually. I think you get what I'm saying. It was pretty awful."

Her eyes filled with tears again.

"James and I became friends with David in middle school, about age ten. David covered up his family situation for a while, then one day it all poured out of him. That's when we went to James' parents and asked if David could stay with them for a while. Old Man Perry was furious and demanded that David return, so I . . ."

"What?"

"I told him that if he insisted on that, I'd tell everyone what he'd done to his son."

Tears streaked down her face as she sat there, fascinated and disgusted at the same time. "David always insisted his father not have any contact with our son. Now it all makes sense. I . . . I thought it was just a case of him not getting along with his dad."

Finch drew in a sharp breath. "Whatever you do, don't let that worthless fucker *ever* touch Davie. You *hear me!*" Finch's voice had risen to a desperate crescendo as he finished his remark. He realized too late how this would sound when they found the old man dead. He was careless, stupid, not at all like his usual, rational self. But she had to, *had* to understand how important it was to shield Davie from the old man.

"Sure, I understand," she said, but looked frightened by his outburst.

"Sorry. I apologize. I get a little carried away when I think about what happened to David. Anyway, all three of us became very close after that. It was like a private club, I guess, where you could tell the others absolutely anything and know it stayed in the circle. Pretty rare for kids that age, I guess, or for any age. Nice thing to have when you're young, knowing that you have people you could completely count on to help you, no matter what. We've never betrayed that mutual trust. Not ever."

Finch pretended to find something interesting to look at, out of the kitchen window, to conceal the depth of his feelings.

She watched him swallow several times, the emotion barely concealed. Taking another spoonful of oatmeal, she chewed on it before continuing. "For a long while I was quite jealous of you, you know. Because my husband shared certain private things with you. Things he refused to tell me."

Finch turned back to her. "It wasn't because he didn't love you. He was in pain and from time to time he needed to talk to someone who knew what he'd been through. A person who didn't require a fresh explanation."

"You loved him, didn't you?" she said.

"Yes, of course."

A tight smile stuck on her face. She reached for Finch's hand. "I thought at one time you must be gay, the way you always took care of him. I once said something to David when I was angry about his dependence on you, and he just laughed at me."

Finch struggled to conceal his private thoughts. "I'm not gay. Hope that doesn't disappoint. I think having the right woman would be the best thing that could happen to a man. Like David felt about you."

Holding on to Nichelle's fingers, he felt her warmth surging through him. He had lain awake most of last night, thinking about her lying there, next door, in her own bed, the one she had shared with David. He cursed himself for what he was thinking, but still wondered what she looked like, what she was dreaming of. Instead of working through obvious contingencies about the upcoming murder, he spent most of the night obsessing over her. He had always secretly loved her, the real reason for his feigning of indifference. No way he could ever hurt his friend, though. Now, with David gone, he was desperate to tell her how he really felt, but this wasn't the time. It was too soon, but, likely, there would never be the right time. She had lost the love of her life in a senseless way, and it would take months, maybe years, for her to come to terms with the tragedy. Perhaps, one day, he could summon the courage to tell her what his thoughts were, but what if she told him she had no feelings at all for him? That would make it even more painful. Better to conceal his emotions, get on with his life, and let her get on with hers.

"Tell me," she said after releasing his hand, "why haven't you found a woman to love by now?"

How to explain, he thought, without telling her the actual truth? "I travel around too much to get serious."

"Ever thought about settling down in one place?"

"Yes."

"Why don't you?"

He exhaled. "Tough question to answer. Many reasons."

"I'm sorry for putting you on the spot," she said, dismissing her previous request. "It's really none of my business. I have a bad habit of being too direct."

"No, it's fair. I used to think I'd die somewhere, alone, when I was old, and that was just fine with me. The more I see, the more I realize that there are places I don't want to go, things I don't need to experience. Mainly, as I get older, I think that solitary ending isn't what I really want."

To change the subject, she said, "You still going over to see David's dad today?"

"Yes."

"Why would you, from what you've just told me?"

Finch considered how to answer. "You probably don't need me to answer that question."

Her face held a startled look, but she said nothing else. Finch knew that, as smart as she was, she now had at least an inkling of what he was up to.

After he finished breakfast, Finch called James and set up the rendezvous. They had clandestinely discussed, as adults, various ways of taking out the old man. That speculation mirrored their juvenile years when, as kids do, they fantasized about improbable scenarios that always succeeded. When they grew older and had the means to carry out their decades-old desire for punishment, David had forbidden it. Now, with David gone, there was nothing to stop the retribution.

•   •   •   •   •

James came by later on in the morning, driving his big black Lincoln SUV, all nice and clean and smelling inside of new leather. The snow from late yesterday was melting off, having flung brownish streaks across the polished running boards, but James didn't seem to care. They drove over to the old man's house and stopped out front.

"Got everything you need?" James said.

Finch said, "Pistol's in my right pocket. The gag and duct tape are in the left."

James nodded. "I brought a small crowbar." He opened his coat, letting Finch see it hanging there, dragging down from the flap of the inside pocket. "In case I need to break something."

"You having any second thoughts?"

"Nope."

"The old fuck is pretty crafty," Finch said. "He may wise up to what we intend to do to him. I'm going to be watching, see if he tries to make a break for a weapon. I'll be on him before he can get across the floor."

James pulled on his gloves and reached for the door handle. "Let's get this over with."

10

Due to Iris' detailed planning, the wedding went smoothly, almost without a hitch. There was a brief mix-up with the caterers about the layout of the buffet, and a few other minor details that needed straightening out, but those issues were soon resolved. Mainly, the couple got to enjoy the ceremony and party afterwards. For Iris, it was the heady climax of a longed-for romantic, public event. David, despite his initial reluctance, had a lot of fun, more than he had expected, except for the worry in the back of his mind about the baby.

A surprise for David was seeing Jackie and her husband, Randall Weir, recently moved back home to take over the family business. When he glanced across the rows of guests, there she was, staring straight at him. Jackie, even more beautiful now than he remembered, sat there in an expensive dress, outshining all the other women. Later on, when he made the rounds, she was friendly enough to him, if distant, saying moving back was an opportunity for Randall to put his law degree to use in business, since her dad wanted to retire in a few years. After Jackie accepted his perfunctory kiss on her cheek, David congratulated Randall, saying nice to meet him. Still, he caught the intense look in Jackie's eyes as he left to greet another table of guests. Glad that's over with, he thought to himself.

David and Iris honeymooned in Antigua at a resort with off-season rates they picked up for a reasonable price. Iris brought three new bikinis with her and enjoyed waggling her ass at her new husband, telling him to get a good look now because soon it would be a lot bigger. He took part in the good-natured fun as they cemented their feelings toward each other while lying in bed with the sliding glass doors open, watching the drifting movements of the long white curtains as they felt the Caribbean breezes wash over them. They made love every day, sometimes twice. David had never seen his wife so happy.

On the plane ride home, he again broached the subject of paying for the child and having to move, things which he said were of significant concern to him. She promised to work right up until the baby was born and get child care after that. He said he so much appreciated that, but, you know, things don't always work out like you want, maybe we should consider an alternate plan if events failed to turn out perfectly. Iris put a finger up against his lips and said instead of talking about money she wanted to snuggle and remember their perfect honeymoon, can't we talk about the finances later? Of course, he agreed, as he was always loathe to disappoint her, and soon she was asleep on his shoulder. She woke up sick before they touched down and had to rush to the bathroom. Back in her seat, she said it must be something she ate, but everything was fine now.

Within a week, Iris became increasingly ill. It's just morning sickness, she said, trying to convince him that this was such a small sacrifice to make, no need to worry. But she started losing weight and soon became nauseous enough that she had to quit work, only temporarily she said, give me a few days' rest and I'll be right back on my feet. She kept saying she was delaying an initial visit to the OB until she felt better. One day, he came home and found her unconscious in bed. During the ambulance ride, he was certain he was going to lose her, and cursed himself for getting her pregnant. Later, at the hospital, the physician scolded them both for not coming in sooner, saying Iris had become severely dehydrated and needed to stay there for a few more days while they monitored her condition. By now, she was three months along and the attending physician asked why in the world hadn't sought care before now, seeing how sick she was? Neither one of them had a suitable answer. The hospital hooked Iris up to a saline drip and gave her medications to help with her cramps and nausea. The day of her discharge, David arrived with flowers. Iris, sitting up in bed, was thrilled to see him, saying the worst was over and she felt great. See, I told you everything was going to work out.

A month later, she lost the baby.

He awoke to her screams that night, reaching for the knob on the bedside lamp, then turned to see her sitting up in bed, a pool of red blood between her legs. She already knew that the baby was gone. Another ambulance ride to the hospital and the inevitable verdict seemed anticlimactic. Iris stayed in the hospital for two more days. David took vacation time and lived in the room with her, holding her hand, telling her how much he loved her, that things would be alright. They would have another child, he said. The important thing now was for her to get well.

David now felt incredibly guilty for ever complaining about baby expenses. He knew, intellectually, that his fretting over money had not caused the miscarriage, but deep down he had always had a sense that the world was out to punish him and, by association, those he loved. Their happiness until now was probably just a setup, an interlude to lull him into believing life could be good and happy, right before the hammer fell.

Iris refused to be consoled. She spent the days in the hospital after the miscarriage crying and staring out the window, imagining a different world than the hell she was living through. She watched people walking by in the distant parking lot, talking, her unimaginable tragedy unknown to them, which made her even sadder. Hating the passersby for their indifference was ridiculous, irrational, she knew, but she felt it all the same. Time should stop for everyone while the world considered her horrible loss. But the world didn't stop, and didn't care, despite her having a hurt down so deep that she didn't know if she could ever recover from it.

"How are you doing today, sweetie?" David asked, as he always did when he came in the last morning, his eyes hoping for a better outcome than the day before.

She was tired of answering him, tired of all of it. If only she could go somewhere alone, crawl in a hole, and have the time to think things through. Instead, there was the constant stream of people coming and going, her parents first, then his parents, next their friends, all supplicants proclaiming a certainty of better days ahead. She caught herself wondering if her husband was pretending sympathy but only waiting for her to get on with her life. Not that he had ever expressed such a thought, but she clung to the possibility.

David sat down on the window side of their bed after kissing her, like he had done each day as she lay in the bed, inert and inconsolable. She didn't kiss him back. Instead, tears filled her eyes. She'd cried so much lately that it seemed like the new normal.

Seeing her distress, he stroked her dark hair. "Do you feel like going home today? The doctor says you've stabilized and can be released."

"It's me," she said.

"What?"

"It's me, my body. I rejected our baby. It's my fault.'

"Of course it isn't," he said. "These things happen. Maybe for no real reason. Don't beat yourself up, ba—" He stopped, knowing as the word slipped out, calling her "baby" was the most hurtful word he could use right now. "Let's get you home and settled, and we can talk this through. Better days are ahead."

"You got your wish," she said.

"Wish?"

"Not to have to worry about paying for our child. You should be happy now."

He protested, but she turned away from him. What she wanted was to push all of her hurt onto his shoulders, see how he dealt with it. Stupid and selfish, she knew, but she could not stop herself.

"That's not fair, Iris. Not at all," he said, a new irritated exasperation filling his voice.

She turned and looked back at him, thinking he only wanted to get this miscarriage over with, put it behind them, then go on like before. Well, it would never be like before. Not for her. At that moment, she hated him.

David was taken aback, shocked by the look on his wife's face.

Iris went home that afternoon and headed straight for bed, believing that she might never get out of it.

11

Finch knocked on the front door while James stood to the side, holding the screen door open. Not hearing anything, they waited and knocked again. Shuffling sounds emerged from inside the house, then the door pulled open.

"What'd *you* want?" Perry said, forcing his head out, acting as if the pair had ruined a serene morning. The stench of whiskey on the old man's breath seemed a perfect companion to the white stubble framing his droopy jowls. His eyes were hard, maybe a dark shade of blue, but it was impossible to tell from the compressed lids. A worn plaid shirt, tail out, and baggy beige trousers completed the appearance of dissolution.

"We're David's friends. Remember us?" Finch said, recovering from the cloud of booze and body odor.

The old man squinted first at Finch, then glanced at James. "Yeah," he said. "I know who you are. I saw you both, after the funeral, at David's house. You're older now, but the same pieces of shit I remember. You're the ones took my boy from me. I figure you're probably the ones hooked David up with that colored woman, too." Perry grinned, his lips curling back to showcase his stained and crooked teeth. "And now my grandkid's a half-breed."

Finch's eyes narrowed. "There's not one damn thing wrong with either Nichelle or Davie. Listen, if—"

James cut Finch off, innately knowing where his friend's rising anger was headed. "Sir, we'd just like to come in, visit with you. See how you're doing now with David gone."

The old man's eyes hardened. "There was no reason, no reason at all, for you two to do what you did, to take away a man's child. Worst thing you could've done." He stopped talking as his eyes shifted between James and Finch. As if he had reached a considered conclusion, Perry hurled a final rejoinder at them. "You can both go to *hell*!"

With that, Perry slammed the door in Finch's face.

Glancing at his friend, James said, "Well, that didn't go as planned. What now?"

"Let's give it another try," Finch said, and started knocking again, harder this time.

When the old man opened the door the second time, he was holding an old double-barreled shotgun. "Can't you fucking *hear*?" he said, raising the weapon to point at Finch's chest. "Trespassing on my property, threatening me, that's what you're doing. I can kill both of you right now. It's the law. I know my goddamn rights."

"We're not threatening you, Mr. Perry. We just want to talk," James said, still holding onto the screen door. "Won't take up a lot of your time."

Seeming to soften, Perry said. "Talk? About what? I've got nothing to say to you two."

Suppressing his rage at Perry's previous comment about David's wife, Finch said, "We're worried about you. David wanted us to look in on you if something happened to him. I think he wanted to know his father was safe."

While pulling back both triggers, Perry said. "I know that's a fucking *lie*. He hated my guts. Now you have to the count of four to get off my property or I'll blow your fucking *heads* off. One...two..."

James and Finch glanced at each other, recognizing the futility of this approach. They headed back toward the street.

Standing on the sidewalk, hands shoved into his coat pockets, James said, "That didn't work quite the way I expected."

"Nope."

"How about we circle around and kick in the back door?"

Finch forced himself to think logically. "He'll hear us. Before we can get to him, we'll probably get shot. The neighbors will call the cops and..."

"Well, what do we do, then?" James said, waiting for the smart one to come up with a new plan.

About that time, a boy on his bicycle almost ran into them, but stopped short, his back tire leaving a black streak as it skidded on the sidewalk.

"Who're you?" the kid said.

Finch pointed toward the house. "We know Mr. Perry. Thought we'd come by and say hello."

The kid, still astride his bike, turned and looked at the front door. "My mom says he's an old rotten bastard. To stay away from him or she'll spank me good."

"Wise advice," Finch said.

"You his kids or something?" the boy said.

"No. We knew his son, though."

"The one who got himself murdered?" the boy said, his eyes widening.

"Yes, that's the one," James said.

"My mom said he didn't deserve it. Said he was a Good Samaritan."

They both nodded.

"What does that mean? Good Samaritan?" the boy said.

"It means you're trying to help another person and not being selfish."

The kid squinted one eye, thinking it over. "Why'd he get killed if he was only helping out?"

"You ask a lot of questions," Finch said.

"Yeah, that's what my mom says." Without waiting for an answer, the boy maneuvered his bike around Finch and James and headed off down the sidewalk.

"Eyewitness," James said.

Finch nodded. "C'mon, let's go."

Once inside the Lincoln, James removed the crowbar from his coat pocket and pitched it into the back floorboard. Finch sat there, quiet, which James knew meant his friend was thinking things over, working on a new plan. "Take you back to the house?"

Finch gave a slight nod.

•   •   •   •

Sitting in the driveway next to Finch's Subaru, James said, "You ever think of driving something that looks decent?"

"Mechanically, it's in a lot better shape than it is cosmetically."

"Like you?"

Finch grunted. "Funny."

"Now what?"

"I've been thinking," Finch started out. "Once a pedo, always a pedo. I bet he's into online porn. If I can hack into his computer, I think I can create some real problems for the old fuck."

"You think he's got a computer?"

"Probably, best guess."

"What would you do?" James said, "If you got in?"

"Clean out his bank account if he's online. Find out his clients, turn him into the authorities, that kind of thing. I think it's worth a try."

James signaled his agreement with a slight movement of his head. "I'd like that. A lot."

"The problem is. . ." Finch began, then didn't finish.

"What?"

"Likely he still has those old photos of David. Maybe on his computer, or could be on a separate hard drive. Or maybe in the cloud, or prints still in a shoebox in the house. That was what I was going to do after I shot him. Go through his shit and see what I could find."

"What makes you think he has anything on David?"

"You remember a few years ago when David said he was going to invest some more money with you?"

James, mildly shocked to discover Finch knew about that proposed transaction, realized he shouldn't be. David had always told Finch everything. For James, David's confidence didn't extend to that depth, but he was fine with their altered relationship. Some things he didn't need to know.

"Yeah, I remember. He said he spent the money on 'unexpected expenses.'"

"His old man blackmailed him. Perry said he'd make the photos public, send 'em to his boss, so David felt he had to pay the old bastard. That's where the money went."

James, in his fury, kicked the inside of the door, the hard plastic ready to crack. "Goddamn that *motherfucker*. Now David's family's going to struggle even more because of him. I'm going back there right now and beat his goddamn *head* in. I don't give a shit what happens to me."

Fuming, James slammed the car in reverse and shot back down the driveway toward the street.

Finch grabbed at his arm. "Stop, James. Please. This isn't the way."

"I'm telling you, I can't stand that fucking *bastard* living one more damn *hour*!" James sped up as the end of the SUV lurched onto the pavement.

"*Stop it!*" Finch yelled.

James hesitated.

"Pull back in," Finch said in a quiet voice. "I know how you feel. I'm the same. But this isn't the way."

James braked the vehicle, hard, a cloud of dust and snowflakes settling on the paint. The SUV sat, for a few moments, partway into the street and partway out, as James' furious breathing subsided. After that, he took his time pulling back into the driveway, the extended time helping to assuage his anger.

"Find a way to get him, get him *good*." James said, gripping the steering wheel. "Or I swear to God, I'll do it myself, regardless."

"Give me some time. I'll come up with a plan."

James rubbed a hand across his face, signifying his grudging acquiescence to the request. "If you say so, Finchie."

"I don't want to see you hurt, is all. I don't need another friend leaving a family without a father."

His adrenaline rush dissipating, James seemed to melt into the seat. "Alright, I get it."

Finch said, "What was the story about David's finances? He didn't fill me in on any specifics."

"David was financially behind in preparing for their future. Way behind. I was counting on that additional money to help them out, smooth over the rocky returns from previous investments. It wouldn't have solved his problems, but sure would've helped."

"How bad of a shape are they in?"

James thought over the question. "I still have to run some more numbers, but even with her going back to work, it's going to be tight. Davie's college fund is also real small. The term life insurance payout will be a godsend, but it won't last forever. I begged him to up the face amount, to at least a million, but he said it was all the monthly payment they could spare. I think they were pretty strapped, but I should've been more persuasive." James paused. "I was thinking I ought to help them out, but I... Well, I can't do much right now. Too many of my own expenses."

"David's family isn't your responsibility," Finch said matter-of-factly.

"I know, but we don't have a lot put back, either. Except for my stock in Dad's company and what automatically goes into retirement, we spend everything I make. I used to think if I had an income like I do now, I'd be set for sure. But a family's needs are never-ending." He paused. "Not very impressive for someone in the investment advice business, is it?"

"Don't beat yourself up," Finch said. "It's hard to say 'no' when you love your family and want them to have nice things."

"You know, I envy you a bit," James said.

Finch laughed. "Envy me? Why the hell would you do that?"

"You're free. Free of all of this social and financial pressure. Go where you want, do what you want. That option looks pretty impressive from where I stand."

"There are drawbacks, my friend," Finch said. "I'm the one who envies you. Settling down, raising a family, having a good woman to come home to. One day, I'd like to have that."

"And Nichelle? How are you two getting along?"

"She'll be glad to see me go. At least that was my first impression. Now, she seems kinda used to me."

James considered his next question before asking. "You're in love with her. How long?"

For anyone else, that remark would have elicited a punch in the mouth from Finch. Coming from James, Finch felt he owed him a decent answer. "Don't know for sure. A while, I guess. I'm crazy about Davie, too, now that I've gotten to know him." He thought about what James had said almost off-hand, dropping a probe down into the well of his deepest secrets. "Is it that obvious?"

"Is to me. Probably no one else. You tell her yet?"

"'Course not. She just lost her husband, for Christ's sake. Besides, I can't tell if she even likes me."

"You going to tell her? Ever?"

"Hard to say. It'd probably creep her out."

"You should," James said, then added, "When you feel the time is right."

"Okay. If you think that's best."

"I do. Trust me," James said, grinning at his friend.

"I always have."

They sat together for a while longer, enjoying not saying anything more.

Finch finally reached for the door handle. "I better head out, get on the road."

"Where to this time?"

"Don't know. Someplace warm. Florida maybe."

"Call me when you get settled."

"I will."

They embraced, grabbing at each other and holding on for a long time.

As they broke apart, Finch said, "You're my best friend, James. The only one I have left now. Take care of yourself, dammit."

James teared up. "You too." He grabbed a few deep breaths as he wiped his eyes. "Better get on home. I figured I'd be through with the old man in time for lunch. They'll be waiting on me."

"Love you, man," Finch added.

James nodded. "Same here. I don't know what I'd do without you."

Finch stepped down from the SUV and waved as James drove away. He wondered when he would see his friend again.

12

After Iris came home from the hospital, she didn't improve and remained sullen and remote. David called her mom, Gayle, who agreed to a quick visit to see if she could be any more successful in persuading her daughter that there could be a brighter tomorrow. Arriving with enough clothes for less than a week, she ended up staying for a month and a half. The first couple of nights, Iris' mother slept on the couch downstairs, but David said that was wrong, so he gave up the bed and traded places with her. Better for you to be with Iris overnight, he had said, since she wakes up a lot now, but doesn't seem too much to want any of my attentions. His mother-in-law said don't be silly, of course she still loves you, but he was having doubts. At least she started eating again, not a lot at first, but a bit more as time went on. She seemed to enjoy her mother's cooking, the familiarity of it, but most nights she sat at the table and said little, then often headed back to bed to watch TV.

David knew Iris was clinically depressed and begged her multiple times to consider seeing a therapist. She always refused, so he quit suggesting it. She was becoming a recluse, maybe thinking that punishing herself would somehow resolve her terrible hurt. He was at loose ends, not knowing how to help his wife, and without acknowledging it, he secretly resented her for ruining their relationship. One night, near the end of Iris's mother's stay, David tried his best to persuade his wife to go out with him, have a pizza or something, anything to get her out of the house. She refused as usual and was dismissive, saying go ahead, don't let me stop you, I know you don't want to stay here with me. By then, he'd had enough of her rejections and resolved to go anyway, even though he felt guilty for it.

• • • • • •

David was sitting at the end of the bar in the small pizza restaurant, taking his time with his beer and the last of his meal, when he heard a familiar voice.

"Hey, sailor, how about buying a girl a beer?"

He turned. It was Jackie, standing there, smiling at him, looking more beautiful, more perfect, than ever. Her winter coat, something he was sure was fashionable, was open. Underneath, above painted-on jeans, the buttons of a mauve blouse struggled to contain the fabric covering her full breasts.

"Hey, Jackie," he said, rising to give her a hug, feeling her ample chest pressed against his own. She hugged him with one arm, holding up her takeout pizza box with the other. "Long time, no see. What're you up to?"

"Same as you, I suspect. Mind if I join you?"

"No, of course not. Please, sit down."

Jackie maneuvered between David and the end wall, squeezing past him as she brushed across his arm. "Where's Iris?" she said.

"She's not feeling well. Decided to stay home."

"I'm so sorry, David," Jackie said, putting her hand on his. "James said she was having a lot of trouble getting over the miscarriage. It's a real shame, too, so soon after your marriage."

David nodded, accepting her concern, then signaled to the bartender. "What'll you have?"

"Whatever you're drinking."

After ordering, David said, "Speaking of spouses, where's Randall?"

"He and Daddy are out on a business trip, visiting their suppliers and customers. He says they're going to be gone a lot in the next year. You knew we're taking over the business, right?"

"Yeah, I heard that at the wedding. Back home for good?"

"Looks like it," she said, opening her pizza box and taking out a slice.

David watched her eat. Jackie, named for Jacqueline Kennedy, a woman her mother admired for her beauty, poise and grace, has grown into the type of woman men always stared at. Long, lustrous chestnut hair, full-figured, with a gorgeous face showcasing those striking cornflower blue eyes. She had it all. He hadn't seen her for years, except at the wedding. Age had improved her, assuming that was possible. He felt guilty, though, enjoying his time with the vivacious Jackie while his damaged wife remained at home, struggling with depression. Looking wasn't a crime, he told himself, as long as you don't touch.

"This is weird," she said, her tongue working to pick up the dangling strands of cheese streaming down from the slice. It was almost erotic, the way she was doing it.

David stammered out, "What?"

"Us meeting like this, you and me. Without our significant others." With that, her free hand drifted down to the inside of his thigh, landing midway to his crotch, and stayed there.

"Right, weird." He busied himself with taking a drink, anything to keep him from staring at Jackie.

She laughed, showing a row of striking white teeth framed by full red lips. He had to stop thinking of touching her back.

"You know, when you were a senior in high school, I had this terrible crush on you."

"I know," he said. "But you were too young for me." Then he added, "Back then."

She took another bite, waiting to respond to his remark. "I used to fantasize about you coming into my bedroom at night and making love to me."

David gulped a mouthful of beer to avoid looking at her. "You did?"

Jackie moved her mouth close to his ear. He felt her breath against his skin, causing the hairs on that side of his face to stand up.

"Of course," she said. "I'd touch myself, dreaming it was you instead of me doing it. Lying there, feeling you on top of me. Sometimes I'd get so wet I'd have to change my panties."

David choked and started coughing. "*Jesus*, Jackie."

"Does that *shock* you?" she said, laughing to him and pounding on his back while he recovered. Jackie had this musical laugh, the exact kind you expected from a woman that looked the way she did. Once he recovered, she kept her arm across him, rubbing his back before settling her hand back on his thigh.

"You did that on purpose," David said, finally able to stop coughing.

"Guilty," she said. "Don't be mad at me. Please." She gave his thigh an affectionate squeeze. "But it was all true. Everything I said."

He turned and looked into her bemused, twinkling eyes. Jackie didn't need false eyelashes. Her eyes, perfectly made up with black eyeliner and thick mascara accentuating her naturally long lashes, were intoxicating. "No way I could stay mad at you." He smiled crookedly, drinking her in.

"You look so handsome when you smile," she said, moving a little closer. "You should do it more often."

"Look," he said, working at extricating himself. "I really better get home."

"Please, stay with me while I finish eating. It'll only take a little bit of your time."

It took little effort for him to agree to her request. They chatted on, about college, spouses, work, and the possibility of having children. Jackie admitted to him she and Randall were trying, but without success. David told her he wasn't sure Iris would ever want to try again, seeing as how her first pregnancy ended so disastrously. Mostly, as the time passed, he enjoyed the camaraderie of being with this beautiful creature that knew him so well, as the hashed over old times and the people they both remembered.

"I'm finished," she said, closing up her box with more than half of the individual pizza remaining. "I'll take the rest home for lunch tomorrow."

"I'll get your beer," he said. "Least I can do for you keeping me company." He signaled to the bartender and slid a credit card toward him.

Outside in the parking lot, David stood next to Jackie's S class Mercedes, the driver's door open and her about to slide in. He lingered there, wanting to say or do something else. He wasn't sure what.

She bent over and ducked into the car, setting the pizza box in the passenger seat. Emerging, she shut the driver's door and stood close to him, looking up into his eyes. He could now smell the delicate perfume she was wearing, previously hidden before by the overpowering smells in the restaurant.

"You better go," he said. "It's getting cold outside."

She nodded, but didn't move. "I should."

David forced himself to break it off. Maybe he should shake her hand. "Well, Jackie, it was really good to see you."

"You too," she said, taking a half step closer to him, her breasts almost touching his chest.

Before he realized it, they were kissing. Not a superficial one, but a deep, passionate kiss. Her arms encircled his neck. He felt himself harden as his hands grasped the middle of her back and pulled her into him. How long it lasted, he wasn't sure. She eventually pulled away and slid her hands down the outsides of his arms, taking her time, looking him over.

"Sorry," he said. "I shouldn't have done that, I—"

"I'm glad you did."

"Look, Jackie, I. . ."

She laid her hand on the side of his face, interrupting his apology. "Don't worry. I won't tell. I never have." Her fingers creased his jaw and pinched the end of his chin before her hand dropped away. "I suppose I better go."

David swallowed hard. "Right, yeah."

Sliding into the seat, she closed the door and started the engine, then rolled down the glass.

"David, if you ever need me, I'll be there. Anytime. You know how I feel about you, how I've always felt."

He stood there, mute, feeling like a bug being pinned to a specimen board, all of his legs struggling in a failing attempt to get free.

Watching his reaction, a conspiratorial smile crossing her face. "It was so good to see you. 'Night." Then she backed out and was gone.

David realized suddenly that despite the cold, he was sweating. Thoughts, crazy thoughts, were running through his head like a herd of spooked horses.

13

David, still unsettled from his experience with Jackie, entered the apartment and tried not to think about what had happened at the end. Gayle sat on the couch, watching TV, and looked up as he entered.

"How was the pizza?" she said.

"Okay, fine. Has Iris come down?"

She shook her head. "No. She'd been in the bedroom all night." An acknowledgement of failure overtook her face. "David, I don't know what to do to help her."

He sat down on the couch and reached for Gayle's hand. He genuinely liked his mother-in-law. Sweet and kind, she tried hard to stay out of their way and not interfere, but now she was visibly upset. David knew she was close to acknowledging that her broken daughter seemed beyond both of their efforts.

"Iris always was a sensitive child, growing up, so loving, but she takes things so personally, so intensely. Once she gets in one of these moods. . ." Gayle's voice trailed off in defeat.

"What do you think we should do?" he said.

Gayle shook her head. "I don't know, David. I've never seen her this depressed before. I'm afraid we're going to lose her." Gayle turned her head as tears dribbled out of her eyes.

"I've got to get her to see there's hope. I'll go up and talk to her."

Nodding, Gayle turned back to the TV, but her expression betrayed the reality that she had no clue what she was watching.

At the head of the stairs, he stopped at the closed bedroom door and knocked softly.

"Iris? Are you awake?"

A mumbled reply came through the door.

"Please, may I come in?"

He heard a rustling, then the door opened. She stood there, forlorn, a waif in a long white nightgown.

"It's your bedroom, too. I can't stop you," she said. With that, she returned to the bed and turned away from him, pulling the covers back over her.

Sitting down on the edge of the bed, he touched her shoulder. "I remember the first morning I woke up next to you after the party. You were so soft and warm."

"That was a long time ago."

"Not really."

"How can you say that after what we've been through?"

Pulling back the covers, he got in bed behind her, and was glad to see she didn't insist he leave. "When I woke up the next day, you were sound asleep, so I moved over behind you and put my hand on your tummy. Like this."

She didn't respond.

"I thought if I could stay like that forever, I'd always be happy."

Her hand moved toward his. He expected she would push his away. Instead, she placed hers on top and held it there.

"You know, you said some awful things to me when we first met." He kissed her on the neck, pleased to see that she didn't flinch.

"I was hurting."

The choice confronting him was one he told himself he would never make. But he had to save his wife, and perhaps telling her his story would convince her he understood how badly life can hurt you. "I know," he said. "You're a survivor. Like me."

She turned her head slightly in his direction. "What does that mean?"

"When I was young, my father rented me out. To other men."

Abruptly turning, she said, "*What?*"

"He was a pedophile. But instead of abusing me himself, he liked to watch other men do it. He took pictures and sold them to his clients."

"You've never *told* me this," she said, her voice urgent, her hand shooting to his neck. "Oh, David, why didn't you?"

"It's very difficult for me to talk about. Plus, I was ashamed for a very long time. I know now that it wasn't my fault, but back when I was a kid, I convinced myself that I deserved everything that happened to me."

"How could you even *think* that? You were a little boy and—"

Interrupting her, he said. "I didn't want anyone to know, ever. If people found out, they'd look at me with pity, then feel secret gratitude that it didn't happen to them. I'm telling you now so that you'll know I understand what terrible emotional pain is. That there are things that hurt us so deeply, things beyond our control, no matter how hard we try to fix them."

"Why didn't you turn him in? That sorry *bastard*!" Iris was furious now, her pupils dilating.

"I was a kid, Iris. Adults didn't believe kids back then. Not about things like that, and not if an adult said it didn't happen. Only your wild imagination, he would've told people, you must've dreamed it all. If it hadn't been for Finchie and James, I don't know what would have happened to me. I probably would have killed myself."

She hugged him to her, crying. "Oh, my *God*, David!"

"My friends were the ones who saved me. And you need someone to save you, Iris. I want to be that person. We could go, together, to see a professional. Talk it out. I think that helps. Finchie was my savior, listening to all of it."

She covered his face with wet kisses. "I can't believe you've held this in for so long. I don't know whether to be angry or..."

"I've told you so you'd know I understand pain so deep it feels like it will overwhelm you. I still think about what happened to me, how awful it was, and I used to believe I couldn't go on, that I had to give up. But you can't, sweetheart, you just can't. You must keep trying. Getting hurt is what I count on in my life. I figure that's a given, that the universe is always against me. I know that's stupid, but that's how I feel. That way, if the awful stuff doesn't happen, I'm surprised and happy." After a pause, he said, "You know, you're not the only one who lost the baby."

"I know," she said, her fingers combing furiously through his hair.

"You must understand you didn't lose it because you're a bad person, or because we wouldn't be great parents, or because I was worried about the money. It wasn't because you didn't deserve to be happy. It just happened, okay?"

She clung to him, shaking, not saying anything more at first. Eventually, she said, "If I'll agree to see a therapist, will you please go with me? I think it would be good for both of us." With that, she started kissing him again.

"I love you, Iris. I always have."

A while later, Gayle heard the two of them on the stairs. Her daughter was clutching David's hand, her face shining like the sun had come up. For the first time in a long while, she looked happy.

Gayle took a long, satisfying breath and fought back tears. Whatever David said to Iris had worked. Things were going to be alright from now on.

She went home the next day.

14

As Finch approached the front door, he glanced up and saw Nichelle, standing in it, hands on her hips.

As he brushed past her, he said, "I'll go get my things together."

"*Wait!*" she said with a concerned intensity.

Her forceful command stopped him. "What's the matter?"

"What did you two do? To David's father?"

"Nothing, actually. He wouldn't let us in the house. Threatened to blow our heads off with his shotgun if we didn't leave."

"I was. . ." she began, reaching out and touching his arm, looking like a person who'd realized that, unexpectedly, the water she'd waded into wasn't over her head. "I was worried. About you. About what was going to happen."

"About me?" he said, trying to determine what she was driving at.

"That you'd do something terrible."

"Well, we didn't, so that's that."

He pushed past her and headed for his bedroom. Mostly packed already, he wouldn't need long to get the remaining parts of his world together. Mainly, it meant gathering up his laptop and the two old, worn suitcases he hauled around. The trailer contained his tools, the small bits of furniture he insisted on holding on to, plus a few other essentials. The surprise was all of his laundry, laid out on the bed, freshly washed, and some of it ironed.

Nichelle appeared at his door. "I need to give you something."

"Cleaning my clothes was thanks enough. You didn't need to—"

"It wasn't any trouble. I wanted to."

They shared an awkward look, then she disappeared from the bedroom doorway. Puzzled by what had just happened, Finch picked up his clothes and started stashing them in the suitcase.

Finished now, he glanced around the room, thinking about his brief stay. It was a habit of his, regurgitating each experience in his head so he could remember it better later on. The places he lived were filed in his memory like index cards, always available for retrieval. Some cards were in better shape than others.

Stopping by Davie's room, he told the bleary-eyed boy he was leaving and he would miss him. Davie gave him a big hug and looked sad, saying, who was going to help me with my homework? Finch said call me, text me, PM me, anytime you get stuck. Davie still clung to him. Giving the boy a kiss on top of the head, Finch broke free, knowing if he stayed much longer, he might never leave.

At the door, Finch found Nichelle waiting for him, a brown paper sack in hand, looking awkward. "I fixed you something to eat. In case, you know, you get hungry on the road. Thought it was the least I could do."

"Thanks," he said. "That's very kind. I've already told Davie 'bye."

"He'll miss you, Finch. He's gotten really attached to you."

"I'm not much to hang onto," he said. "Probably he only misses his dad and I'm the stand-in."

"It's more than that."

Finch had nothing else to add, so he headed out to the trailer with his suitcases. Nichelle followed with his lunch sack and watched as he loaded the trailer, making sure everything was in its place.

"That's very organized," she said, appraising the interior. Custom metal shelving faced each wall. Retainer bungee cords held boxes and cartons in place so they wouldn't shift in transit.

"Helps me to find things. Probably not what you expected."

She ducked her head as her foot found some gravel to poke through.

Finished, he closed and locked the trailer door and added the padlock. "Well, guess that's it. Thanks for letting me stay here. I know I was in the way, but. . ." His explanation stopped, then started again. "I wanted to be helpful to you and Davie."

"You were," she said. "Very. I want. . ." She didn't finish her thought.

Nichelle had this strange look about her, as if she couldn't decide what to do next. When she glanced up, it surprised him to see her eyes tear up. Still emotional, he decided, not unexpected after losing her husband. Time to go. He reached for the sack.

"Thanks for this. I'll. . ."

By then, she had her arms around his back, the side of her face against his cheek. She held on in a desperate sort of way. He stood there awkwardly, not knowing what to do. His first reaction was to crush her to him, but he knew that was not appropriate. Instead, he delicately placed his arms around her. She continued to hold him. As she did, he tightened his grip, pressing her against him. She didn't pull away. For Finch, it was all magical, unexpected.

"I haven't been very nice to you," she said, apologizing once more.

"You were fine. I don't deserve—"

She pulled away, instantly rebuffing his apology. "Don't *say* that! Don't *ever* say that." Flustered after their embrace, she struggled to regain her composure. Glancing at his rig, she said, "You should get an RV."

"They're expensive," he said. "Besides, this way I can park the trailer and drive my car to the job sites."

She shifted her feet and hooked her thumbs in the back pockets of her jeans. "I guess that makes sense." Then she added, "When are you coming back to see us?"

"I don't have plans. Why?"

"I'll miss you, Finch. Both of us will." The tears that had filled her eyes started rolling down her cheeks. She looked miserable, standing there in the cool wind, acting like someone she really cared about was leaving. But that wasn't possible. She loved David instead. It was just a couple of weeks since she had lost him, and. . . An impossible thought crossed his mind. Could it be that. . . No, of course not, don't be so stupid he told himself. Nichelle's just lonely, filled with emotion after the tragic death. That had to be it.

"Call me Finchie," he blurted, not knowing where the thought came from. "Only David and James can do that. I'd. . .I'd like you to do the same."

A hand flung up to chase away her tears. "Call me when you get to where you're headed. Please. I *mean* it." Her tone was insistent, bordering on panic.

"Sure, okay."

"Come back to us," she said, already backing up. "Goodbye, Finchie."

He scanned her face, noting every detail. "Sure, see you later."

Nichelle turned and hurried back into the house and closed the door.

He stood there, holding the lunch sack, as hope rose in him like an explosion he didn't want to stop.

15

David Perry upended Jacqueline Randolph's serene, stable world the moment he came to live with them. Before, she had her corner of the second floor all to herself. James' own room was at the opposite end of the same level, leaving two intervening bedrooms and baths, almost never used. Not that Jackie had to make much in the way of accommodations. One day he wasn't there, then he was. When he arrived, she figured him for eleven or maybe twelve, but she wasn't sure about his birthday. The good news was that she now had a pseudo-older brother, someone to alter the monotony of her privileged life. David seemed apologetic and intensely grateful to her parents. There wasn't any problem with how he behaved. The problem was her immediate attraction to him.

David soon melted into the Randolph family like he had always been there. He was courteous, easy, the perfect houseguest, the kind you almost forgot about being there. Not that she could forget him. Over the next few years, she grew steadily more interested in their relationship.

One evening several years later, about the time Jackie started high school, her mother said she had an important question to ask her. Her parents were thinking of adopting David, seeing as he was practically the same as family already. What did she think about that? Wasn't that a good idea? Instead of agreeing, Jackie threw a fit. The stated reason was she didn't want to share her inheritance with some person not related to her. It wasn't fair, she said, him not being a real Randolph. The hidden reason was that she wanted to keep the option open to marry David, and she certainly couldn't very well marry an adopted brother. Seeing her vehement rejection, her mother never mentioned it again, and the family dropped the matter.

By the time David was a senior in high school, Jackie was madly in love with him and determined they should wed. Sure, she was sixteen, really too young, but state law allowed it with parental consent. Besides, she was mature for her age, so it would all work out. She knew how David looked at her when she swam laps in the backyard pool. She enjoyed acting like she didn't know he was lusting after her. It all seemed preordained, so simple. David graduated this year and her father would immediately put him to work in the family business. They would get married as soon as practical after that. It would be this huge wedding, the envy of the social scene. Soon, he would rise in the company, way up, and eventually run the place. At night, alone in bed, she fantasized about him and their future, often thinking about him making love to her, wondering how it would actually feel. She needed to make sure they had sex before he graduated so she would have a special hold over him, the taking of her virginity. Exactly how this was going to happen, she wasn't sure. Early on, David adopted a distant pleasantness toward her, but she knew, deep down, he shared her feelings. She even thought of going down the hall and getting into bed with him one night, but she fought the impulse. He needed to make the first move, to prove his love for her.

One reason she was certain of his true feelings was that special afternoon late last summer, when her parents were away for the weekend and James was at a baseball game across town. Jackie and David were the only ones in the house. She was standing in her bathroom, down to her low-cut panties, assessing herself. You're gorgeous, her mother told her repeatedly, going to be the ideal woman. Confident in her fortunate genes, Jackie didn't dispute the assessment. Her perfect breasts were already full and firm, "perky" her mother said. She had her hands up, cupping them, trying to decide how much bigger they might get. By now, she was already larger than her mother and was going to need new bras next month. She was turning this way and that, admiring her silhouette, when she heard a sound out in the hall. Looking up, she saw David, visible through the partially open bathroom door, his mouth slightly ajar. She turned to face him and dropped her hands. She watched him stare at her, drinking her in. Taking her time, she walked to the bathroom door, looking him in the eye the entire time until she eased it closed.

Jackie went to her closet and put on her skimpiest bikini, the one her mother forbade her to wear any place except the backyard. As she descended the stairs, he was there, at the bottom, looking up at her, his face flushed. She took her time and pretended nothing had happened as she brushed past him.

He said, "Jackie, please. . ."

Turning to face him, she said, "Something wrong?"

"I want to, need to, apologize for what I did."

"What's that?" she said, standing on the step above him. He glanced at her full breasts, barely covered by her top. As if caught with his fingers in a fire, he immediately switched back to her face. She could see small droplets of sweat appearing on his forehead.

"Looking at you when I was out in the hall. I should never have done that."

Even at this age, manipulating men came easily to her. Appraising him with her big blue eyes, she said, "My fault, really. I should have closed the door all the way."

"But, I mean, if your parents ever found out, I'm sure they would. . ."

She put her hand on the side of his face. "Don't worry, David. It'll be our little secret. I won't ever tell. Will you?"

"No, of course not. I mean, I, uh. . ."

"It's settled, then," she said. "Put your trunks on. Let's go for a swim."

He stared at her. "I, uh, I have some homework to do."

"Don't be silly. You have the rest of the weekend. Besides, it's just you and me here now." With that, she reached for his hand, which was already sweaty. "Come on, please. I need you to keep me company."

David shifted his weight, his face betraying the turmoil between what he wanted and what he was afraid might happen. Jackie felt this was the perfect time for them to make love. She fantasized about them, poolside, kissing and caressing, then taking off their clothes and having sex. It would be magical, incredible, something they would both always remember.

"No, I, I can't," he said, the distress of the decision tormenting his face.

"When you change your mind, I'll be waiting," she said, giving him a broad smile, then headed for the pool.

Jackie expected him to follow her in a few minutes. How could he not? She knew how desirable she was, how much he wanted her, how open she was to his expected advances. But, after some time passed and the swimming of laps ended, no David appeared.

She toweled off and laid down on a beach towel, then undid the string that attached the top of her swimsuit. Soon, he would emerge from the house and see her lying there, half-naked, soaking up the sun. He wouldn't be able to resist. She would ask him to put lotion all over her back and legs, then turn over when he finished. Once he saw her, he wouldn't be able to resist. They'd make love right out there in the open. It would be so passionate and totally scandalous.

But no David appeared. It became obvious to her that he really *was* going to avoid her. The destruction of her romantic idyll pissed Jackie off. Getting up, she reattached her top and reclined in one of the pool lounges, plotting how to best show him how his unexpected behavior caused her to not be happy, not one damn bit, him leaving her hanging like that. How dare he upend her perfect plan?

Afterward, she returned to the house and discovered that his bedroom door was closed. Angry now, she wanted nothing more than to charge in and have it out with him. They'd fight at first. Maybe she would slap him and he would retaliate by holding her hand as she struggled to hurt him again. Then they would silently admit their shared passion, start kissing, and then make love, right there on top of his bed. She hesitated, though, not wanting to show her true feelings first, needing him instead to acknowledge how disappointed she was in his failure to appear poolside. Torn between passion and revenge, she paused at his door. After choosing to leave David to his own selfish pursuits, Jackie headed for the shower, making sure the door was closed this time. She leaned forward, hands on the wall, and let the warm water wash over her.

Unable to come up with what she considered an appropriate payback, Jackie decided instead to not speak to him for two days. She knew he would spend the whole time worrying that she could tell her parents at any moment about their brief liaison. David was tougher on himself than anyone else. Let him twist in the wind, she decided. Proper punishment for rejecting her.

Despite the breakdown of her pool day plan, Jackie still wanted David, and she knew he remained infatuated with her. As the school year went by, she flirted shamelessly, increasing the pressure by touching him and saying suggestive things when no one else was around. David worked tirelessly to resist her charms. But he wouldn't, couldn't, outlast her, she told herself. She would have him. The specifics of when and how weren't clear, but it would happen.

Everything was going to plan until, late in the school year, she forced herself to rethink her David strategy. That day, she found her friend, Camille, alone on a bench outside of school, waiting for her ride. Jackie was leaving a cheerleader meeting that took longer than expected. Camille was trying to hide the evidence that she had been crying.

After some prodding, it all came out. Camille was pregnant by her boyfriend, Paul. Camille's parents, committed Catholics, forbade her to use birth control. Abstinence, her mother had told her, was the only acceptable way to behave, especially at her age. Paul was sympathetic, Camille said, and madly in love with her. He insisted he would quit school, get a job somewhere, support her and the baby. They could make it work if she wanted to keep the child. Of course, she would keep it, she told Paul. Abortion was out of the question.

Jackie asked her how this had happened. Hadn't they used protection? Yes, she said, he'd used a condom, but something had gone wrong. Maybe it tore, or maybe he didn't put it on right. She didn't know for sure. All she knew was that she too young to be pregnant. Had she told her parents, Jackie asked? No, she had to tell them tonight and was dreading it. Almost three months along and soon to be showing, she couldn't hide her condition much longer. Oh God, what was she going to do? Jackie held Camille as she cried. Cracks formed in Jackie's determination to trick David into having sex with her.

Her parents' demands immediately overrode Camille's resolve. Paul's own wishes were cast aside. They threatened him with a charge of rape if he persisted. The parents sent their daughter away at once, telling everyone she was spending the end of this semester, as well as the coming summer and fall, at a special school to expand her educational experience. That explanation, though suspicious, was enough for the parents' friends and acquaintances to at least socially accept. Apparently, Jackie was the only outsider who knew the truth. From time to time, Camille sent her clandestine, sad letters from the unwed mother's home. She was doing alright, she said, but was lonely for Paul, school and her old friends. Getting larger every day, she wanted more than anything to have the baby and come back home. After that, she said she was sure she would reunite with her boyfriend. Paul, unknown to Camille, was forbidden to talk about the situation or contact Camille in any way, under threat of legal action. Jackie watched him the next semester, going about his classes, often looking dejected and miserable. Later in the year, Camille had her baby, and despite her pleas, it was put up for adoption. She returned for the spring semester a changed woman. Every once in a while, Jackie would see Paul and Camille talking quietly together, but the two of them never reestablished their prior relationship.

By then, David had headed for college and was inaccessible to Jackie, which made her furious. He replied to each of her letters, only letting her know, without specific details, how things were going, but made no acknowledgement of an undying love for her. Dammit, she had told him she was in love with him before he left, but he had gone anyway. Now, at night in her bed, rather than fantasize about him making love to her, she seethed at the thought of him having sex with various college girls, knowing that she was powerless to prevent it. As the year went on, he continued to stay away, seldom coming home, even for holidays, and mostly avoided her when he did. Now entering her last semester as a senior in high school, Jackie was in full bloom. All the boys wanted her, and all the girls envied her. She would wait until college, she decided, to experience sex. These local boys were not what she needed. David, well, she wasn't sure what she was going to do about David.

The day after she registered for her freshman year at the private university, Jackie visited the health department and got a prescription for birth control pills. She also signed up to pledge the correct sorority. With a few weeks, she was a new initiate. She had picked the organization carefully, making sure it consisted exclusively of women like herself, scions of rich, socially prominent families with certain expectations. The parties with the frats were never-ending, and Jackie understood quickly that she enjoyed sex. But she was picky. Her mates had to be good-looking, tall, preferably rich, and reasonably good in bed. She decided to marry either a future doctor or lawyer, or perhaps, if that didn't work out, someone with strong connections to a successful business. By her senior year, when she was president of the sorority, she settled on Randall Weir, of the Boston Weirs. His father was a well-known lawyer, and Randall's own future with the eponymous firm was preordained. All Randall had to do was finish law school and pass the bar.

After college graduation, Jackie had a huge wedding, her mother sparing no expense. The guest list stretched out to five hundred and the writeups made the local paper two weeks in a row. Her mother insisted they invite David, who begged off, saying unfortunately he didn't have time to come, being too busy with work deadlines, and sent a gift instead. It was a kitchen appliance, one not on her detailed and extravagant gift list, so Jackie added it to the charity pile as soon as she opened it.

As expected, Randall's career moved along on greased skids. He went to law school and graduated comfortably in the top quarter of his class, while she set about becoming the perfect society wife. Other women might aspire to a career, but Jackie was more interested in following her mother's lead, only doing a much better job of it. There was a certain satisfaction, she felt, being part of the upper crust of society. Giving parties, being seen in all the right places, wearing the right clothes, living an exciting and enviable life. Her trust fund income supplemented Randall's earnings, meaning that, for now, she could spend pretty much what she wanted. Life was perfect, except for one thing. She needed children, two to be exact, preferably one of each, to complete the ideal nuclear family. They were trying, without success, to get pregnant. Her checklist included having the first child no later than age twenty-eight, but now she was crossing thirty with no baby in sight. Recent fertility tests indicated Randall had a very low sperm count. You could get lucky, the doctor suggested, if you want to keep trying. Or we can try IVF. The cost wasn't a problem, but Randall hesitated. Can't we wait a while longer and see what happens, he had said. Jackie knew the real reason for his hesitation—a male's reluctance to admit he wasn't fertile, especially if his friends ever found out. She grudgingly agreed and reworked her timetable. Adoption was out of the question. Her children were going to be genuine Randolphs or nothing at all.

About that time, her father called and asked if they wanted to move back and take over the family company. James, he said, wanted to stay in finance and wasn't interested. Jackie, content climbing the social ladder in Boston, was not terribly interested in the move until her mother told her how much money the company made, and that Randall probably wouldn't have to work all that hard to keep things going. Right now, Jackie's husband was working ridiculous hours at the law practice, leaving very little time for her or procreation. This new opportunity would raise their income substantially and free up a lot of his time. Besides, her chances of making it to the epitome of society back home were much better than with all the competition in Boston. A win-win, she decided.

The next time Jackie saw David was at his wedding to Iris. She remembered sitting there in the church, watching them at the altar, seeing the way he looked at his bride, like she was the only woman in the world. Jackie's emotions alternated between intense jealousy and patrician dismissal. Later, she concentrated on the first dance of husband and wife. As she watched them move against each other, those earlier years of desire came back to her in waves as she remembered all those previous attempts to capture David, now gone to waste. It made her angry, the dredging up of old feelings she would rather forget. Despite being in a much better social and financial position with Randall instead of David, she hurt from what she was observing. Catching her brother James looking at her, she knew he knew what she was thinking. Angry at herself for revealing her true feelings, she insisted to Randall that they leave the reception early.

Seeing David that night at the pizza place was a watershed moment for Jackie. At first, she thought of being shitty to him, saying some unkind things and watching him duck his head and stumble over his words, giving her cold satisfaction for him standing her up when she so desperately wanted him years ago. She heard he now worked for some kind of consulting company, a job distinctly inferior to the position that Randall now enjoyed. Yes, she was better off, much better off, with her second choice. Still, she had never quite gotten over David, and seeing him sitting there felt like a small dagger digging into her chest.

As she waited for her takeout, she realized he was there solo like herself. Apparently, that neurotic wife of his was staying home, still clinging to her lost child, from what James had said. Maybe their marriage wasn't that great after all. Then the perfect idea occurred to her. If Randall couldn't father her child, David could be her baby daddy. He looked enough like James to be his brother, so no one would suspect. Plus, David had already proven his own fertility. And he wouldn't be able to resist her charms for long. She could arrange for him to make love to her, even if he resisted, because she was good at male manipulation, very good. Whether it was talking her way out of a traffic ticket or scoring a table at a crowded restaurant, being a striking woman with a sexy voice carried with it major advantages. She just needed to be careful and not scare David off before she could get him into bed. Iris, and whatever muddled life she was leading, Jackie could care less about. Time for Step One.

Once she had her order in hand, she walked up behind him and said, "Hey, sailor, how about buying a girl a beer?" The perfect light-hearted intro line. When he turned around and looked at her, that old longing immediately visible on his face, she knew she had him, at least for now. David, though, was like a twitchy deer, his eyes and ears constantly scanning the environment, alert for danger, wary and ready to bolt at any moment. She had to be careful and not press him for too much too soon. All it would take was the right amount of finesse and she'd get him into bed. At the right time of the month, when she was the most fertile.

16

Finch, temporarily settled in Miami, had a construction job lined up that started in a couple of days. For now, he was cyberstalking David's father. He had contacted Perry through the dark web using ProtonMail's encrypted email. Finch concealed his own identity by using a 256 bit encryption VPN over Tor, which, though more complicated to set up, prevented a malicious exit node from spying on his internet activity. The previous course he took in encryption, enrolled in because of his natural curiosity, was coming in handy. As usual, since the Tor messages bounced through servers all around the world, the browser operated slowly, but that wasn't an issue with their plodding messages.

—*Are you interested in trading some photos, maybe selling some? Confidential, of course. I'm in the market.*

Figuring it might be days before Perry responded, Finch was about to close his laptop when he received a reply.

—*Who is this?*

—*Friend of a friend. We share a particular interest.*

—*Yeah, what interest?*

—*Let's say one best kept private.*

—*Are you in law enforcement?*

—*Of course not. No way.*

The last message didn't receive an immediate reply. Finch waited a bit, then sent,

—*Check with you later. Think about it. I'm not in a hurry.*

—*Yeah, later.*

That was enough for now, Finch decided. Let the old fuck wonder who he was and what was going on. He'd give Perry time to think over his offer, then re-contact him again in a few days. From now on, whenever Perry opened an email from Finch, a few fragments of software would be deposited, without his knowledge, into his laptop's operating system. After multiple emails, it would add enough fragments together to create the kernel of a program that would surreptitiously download spyware and keylogging software onto Perry's computer. That would allow Finch to browse the internal hard drive without Perry's knowledge, even with the laptop officially in shutdown mode. The power light would extinguish and the screen go dark, but he'd still be inside the machine, sifting through its contents undisturbed. Finch would need to be careful, though, and make sure he was out of the laptop before Perry turned it on again. In that case, touching the power-on button would immediately make the screen come alive, proving that the laptop wasn't truly off to start with. Details, Finch decided. He had time to be patient.

Finch thought back to the morning that he and James intended to kill the old man. Ordinarily, Finch would never have considered such a thing, but Perry was evil enough that Finch had no moral qualms about taking the old bastard out. He didn't look upon himself as a vigilante or a person consumed with revenge. No, he was only doing what needed to be done, to free society from a predatory pervert. Morally, he knew this was a dubious position, but over the years, he had convinced himself that if the Perry opportunity ever presented itself, he would take it. First, he needed to make sure that any old photos of David were off the hard drive, or not stored in the cloud, though he considered that last possibility unlikely because of potential liability issues in case the cloud provider scanned for such images. Being inside the laptop would also tell Finch if Perry ever plugged in an external hard drive. He expected that would be the case, as the old man wouldn't want to lose any precious pics that he could sell in the future. Once he discovered the location of all the files, he could take action.

Finch closed his eyes and remembered his conversation with David from a few years back. David panicked over the possibility that the photos, which his father had so diligently saved from when he was a young boy, might get out. David wasn't specific about exactly what they depicted or how many of them there were. He's blackmailing you, Finch told him, the worthless piece of shit. Blackmailers never stop with just one ask when they figure the sucker will continue to pay. Please don't do this, Finch had pleaded. We can go to the police or the FBI, tell them your story. They can put him behind bars for good. No, David said, I couldn't bear it if

Nichelle and Davie found out what had happened to me. Other than Iris and the therapist, you and James are the only other ones who know, or who will ever know.

David gave his father the thirty grand, negotiated down from the original ask of fifty. That money should have gone into conservative investments for David's family's future, to balance out the misplaced risk he'd taken before. Unexpectedly, Perry hadn't asked for more money right away, but told his son that he'd be contacting him in the future for further negotiations. David hadn't lived long enough to get a second demand. Finch wondered if Nichelle had any idea, now that he had told her a bit of the truth about her husband's past, of what David had gone through.

Nichelle.

Finch tried his best to purge her from his thoughts after he left her house, but so far was unsuccessful. As promised, he told her right away where he landed. I'll be here about six months, he said, maybe longer. She seemed eager to hear from him, but Finch had little understanding of what, deep down, motivated Nichelle. He thought her appraisal of him had moved too rapidly from unwelcome house guest, to gratitude for fixing her house, to confider of hidden scandals, to, at the end, perhaps something more than that, maybe even a real attachment to him. He relived their parting a thousand times in his mind. Was it misplaced loyalty on her part? Maybe only the emotional relief that he was there, a person to be relied on, disguised as a false affirmation of him? Or could she possibly have genuine feelings for him? No, he told himself, that's not likely. She's only upset about the tragedy and clung to him as a last resort. But she said, as he left, that she wanted him to come back to them, to both of them. And he remembered the hug in the driveway, especially since he relived it, over and over, constantly searching for its exact meaning.

He unlocked his phone and texted Nichelle, asking if he could have her email address, if that was okay with her. In case Davie needed help with his homework, he said, or if she needed anything. After hitting the Send button, he stared at his phone, not knowing exactly what type of reply to expect.

17

Encouraged by how quickly Iris seemed to recover from her depression, David grew cautiously optimistic. Progress at recovering from such deep hurts would, he knew, be long and prone to regression. Beginning with the first visit to the therapist, though, Iris was open to discussing her anguish over losing the baby and her concurrent, if unfair, rejection of David. David, his defensive wall up, revealed only parts of his earlier abuse, but enough to convince both of the other parties that he understood the nature of painful pasts. Within a month of starting their joint therapy, things improved enough that Iris went back to work in the event planning business. After some serious, open discussions between David and Iris, they jointly agreed to put off trying for another baby until their finances improved. David was relieved to see that she no longer blamed him for not wanting a child. He was, he decided, more in love with his wife than ever.

Iris, though, never returned to having much interest in their sex life. David waited to make sure she was ready, and the first time they made love, he was extra attentive. Still, he sensed she was uneasy, even fearful of having sex with him. He assumed it was her constant worry about accidentally getting pregnant again, so both of them agreed to use birth control. But despite their best intentions, sex was never the same as before. She was often tentative, uncomfortable, and more than once, they broke off making love when she changed her mind. Her repeated apologies and assurances that this was all her fault only made him feel like a bad husband covering up his own sexual frustration. Often, after a broken romantic interlude, he caught himself thinking back about Jackie and how desperately he had wanted her when they were younger.

As time went on, David stopped going to therapy with Iris, feeling he had exposed himself enough. Intensely private and uncomfortable about his past, he felt his recent revelations, though incomplete, left him exposed, naked. Still, he encouraged Iris to keep attending the sessions, saying it helped for her to have a third party to confide in, to tell things she wasn't quite prepared to share with David. This seemed to mollify her. In the meantime, he regretted selfishly wanting his wife to return to the carefree, loving woman he knew before the miscarriage. But he knew Iris had experienced a terrible shock, one which left lasting scars. She *would* get better, he told himself, things *would* be back to the way they were before. But as time went on, he faced the reality that their intimate relationship had forever changed.

Throughout his therapy, David kept his indiscrete kiss with Jackie a secret. He didn't see how this pertained to Iris' present issues, and admitting to the unwise liaison would only further damage her opinion of him. Fortunately, Jackie stayed out of his life for over a month, until the day she called and invited him to lunch.

Immediately on edge, his voice firmed after returning her greeting. "Look, Jackie, I don't think we should go out, just the two of us. I don't feel comfortable doing that. Is Randall out of town again?"

She laughed into the phone. "I'm flying solo this week, but don't worry. We'll go someplace public, very public. How about the country club? You know the food is always good there."

"You're a member now?"

"Of course," she said. "We joined as soon as we moved back. Come on, *please*. I'm lonely."

"I don't know about this."

"Look, I promise not to attack you, if that's what you're thinking."

"No, that's not it." Of course, that was exactly what he was worried about.

"Invite Iris if you want. She can come, too. It's fine with me."

He felt himself relaxing. "She's busy with a project today. I don't think she has time."

"We can wait, I guess. See when her schedule will free up."

Capitulating, he said, "Not necessary. I'll go."

He heard relief in her voice. "I'll make reservations for 12:30. Will that work? How much time to you have for lunch?"

"I don't have a definite lunch hour."

"Great. See you then." She hung up.

David put his phone down, trying to decide what Jackie really wanted. He wasn't afraid of her, but also knew her well enough to understand that she was determined to get her way, whatever that was. What could it hurt, though, a simple lunch out in public?

• • • • •

He found Jackie sitting at a table next to the large sectional glass wall that looked out onto the first hole's tee box. It was still too cold for the regular golfers, but a few hardy souls practiced their swings at the adjacent driving range, located off to the side of the restaurant. Jackie got up and gave him a friendly hug before he sat down.

"Thanks for coming, David. I really appreciate this."

"Sure," he said, scanning the room before he sat down.

A few of the diners' faces looked vaguely familiar, but it had been years since he was in this room. He remembered the previous times when he often tried to disappear into himself, feeling desperately out-of-place while the Randolphs glided through the social mix with nary a pause. Good for them. He was glad he didn't have to pretend anymore.

The refreshed dining room sported a more contemporary flair. Gone were the heavy wood paneling and the dark carpet. The new décor included light gray painted walls plus a carpet with a custom pattern repeating the club's logo. Much more inviting and open, he decided, though he was sure that the men's cardroom was just as clubby, dark, and smoke-filled as always.

"Looks like they did a big remodel," he said, trying to think of something to say. Normally, he would offer thanks, great to see you, looking forward to lunch, but he felt ill at ease. Jackie looked stunning in her stylish maroon dress. He caught himself wondering how much it cost and what she looked like underneath it.

The server came by, left menus and took their drink order. Time for idle conversation.

"How's Iris doing?" Jackie said, looking out the window before turning to him.

"Fine, good. Much better."

"I hear you're both going to therapy."

"That's right. Well, we both did for a while. Now she's going by herself."

"Well, I hope that does the trick."

"I think it will."

"You two planning on having another child soon?"

"No," he said. "Iris agreed to wait for a while. We need to get our finances in better shape first."

Jackie nodded. "I can see where that would be a problem."

Not for you, David thought as he picked up his water glass. Nothing much is ever a problem for you.

Changing the subject, she said, "See anyone here you remember?"

He scanned the room again. "I think so. But it's been a good while." He started naming off the few people he remembered or wasn't sure about.

Jackie either confirmed or corrected his various observations and offered updates on everyone he used to know. She takes to the social scene and underlying gossip like a pro, he decided.

A woman who had caught his eye earlier came over to their table.

"Mrs. Stevens," Jackie said, holding out a limp hand. "So good to see you. Do you remember David Perry?"

"Yes, of course," the woman said, barely grasping Jackie's offered paw. "David, it's been a long time. Good to see you here at the club."

David stood up. "Mrs. Stevens. How nice to see you again."

"I saw you two here and just had to come over," she said. "Where's Randall, Jackie?"

"He's out of town on business with Daddy. I needed a lunch companion, and David here was sweet enough to keep me company."

"Is that right?" Mrs. Stevens said in an off-hand way. "If I remember, David, you're married, correct?"

"Yes, ma'am. To Iris. She's busy today and couldn't come. Jackie asked us both."

"I see," the woman said. "Well, enjoy your lunch. Good to see you, David. Jackie."

David sat back down and retrieved his napkin. Mrs. Stevens returned to the table filled with her privileged friends. He still felt out of place here, where the Randolph family often came for lunch after church on Sundays. Jackie's parents were always interested in being seen at the club, schmoozing friends and business acquaintances alike. David had cared less about the social implications, instead being more interested in blending in with the furniture. He never gained the comfortable façade of wealth and privilege, especially since he was essentially a house guest at the Randolphs. A good thing, in the long run, he decided, since he lived a much more modest life on a middle-class income.

"In case you're wondering," Jackie said, laying her hand on David's arm. "She's still the same old gossip."

"She was checking us out?" David said.

"Of course. Looks like we're safe now. As long as you don't throw me down on the floor." She said the last of her words with a twinkle in her eyes.

"Don't think I'll be doing that," he said, blushing despite himself.

"Oh, one never knows."

David blanched.

She patted his hand. "Only kidding, David. Don't be so serious all the time. Now, what are we having for lunch?"

• • • • •

After their prolonged meal, David grew antsy to get back to work. He had several projects that needed his attention.

"Well, thanks again," he said, awkwardly extending his hand to Jackie as they stood out on the sidewalk.

"Aren't you going to take me home?" she said, looking at him with reproach.

"What?"

"I don't have my car here. I caught a ride. Can you take me home? Please? If you can't, I'll have to call a taxi or something, and those things are always so dirty and gross."

Realizing he had no viable social alternative, David agreed.

After they got into his car, he started the engine, letting it warm up. He drove a white midsize Chevy, an everyman car, not nearly as expensive and glamorous as Jackie's black Mercedes. Relief that the vehicle was actually clean today reduced his nervousness, though he immediately upbraided himself for having these thoughts. No need to feel that way; Jackie is damn lucky to get a ride from you. Still, he couldn't help thinking the ridiculous notion that such a beautiful woman should only be driven around in a suitable vehicle.

Jackie buckled her seatbelt and then folded her hands in her lap. Apparently, she was ready for the chauffer to do his duty.

"Where to?" he said.

"Don't you know where I live?"

"No, why should I?" he said.

The musical laugh rang in his ears. "Sorry, I just assumed. Turn left out of the parking lot."

18

James prepared a set of printouts for Nichelle, including several graphics. He wasn't sure how financially savvy she was, but didn't want to appear condescending. After seeing too many of his male colleagues act this way toward women, especially widows, he was sensitive to the issue and didn't want to offend Nichelle.

With his materials spread out on the breakfast table, James explained Nichelle's and Davie's future prospects. Despite David's life insurance payout, without her earning an income, they would be out of money within three years.

"I see," Nichelle said, a taciturn expression crossing her face.

"I know that's not the news you hoped for," James said.

"Now, from what you've told me, part of the shortfall is because of the earlier investments selected in the portfolio. Ones that didn't work out, right?"

James nodded. Nichelle had a much clearer idea of their situation than he expected. He shouldn't have been surprised. Nichelle was extra sharp and held a master's degree. She was a successful physician's assistant before taking time off to be a stay-at-home mom to Davie.

She continued, "And because of those selected investments, their return hasn't done as well as the overall market?"

"Yes, that's exactly right. I selected the prospects. Then David and I would go over them. He was short on funds, so the theory was we needed to take extra risk for extra reward." He stopped, thinking about the unfortunate choices they made several years ago. "We discussed it, and he wanted to take the chance. Said it was okay with you. On balance, it was the wrong move. We took the risk but saw little of the reward. I'm sorry, it's my fault."

"Why would you say that?" she said, looking him in the eye.

"Well, if you'd instead had your money in a passive fund, invested in the whole market, you'd be significantly better off by now. By at least thirty, forty percent more."

She considered his response before replying. "But if the strategy had succeeded, we'd be a lot better off than that, right?"

"Yes, of course, but it didn't—"

She patted his hand. "You think you're responsible for this, don't you?"

He nodded. "David and I discussed the strategy. He felt it was the best course of action, and I agreed. The thing is, we rolled the dice and lost. All of those investments seemed promising at first, based on what we knew when we invested, but most didn't do well in the long term." Sitting back in his chair, James added, "I should have advised both of you both against it. I know that now."

"But you didn't know that before."

"No."

"You can't beat yourself up because chance didn't fall our way, James. David never felt that fortune favored him, and I'd have to agree that was mostly the case for him. Things happen we can't control. If I could do that, I'd still have a husband." Nichelle abruptly got up from the table and headed for the kitchen. "More coffee?"

"Yes, thanks."

After she returned with two cups, she said, "Something you need to know. Finch told me, before he left, about what happened to David when he was a little boy."

"He did?" James said, an incredulous look on his face.

"I insisted he tell me the truth. I think he felt that since David was gone, he could be honest with me. He didn't say that much, but I understood what he meant. I think he wanted to spare me the terrible details."

"Glad he did."

"David refused to tell me what the cause of the rift was with his dad. That certainly cleared a lot of things up." She straightened her back, as if she had put something behind her. "The good thing is we have that last thirty thousand working for us now. Tell me what it's invested in."

A shadow crossed James' face.

"What?" she said, concerned by what she saw.

"That, uh, extra money. I never received it."

"What are you talking about? I've seen our savings account statements. The money was withdrawn. Don't kid me, James."

"Look," he said. "I don't know how to tell you this, but that money didn't end up in your investment account. David gave it to his father instead."

"His *father*? What the hell for?"

"I didn't know about this until Finchie told me the day he left. Turns out, uh. . ."

Fuming now, Nichelle said, "Tell me, *dammit*."

"David's father blackmailed him, okay? Said if he didn't give him the money, he would publicly expose David's past, make sure that his employer and all of his friends knew. David believed it would ruin him, and you as well. So, he gave his father the money instead."

Her eyes widened in hurt and disbelief. "But half of that was *my* money, what I'd saved from my job before I quit. And he did this without even fucking *talking* to me?"

"All I can say is that he was very ashamed about his past. He didn't want anyone to know what he'd been through."

She hurled herself out of the kitchen chair and headed for the front door, wrenched it open, and stormed out. James leaned back, waiting, not sure what was going to happen next. He had seen this situation before when people realized their inheritances were not what they expected. Anger would follow the hurt. Hopefully, hatred, the last emotion in the chain, wouldn't apply here. Either way, it would take time for her to work through her feelings.

After a while, she came back in, still flushed but calmer. She sat down and took a sip of her rapidly cooling coffee, barely concealing her emotions.

"It was like living with a stranger," she finally said.

"David loved you, loved Davie. He was very proud of the life you two built. He just. . . He couldn't come to terms with his past. It was his constant worry he would one day be exposed and humiliated, and that you and Davie would hate him for it."

"You always think you have to take up for him," she said, giving James a fierce look.

"No, I'm telling you what I truly believe."

The weight of what she had learned seemed to lift. She squared her shoulders and said, "I know I can't spend forever being hurt about this. I have to be strong for

Davie. I know that's what David would have wanted. Let's move on, figure out a path forward."

"Good choice," he said as he gave her hand a squeeze.

She continued, "I think women are often more conservative regarding finance. We worry about being stuck with little money and a family to take care of. I want less risk from now on, but I realize that I also need a decent amount of growth prospects as well. Can we revise the investment mix and opt for a compromise, a middle strategy?"

"Yes, of course. I've already got some ideas along that line. We can harvest the losses and save on taxes. Plus the term life insurance policy will give you a nice cushion for awhile. I wish now we'd agreed on a higher value for the policy. At least a million, maybe two."

"I know that's what you recommended, but we didn't have any extra money. It was what we felt we could afford. With me not working and saving up for the added investment. . ." She stopped and clenched her teeth before speaking again. "Damn, what a mess."

"We'll figure this out. We have to," James said.

"David insisted I stay home with Davie. That's been good for Davie, but with only one income these days, well, you make sacrifices. Besides, nobody thinks they'll die this young."

"I know this is awfully difficult," James said. "I wish it could be easier."

"Come on, let's quit talking about what could have been." Nichelle offered him a tired smile. "We have a problem that needs solving."

For another hour, the two of them worked through what to sell and which new investments needed to be added to her portfolio. When the session finished, James felt they had achieved their goal.

"I think, overall, this will put you back on track," he said.

"Good. That's what I wanted," she said.

"But you understand you'll still have to go back to work. Eventually."

She hesitated. "Yes, I know that. I'll need to get my license current. But I want to stay home a little longer with Davie, help up get through the transition without David. Maybe another few months would help."

"That makes sense," James said. "Well, guess that's about it. I've taken up a lot of your time."

"We had important things to discuss. It was no imposition."

James set about gathering up the materials to take with him and left out what was to remain. "Anything else I can help you with?" he said.

"Wait. If you will."

"Alright, sure." He searched her face for a clue for what she was angling for, but her countenance remained impassive.

"That day, the morning of the day Finch left, I had this impression that you two were going over to Perry's house and do something terrible to him."

Considering how well he knew Nichelle, and how fond of her he was, James didn't want to lie. "Yes, that was our plan."

"I thought so." She looked off, thinking.

"When David was alive, he insisted we not retaliate against his old man. I think Finchie and I, well, we figured it was way past payback time. Maybe it was a dumb idea, but we were both committed."

"I wish. . ." She stopped, then added, "I wish you'd succeeded."

"You don't really mean that," James said, surprised by her reply.

"People who do that to children need to burn in hell. Or the next best thing."

James reached out and pried her whitened fingertips away from her cup. "It's probably a good thing we didn't go through with it. Really."

"Maybe." She gave up her cup and sat back, looking a little exhausted. "Have you heard from Finchie lately? He has our email addresses and I hear from him every weekend, but he doesn't say much about his personal situation. He's been a godsend to Davie, helping with his classes. His teachers say he's really smart, but he learns in a different way from other kids."

"Finchie's the quiet type, so I don't have any personal updates," he said. He didn't need to fill her in on Finch's cyberstalking progress, at least not yet. James paused, thinking about what she had said. "Finchie, huh? He asked you to call him that?"

"Yes. That's what he said when he left."

"Impressive."

"How so?"

"He only let me and David call him that. Nobody else."

"I see." Nichelle rose and took their cups to the sink.

After that, James finishing stacking up his materials and headed for the front door. Nichelle trailed along behind, wanting to say something but not yet ready to.

"Well, I better get going," he said, holding the door open. "You know you can call me anytime, right?"

"Yes. There is one thing. What does Finchie really think about me? And about Davie?"

Chewing on the inside of his lip, James considered several replies, each fraught with consequences.

"Please tell me the truth," she said, her eyes pleading with him.

"He's crazy about you and Davie."

"Then why did he leave?"

James gave her a sad smile. "Same reason. He felt he couldn't express what he really feels. At least, not yet."

Nichelle turned James' statement over in her mind before commenting. "When you talk to him, would you give him a message?"

"Sure."

"Tell him how much we miss him. And that we want him to come back to us."

19

Step Two was going according to Jackie's plan. She and David were on their way to her house. She considered several options about what to do when they got there, each choice dependent on how David reacted.

As he pulled into the driveway, he said, "Nice place."

"Thanks," she said.

The car coasted to a stop. "Well, I better get back to work."

Jackie expected this. "I'm so glad we had lunch and a chance to talk. Walk me to the door?"

David reluctantly unbuckled his seatbelt and headed up the walk. At the door, he tried to pull away again.

"Please, come in," she said. "Just for a minute. I want you to help me check the house."

"Check it? What for?"

"I believe there's been someone lurking around recently."

"Really?"

"It's probably nothing. There are a few things out of order or maybe missing, here or there, mainly in the backyard. I don't think it's for sure enough to call the police about, but the thought of someone... Well, it scares me, David." She looked up at him, eyes pleading. "If you don't mind. Please?"

"Didn't you set the alarm?"

"I don't think so. I'm afraid I forgot."

David shrugged. "Sure, that's fine."

Jackie opened the front door and entered with David close behind. They both noticed that the security panel was unarmed. Jackie crossed the foyer and living room in a hurry. For a long while, she looked out the French doors into the backyard.

"Anything out of place?" he said, standing back.

"I. . .I don't think so. But I need to check all the rooms. Can you please go with me?"

David mumbled an affirmative grunt. Together they surveyed the house and ended up upstairs in one of the several bedrooms. Looking worried, Jackie sat down on the side of the bed. David joined her.

"Well, is that everywhere?" David said, glancing at his watch.

She sniffled, then her reserve broke and big tears streamed down her cheeks.

"Hey," he said, sitting down next to her. "What's the matter?"

Between sobs, she said, "You think I'm crazy. Admit it."

"No, of course I don't."

Jackie leaned into him, her head on his shoulder, and took his hand. "I'm sorry. I get so lonely when Randall's gone. It's probably only my imagination. This house is too big when I'm here all by myself, especially at night."

David put his arm around her back to support her. "That's natural. Don't regret asking for help."

"Thank you for being here," she said, reaching across his chest. "I don't know what I'd do without you. You've always cared about me. Most people don't."

"That's not true. Everyone loves you."

"Not really. I have a lot of casual friends, but there's hardly any I can really count on." She raised her head and looked at him with an intense expression. "You're about it."

He stared down at her, her full lips within a few inches of his. She knew he wanted her, so she lifted her hand and put it on the side of his face. "Thank you for everything."

They shared a long, passionate kiss. After they broke apart, she snuggled closer to him, a satisfied smile on her face. David looked guilty, very guilty.

"You know, I always wondered about us. . ." she said.

David swallowed. She could see his trepidation rising. Better to head this off, keep the deer from bolting.

"I'm sorry," she said, disentangling herself from him. "That was all my fault. You must think I'm a terrible person."

"No, Jackie, but we can't. . .we can't do this. We're both married to. . .to other people."

She nodded, wiping away her earlier tears. "You're right. I know you're right." She paused for effect. "But I'm so. . ."

"What?" he said. "What's the matter?"

"Things aren't going very well in my life."

"What do you mean?"

"I'm supposed to have the ideal marriage, right? Successful husband, big house, social standing?" She waved her hand in the air for emphasis. "But there's one thing missing. One big thing." She leaned into him again.

"What's that?"

"I want a baby, and Randall, well, he's. . ." She stopped talking and looked guilty for revealing family secrets.

"Tell me what's the matter."

She sniffled. His hand moved across her back again. A good sign. He would be sympathetic now.

"I don't think we can have children. We've talked about other things, like adoption, but he's very against that." She stopped, acting as if a terrible secret was inadvertently revealed. "Oh, David, I'm so sorry for being a burden to you. I shouldn't have said anything about our personal problems."

She started crying again, sobbing into his coat. He reached his free hand across her front to stabilize her body. It slipped off of her shoulder and moved down to her breast. He held his hand there, uncertain of what to do next, but not breaking away, either. Jackie moved her hand over to his and pressed it against her.

"Kiss me again. Please," she pleaded.

Then they were kissing, longer and more passionately than before, his hand massaging her breast. It was her that broke off the embrace, abruptly standing up.

"I know what you must think of me now," she said, facing away from him.

David, still recovering from their sensual contact, seemed disoriented. "I'm to blame, too."

"No, it's all me," she said. "You need to go before I get us both into trouble."

With that, she left the bedroom and headed downstairs.

"Jackie? Wait!" he called after her.

When he caught up with her, she was standing with her back to the front door, hands tucked behind her bottom, her shoulders back and chest extended. She looked confused and uncertain.

"Hey, look, it's not just you—"

"I was feeling so vulnerable and there you were, being a wonderful man, trying to comfort me, and look what I did."

"Jackie, it's. . . Look, my feelings for you are complicated. They always have been."

"What does that mean?"

"I've always cared about you. You know that. But you were too young for me."

"I'm not too young now."

"But it's too late. Don't you see? We've both made choices, choices that are impossible to undo."

She stared at him. "Are they?"

"Yes, and. . ." He hesitated, unsure of what else to say.

She turned petulant. "You'd better go. I've been enough of a burden for one day."

"Jackie, look, I. . ." He stopped mid-sentence.

"What?" she said, doing her best to look sad and hurt. "Are you going to tell me the truth? That you aren't interested in me or my problems?"

"No, of course not. I mean. . . I better go."

She turned and reached for the door handle. "I'm sure you want to get away from me as soon as possible."

His frustration peaked. "We can talk about this later, okay?"

She unlocked the door and opened it. "Sorry I ruined your day."

"You didn't. Listen, I better go." With that, he exited the house and headed quickly to his car.

Jackie closed the door. A broad smile crossed her face. Step Two, setting the hook, was complete. Let him run from her, let him believe that he wasn't caught. She would ovulate in about two weeks and needed to settle on a trumped-up reason for David to have to return.

Elated at her success so far, Jackie went to her side of the enormous master closet and pulled out the remains of last season's outfits. These clothes she would take to the consignment store. For now, she needed to replenish her wardrobe.

• • • • •

The sales clerk at the upscale specialty women's clothing store mentioned what a good mood her customer was in that day, and was quite pleased to collect the hefty commission on all the things that Mrs. Weir bought.

20

Decked out in the accouterments typical of a successful financial advisory firm, the conference room waited patiently for the occasional meeting. Full height continuous glass windows formed one side of the large room, while the other three borders were outfitted with oil paintings and a long bookcase that faced the windows. The signature bookcase, filled with miscellaneous and brightly colored books that no one had read, also contained various knickknacks and souvenirs purchased during previous overseas trips taken by the managing partners. Tax deductible business expenses, of course, as the stuff eventually found its way to the conference room once the purchasers grew tired of admiring the items in their own houses. In the center of the room was a large, custom-built mahogany table with the usual array of expensive leather chairs paying homage to the central artifact.

When James entered, Michael Anderson, the lead partner of Anderson-Markum, was already there.

James glanced at his rose gold Piaget watch. "Sorry, I thought I was early."

"You are. Finished up my last meeting a few minutes ago." Michael, ensconced at the head of the table, the same place he always sat, looked like a bullfrog untroubled by lesser beings.

"What's up?" James said.

"Shut the door, please," Michael said, extending a finger toward the entrance.

James' blood pressure went up a notch or two.

"Anything wrong?" he said as he grabbed a chair.

"Nothing that can't be fixed."

Frowning, James laid his forearms on the table and folded his fingers together. "Fixed?"

"James, when we hired you at this firm, you weren't the brightest or best financial candidate out there."

So, getting right to it, James decided. "Sorry if I've disappointed you."

"Don't take it that way. You have other skills we needed. Still do. You're wonderful with people. You have this effortless charm everyone likes."

Despite a conscious determination not to look nervous, James combed the fingers of one hand through his hair. He had to wait to let Michael say what was on his mind. The man hated being interrupted.

"The issue is, if you hire a rainmaker, you expect him to perform as intended. The partners and I have examined the assets under management that you're directly responsible for acquiring, and frankly, we have seen very little growth recently. To use a metaphor, there's been a long drought. The skies don't look very cloudy, either."

James said, "I know my book hasn't grown as much as I'd prefer. But I'd like to say I'm working on several possibilities that, if they come through, could be quite beneficial to expanding the firm's revenue."

"Glad to hear that. I knew my faith in you wasn't misplaced."

"I understand my obligations to the firm, sir. I won't let you down."

"Excellent, James, excellent. That's all I needed to know. Well, back to work."

With that, Michael shook James' hand and left the room.

James remained seated, thinking through his options. Sure, he had been coasting for a while, maybe too long. He had grown tired of the constant pressure to sell the firm to an ever-expanding list of potential clients. Unless the wealth management services were incompetent, most clients would, absent some brief turmoil or foolish behavior, see at least a gradual rise in assets as the markets eventually produced some measure of wealth generation. But his stated mission was to seek out new people to bring into the fold, not babysit the current clients. Despite that, he often found himself chatting with the people he knew and asking how they were doing. He had been told more than once that his efforts in that direction weren't necessary, that the firm had other people to handle that. But he resisted, making sure he was always available if his earlier clients needed to speak with him after the handoff, or to talk someone off of a ledge when they wanted to sell everything during a sharp downturn.

Unfortunately, James' professed expectation of imminent new money was an empty promise, at least for now. He didn't have any whale prospects. The previous glad-handing at the country club, his health club and the arts performances had by now tapped out the usual possibilities. The easy opportunities from his age group, mostly resulting from conversations started by common interests and kids in sports together, were gone. While previously quite productive, his contact list had grown stale and needed refreshing. The pressure to perform was always there, never-ending. He tried not to think much about it before, but here it was, demanding a resolution.

Then he had an idea. Previously, he concentrated on the new money people, those up-and-comers without historical roots in established wealth management. But there was a vast pool of older, rich people. Most, of course, were circumspect about their fortunes and only trusted people with whom they had a long-term relationship. Surely, a few of the patriarchs or matriarchs might consider a change, or, absent that, their kids would need someone to turn to when the inevitable happened. He knew from his experience with Nichelle, as well as with several other widows, that these women wanted a person who would actually tell them the truth and not demean them. James expected some survivors were being ignored and marginalized by the patronizing representatives of the firms their deceased spouses were comfortable with. He saw it often, even in his own firm, the careless certainty that those left behind would have no choice but to stay with whomever the original investors had originally selected. And he knew he could capitalize on the disparity between what those lazy fucks were doing and what people needed.

First, he would check with his father and see if he had any ideas about prospects. Then, remembering that the local charity circuit was a mélange of both old and new money, he would give Iris a call. She set up events all the time and knew a lot of rich bastards who enjoyed wasting money on galas so that their wife could buy a new, expensive gown and flash the jewels while simultaneously donating a dab of their money, all the while pretending to care about poor people. If he could just pry some of those substantial assets away from their current advisors, he could be back in front in no time. He had a generous expense account, and his wife, Jeanette, enjoyed dressing up and attending events, though not nearly as much as she once did. Maybe he could even get Jackie to come up with some new contacts. She was always on board for anything that was socially prominent. Yes, he decided, that's the ticket. Why hadn't he thought of this before?

As he considered the whole procedure, though, a realization came over him. He wasn't a hustler, didn't have the right personality to prey on people, to promise fabulous results, then not deliver. The approach his own firm used also seemed short-sighted and mercenary. What he wanted was to make a real difference in these people's financial lives, to help them, tell them the truth, all the while avoiding taking too much of their money for mediocre results.

He sighed, knowing there wasn't a way for him to achieve what he wanted, at least for now. Maybe he could come up with an alternative. He should call Finchie, discuss where he wanted to be, bounce some ideas off him. Finchie, he thought, rubbing his chin. The Keeper of the Keys, The One Who Can Always Be Trusted. Where would he be without such a loyal friend? And how even more difficult would David's life have been?

21

Sitting in his cramped apartment, Finch continued to search through Perry's laptop's internal hard drive. After logging off an hour ago, Perry likely headed for bed. Finch was having issues getting access to several of the password-protected files that Perry had yet to open, but so far, he could see that the old bastard served as a national clearinghouse for child pornography. There were many detailed notes confirming transactions with fellow offenders, so it was obvious this was how Perry made his living. Only a portion of the photos themselves, ready for immediate transfer to an interested buyer, resided on his laptop. Finding no evidence of cloud storage, Finch suspected most sat on an external hard drive that Perry only accessed when he needed to send or retrieve stored files. By tracking Perry's actions over time, the keylogger Finch installed should be able to intercept the password and access the missing drive. He needed to be careful, though. He had to come up with a way to copy and delete the David files, unnoticed, when it was time. If the old man was paying attention, he might see them disappear in front of him, instantly alerting him of the online theft. Besides, Finch still needed access to where Perry stored his funds.

Finch thought through his present plan and realized there were significant holes in it. Changes needed to be made to facilitate a better-organized attack on Perry's stashes of porn and money. After a lifetime of skirting the law, Perry officially had only a small checking account at a local bank, used for paying miscellaneous bills, such as utilities. Perry added cash only when that account got close to zero. Finch suspected Perry was using a cryptocurrency bank to hold most of his assets, possibly in an off-line cold wallet, but he had not accessed such an account since Finch had been snooping. He needed to be patient, though, stringing the old bastard along, teasing him about future purchases. The very delay in Finch needing to complete a transaction seemed to make Perry less suspicious of Finch's motives.

This evening, Finch opened his browser and typed a message. He knew Perry was online because he could see his computer screen in a side window.

—*Contacting you again about a future purchase. You there?*

—*You again.*

—*Like I said, I'm not in a hurry, but there are special things I want to buy.*

—*Like what?*

—*I prefer a male, maybe five to ten, dark hair.*

—*That right?*

—*Yep.*

—*I may have something. I'll let you know.*

Finch watched as Perry got ready to sign off. He hoped Perry would plug in the external drive then, but that didn't happen. Finch spent the next hour working through the limited porno material on the internal hard drive, making a list of each file, encrypted or not. Satisfied with the night's work, he signed off and used his smart phone to call James.

"Hey, buddy, how's the construction project going?" James said.

"It's on track, but the foreman's on everyone's ass to keep it that way. Same old shit."

"When will you be finished?"

Finch thought it over before answering. James had already told him about Nichelle's request.

"You still there?" James said.

"Yeah. I'd say three, four months more."

"And?"

"And what?"

"What do you think I mean? Are you coming back to see Nichelle and Davie?"

"I don't know. I'm thinking it over. It seems too soon."

"Alright, take your time. I've told you how she feels about you. Any news on Perry?"

Finch brought James up to date. He said he felt like in another week or two he'd be in deep enough to screw Perry over good.

· · · · · ·

Finch should have been paying more attention. Normally very careful, especially when working this high off the ground, today he found himself distracted. He was assisting the non-union steel erectors since they were shorthanded today. The crew was setting a large steel beam that would complete the steel skeleton of this floor. He watched as the crane slowly lowered the massive weight. Finch stood at the perimeter of the structure, ready to reach up and grab the end of the slowly rotating steel. But thoughts of Perry and Nichelle kept interrupting his concentration. He didn't remember, later, exactly what happened when the beam unexpectedly swung into him after a gust of wind. Finch reached up to stabilize it, then realized too late that he wasn't braced properly. The inertia and weight easily overpowered him, knocking him off the structure. As he fell, his safety harness unlatched. Perhaps he had not been thorough in his morning safety check. Or maybe he hadn't snapped his harness to the perimeter safety cable correctly. Whatever the reason, his hands slipped off of the beam and he fell backwards into nothing but air. As he hurtled down to the stack of gypboard on the floor below, he thought only of Nichelle and Davie, and knew he was going to die.

· · · · ·

James was in the conference room with Michael and the older couple, Adelle and Richard Sinclair, when the call came in. The Sinclairs were one of James' recent contacts, representative of the new type of clients he wanted to develop. After years of being with a competitor firm, the couple had expressed some discomfort with their present asset management arrangement and were tired of being handed off to a succession of younger advisors. James was going over the details of what the firm could offer if the couple transferred their sizeable assets to Anderson-Markum. James had spent two weeks working through new investment possibilities and had a professional brochure printed up to give the couple. They were conservative and hesitant to change advisors, thinking at first that no change was the preferred decision. James was explaining the details of the asset transfer in a confident, smooth manner as Michael looked on approvingly. In the middle of the discussion, Madison, James' assistant, awkwardly entered the room and motioned him over. He excused himself, then conferred with her in whispers for a few long minutes. James glanced back. Michael became agitated as the couple exchanged knowing glances. The looks were, Michael knew, the herald of unspoken but concerned communication often shared by long-married couples.

James returned to the table with a set jaw. "I'm sorry, but I've had an emergency come up. There's been a terrible accident."

"Your family?" Michael said.

"No, my best friend. He's in Miami, working construction."

"How badly is he hurt?" Adelle asked.

"Don't know yet, ma'am, but it sounds pretty serious. I have to leave immediately."

Michael's frown deepened. "Look, James, we need to finish this. In another hour, we'll have this done."

"It can't wait," he said.

Rising, Michael said, "I'm sure this—"

James wasn't about to be dissuaded. "Sorry, but this isn't up for discussion."

Michael tried not to show his growing impatience in front of the couple. "This is some *friend*, you say? Can't someone else handle this?"

"There's no one but me." James turned to the Sinclairs. "I'm very sorry, Mr. and Mrs. Sinclair, but I must leave. Can we reschedule for next week?"

Michael's eyes narrowed. "Next *week*?" He asked the couple to excuse them.

Out in the hall, Michael punched his finger into James' chest. James knew how angry the senior partner was.

"Look, I don't know what you think you're doing, but you better not *fuck* this up." Michael's face was turning red.

James said, "I know how important this is to the firm, sir, but this other obligation comes first."

Michael took a long breath. "First? Maybe if this was your family, I could see—"

"*Maybe?*"

"Perhaps I should be blunt. If you leave now, and we lose this account, you'll need to look for another job. Do I make myself clear?"

"Yes, sir, very clear." James said, staring back at the older man.

"Good. Let's go back and finish this."

James followed Michael back into the conference room, but stopped just past the entrance. "As I mentioned, Mr. and Mrs. Sinclair, we're going to have to postpone our discussion. Perhaps you have a time next week we could reconvene?"

A dark scowl crossed Michael's face. "What he means is that we need to conclude our business here first."

"No, that's not what I mean." He looked around Michael toward his potential clients. "I've very sorry, but the injured man is a very close friend. I'm all he has, so I have to go." He glanced at Michael. "Mr. Anderson here can handle the transaction without my assistance."

"But you're the man we're trusting with all this, James," Richard Sinclair said, glancing over at Adelle. "This could be quite tricky with all the trust fund constraints, and if you're not here, I don't think we want to proceed."

A fixed smile consumed Michael's face. "Nothing to worry about. We can finish up things now. *If* James ups and leave us."

"I'm not so sure," Adelle said, frowning. "I think we better think about this some more, don't you, dear?"

James said, "I completely understand. You need to be comfortable making a big decision like this. And I apologize again. Hopefully, we can get back together soon. This firm has a lot to offer, and I sincerely believe we can be of help to you both." With that, he turned and headed for his desk to grab his laptop.

Michael caught up with James as the elevator doors were opening. "*Goddammit*, James, what the *hell* do you think you're doing, leaving in the middle of a big negotiation like this? Some fucking *friend* of yours is in trouble? You know if they have time to think about it, they'll probably stay with Abbott Advisors. This is our chance, our only chance to reel them in. You better *not* blow this. I don't have to remind you that your bonus this year will depend on completing this deal."

The elevator chime sounded as the doors opened. James stepped into the elevator. "I'll let Madison know where I am, how to contact me, in case you need me. I'm heading for the airport as soon as I pack."

Michael's eyes narrowed to accompany his scowl. "You leave now, don't bother coming back."

"Understood, sir," James said as his finger punched the button for the first floor.

22

Jackie called Iris' event planning business to check on her schedule. "Yes, is Iris Perry available later on today?"

The woman on the phone said, "Let me check her schedule." After a few moments, she came back to the phone. "She's setting up for an event this afternoon. It's a dinner for a large group."

"When's the dinner?" Jackie said.

"Tonight. She'll be there until pretty late. Can I have her call you on Monday?"

"No, that's fine. I'll give her a ring back." Jackie ended the call.

Holding up the ovulation stick she had peed on this morning, she checked again and smiled. Time for David. She went to the backyard and turned over a couple of pots of ferns, letting the dirt spill out onto the patio's flagstones.

• • • • •

David's phone rang that evening while he was working his way through a popular series on Netflix. He noticed Jackie was calling and started not to answer. What could she possibly want this time of night? Still, he felt obligated to take her call, so he paused the feed and answered his phone.

"Jackie," he said.

"Oh, David, thank *God* you answered! I'm so *scared!*"

He sat up on the couch after hearing the terror in her voice. "Hold on, what's the matter?"

"You know I told you about me thinking someone is lurking around the house? Well, I just heard crashing noises on the patio and I, I thought I *saw* someone. . ." She started sobbing and her next words became muddled.

"Look, did you turn the light on? See if someone's really there?"

"God, what if he's out there right now, looking in at me? I don't know what to do. Can you please come over? I know it's terrible to call you in the middle of the night, but Randall's gone again and I. . .I don't know what else to do."

"Okay," he said. "Go over to the alarm panel and get ready to sound the siren if you hear glass breaking. And call 911. Now. I'll be right over."

As he grabbed for his coat, David wondered what kind of mess Jackie was really in. Wasn't her damn husband ever home?

· · · · ·

Watching through the window with the light in the bedroom off, Jackie saw David drive up and jump out of the car. He stood there momentarily, his short hair lifting slightly in the chilly breeze as he surveyed the site for a phantom intruder. Good, he believed her so far. She began working up her emotions as she hurried to the front door.

He rang the doorbell. She opened the door immediately, grabbing onto him as he entered the house.

"Oh, David! I've been so *afraid*!" She hugged him to her, feeling his arms encircle her back.

"It's going to be alright," he said. "I'm here now. Did you call the emergency number?"

"No, I wanted you to look first."

He frowned. "I told you to *call* them Jackie. What the *hell*—"

She started sobbing. "Don't be mad at me, *please*. I'm so sorry if I'm not doing this right. . ." She expected this initial reaction, so more tears and a petulant look were required. "I know you must *hate* me for asking you to come over. Maybe you should go back home and I'll call the police. I should have done what you said, but I was so *scared* that I waited until you got here, so I could be with someone I trust. Now, I feel so much better, in case. . ." She swallowed hard as the tears continued to roll and her breath came in quick gasps.

David's expression softened. "I didn't see anyone out front. Let me look outside and see what's going on."

"I couldn't possibly ask you to do that. It's too dangerous."

"It's okay. I'll be careful."

She followed him to the back doors, holding onto his trailing hand with both of hers. David turned on the patio exterior lights and saw the overturned pots.

"Humm. Two of those are knocked over. Sure it wasn't the wind?"

"I don't know. I heard this crash, so I thought. . ." She grabbed for his arm and hung on.

"I'll step outside, see if—"

"*No!* If anything happened to you, I couldn't *bear* it." She looked up at him with terrified blue eyes.

He smiled back. "Dial 911 on your phone and get ready to punch the Call button in case something happens." With that, he unlocked the doors and walked outside.

A few minutes later, he was back inside the house. "Backyard's clear, Jackie. Nobody's here now."

She let out a deep sigh. "That's good, I guess."

"Sure. I think everything's probably fine."

Putting her lips into a tight grimace, Jackie said, "You think I'm just a stupid woman, don't you?"

"No, of course not."

"That all I am is a burden to you. Calling you up in the middle of the night with some fake story."

"Please, Jackie, that's not what I think."

She turned her back to him. "Go ahead, leave. I know that's what you want to do."

He moved up behind her, putting his hand on her shoulders, his face near her neck. Dressed in black leggings hugging her shapely form, with a close-fitting knit top over that, she presented just the right mix of showing off her body without looking purposefully slutty.

He said softly, "I'd never think that. I've known you for too long."

Turning around, she presented him with a sad face and the remnants of her previous tears. "You've always been so good to me."

With that, she reached up and kissed him and, as expected, he kissed her back. She broke slightly away, then kissed him again, this time long and passionately. He responded by hugging her to him. She reached down and lifted his hand to her breast and pressed it against her, then continued to kiss him. His hands drifted down to her bottom and squeezed her tight butt as she pushed her crotch against his. Feeling his erection, she knew he wanted her.

Unexpectedly, he let go of her. "I, I can't do this," he said, his breaths rapid and uncertain.

"What?" she said, feeling his passion slipping away. Fuck, she thought, this was all going wrong. David was growing a conscience instead of a sustained hard-on.

"I can't *do* this," he said, pushing her slightly away from him.

"You don't care about me, do you?" she said.

"Of course I do, but I can't. Not to Iris. You, *we*, have other obligations. To Iris and Randall."

Jackie realized that the more he talked, the more likely he was to convince himself that he couldn't have sex with her. Time to change tactics.

"I've always loved you, David. Always. But I can see that you don't feel the same way toward me. I realize that now."

"No," he said. "That's not it. I've loved. . ." He stopped, flummoxed, unsure of how to go on. "I've always loved you. There, I've said it. It's true. But we can't do this."

She shook her head. "That's nice of you to say, to not hurt my feelings, but I know you don't mean it. Not really."

"But I *do*!" He grabbed her arms. "Please believe me."

"Why should I?"

As he grew more frustrated, trying to come up with a new angle to convince her, she returned her arms to his back.

"It's okay, David. You can be honest with me. I know you need to go, but if you could just hold me for a little while, maybe I'll be alright."

He clutched her to him. She sniffled along for less than a minute, then suddenly pulled away. "I'm so *sorry* about all of this! I'm such a terrible person." The tears starting up again as she ran toward the downstairs master bedroom.

"*Jackie!*" David called after her.

When she didn't respond, he hurried after her.

23

After re-checking the calendar, Jackie smiled to herself. She was always regular, right on time, but this month her period was a week late. Unwrapping the home pregnancy test, she headed to the bathroom. Fifteen minutes later, she knew she was going to have David's baby. Randall, of course, must always think it was his. He returned home a couple of days after Jackie had sex with David, and she made sure they made love that night. She told her husband that she had a special feeling about this time, which would make the result even more believable.

Jackie thought back on that night she lured David to the house. He was his usual reluctant self, but the fleeing to the bedroom routine had done the trick. She fell on the bed, crying, and, of course, he came after her. It wasn't long before Step Three was complete. Their lovemaking was more of a rushed imperative than the extended coupling she would have preferred, but she knew David, and she couldn't let him get distracted and reconsider. When he entered her, she thought of the time years before when this was all she wanted. The sex that night was satisfying enough, but not quite the life-changing experience she always contemplated. She was more experienced with such things now, so she judged the act more objectively than her teenage hormones would have done.

Afterward, they laid together, him still inside her, both of them breathing hard. His expression was somewhere between intense satisfaction and extreme guilt, despite their fervid kissing. She talked to him afterward, reassuring him that, as always, she wouldn't tell. He could trust her, she said, you know you can. I've never, ever told about us before, and never will. He left, looking dazed and confused. Her decision now regarded whether she wanted to continue to have sex with him, or consider Step Three the end of their relationship. She would have to think on that, now that Randall would soon quit traveling as much. Any future liaison would need to be carefully planned. Tomorrow, she would call their special occasion chef and tell him to fix a fancy meal for them tonight. Time to tell her husband he was going to be a daddy.

• • • • •

The next month, Jackie called David's office. After ringing several times, he picked up.

"Hello, Jackie." His voice was flat, unemotional.

"David. I wanted to call and give you an update."

She heard an involuntary intake of breath. "Update?"

"Yes. Randall and I want to take you and Iris out to dinner. At the club."

"Why us?"

"I thought we were all friends."

"Look, Jackie," he said, sounding like he was talking through closed teeth. "I think it's best we both don't see each other again. Considering."

"That would be a shame," she said.

"I'm sorry, but I think that's best."

"Then you need to discuss that with your wife. She's already accepted."

• • • • •

The weekend dinner at the country club went reasonably well at first. The Perrys felt out of place when compared to the better turned-out diners, including Jackie and Randall. Jackie, looking sexy and rich as always, was poured into a beautiful cream-colored dress enhanced with expensive emerald jewelry. Randall, as usual, had on an equally costly suit. David fidgeted in his inexpensive sport coat while the plain azure blue dress that Iris wore spoke more of sales rack than haute couture. The conversation stumbled along, stilted and halting, as each side struggled to come up with innocuous questions and comments.

"Say, I wanted to thank you, David," Randall said as the server took their dinner plates. "For helping Jackie out the other night when she thought there was a burglar."

"Yes," Jackie said. "It was so sweet of him to come over. Good thing it was a false alarm."

Iris turned to David, her gaze level. "You didn't tell me about that."

David's face reddened. "Sorry, I forgot to mention it. It was no big deal. You were working that night, at an event."

Iris didn't reply. She looked her husband over for a moment, then took a drink of her ice water. Jackie watched the couple, trying to avoid a smug smile, thinking that Iris looked like she would rather be anywhere else but here. Did Iris suspect they had sex that night? Not likely, Jackie concluded, as long as David didn't blow it.

Looking pleased with himself, Randall announced, "Desserts for everyone."

"That's unnecessary. It's time we went home," David said. Clearly, he wanted this evening to be over with. Jackie enjoyed watching him trying to make small talk and fit in. Her memory flashed back to when David lived with them, and how often the family ended up at the club. Regardless of the number of trips here, he never seemed to be comfortable amid the rarefied social atmosphere. Of course, everyone knew by then that David was their charity case, so no one expected him to act like a real Randolph.

"Nonsense," Jackie said. "There's no rush. It's our treat." She handed the Perrys the evening's dessert card. "Get whatever you want. Please, I insist."

Iris and David conferred and decided to split a slice of chocolate cake. The Weirs ordered coffee for everyone when the server returned. Once the desserts and drinks arrived, the four of them started eating and the conversation lagged.

Randall couldn't wait any longer. "We have some great news," he said, leaning forward. "But it's confidential for now."

David and Iris both looked up.

"We're *pregnant*! We're going to have a *baby*!" he said, knocking his fist on the table for emphasis.

Jackie's face broke into a broad smile, showcasing her perfect white teeth. David sat mute. Iris looked like someone had put a stake through her heart. She laid her fork down beside the dessert plate, taking her time with the motion, and said, with her head down, "Congratulations."

David grabbed for Iris' hand. "Yes, that's good news for you both."

Randall continued to gush. "We've been trying for a while. A good while. I'll admit I was the problem. But I guess we got lucky last month. We're so excited. Jackie's already started planning on how to furnish the nursery. She's going to hire an interior decorator."

Staring at David with a self-satisfied look, Jackie said, "Fortune was on our side last month."

Randall's admission was unplanned, but since it happened, Jackie enjoyed the secret power she now had over David, watching him squirm with the news that he was likely the father of the baby she was carrying.

Iris abruptly stood up. "Excuse me," she said, and headed for the hallway.

"I'm sorry. Did I say something wrong?" Randall said, turning to watch her go, genuine concern now replacing his previously thrilled expression.

"Iris recently had a miscarriage," David said.

Jackie eyed David, sure now that the visible jaw muscles of his cheek meant he was gritting his teeth. "Sorry, David, but Randall wasn't aware of Iris' history."

"Yes," Randall said. "That was very insensitive of me. I apologize."

"Not your fault. I better see how she's doing. Excuse me." With that, David hurried after Iris.

Randall turned to Jackie. "I guess I messed up, babe. But I'm so thrilled I didn't think that..."

"Not to worry," Jackie said, patting his leg. "Every couple has their own set of problems. How's your peach-ricotta cheesecake, Daddy?"

Grinning, Randall said, "It's perfect. Same as you, Mommy." He gave his wife a big kiss, then added, "This is going to be so great."

Jackie acted a bit embarrassed by Randall's unusual public show of affection, a guilty look initially crossing her face, but after the kiss, she patted the side of his face. "I'm happy, too, sweetheart. You're going to make a wonderful father."

24

As soon as he entered Finch's room, James knew his friend was in a great deal of pain. Finch's eyes remained squeezed shut as his slightly opened mouth emitted a low moan.

"Hey, Finchie," James said. "You look like shit."

Finch cracked open his eyes and took a ragged breath. "What're you doing here?"

"Why do you think? I got a call that you took an unannounced swan dive off of a building. Unfortunately, there was no water in the pool. You better check next time."

"It wasn't necessary. . ." A strong enough pain spasm went through Finch's body that he grimaced, unable to speak.

"I'll get the nurse," James said.

"Not much they can do for now." Finch struggled with each succeeding breath. "Don't want to give me. . .much before the operation. For now, I. . ." He stopped again, tears springing from his eyes. "Damn, that really. . .*hurts*."

James headed for the nurse's station.

Later, his pain eased by a modest dose of painkillers, Finch provided a semi-coherent narrative of how he broke his leg and cracked two of the vertebrae in his back, plus the associated disc damage. The leg was already in a cast and the back surgery was scheduled for early the next morning.

James said, "I talked to your parents. They send their love and best wishes. They wanted to come, but, you know, the cost of last-minute plane tickets. . ."

Finch nodded. "No problem. I'll be out of here in a week, maybe less. You know me."

"No, you won't, not without an ambulance."

"What does that mean?"

"I talked to your doctor. Said I was your brother so he'd give me the details. You're in worse shape than you're admitting."

Finch took a deep breath. "They said if the surgery doesn't work, I'll end up paralyzed. I can accept that. Not how I figured I'd end up, but I guess no one does."

"Assuming a decent outcome, you're still going to need some serious rehab, buddy. Workers' comp won't pay for all of it."

"I've got some special rehab insurance," Finch said, resigned to his situation. "Thought maybe someday I might need it. Just didn't expect the damage to be this bad." His eyes squeezed shut as a fresh stab of pain coursed through his back.

"Soon as the surgery is over with and we can move you, I've got a plane lined up to fly you home."

Frowning through a grimace, Finch said, "You get a big bonus?"

"Nope, but I have some wealthy clients. Ex-clients, that is. I called around. One of them needs a tax write-off."

"Look, James, this won't be a quick fix. It's better if I stay here and get in some kind of facility. I can't go home and stay with my parents. No way they could take care of me with both of them working. And you don't—"

"Shut up. It's all worked out. You're staying with Nichelle and Davie. Right now, she's getting a hospital bed with attachments set up in the spare bedroom."

Finch shook his head. "*No!* No *way* I can stay with them. I'll be helpless for a while, can't even get up and go to the bathroom." Finch paused, considering what he'd said. "It's not right to burden her like that. Not right at all."

"Quit complaining, okay? It's a done deal. Once I told her what had happened, she insisted. Personally, I can't see the attraction." James grinned as he patted his friend's arm. "If it was up to me, I'd get you a tent for the backyard, but she said that might be a little cold at night. I told her a dog could keep you warm, no problem, but she put her foot down. Said you had to stay in the house. We'll put a corkscrew in your butt so she can turn you over."

Finch, his eyes tearing up, said, "Thanks, man. Tell her I'll try not to be a lot of trouble."

"I'm sure you'll be a complete pain in the ass," James said.

"How long are you staying?" Finch said, wiping his eyes.

"Long as it takes."

"Don't you have a job?"

"That's not an issue right now."

Finch gave James a long look, but didn't reply. He later closed his eyes and drifted off into a troubled sleep. James went outside the room and called Jeanette, filling her in on the situation. She told him to stay as long as necessary and hoped Finch would recover soon. They discussed the certainty that he had lost his job. Jeanette said she was glad he wasn't working for that jackass Anderson anymore, and that they'd figure something out since she had complete faith in him. Her warm, supportive words gave him the confidence boost that he needed. Next, James called Madison, giving her a brief review of the situation. She also expressed her belief that he would land on his feet. After that, he set himself up in the hospital room chair and got out his laptop. Time to get to work on his resume'.

• • • • •

True to his promise, James arranged for Finch to be flown home and set up in Nichelle's spare bedroom. Finch protested vociferously about all the trouble he caused. Nichelle kidded him by declaring she had agreed to the arrangement only because Davie needed help with school. She constantly fussed over him for the first few days until they settled into a routine. Finch, a natural loner, was mortified by all the attention and the fact that he couldn't take care of himself, but the secret thrill of being so near Nichelle and Davie buoyed his spirits. His surgery had been a success, and his local doctor said he could start rehab in a few days. His long-term prospects for recovery were good, but he wouldn't be returning to construction, not considering how badly he had mangled his back.

• • • • •

James called the Sinclairs to apologize again for leaving so abruptly. Adelle thanked him, then surprised James by saying that Richard also wanted to talk to him.

"James? Richard Sinclair."

Smiling to himself at the formality of the older man, James said, "Mr. Sinclair. I only wanted to apologize again for leaving our recent meeting so abruptly."

"Yes, that was quite a surprise."

"Did you get things worked out with Mr. Anderson?"

"We've decided to stay with our present advisors. For now."

"I understand."

"Your boss, Anderson, was pretty upset when we let him know our decision. That's when he said that you didn't work there anymore."

"We've had a parting of the ways. But I wanted to say I'm sorry I put you through that. Anderson-Markum *is* a quality investment firm, if you're ever ready to switch. I want you to know that I still believe they can do a good job supporting you and Mrs. Sinclair."

"I suppose so," Richard said, dismissing the previous commentary. "You said before this was a friend of yours that got hurt?"

James gave Sinclair a brief run-down on what had happened.

"You sound like a very loyal man," Sinclair said after James finished his story.

"We're old friends, since we were kids. There were originally three of us, but there's only two of us left. We're as close as brothers, maybe closer. Fact is, I couldn't let him down. He's always been available before when I needed him, so I had to do the same. Not being there for him wasn't really an option."

"Well, Adelle and I feel that loyalty isn't something that most people value that much anymore. To lose your job in order to help your friend is quite impressive."

"Thanks for saying that, but that decision probably wasn't the smartest one I've ever made. But I felt like I had no choice. Under the circumstances."

"Yes, I see," Sinclair said. "So, we were thinking. . ."

Surprised by how long the conversation was taking, James said, "Yes?"

"Adelle and I want you to take on our account."

Stunned, James said, "But, sir, I'm not set up to do that. Not personally, not right now. Maybe a little later on. . ."

Sinclair said, "If you want to start your own firm, I believe I can round up some investors, in case you're interested. Take your time deciding, James. You already have our recommendation. Good day." With that, Sinclair hung up.

After thinking the conversation over and doing some quick mental calculations, James called his ex-assistant.

"Madison? James. Would you ever consider leaving Anderson-Markum and coming to work with me? I want to take a different approach to investing, one that benefits our clients instead of maximizing the fees."

Madison didn't hesitate. "When can we start?"

25

Iris hurried through their apartment as soon as David unlocked the front door. Her first action was shedding the simple dress she knew Jackie had surreptitiously viewed with contempt. After that, she had little interest in his continued defense of Jackie. David followed her into the bedroom, listening to her renewed complaints about Randall's insensitive revelation about Jackie's pregnancy. She didn't blame him, she said. Maybe it was an insensitive remark, but it was also entirely possible Jackie put him up to it. David demurred, saying he was sure it was an unplanned reveal. Yes, I know that's how Jackie can seem, he said, but she has a sweet side, too. Oh, really, Iris replied. If it's there it seems well-hidden to me. The solid conclusion that Iris settled on was that Jackie was a certified, stone-cold bitch and David was too naïve to see it. You just don't know her like I do, he protested. Eventually, mollified by his lengthy entreaties, she finally agreed to disagree, kissed him goodnight, and went to sleep. David, thinking over the consequences that he was likely the father of Jackie's child, stayed awake most of the night, considering what that might mean for his future.

The constant thoughts of Jackie and his potential child receded from David's mind as time went on and his own life with Iris settled back into its predictable routine. They had no further contact with Jackie or Randall. Iris was busier than ever and looked forward to going to work every day. She was happy most of the time, if still unsettled with their sex life. In guilty moments, David remembered the night with Jackie and how satisfying the sex had been, despite the complete failure of his moral standards. He knew he needed to forget about that indiscretion. Surely, like Jackie said, it was Randall's child. Surely.

David and Iris both agreed that a discussion about them having another child should be postponed. They would go on with their lives and revisit the decision later on. Iris no longer seemed so sad about losing the first baby, but he felt she needed more time to heal. She agreed, saying that she was content to wait until they were more financially secure before trying again. A good thing, David thought, since the rent on their new downtown apartment was about to be jacked up ten percent whenever they renewed the lease. After moving out of his previous one bedroom, they had rented a significantly larger two-bedroom single level unit in a nicer building. The other bedroom was, both knew, for a future baby, though neither one of them officially acknowledged the reason for the change. More room, a place for visiting family or friends, a temporary office, whatever, formed the shifting rationale for the extra space. Since most of the furniture from the previous apartment didn't fit or wasn't suitable, a slate of new furnishings added to the moving cost. David, uncomfortable with facing several years of high interest monthly installment loan payments, raided their savings to pay cash for all the new items.

The apartment change thrilled Iris. Gone was the cramped space from before, and the new unit had large windows that let in lots of light. Living downtown near wonderful restaurants and entertainment made her happy. David, as always, worried constantly about the costs. Having a child, along with the associated expenses, seemed further away than ever. Several times, he broached the idea of moving out to the suburbs. Yes, they'd both have to commute, but when the current lease was up, he suggested they see what was available, maybe get a bigger place for less money, even buy a house. Nonsense, she had said. This place is perfect. Besides, most of the events she worked on were nearby. How could living so far away from work be a good plan?

A few months later, after the last of the new furniture arrived and the entire place had a coat of fresh paint, Iris told David she wanted to have a house-warming party, a small get-together with a few friends. He agreed, happy that at least she wasn't planning a big blowout. Then, as they were listing potential invitees, the names of their previous dinner hosts came up.

"We probably need to invite Jackie and Randall," Iris said, a resigned look on her face.

"What for?" David said, turning sour. "We don't run in their circles, Iris. If they came over, they'll probably make fun of our place, even with all the new stuff.

It's not much compared to their mansion. And no way they'd fit in with our friends. Besides, you said before you can't stand her."

"I can put up with her for an evening. We have to at least make an effort to pay them back for that expensive dinner."

"Let's pretend that night never happened," he said. "I'm sure they have."

"David, for Christ's sake, it's the only social thing to do."

"Screw social," he said, and got up from the table.

David and Iris didn't have a large circle of friends, so it wasn't difficult to limit the list. Eventually, they narrowed the number of invitees to twelve. They would ask James and Jeanette, of course, and Max and Ja'Neel, plus a few work friends of both David and Iris. The last two spots were open, so Iris wrote in Jackie and Randall, overriding his objections.

"Don't worry," she said. "They won't come, and it gets us off the hook."

David grumbled his agreement.

· · · · · · ·

Two days after the invitations went out, Jackie called David at work.

"David, it's Jackie."

"Hello," he said, noncommittal.

"I got your invitation in the mail. It was so kind of you and Iris to invite us to your little party."

"Sure, I doubt you can come, though," he said. "You and Randall are so busy socially. Iris and I will completely understand if you have other commitments."

"Don't be silly," she said. "We'll be there."

"You *will*?"

"Yes, of course. Why wouldn't we?"

"I, uh, I just thought this wasn't really your kind of thing. It's very informal, Jackie. Nothing fancy at all."

"Sounds marvelous. I'll wear my new jeans. Tell Iris we're thrilled to be invited."

David hung up. Nothing about hosting a pregnant Jackie and her clueless husband sounded like a good thing.

· · · · · · ·

As expected, Jackie and Randall showed up an hour late. Jackie breezed in like she owned the place, with Randall close behind. The rest of the guests were, of course, already there, so David introduced the new arrivals all around. Despite their attempts to tone down their appearance, Jackie was striking, as usual, causing several of the wives to elbow their spouses for staring. Randall, dressed in an expensive Polo outfit, was a standout from the rest of the men, mostly attired in jeans and short-sleeved department store shirts not tucked in.

"Get you a beer?" David asked Randall.

"Do you have any wine?" Randall said, then corrected himself. "Sure, a beer will be fine."

"I can open a bottle," David said. "What do you like?"

"No, don't bother. I'll have what you're drinking."

Randall took one sip of the offered beer and had difficulty not grimacing at the taste.

David said, "Look, let me open some wine for you and—"

"No, no. That's fine," Randall said, cutting off his offer. "It's just that I haven't had a beer since maybe college."

The other men looked at each other before David steered the conversation away from beverages.

"Tell the guys what you do for work," David said, giving Randall an opening.

"Oh, not that much. I'm running Randolph Enterprises now."

"Wow," Stewart said. "Impressive. That company's a pretty big employer here in the city."

"Actually, Jackie's dad started the company. I'm only the hired hand."

David gave Randall marks for modesty. The fact was, Randall brought many new ideas to the company, such as increasing the company's on-line presence and reworking its clunky website. David understood sales had recently increased by a third or more. While Randall gave detailed answers to the various questions the group of interested men posed to him, David snuck a glance at the women's circle. Jackie, as expected, was the center of attention, and the women were trading stories about having babies. She was five months along, he guessed, based on her previous announcement. She had a nice bulge but wasn't that big yet. Iris, one of the few women without children, looked vaguely bored and pissed off at the non-stop chatter about kids.

After David and Iris set out the last of the food on the kitchen island, the conversation clumps drifted apart. Some sat in the living room, listening to and arguing over the merits of various types of music sequencing through the playlist, while others remained congregated in the kitchen. David looked up from the chips and dip and saw Jackie looking at him. He forced a return smile.

Jackie disengaged and came over to stand beside him, both of them surveying the living room as they each pretended that being close didn't matter.

"Thanks again for inviting us," she said.

"Sure. Iris thought you might like to come."

Jackie turned to him. "And you didn't?"

"I didn't say that."

She grunted. "But it's what you meant."

David grabbed a chip and drug it through the bowl of dip. "Jackie, we're from two different worlds."

"We don't have to be." She turned and glanced down the hall. "What's down there?"

"Bedrooms and baths. Iris is using the second bedroom for a home office right now."

"Can I see it?" she said.

"Sure, go ahead."

Dropping her hand to grab onto his, she said, "Give me the tour."

Resigned, he downed the last of his chip. "Alright."

As she pulled him toward the hallway, Jackie murmured to Randall in passing. "David's going to show me the rest of the apartment."

Randall nodded, then returned to answering a question about the best way to fire an employee. David noticed Iris giving him an odd look as he and Jackie headed down the hall.

The tour lasted less than two minutes.

"That's about it. Not much to see," he said, stuffing his hands in his pockets.

"Nonsense," Jackie said, standing inside the master bedroom while David lingered outside. "Half the time, I think our house is too big. Show me the closet."

David entered and opened the door. Crammed with clothes that Iris insisted on keeping for years, the racks billowed outward as garments fought for space.

"How cozy," Jackie said, surveying the clutter.

"Our apartment would probably fit in your living room."

"Don't be silly. This place is delightful. And, yes, I remember that you've seen my house. You were so sweet to come over and save me. And afterward was pretty nice, too."

David, feeling his face redden, was grateful that the only light in the room came from a small table lamp by the bed.

"I think we should forget that ever happened," he said in a flat tone.

"Hard for me to," she said, putting her hand on her belly. "This is a constant reminder."

He knew she loved torturing him, watching him squirm. She always had.

"You don't know it's mine," he said in a tense whisper.

"She started kicking last month." Jackie rubbed her belly. "Would you like to feel your baby kick, David? Maybe she's going to be a famous ballerina."

"Jesus, don't say that." David's jaw clenched. "What happened between us before needs to stay a secret. Nobody else can ever know."

"Don't worry," Jackie said, giving him a conspiratorial look. "Here, give me your hand." She lifted her top and placed his hand on her rounded stomach. "Feel that?"

His hand moved toward the motion as he felt her skin undulate with the baby's moving foot. "Yes," he said, swallowing. "I do."

"She wants to say hello to Daddy."

David's hand pulled back as if scorched by a fire. "Please, Jackie, I . . ."

"Our little secret, remember?" she said. "I miss you, David." She turned into him, pressing against him. "I think about you all the time." Jackie's hand dropped to his crotch and started massaging him. "I have very fond memories of that night."

"I can't do this," he said, but made no real attempt to disengage.

Her hand left his crotch and, taking one of his hands in hers, she placed it on the side of her breast. "Kiss me. Like before. You know I love you."

Her mouth found his. He greedily accepted it.

"See what you've been missing?" she said, before kissing him again.

David's peripheral vision detected motion. He glanced toward the open bedroom door. Iris was standing in the dark hallway, eyes flung open, a hand over her face to cover the scream.

26

Today presented an important milestone in Finch's recovery. He was going to get out of bed.

Before now, the physical therapist worked him over while he lay in bed, stretching and moving his legs in a practiced routine to keep the muscles from atrophying while his back healed. Some days were more painful than others, but he became used to the process. He was now ready for the next step.

Nichelle and the physical therapist positioned him to turn and sit up. He knew that if he turned even slightly the wrong way, a stabbing pain would bring him to tears, so he took his time, a lot of time, getting it right. Eventually, as he slid down across the sheets, his feet found the floor for the first time in days. It felt like a great triumph, even if he remained stooped over.

"Lean on us," the therapist said, hooking his arm over her shoulder. Nichelle took the other arm. Instead of using a walker, Finch insisted on trying to support himself, aided by the help of the two women.

Finch felt elated by the simple act. Maybe soon he could make it to the bathroom by himself. Using a bedpan had been intensely humiliating for him, but Nichelle acted like it was no big deal to empty it and wipe his ass. She said she had seen a lot worse, so quit complaining. How she could do this for him, day after day, he wasn't sure.

"First step," the therapist said. "Easy, take your time."

He nudged his foot forward less than twelve inches.

"Good, good. Now the other one."

Finch repeated the procedure.

"Very good, Mr. Finch," the therapist said, smiling up at him. "A milestone."

Mumbling his thanks, Finch was instead looking into Nichelle's eyes, those wonderful brown eyes full of tenderness and caring. If only he could kiss her, he thought. They slow-walked around the room instead. Finch found it exhausting and was panting when they returned to the bed.

"Sorry, I'm worn out," he said as he eased back into the bed, breathing hard.

"That's expected," the therapist said. "I'll come back tomorrow, and we'll make some more progress. Maybe go down the hall."

After Nichelle saw the therapist to the front door, she came back in and sat on the side of his bed.

"I'm so proud of you," she said, smiling down at him while she held his hand.

Finch's heart caught in his throat. "There's. . .so many things I need to say to you. Tell you how good you've been to me. Why in the world you took me in, I'll never understand. You're the most wonderful. . ." He looked away to keep from tearing up.

"I'm glad to do it. You meant so much to David." She stopped, then said, "And to me." She moved her hand to his chest and kept it there.

"I thought you hated me," he said. "At least at first."

"Let's say you've grown on me." She patted him and gave him a big smile.

"You mean like a fungus?" he said.

She laughed like she meant it. "Better than a fungus."

"Look," he said, taking her hand in his. "I can't ever repay you for your kindness. Ever. For whatever crazy reason, you've been so nice to me and I. . ." He stopped talking, the tears filling his eyes.

"You don't have to repay me, silly," she said. "It's what I wanted to do. When James told me you were badly injured, and you were so far away from me and Davie, I knew for certain that I wanted you here, with us. So we could take care of you."

"I never figured to end up like this," he said, still avoiding looking at her. If he did, he didn't know what thoughts might spill out of his mouth. "Guess you never know."

"No, you never know what will happen."

Nichelle looked away, too. While she did, Finch wiped his own eyes and watched her, knowing she was thinking about David, her lost husband. He could see the deep hurt settling on her face.

After composing herself, she turned back and said, "I think your wandering days are over, Finchie. Remember what the doctor said about not working in construction again?"

"Yeah, says him. Once I get better, I'll get back on the road."

A worried look crossed her face. "I don't want that."

"That way you'd finally be rid of me," he said, trying to sound like he was half-kidding.

"You should know by now that I want you here. So does Davie."

He reached again for her hand and squeezed it. "How can you be this nice? To put up with a stupid invalid like me?"

"I care about you. A lot. That's why."

He ached to tell her he loved her, but he couldn't possibly, since he was sure a confession like that would ruin their relationship.

"What?" she said.

"I want to say how much I care for you and. . ." He stopped again, frustrated.

She got into bed and stretched out beside him. "Put your arm around me."

He held her, thinking maybe a miracle had occurred. As they lay there, he felt his erection growing and was powerless to stop it. He remembered the times she bathed him in bed, and how often he sustained the same inadvertent reaction, and then how she seemed unaffected. This is natural, she said, nothing to be ashamed of. But with her so close to him, he remained intensely embarrassed.

She reached down and put her hand over his crotch. "I can tell you're glad to see me."

"I'm sorry," he said. "I shouldn't be doing this, but. . ."

Leaning into him, she kissed him. For a long time. After it was over, he struggled for a breath. "Do you, could you. . ."

Continuing to caress him, she said, "Finchie, my feelings for you aren't based on you being David's best friend. I care about *you*, because of who *you* are. You need to quit thinking you're a charity case. Understand me?" To reinforce her words, she squeezed his cock.

He grimaced with pleasure. "Nichelle, I, oh, God, that feels so good."

Her face opened in a broad smile. "I think you need a little reward for working so hard today. To give you an extra incentive to get better." She sat up and shifted his jogging suit pants and underwear off his butt and up on his legs. "Now, pull your legs up to relieve the pressure on your lower back. That's right."

He did as instructed, unsure of what would come next.

"This way, when you ejaculate, your lower back won't spasm."

"What?" But he closed his eyes again as she stroked his shaft. "Nichelle, I . . ." Finch stopped talking, consumed by the intense exhilaration.

"Be quiet," she said as she laid back down and pressed against him. "Enjoy the moment."

After his intense climax, she said, "My, you must've been all backed up." She got out of bed and returned with a warm cloth, then cleaned him up and rearranged his clothes.

"Feel better now?" she said, bending over and kissing him again.

"Much," he said, reaching for her. "That was incredible. Thank you. I don't know what to say."

"I enjoy helping you, Finchie. Very much. And having you here, with me and Davie, for as long as you want to stay." She ran her fingers through his hair, then let go of his hand.

"Maybe you could do that again tomorrow," he said, grinning at her. "I promise I'll walk all the way to downtown if you do."

Nichelle laughed. "If you get cake every day with your lunch, you'll start thinking the treat's nothing special."

"How about another kiss?"

"I need to get ready. Your parents are coming over." She looked at her watch. "In about fifteen minutes."

"Today? It's Thursday."

"They both took the day off. We're celebrating your progress, your first walk. Your mother and I have it all planned."

"Do you tire of having them over?" he said. "I've only been here for a short while, and they've already come over a lot after work. If they're annoying you, please say so. I can—"

"Nonsense," Nichelle said as she rearranged his sheets. "I'm always happy to see your parents. They're so sweet to me."

"They're crazy about you," he said.

"Really?"

He reached for her hand. "What's not to like?"

"Well, I'm the person taking care of their son. I'm sure that's it." She lingered, looking at her hand in his.

Finch chuckled. "What you don't know."

She gave him a quizzical look, then headed for the closet and started pulling out the card table and folding chairs and setting them up next to his bed. When the Finches visited, they always had a little celebration in Finch's room to cheer him up. His mother brought a delicious treat, and Nichelle made the drinks. Because of his medication, Finch got grape juice while the rest enjoyed an inexpensive bottle of wine. Nichelle knew he loved his parents deeply, and that their visits were always a source of encouragement for him to get well.

"What's that?" he said, as she returned with a box he hadn't seen before.

She sat the box on the card table and opened it, displaying a set of tiny conical party hats adorned in gaudy colors, complete with thin elastic neck bands. "We're going to celebrate."

"No way I'm wearing one of those," he said.

"You will. And I'm taking pictures," she said, then laughed.

He watched as she headed for the kitchen. All he could think about were her words, the loving things she said to him, the unexpected pleasure she had just given him, the statement that she wanted him to stay. Could she possibly have meant that? A wild thought careened through Finch's head. What if someday she could feel the same way about him that he already did toward her?

27

The guests hustled out of the apartment, almost bumping into each other, as Iris fumed, her anger barely contained. Except for Jackie, the rest of the invitees were clueless about why the party had suddenly ended. David refused to answer anyone's questions, only saying something had come up. As soon as their front door shut, Iris lit into David.

"You fucking *asshole*!" she screamed. "How *could* you?"

"Look, Iris, it just happened. It wasn't serious," David said.

"Not serious? Kissing the pregnant wife of another man in our bedroom? Feeling her up while you're at it? You call that *nothing*?"

"It wasn't like that. She wanted a tour of the back rooms and then told me she wanted me to feel the baby kicking. That's when I messed up. Iris, I'm so sorry about this. It'll never happen again."

"You've always been in love with her, haven't you?" she said while throwing the paper party plates into a trash bag.

"No, I'm not."

"Don't lie to me. *Not anymore!*" she yelled.

David realized Iris was so angry that she couldn't cry. He watched as she used her forearm to scoop food and condiments alike into the garbage.

"Okay, yes, I've had feelings for her," he said. "In the past. But I don't love her, Iris. I love you."

"You know she's just using you, don't you?" Iris said.

David seemed to miss the point. "What? Using me?"

"She's a devious fucking bitch, David. And you fell right into her trap. Men are so *fucking stupid!*"

"It's not like that, Iris. We go way back. I lived in the house with her for years."

"Did you fuck her when you lived there?" Irish was stomping on the trash sack, reveling in the splintering sound of plastic cups and paper plates being smashed into formless masses.

"No, of course not."

"But you *wanted* to."

"Jesus, Iris, I was eighteen. Jackie was beautiful even then. Of course, I thought about her, but I never touched her. No way I'd risk getting thrown out of that house."

She stopped and looked at him, temporarily mollified by his comments. For a short time, she remained silent and worked on cleaning up the party's remains. Then, she stood still as an odd look took over her face.

"Did you sleep with her? Before now?" Iris said, facing him.

"Why would you ask me that? We were only kissing, Iris."

"Did you or did you not? Tell me the truth."

She could see the answer hanging on his face. He never could conceal his worst deeds from Iris.

"So you *fucked* her. When?" Iris said, pushing the trash sack up against the cabinet with her foot before folding her arms.

"Jesus, Iris, it was a terrible mistake. It just. . .happened." David thrust his hands in his pockets, not knowing what else to do.

"*When!*"

"A while back. Not recently."

"*When!*" Her eyes were bright and narrowed, her arms open now and fists clenched.

"Several months ago."

"Several months ago, huh? As in five months ago?"

He turned his head. He couldn't face her.

Iris' face drained of color, then displayed a desperate, faraway look, a look he hadn't seen before. "Randall said that night at the country club that he was infertile. So you're the father of her damn baby. That's why you were kissing her. It all makes sense now."

Iris floated into the living room and collapsed onto the sofa. David hurried after her.

"Look, sweetie, it was a terrible thing for me to do. It's not like I planned it. It was the night she called me over to her house, said she was scared, that she thought there was a burglary, and I. . .we. . ." He stopped, thinking about what to say next. He realized he couldn't dredge up a suitable explanation, not one that would make any sense to Iris.

She looked off and saw nothing.

"No, it's impossible. I'm sure I'm not the father." David said, trying to upend the obvious. He grabbed for her hand, but she pulled it away.

Iris' face moved into a wry smile. "Don't you see? She lured you there. To impregnate her. She planned to get you there at just right time. Husband's out of town and he's shooting blanks, so she gets her old roommate David to fuck her because she knows he's got swimmers. After all, there's proof. He'd already gotten stupid Iris pregnant."

"No, that can't be what happened," was all he could say. But he knew Iris was right. Jackie had planned it all along, acting helpless, then rejected. She knew he would respond the way he did.

"It *can* be what happened," she said. "And it *was*."

Iris launched herself from the sofa and headed down the hall, not saying a word. When David caught up with her, she was already packing a suitcase.

"Please, Iris, *please*. We can work this out."

She didn't reply. He moved up behind her to try and comfort her. She shook him off. He stood back, watching her pack, his repeating entreaties receiving no reply. Jesus, he thought, she's going to leave me. And I deserve it.

Finished, she closed the suitcase and announced, "I'm going to Mother's. Don't call me."

"Iris, come on. Let's discuss this. You're my wife and we. . ."

She headed toward the front of the apartment, pausing at the door to get her coat out of the closet.

"Can't I say anything to change your mind?" he said in a last-ditch effort to stop her.

"No, you can't."

He watched her call for a ride from her cell phone.

"I'll wait downstairs," she said. "Don't follow me."

"Iris, I. . . When are you coming back?"

She turned and stared at him. "You've broken my heart, David. I thought I could trust you, you of all people. My advice is to stay away from Jackie." She let out a strangled laugh. "Not like you'll listen, though."

He ducked his head. "You're right about her, Iris. She's bad news. I see that now. But I won't ever again—"

"Guess I was right before. You are *all* worthless fucks."

The door slammed, and she was gone. David leaned his head against the closed door, trying to think of what to do. He had to call Finchie, get his advice. One thing was for sure: James must never know what he had done.

28

David tried repeatedly to contact Iris, but his phone calls all went unanswered. Finally, he called Gayle instead and was relieved when she picked up.

"Gayle? This is David. Is Iris alright?" he said.

Gayle took a few moments to reply.

"Yes, she's okay, David. Physically. But she's very hurt, emotionally."

"This is all my fault."

"Oh, David, how could you do that to her?"

"I really screwed up. That's my only excuse. I *do* love her, Gayle. I really do. And I'm so very sorry for the hurt I've caused her. Do you think she'll ever forgive me?"

"I don't know. Maybe. Not yet."

"Would you tell her I called? And that I'm thinking of her?"

"Yes, I'll do that. Goodbye."

David stared at his phone after the call ended. Funny how human relations are so ephemeral. Two weeks ago, he had a happy, loving wife, blissfully unaware of his single indiscretion with Jackie. He knew Iris all too well. She likely hated him now. Maybe she was already set on divorcing him. Yes, he was guilty of a terrible mistake. He regretted it every day. But should she forever punish him for one stupid indiscretion, even if it was a big one? He loved Iris as much as he ever did, maybe even more when he considered the prospect of losing her. Couldn't she see that?

As he fixed himself breakfast, thoughts of her rolled through his head. If Iris had an affair, could he forgive her? Yes, he instantly decided. I'd deserve to be cheated on. I'm not the easiest man to love. My history is terrible and I have many faults. She would be perfectly justified finding solace in another man's arms. He always knew, deep down, that he was a psychological wreck, with only a thin veneer of normality, a sheet of opaque plastic stretched thin, barely covering the lumps of the terrible secrets inside, forever keeping his public face from showing the awful things that remain hidden.

His thoughts returned to Jackie. He had always wanted her, so close and yet forever inaccessible to him while he lived in the big house on Searcy Circle. That house, that family, his friend James, had saved his life. He felt nothing but kindness and respect for the Randolphs for taking him in. He worked hard to prove they had not made a mistake. But a secret delight was being close to Jackie, watching her laugh, drinking in her beauty and charm as her self-awareness increased each day. His infatuation with her jumped as soon as he reached sexual maturity. When she told him in the pizza restaurant about her touching herself, wanting him to come into her room and make love to her, it shocked and thrilled him. That was the same fantasy he had, almost every night, wondering what it would be like, how she might taste and feel. His musings resulted in many nighttime trips to the bathroom to clean himself up. He obsessed over her and often thought he would go crazy because of it. Every day, he forced himself to focus once again on school, on being a good houseguest, on behaving himself, when every day all he wanted was to make love to Jackie, feel his cock inside of her. Denial of his needs became an immense, never-ending effort. Some days he thought it would drive him insane, but he managed it somehow throughout high school. After that, he fled to college when he realized he could no longer prevent his attraction to her from becoming overwhelming.

He often thought back to that day when he saw her half-naked in the bathroom, admiring her breasts, how he couldn't look away, and how she let him look her over, knowing even then her power over him. Don't worry, I'll never tell, she said more than once. But she also flaunted herself in front of him, seeing the desire burning in his eyes. Randall must not be enough to satisfy her. Or maybe Jackie only wanted a different dessert, a taste out of the ordinary, from time to time, confirmation that other men still wanted her. Their coupling in her house had been fast and furious, more of an animalistic release than measured lovemaking. After it was over, part of his regret was not taking his time. Now, he admitted to himself, for the first time, that he still lusted after her. The next time would be better, more satisfying. . . *Stop* this, he told himself. You have a wife that you need to find a way to make up with, to see if she could forgive you. You need to forget Jackie. Forever.

All of this he had discussed with Finchie. His friend was direct, to the point, knowing David as well as he did, reminding him of the obvious conflicts, the buried secrets, and helping him recognize the trap that Jackie had set. Iris called her a manipulative bitch, and Finchie agreed. Funny how women see through other women, almost automatically, so obvious to them but so obscure to men. It was all so simple. Jackie needed a biological father for her child. Jackie had planned the whole thing, probably even turned over the pots on the patio to set the scene. Yes, that sounded just like her. She had a goal and developed a scheme to achieve it. He fell into her trap, stupidly unaware, and in a few months she would have the baby, *his* baby, and pretend for the rest of their lives that it was Randall's child. The little girl would rise into the rarified social circle of her mother, and the girl, *his* daughter, would grow up believing her journey through life was preordained, the obvious product of rich parents. David could watch only from a distance, perhaps glimpsing her from time to time. If only he and Iris had had a child, he thought he could bear it easier. But they hadn't yet because he insisted on waiting. Perhaps this was God's punishment for him. It would fit. He would deserve that.

Finished eating, he rinsed his cereal bowl out in the sink. He hoped, more than anything, that Iris would come back to him. He would do whatever it took to make her happy. But Jackie... He had to stay away from her. Forever. He knew he could. He had done it before, for years. All it took was more self-control.

At the door into their room, David stopped, looking at the bed, thinking of Iris as she was before, waiting for him, happy, her arms open and a big smile on her face. Despite the reduced intimacy they recently shared, he loved Iris and tried his best to make her happy. Even now, as he agonized over his wife's departure, Jackie kept returning to his thoughts. He remembered how she felt and tasted. Then his mind switched back to Iris, how happy they were after her recovery. And he screwed it all up. His fate was to love one woman because of who she was, and simultaneously to be obsessed by another who could probably care less about him, despite what she claimed.

He headed for the closet. He had a lot of work to do at the office today. Maybe that would keep his thoughts occupied, but he knew better. There was no getting over Jackie. Not for him.

29

The letter from Iris' attorney included a separation agreement. Each could go on with their disconnected lives for now, a future resolution of their marriage to be determined later. David re-read the agreement, relieved that it was not the divorce papers he had feared. Iris still refused to take his calls, but Gayle operated as a sort of intermediary, so the document was not completely unexpected. But it was still a blow and reminded him again of the reason his wife was back living with her mother.

He started seeing the therapist again, the one he and Iris had initially gone to. Her questioning helped him see how his earlier experiences made living a normal life difficult. You have self-destructive tendencies, the woman told him. Perhaps when things are going well, you feel you don't deserve it and unconsciously sabotage your own happiness. That could apply to the indiscretion with Jackie, but Jackie was also to blame. Likely she enjoyed screwing with him, professing her love while remaining married to Randall. Maybe it was payback for the years he had ignored her sexual needs, but realistically, there had been no way that he could have responded to her back then. She had to understand that, now that she was married, just as he was, at least for the present. They needed to live their separate lives, embrace reality, and stop this fantasy driven by some twisted, long-lost love. Jackie hadn't contacted him since Iris caught them kissing, which was just as well. He could forget her. He *could* do this. But as he told himself those words, the self-doubt flooded over him. All he could think of was Jackie, naked and underneath him, and how much he enjoyed finally having her.

•　•　•　•　•

Randall and Jackie sent David a birth announcement for Charlotte, complete with photos of a smiling father and mother holding their new baby. David sifted through Jackie's social media pages, taking his time, trying to decide who the little girl looked like, but it was fruitless at this age. Later, as she aged, it might be more obvious. The announcement ended up buried in the bottom of one of the dresser drawers. He would send them a gift, and that would end it.

•   •   •   •   •

Several weeks after the baby was born, Jackie showed up at David's house on a Saturday afternoon. He started not to open the door, but he knew he was only delaying the inevitable.

"Jackie," he said. "What are you doing here?"

"I was downtown anyway. Thought I'd stop by."

David knew she was lying. There was no reason she would end up in this high-rise neighborhood, other than coming to see him specifically. He hesitated.

"Can I come in?" she said.

"Sure, alright." He opened the door and smelled her distinctive perfume as she drifted past. He appraised her shape from the back. Jackie had already lost almost all of her baby weight. She looked as striking as ever.

She stood in the living room, giving the room a careful once-over. "Your apartment looks so nice, David. Everything's neat and clean."

David nodded his thanks.

"I wanted to tell you we appreciated the baby gift."

"You could've sent a note."

"I like the personal touch."

"Would you like to sit down?" he said, to be polite. "Something to drink?"

"Thanks. Some iced tea would be nice. If you have it. Unsweet."

So, she was going to stay. David headed for the kitchen and fixed them both a glass, then presented one to her.

"Would you sit with me?" She patted the sofa cushion next to her.

"Why?"

"I wanted to talk is all."

He sat near her, but not too close. "About what?"

"About what happened. What Iris thought happened."

David said, "She saw us, Jackie. Her reaction wasn't exactly unexpected."

"Did you tell her we slept together?"

"No. Well, not at first. She figured it out by seeing us together that night, from what we were doing. She put two and two together and thinks I'm the father of your baby. That's why we're separated."

Jackie sipped her tea, taking her time. "What do you think? About the baby?"

"She's probably right."

"How would you know that?"

"I don't."

A long silence passed between them. Jackie broke the tension.

"You think I used you? To father my baby?"

"I'm saying it's possible," David said.

"My husband makes love to me regularly, in case you might wonder. And what he said at the club, about us not getting pregnant being his fault? That's not really correct."

Surprise and relief washed over David. "It's not?"

"He has a low sperm count, that's all. It doesn't mean we can't conceive. It only takes a while longer. We made love right after you and I did. I'm sure that was what got me pregnant, not our little indiscretion." She watched the relief wash over David's face. "Feel better now?"

"Well, yes, sort of."

"I was teasing you before, that night, about being the father. I know I shouldn't have, but I admit I wanted to see how you would react. Now I realize it was mean of me, so you don't need to worry. It's not like I'm going to say that again."

"Okay."

"Would you like to see her sometime? Charlotte's so pretty. Right now, she's home with the nanny. I don't want to get her out until she's a little older. Besides, I've quit breastfeeding. It was too much trouble, all that hassle and getting up with her at all hours. Randall now takes over at night so I can get some rest. Anyway, I had some time to myself today, so I wanted to come see you, patch things up."

He nodded, not knowing what else to add.

"If you believe I trapped you into having sex with me, well, that's not true, not at all. It's that I've always cared about you. You know that. What happened between us wasn't planned. It came about only because of my, our, old feelings."

David didn't reply.

Jackie set her glass down on the coffee table. "I suppose I should go. I'm not sure if you want me here."

"You can stay as long as you want," he said. "I'm glad to hear you didn't use me."

"How could you think that?" she said, her face contorting into a dismayed look. "After all the years I've loved you?"

"Jackie, look, as I've said more than once, we're both married to other people. We need to move on with our separate lives. It's the best thing."

"Is it what you want?" she said. "Never to hold me, never to kiss me again?"

"It's not a question of what I want. It's what has to happen."

She stood up and reached for her purse. "If I thought for one second you actually cared for me, it would be such a wonderful feeling that I. . ." She stopped and brushed at her eyes. "I better go. I'm sorry to have bothered you."

He could see the obvious hurt in her eyes as he rose from the couch. "Jackie, I do care for you. You know I've always felt that way."

She paused. "Maybe so, maybe not. That's what you say now, but how do I know what's true?"

"I mean it. I do. I care about you. A lot."

Moving over to him, she dropped her purse and put her arms around him. "Could you hold me? Just for a minute? Please?"

David obliged her, feeling her body pressed against his, her warmth, the smell of her, the softness of her skin. He caressed her back. The old longings came surging back. It was all he could do to keep from kissing her.

"Do you remember the night we made love?" she said, murmuring into his chest.

His reply caught in his throat. "Of course I do."

"I think about it constantly. Making love to you was everything I ever dreamed it could be." She kissed him on his neck. "Was it special for you, too?"

"Jackie, you know. . ."

She whispered in his ear. "I waited so long to feel you inside of me." Her head drifted across the side of his face, kissing him as she went, then found his mouth with hers.

Despite his reservations, David kissed her back, reveling in the taste of her, the understanding that, as beautiful as she was, she had always wanted him.

When they broke apart, she moaned with pleasure, eyes still closed. He was breathing hard, wanting to say something but not knowing what, or how, to reply.

"Tell you what I'm going to do," she said, patting his chest as she opened her eyes.

"What?"

"I'm going to go down the hall, take off my clothes, and get into your bed."

His eyes widened. "Jackie, I, we, don't. . . Please. . ."

"I only hope you understand how much I need you, David. How much I've always needed you."

She gave him another kiss, then turned and headed toward the back of the apartment, stopping once and glancing back at him. She had a soft smile on her face as the tip of her tongue moved across the center of her upper lip, expressing her unconstrained desire for him. Then she headed into the bedroom.

David stared at her back as it disappeared into the room. Terribly conflicted, as always, he considered asking her to leave, but he knew there was no question about what was going to happen.

30

Finch recovered enough to ditch the hospital bed. Despite his earlier reticence, a walker provided the temporary support he needed, but was now added to the growing list of relics thrown off by his rapid recovery. He got around with a cane now, still taking his time, being careful and holding on to door frames and walls, though determined as ever to overcome this latest assistance aid. Finch amazed the local orthopedic physician by his speed of recovery. Finch said it was only putting your mind to what you wanted, and then wanting it badly enough to make it happen. This afternoon, Finch and Nichelle had visited the doctor's office, where Finch was cautioned again about expecting a full recovery.

Finch was sitting in the living room now, working on his laptop, when Nichelle came in with two glasses of iced tea.

"You doing okay?" she said.

"Sure. Perfect." He took the glass, then stopped, considering what to say next. "I don't know what I would have done without you."

"Stayed in some sleazy rehab place, I suspect, where people wouldn't baby you like I do."

"No doubt. Could you come over and sit by me for a minute? I like it when you're close to me."

Nichelle plopped down beside him. "What're you working on?" she said.

Finch closed his laptop. "Just catching up with things." She didn't need to know that he was corresponding again with Perry, apologizing for his absence because of a need to lie low. Let the old fuck think he was avoiding the law. That comment would make Finch seem more legit.

"Secret stuff, huh? What would you like for dinner?"

"Anything you fix is fine with me."

"Well, I better go see what we have."

As she started to get up, he grabbed for her hand. "Wait. Please."

"Alright."

She sat back down, giving him a curious look. Davie was still at school, due to be picked up in about an hour. Finch couldn't imagine not seeing the boy every day. They became fast friends early on, and now that close friendship had strengthened into love.

He continued to hold her hand. "Nichelle, I can never thank you enough."

She snuggled against him. "Aww, Finchie, is it that hard for you to say?"

"Not to you, it isn't."

He could tell she was getting the impression that this was going to be more than a verbal jousting.

"Finchie, what's the matter?" Her eyes widened. "You're not thinking of leaving us, are you? Because if you are—"

He cut her off. "No, of course not. Well, not now."

She covered up his hand with both of hers. "I want you here. As long as you want to stay."

"That's what I wanted to talk to you about."

Nichelle gave her head a little turn. "And?"

"I think you know how happy I am here, with you both, despite all the trouble I've caused. I'm crazy about Davie. He's the greatest kid ever, and so smart. . . Must take after his parents."

"Or got lucky," she said, a rueful smile crossing her face.

"I wanted to say. . ." He stopped, groping for the right words. "This is hard for me."

"Take your time."

"I wanted to say I have strong feelings for you. Very strong. And it's not a caregiver kind of thing, being obligated to the person who is the kindest, sweetest, most wonderful woman I've ever known." He stopped. "You probably don't want to hear this, but I'm. . .I'm in love with you."

She said nothing at first, but didn't jump and run, either. "Your mother already told me."

"When?" he said.

"The day we had your getting-out-of-bed party."

"So, you knew?"

She laid her head on his shoulder. "When David and I first started dating, he was still getting over Iris. I'm not sure he ever did, really, just found another place in his heart for me." She settled against him. "David was a complicated man, sweet and loving, but always troubled. We had our difficulties. After you told me more about his past, more of his behavior makes sense. That knowledge helped me come to terms with who he was. I think maybe he thought if he told me his entire story, I'd think less of him, but that's not true." She took a deep breath. "I miss him, and probably always will."

"Yeah, I miss him too." Finch said. Well, now he had his answer. There wasn't any use pursuing Nichelle. He could see that now. She was still in love with David and until she made room in her heart for another man, his own professions were useless. Maybe even worse, an unwelcome thorn that pricked at her memories. He released her hand. "I understand where you're coming from. I shouldn't have said what I just did. It was unfair. Please forget it."

"Don't say that," Nichelle said. "It's not like that."

"Like what?"

"David's gone. He's never coming back, and that's something I've learned to face. It doesn't mean I can't go on. It only means I still remember."

"You should. Remember him always, that is. He was one in a million." Finch slid his computer off his lap. "I'll put some more money into your account in the morning. I figure I owe you another six hundred. Besides, I need to go make some plans to get out of your hair." He leaned forward, readying the effort to sit up. The couch cushions were the kind you settled into instead of sat on, and it took a coordinated effort for him to get upright. With his bad back, he'd learned a rocking routine that, with the aid of the cane, launched him off of the sofa in a smooth motion.

Grabbing for his arm, Nichelle said, "Stop it."

"What?"

"Stop avoiding me."

He turned back to her. "I'm not avoiding you. I don't need to burden you with my stupid confessions. Like I said, I'm sorry for what I said. It put you on the spot, and you don't deserve that. I shouldn't have done that, not considering how you—"

"Shut up, Finchie."

Taken aback by her remark, he glanced back at her. She took his face in both of her hands and kissed him. He felt powerless, limp, the display of her affection like nothing he expected.

"I thought you didn't feel that way toward me," he said after their lips parted. "What you said, about David—"

"Just because I loved David doesn't mean I can't love another man. A good man, one that apparently has a helluva time showing his true feelings. A man that could actually experience some happiness, if he let himself, besides being dedicated to the people he cares about. One that, down deep, is kind, loyal, and can't seem to understand that a woman like me could truly care for him."

"You mean. . ." He paused, thinking through what she'd said. What was she telling him, exactly?

"David wasn't perfect, Finchie. Nobody is. Most of what we fought over was him trying to tell me what to do and refusing to reveal his secrets. But I went along with most of it to save our marriage. That doesn't mean I didn't resent it. If you're going to be my man from now on, you better not treat me that way. Ever."

"I won't," he said. Seeing his opportunity, he added, "I love you, Nichelle. I have for a long time."

Her eyes twinkled. "Good. I'm glad we've got that settled. Now, there's less than an hour before we pick up Davie, and unless you want to waste even more time, you better start kissing me."

31

When David entered the bedroom, Jackie was lying in bed, her eyes closed, her hand busy under the sheet. Fascinated by what he was witnessing, he stood beside the bed, mute, watching her and listening to her soft moans.

Jackie opened her eyes. "Remembering the old days," she said. "When I used to think about you all the time."

He sat down on the edge of the bed, pulled the sheet back, and ran his hand along the inside of her thigh. She opened her legs wider to give him a better view. "Touch me there," she said. "I love it when you do that."

She enjoyed watching him look at her, seeing the unconstrained desire in his eyes, enjoying the power she had over him. His hand moved to her crotch as she closed her eyes. "That feels so good. Keep me company?" she said, reaching for him with outstretched arms.

After nothing happened, she opened her eyes to see the conflict showed on his face.

"Just for a little while? Please?"

David's hesitation was short-lived. He undressed and got on top of her, kissing her over and over. Jackie reveled in his attention, caressing him amid murmurs of her appreciation.

"This time, let's not get in such a hurry," she whispered to him. "Maybe try it in different positions?" She knew David would do everything possible to satisfy her. She only needed to tell him what she wanted.

"What about, you know, you getting pregnant again?" he said as he kissed the side of her neck.

"I'm using birth control now, so you don't have to worry." She moved her head and started chewing on his earlobe.

"Jackie, I've always wanted you," he said between breaths. "So much."

"And now you can have me." She reached down and guided his cock inside her as they both moaned from the pleasure of it.

As David moved inside of her, his head buried in her neck, Jackie checked her diamond-studded Rolex. Plenty of time after this for her to get home and shower off the smell of David and their lovemaking before Randall came home. She relaxed and told David how good he felt, how much she needed him, knowing that would only enhance his performance. Right now, what she wanted was for a man to make love to her. Randall avoided sex with her during the last stage of her pregnancy and had not started back after the baby was born. Jackie needed sex, and David could provide that. Yes, she knew she was using him, probably helping destroy the chances of him getting back together with Iris. But he was a grown man and able to make his own choices in life. She knew exactly what she wanted and was determined to have it. It was time for him to get on board.

•   •   •   •   •

Later that night, Jackie and Randall were in bed. He was busy reading over some company papers. She pressed against him while offering hesitant kisses.

"Can't you put those down, sweetheart, and pay a little attention to your wife?"

He said, "I need to review these before the meeting tomorrow."

"So your work is more important than I am?"

"Don't say that. You know how I feel about you." He gave her a brief kiss, then returned to his reading.

"You didn't want to make love to me for the last few months I carried Charlotte. I understood that, considering how I looked. But now I think this means you aren't interested in me at all anymore." With that, she got out of bed, sniffling, and headed for the bathroom.

As expected, he followed her.

"Jackie, please, that's not it at all. I told you I didn't want to risk doing anything to hurt the baby. Considering how long it took us to get pregnant."

She made a petulant face. "That's what you said, but I know that I probably disgusted you with the way I looked. Maybe I'm still not attractive to you."

"Of course you are. Don't be silly. You're as sexy as ever."

"I'm working hard to get back my shape, Randall. The personal trainer is here every day. Still, I don't know if that's enough for you. . ." That should do the trick, she thought. Her interest in getting completely back to her previous appearance was more of a selfish one, but Randall needed to think it was only because she wanted to please him.

He pulled her to him, kissing her. "Never say that. It's not true. You know it's not."

"Maybe," she said, hanging her head, her lower lip now protruding. "But that's how it feels."

Reaching down, he picked her up and carried her back to the bed, tenderly setting her down and kissing her.

"I've missed you so much," she said. "I was sure it was all *my* fault."

"Don't be silly," he said, undressing her. "You're the most beautiful woman I've ever seen."

She gave him a coy smile. "Do you really mean that?"

"Of course."

"I like it when you look at me like this," she said, opening her legs.

"Me too." With that, he started kissing her breasts.

"Be gentle," she said. "It's our first time since the baby."

As Randall made love to her, she mentally contrasted the styles of the two men. David was an obsessive type of lover, constantly kissing, almost smothering her, always making sure she was enjoying everything he was doing. Randall instead loved to look at her as they made love. Regardless of whether she was on the top or bottom, his eyes drunk her in, admiring her like he was appraising a fine painting. Both men satisfied her in different ways.

After it was over, Jackie laid against Randall, who had pulled out his papers again.

"I went by to see David this afternoon," she said.

"Oh? How come?"

"I wanted to see how he was doing. He and Iris are still separated, and he's taking it pretty hard."

"That's too bad," Randall said, sifting through the documents. "Did you ever find out what happened that night at their apartment?"

"No, not really. Whatever it was, I guess it was simmering in the background and finally came to a head."

"So how is he?" Randall's distracted comment indicated he was already moving on, concentrating on his reading.

"Pretty lonely. If it's okay with you, I think I'll go by and see him from time to time, maybe take Charlotte with me when she gets a little older. That might cheer him up. She's such a sweet baby."

"Sounds like a good idea. You know," he said, giving her a kiss on top of her head, "you're such a good friend to him."

"It's the least I could do," she said. "I still feel a certain attachment to him. I want him to be happy."

"You're a wonderful person, Jackie."

"Oh, don't be silly. I just like to help out when I can." Jackie reached up and kissed him on the cheek. "I'm so glad we're back together."

"Of course we are."

"My reward is knowing you still love me," she said.

"Was there ever any doubt?"

Jackie gave Randall a final kiss goodnight, turned over, and settled into the mattress. Randall returned to his reading after giving her bottom a last pat. She was content. Today turned out exactly as she had planned. She wanted to make love to both men and determine if the combination was better than either by itself. David was trapped by his love for her, so she could have him whenever she wanted, and he was certain to keep their affair a secret. If Iris returned to him, Jackie would deal with that issue when it happened. These days Randall was busy running the company, and she now often experienced the same loneliness her mother felt while her father was away at work. But she had her baby, something she always wanted, and life was going well. As she drifted off to sleep, she realized she had made a decision regarding her lovers.

For now, she would keep them both.

32

David understood Jackie was serious about establishing an affair with him soon after he opened the door to a delivery man.

"David Perry?" the man said.

"Yeah, that's me. But I didn't order anything."

The man shrugged and said, "Says to deliver this to you at this address." He repeated the address, so David shrugged and signed for the rectangular box. He lifted the heavy package and walked it into his living room. Attached to the box was a note, which he opened.

David. For when Charlotte visits.

He read it through again, then opened the container. Inside was a small crib, ready to assemble. He wasn't sure how long he stared at the contents before he went to the closet and got out his small set of tools.

Jackie called later on.

"David? Jackie. Did you get the package I sent you?"

"Yes, but—"

"Charlotte will need something to sleep in when we visit. I'll bring the rest of her supplies next time. You know how much paraphernalia a baby takes. . ." She stopped, then said. "I don't mean to be insensitive. Is it okay if I come by Saturday afternoon?"

"Look, maybe we shouldn't. . ." His voice, truncated from a lack of conviction, faded to a whisper.

"I thought you'd like to see the baby for the first time. Say so if you don't."

"Yes, sure I would, Jackie. I mean, if that's all we're going to do."

"We'll see you about 2:00." She hung up.

• • • • •

David moved Charlotte's crib into the second bedroom and partially closed the door. While the baby slept, David and Jackie spent an hour enjoying hot, sweaty sex, so intense that afterward Jackie insisted on showering before she left. He watched her from the bathroom doorway, standing there naked, combing through her long, beautiful hair, smiling back at him from time to time, obviously enjoying him appraising her. Despite their recent tryst, David felt a new erection growing, wanting her again. She glanced over and noticed his obvious desire for her, smiled, then kept on brushing. Then the baby started up, her plaintive cries still loud from behind the closed door.

David pulled on a pair of sweatpants and headed into the bedroom, then reached down and picked up Charlotte, holding her close, watching her squinched eyes tightened in discomfort. He felt her warm skin against his chest and automatically kissed her. Was this tiny child part of him? He experienced a surging, desperate need to know that supplanted his previous erotic thoughts.

"What do I need to do with her?" he said.

Jackie's voice floated in. "It's a wonder we didn't wake her up before, with all the noise we were making. She probably needs to be changed. The diapers are in the bag by the crib."

David retrieved the diaper bag and laid the baby on the bed, unsure how to change her.

"Now what?" he said, feeling helpless.

From the bathroom, Jackie said, "Don't you know how to change a diaper?"

"Never done it before."

"You're just like Randall. It's easy. Let me show you." She came into the room, still naked. As she bent down, David's greedy eyes scanned her form. If she hadn't already showered, he would ask her to have sex again. Instead, he stroked her back as she unfastened the diaper. "Put this in the trash, then come back."

After he disposed of the diaper, she showed him how to clean Charlotte, put on a new diaper, then redress her. The baby looked contented immediately afterward, but only for a few moments, after which she began to cry again.

"What's wrong now?" he said.

"She's probably hungry." She gave him instructions on how to warm a bottle and how to hold her when he fed her. David carried the baby to the living room and set her on the couch, then hurried to the kitchen.

Jackie stayed in the back, getting dressed. Finally finished, she headed toward the front of the apartment to check on them. Charlotte was finishing up her bottle and David was talking to her, making silly baby noises, while Charlotte sucked on the bottle. After she was full, Jackie showed him how to burp her.

David gazed down at the baby, love filling his heart. "Could you stay a while longer? I enjoy taking care of her. She's so sweet and innocent."

"Sorry, but we need to go."

David looked up at Jackie. "Is she. . .is she mine?"

"We've already talked about that," Jackie said, a scowl crossing her face.

"I mean, she could be."

"I told you I also had sex with my husband about the same time."

"Well, I need to know. Is she mine or Randall's?"

Jackie picked Charlotte up and kissed her in the crook of her neck, causing the child to squirm. "She's *my* sweet baby. And the cutest thing there ever *was*!"

After placing Charlotte in her carrier, Jackie retrieved the diaper bag. David watched the baby kick and wiggle in her excitement as Jackie cooed to her.

"Time to go, sweetheart," she said.

David reached for the carrier. "Let me get that." After she handed the baby over, he said, "What do we do now?"

"What do you mean?"

"You and me. What's our situation?"

"I don't understand."

"Shit, Jackie, we're carrying on an affair here. Aren't you concerned?"

"About what?"

He found her nonchalance maddening. "Damn it, about us getting caught. About this. . .this thing ruining our marriages."

"Who's going to catch us? Besides, I only came by today to check on a family friend." Her quick smile disappeared as she headed for the front door and then opened it. "Come on, I need to get going. Bring the baby."

All three of them walked over to Jackie's Mercedes, which straddled two spaces in the adjacent garage. David took his time placing Charlotte in her car seat and testing the seat belt attachment.

"Wouldn't want anything to happen to her," he said as he closed the door and waved to the baby. She wiggled in response. As if the finality of their situation had just dawned on him, David added, "So that's it. We just keep screwing each other?"

"David, stop this. You and I both know what this is." Jackie opened the front door and got in, then started the engine.

"When will you come back?" he said.

She stared at him. "Right now, I can't tell if you want me here again."

"You know I do. I think about you every day. All the time."

That remark seemed to confirm what she already knew. "I'll call you. Charlotte, tell David bye-bye."

He listened to the spit bubble noises coming from the back seat. Then the window rolled up, the car pulled away, and he watched as they drove off. David gave them a half-hearted wave, which he doubted Jackie even saw.

Back inside the apartment, he turned the afternoon over in his mind, reliving the entire time. The sex was incredible, even more exciting than he had expected. He was now living out his earlier fantasy about Jackie, but with a dangerous new twist. He didn't know what to think about that, except that he wanted Jackie now more than ever. And Charlotte? He could not get her out of his head, either. His gut told him she was his daughter, a certainty as sure as anything he had ever felt.

33

The people around the table were uniformly older, representing the benefit of years of both accumulating wealth and legacy inheritances. Richard and Adelle Sinclair, as promised, had brought together a group of their equally well-off friends. Apparently, Sinclair's statement of faith in James had been enough for them to at least consider his proposal.

James and Madison handed out brochures which designated their proposed investment firm type and what made it especially suited for a particular type of client. Modeled after a private physician's practice, the arrangement entitled its clients to all the firm's services, including house calls. Whereas most investment houses concentrated on gathering assets, then left the actual decisions to pre-made plans, computer algorithms, or back office eggheads, James' alternative idea pledged a boutique experience, almost like a family investment office, complete with fully customized portfolios for each couple's particular needs.

The PowerPoint presentation went through the basics of traditional asset management, including fee-for-service and charging a percentage of assets. Their new firm instead proposed to collect an annual fixed fee and thereafter provide whatever range of service the clients needed, based on a three-tiered structure conditioned on the level of service requested. That way, if the couple's assets increased over time, there was no associated automatic increase in fees, except for adjustments for inflation. Based on his projections, James could make this work only if a certain number of prospects signed up to cover the overhead.

One man raised his hand immediately after the presentation was over.

"So, you're saying that we'd avoid our current percentage expenses?" the man said.

"There's always a cost involved in managing money," James said. "I can't prevent that. Part of your expenses come from the fund or brokerage you end up choosing. In most cases, I'd recommend you tailor your portfolio using low-cost index funds or ETFs. Studies show that expenses, on average and over time, matter more than anything except asset allocation. For some of you, a more customized approach, perhaps based on tax-loss harvesting or finding a tax-efficient way to leave money to heirs, might be preferable. If we need to bring in lawyers or accountants to help with setting up things, then that additional charge will be passed on to you at our cost. We don't expect any two of your situations to be the same. Our part of the proposed fee structure is based on what your needs are, not the size of your assets. I think that's a fairer way of assessing costs."

"But once this gets set up, what would we need you for?" the man said, only half kidding.

James smiled, having expected the question. "Different tax laws get dreamed up or repealed every year, people's families change, and interest in leaving a legacy may vary. But you're right. If all you want is to get a suitable investment portfolio set up, we'd be able to do that the first year, and if you wanted to discontinue our services after that, you're welcome to do so. If you need us later, we can work hourly. Our proposed rates are in the brochure, and I think you'll find that low overhead means you'd pay a lot less than a typical hourly for this type of service. The main thing to remember is that different people prefer different approaches. Our goal is to provide full transparency for a service that's often full of conflicts of interest."

The man persisted with his questions. "If the market crashes, you'll promise to be there to help us with damage control? Not be on some beach conveniently out of cell phone range?"

"Yes, of course. Though in a lot of cases, the best action in a crisis may be to do nothing at all."

"You mean we just hold on and watch things fall apart?"

"Everyone needs to take a long-term view."

A smartly dressed lady raised her hand. "Maybe for some of us, the 'long term view' is getting pretty short."

Laughter chased around the table.

"I understand your concern," James said, "but what I'm looking for are clients that, regardless of age, are interested in both preservation and growth of their assets. If you want to go spend it all, that's certainly an option to consider, and please enjoy yourselves if that's what you want. But I think most of you here have different motives. Maybe you want to leave your remaining assets to your children or relatives, or perhaps provide an endowment for a charity or an institution you admire. That means not bolting at the first hint of a bad market."

A member of the group seemed confused. "But how do we know how much to spend, and how much to keep? Who knows how long we'll live?"

James nodded. "No one knows the future. I certainly don't have a crystal ball. But I believe there are prudent ways to enjoy your assets without constantly worrying about not having enough money. Besides, no matter how much people have, studies show people always say they need just a little more than they currently have to feel comfortable."

Another set of chuckles.

James continued. "For those of you who've spent their entire lives being frugal and building up your fortunes, to not take time and enjoy your money would be a mistake. First, we can figure out what your expenses are. Then, after we arrive at a spending plan and calculate an estimate of how long your assets will last, you can plan what else to spend your money on."

"That means I get to buy the new Lamborghini?" one man said, right before his wife elbowed him.

"Maybe so, it that's what you've always wanted."

"See?" the man said as he turned to his wife. "He said it was okay."

James laughed. "I think I've been set up. First, I'd need to check on your situation before I endorse your idea. Then we can talk. If you'll all open the brochure, we've prepared ten different scenarios for an older couple with substantial assets. There's a fair amount of information in there, but basically these scenarios deal with market crashes at the wrong time, as well as market gains at opportune times. It lets you know what the range of outcomes could be, based on various spending patterns and what happens with the market. These are called Monte Carlo simulations and consider thousands of possibilities based on historical returns. You may find a situation in there that resembles your own."

James and Madison waited as the attendees paged through the materials. She said, "Keep in mind, these are representative only, and your conditions will not be exactly the same as any of these examples. We won't treat them that way, either."

"What happens if you fall over dead tomorrow?" one person said.

"I'm working with my early investors to determine a succession plan. Madison. . ." He nodded to his associate, "will complete her security licenses in the next two months. She's fully committed to this strategy and can take over if something unexpected happens to me. And if our asset base grows enough, we will add additional personnel as needed." He paused. "Besides, studies show that women managing assets are more conservative and often achieve better results than men."

Most of the women nodded, like such a verdict was a foregone conclusion.

Another hand raised. "What happens when we all croak? Who'll be your next clients?"

"We have a strategy to expand the business. Many people these days have significant assets, even when younger, and they worry about who can tell them honestly what they need to know, just like you do. Only by being good managers and providing a decent track record can we keep your trust, and hopefully also assist your heirs as well."

Finally, a man who had been quiet so far said, "What type of firm did you say you would be?"

"A registered investment advisor. RIA for short. It's becoming a lot more common. As I mentioned previously, it carries with it a fiduciary obligation. Our strategy is to use that model, but to charge in a way that's different from most firms."

The man stroked his chin. "Your proposed annual fee at first seemed expensive, but I guess when compared to what we're paying now. . ." He did some mental math after conferring with his wife. "Looks like it would be maybe half of what we're paying on our current one percent management fee. I guess seeing the fixed number makes it more obvious."

"Some advisors do their best to hide their fees, but most just stick to standard ways of charging you. Each alternative has its pluses and minuses. Our proposed fees are fixed and out there for everyone to see and evaluate. Clearly, the more assets you bring to the table, the more attractive a fixed fee would be. And, at some point, if a client's assets decline enough, it wouldn't make sense to continue to pay the fixed fee."

"Then what happens after the market crashes and our assets go way down? Do we get kicked out after that?" The woman asking turned to her husband, both of whom looked worried.

"Absolutely not. If you're an existing client and your assets have dwindled below a certain point, we'll commit to reduce the fixed fee proportionately and continue to help you. That's our promise. We won't abandon you, even if you fall on hard times." James could see that the frequency of questions winding down. "It's simple arithmetic, folks. If you have twenty million instead of five million in assets, then the fixed fee will look completely different. The idea here is for us to cover our costs, make a decent profit, and not have a conflict of interest by encouraging you to do things that increases our fees, or allow us to free-ride on a percentage of assets that goes up simply because your fortunes continue to grow on their own."

A woman who hadn't spoken before raised her hand. "How is this different from a wrap fee?"

James nodded for Madison to answer the question. She said, "Traditional asset managers have several built-in conflicts of interest. If they charge you for each buy and sell, their incentive is to encourage you to trade a lot. If they charge you an overall percentage of assets, such as a wrap fee, then their incentive is to do nothing and get paid the same amount. Think about it this way. You require a certain level of service for your investments. However, the incremental cost of managing another dollar of your money is essentially zero unless you want to expand into more complicated investment ideas. Some are happy with just a few investment categories, whereas others like to dabble in a number of different types. That's the reason for the tiered structure we're offering. You can choose whichever version you feel fits your situation. And we can change to another tier if what you thought you wanted isn't what you really need."

"So, is this a unique investment management approach?" The question came from a member of the group who had said nothing yet.

Madison smiled. "No, not unique. Unusual, I'd say. Our goal is to have a transparent relationship with our clients, based on what's good for them, not what brings us the most in fees. That way, we always look out for your interests and not our own. Any more questions?"

The members of the group glanced around, but no one else spoke up.

"Madison and I will be available to answer any of your individual questions in case you wanted to discuss things in private. We can stay as long as you'd like to visit. I also want to thank the Sinclairs for their hospitality in hosting this meeting.

We've arranged for caterers to provide some refreshments and treats, which are set out in the kitchen. Please help yourselves."

As the couples got up from their chairs and started socializing, James had a good feeling about the outcome. Maybe this would work. He had always wanted to try an alternative to traditional investment management, and this was his opportunity to do so. If only enough people signed up.

Richard Sinclair came over and shook both of their hands. "Nice job, James, Madison. I think you both created a lot of interest here today. You've likely found both investors and clients."

James nodded his appreciation. "Thanks, Mr. Sinclair. I hope we've kept the trust you've placed in us. Maybe this will work."

Sinclair grinned. "I'm sure it will. I've heard a lot of positive feedback already. And call me Richard. Now let's all go have us some of that champagne."

34

When David pulled into the apartment building's garage, it shocked him to see Gayle's car sitting in a visitor space. The realization that Iris, and possibly her mother as well, were both here, filled him with a mixture of dread and relief. He couldn't wait to see Iris again, but he worried about what she had decided about their relationship, since he had yet to actually talk to her. If they could get back together, he resolved immediately to banish any idea of sleeping with Jackie ever again.

He found Iris at the back of the hall, standing in the spare bedroom, her back to him.

"Iris, sweetie, thank God you've come home. Is your mother with you?"

"No, only me."

He moved up against her and rested his hands on the side of her shoulders. She stood still, stiff to his touch. Maybe she wasn't ready for him to touch her. He probably needed to give her more time. He let his hands drop.

"Could you look at me? Please?"

When she turned around, he could see that she had been crying.

"What's the matter?" he said.

Without replying, she turned and headed toward the living room, David in pursuit.

"Please, Iris, talk to me. I've missed you so much."

Near the front door, she hesitated, then turned to face him. "I thought maybe if I was gone a while, you'd get over her."

"Over who?" David said, but he knew exactly whom she was referring to.

"Jackie, of course."

"What do you mean? Over her?"

"The crib," she said. "Let me guess. The baby stays in there while you two have sex. In our bed."

"What would make you think that?" he said, but he knew he looked guilty. Iris had an inherent sense of knowing when he tried to conceal his dirty secrets.

"Tell me the truth," she said. "You owe me that."

"Okay, she came over once. Said she wanted to show me the baby. That's all. And then. . .well, you're right. We had sex."

Iris stared at him, not replying.

"It happened, okay? You had left me. You wouldn't talk to me, and I didn't know if you were ever coming back. Doesn't have to mean that will happen ever again." Even as he spoke those words, he realized he was deliberately lying to Iris. Jackie had visited his apartment not once, but multiple times since their initial encounter, usually on a Saturday afternoon. Each time they made love, the sex seemed more sensual, more intense than the last. But he couldn't admit that to Iris, not now, not when a chance remained for them getting back together. But did he mean it? Could he give Jackie up? Dismissing that conflict for now, he clung to the diminishing possibility of saving his marriage.

Iris scanned his face, a coldness taking over her own. "You still want her. I can tell. Not that this is a surprise—you've always wanted her. And now, after having your child, she has a permanent hold over you."

"No, that's not it. I asked. She said I wasn't the father."

"And you believe that?"

David looked down, embarrassed. "I don't know what to think, Iris. I don't know what to do about it."

After considering his reply, Iris said, "Maybe if we'd had our own baby, things would have been different. Or maybe you'd have found your way to her, regardless. I don't know anymore." She paused. "How is your daughter?"

"She's so beautiful, a little angel. I got to hold and feed her. It was. . ." His voice trailed off as he realized his overt enthusiasm was causing Iris additional pain.

"David, I want a divorce."

"Please, *please* don't do that," he pleaded. "You're the one I want, the one I need. I've always loved you. I promise I'll never see her again."

"I suppose you mean that," Iris said. "At this moment."

"I don't know if I can go on without you," he said, tears forming in his eyes.

Iris moved over against him and put her arms around his back. He hugged her fiercely to him, feeling her thin body pressed against his. She had lost weight and was smaller than ever. No doubt this was his fault as well, for all the misery he caused her.

He continued to cry into her shoulder. "I'm so sorry, Iris. I've failed you, been a terrible husband, but I still love you. I really do."

"I love you, too, David," she said before kissing him on the cheek and disengaging. "But that's not enough. I can't live with you, not anymore."

"I'll change. I promise I will."

She stood back. "There's not room in our marriage for three people. I drove here today to have an honest talk with you about us, about our future, see if we could work things out, if you could give her up. I see now that I'm a little too late."

"You can't *do* this. I *need* you," he said, completely distraught. "I *can't* lose you. Not like this. I can't. . ."

She gave him a faint smile. "You've already lost me. You just haven't admitted it to yourself." She turned toward the door. "I'll come back with some moving people in a couple of weeks to get my things." Her eyes scanned the living room. "Most of this you can keep. I'll let you know ahead of time when I'll be here. It would be better if you weren't."

"Please, *please*, Iris, don't let us end like this." he said.

"Watch out for her, David. She's nothing but trouble. In the end, she'll only be there for herself." She paused. "About the divorce. I'll tell the attorney to put it down to 'irreconcilable differences.' If you contest it, I'll go to court and tell them about how you've behaved. That will be very messy for everyone, so I suggest you don't go that route." She gave him a last look, appearing as if she wanted to say more, maybe tell him about her feelings, her regrets, what a shithead he was for doing this to them, but all that came out was, "Goodbye, David."

With that, she exited the apartment, leaving him standing there in the doorway, watching her walk down the hall to the elevators, wanting to say something, anything, to get her back. But she was right. He couldn't give Jackie up, not yet anyway. Even though his obsession had ruined his marriage.

Later, as he sat on the sofa by himself, he thought about what he had done, the hurt he'd caused Iris, and he cursed himself for the millionth time. This was all his fault. Maybe if he went after Iris tomorrow, made her see that he had changed, that he was over Jackie. Maybe that would work. They could move away and he would get a new job. They could try to have another child. It could work. All the while, visions of Jackie kept popping back up in his mind as he remembered the amazing sex, the longing for her that had never abated, and the pleasure he had in holding the child. He knew it was his baby. It had to be. He also realized that he could not bear to leave the little girl, not now, not permanently, even if he seldom saw her. It was all driving him crazy. This disaster, this enormous mess, was all his fault, the result of his inability to do what was right, to take control of himself, the same way he could not stop what his father forced him to do. Maybe he secretly liked the abuse, that he deep-down enjoyed destroying his life. That would fit. And his weakness had hurt everyone around him that mattered.

That night, for the second time in his life, David Perry seriously thought about taking his own life.

There were two things that kept him from doing so. The first was Iris. She would see his death as all her fault. He couldn't do that to her, especially when she was in such a fragile emotional state. The second reason was his need to see Charlotte again. Yes, Jackie had said she wasn't his daughter, but every time he saw the child and watched her grow, he became more certain that she was his. He needed confirmation, one way or the other, and he knew how he was going to get it.

First, he had to call Finchie and talk this out, see what he thought. What would he have ever done without his friend?

35

David signed the divorce papers in his attorney's office on a Friday afternoon. The lawyer said it was one of the easiest ones he ever worked on since the couple didn't fight over anything. David would get his bill by the end of next week.

After he left the attorney's office, David drove around, not having anywhere in particular to go. He had asked his boss for the entire day off and had nothing else planned. He headed for the house on Searcy Circle, the one the elder Randolphs sold after Jackie's and James' dad retired. Last David heard, they had moved to Florida, but kept a condo in the city so they would have a place to stay when they came to see their children and grandchildren.

David lingered in front of the house, thinking about better days and all the memories the place held for him. Better not to stay too long, though, since his car looked out of place. If the neighbors were anything like they used to be, an unknown vehicle with a man in it, stopped for more than a few minutes, would guarantee a prompt call to the police. David put the car back in gear and headed out.

As he drove, he thought about Jackie. Again. From all he could tell, Randall was doing a great job running Randolph Enterprises, constantly expanding the company and increasing sales year after year. Jackie, balancing out her successful husband, often appeared in the local society postings, arranging and pulling off one social event after another. The newspaper and social media often gushed over the couple's philanthropy. One day it was unwed mothers, the next cause was the homeless, after that support for food pantries. That made him, for whatever reason, decide to drive by Jackie's house.

David wondered, as his car idled in front of the Weir house, how much Randall would have to earn to cover all those expenses. Jackie certainly wasn't cutting back. She always dressed in the latest fashion, including when she came to see him. They still kept up a regular schedule of sleeping together on weekend afternoons. Each time he promised himself this was the last one, that he needed to get over Jackie, that he absolutely must move forward with the next part of his life, but the lure of Jackie and Charlotte was real. He knew he wasn't ready to quit either of them.

A gaudily painted catering van sat in the driveway, ready to deliver another event, another notch, in her belt. He watched the workers carry in flowers, trays of pre-cooked foods and heaping cellophane-wrapped platters of cheese and finger foods, all ready to feed the hungry elite. He wondered what he would do if Jackie came outside, what he would say, what kind of remark she might make about him spying on her. But no Jackie showed. She was inside, doubtless consumed with final preparations. A maid would be busy getting her new formal dress ready. He wondered what her society friends would think if they knew she was fucking an ordinary man way below her social class. Appearances, he decided, seldom reflected reality. Maybe he should take out a notice in the paper and let everyone know.

He circled the cul-de-sac, speeding up as he headed for the central park.

As the days grew warmer, the budding plants, responding to an expectation that the last freeze was over, put on blooms. Even the grass was turning. It was the end of the work week and people were already out all over the park, walking, playing with their dogs, lying on the emerging green shoots and enjoying casual conversation. He wanted to be there with Iris, enjoying the weather with his sweet wife. But Iris was gone, all because of his obsessions and his carelessness. He parked in the lot and rolled down the window, content for now with people-watching.

How long he sat there he didn't know, but soon it grew colder. The skies quickly clouded over and signaled that no, it was still early spring and the weather was just kidding about it being a glorious, sunny day. Soon, the scuttling clouds darkened and stinging rain fell, first in a few big drops and then, unexpectedly, in a fierce, all-consuming pattern that got everyone and everything soaked. David rolled up his window and watched people run for cover. He should go home. But to what?

His phone rang.

"David? Ja'Neel. Max and I were wondering if you'd like to come over for dinner."

"Tonight?"

"Yes, unless you have plans. We'd like to see you. Frankly, we're worried about you. Are you doing okay?"

"My divorce from Iris was final today," he said.

"David, I'm so sorry. You two were. . ." Ja'Neel stopped, obviously unsure of how to describe the vanished couple. "Well, it's done. Let's not dwell on that. Come by early and we can open some wine. We'd really like to have your company."

He opened his mouth to say no, he wasn't in the mood, or to come up with a myriad of other excuses so he could go home and have a frozen dinner and dedicate the evening to feeling sorry for himself. But, on a whim, he agreed.

"Great. See you about seven?" she said.

"Fine. I'll be there."

"One other thing. We invited someone else. I didn't know if you could come, so I..."

"Look," he said, "maybe I better take a raincheck. I don't want to make your other guest feel uncomfortable. I'm not in a great mood right now."

"No, please don't do that. It's not a setup at all. Just a coincidence. I promise," Ja'Neel said. "Besides, she's not looking for a man."

"What's the matter, she prefer women?"

"David, that's a very insensitive thing for you to say."

"Sorry, I'm in a shitty mood right now. I probably need to go home instead."

"Come anyway, please? I mean it. I won't take 'no' for an answer."

"The last time you talked me into coming over for a party, I got married because of it."

"This isn't a party, only a quiet dinner, so you're safe. The fact is, I've already made too much pasta. I need someone to help eat it all up. I'm not so keen on leftovers, and I'd hate to waste it."

"That means whenever you have excess food, you think of me?"

He could hear her talking to someone out of earshot. "Max said to tell you we've run out of all our other friends to invite. You're the only one left, so you have to accept."

He had to laugh. Ja'Neel and Max had this way of making him always feel comfortable at their place, something that right now he needed. "In that case, I guess I have no choice. I'll be there."

"Thanks. Love you," she said.

"You too. 'Bye."

David headed back to his apartment. He needed to take a shower and change clothes. Who knows, he thought, maybe a quiet evening with two good friends would be just the thing to improve his mood. Assuming he could avoid the other guest, that is.

36

After Nichelle and Finch delivered Davie to school, they returned home. Nichelle declared she was hungry and wanted a big breakfast, so Finch helped her fix the meal.

"You seem to know your way around the kitchen," she said.

Finch dropped bread into the toaster before reaching over to flip the bacon. "I was a line cook for a while. The diner mostly favored speed over quality, but I can make a mean chicken-fried steak."

"Is there anything you haven't done?"

"Lots. But I've always enjoyed getting to know new things along the way." He returned to stirring the eggs while glancing over periodically to see how Nichelle was coming with her part.

"What?" she said, catching his eye.

"I enjoy looking at you."

She had to smile. "I have a question for you."

"What's that?"

"Why haven't you made love to me yet? You told me yesterday that you loved me."

Finch didn't reply at first. He was still getting used to the direct way that Nichelle talked to him. He had never experienced a woman who was so open with her feelings and opinions.

"Well..." he said.

"Don't you find me attractive?"

"Yes, of course I do."

Finished with frying the bacon and making toast, he placed the finished parts of the meal on each plate. Usually, they ate little or nothing for breakfast. He never liked to fill up early unless he was doing manual work that morning, in which case he needed a substantial breakfast to last him until noon. Lately, all he did was sit around the house, waiting for his back to heal. He felt like he was getting fat. Today, despite their usual reluctance to eat a big breakfast, they were both hungry, a harbinger of serious discussions to come.

"I meant what I said. I do love you. It's..." He used the spatula to ladle the eggs onto the plates. "I've hesitated to go that far."

"Do you have some reservations about having sex with a woman?" she said, heading over to the grab the pot so she could pour coffee for them both.

"You always come to the point, don't you?" he said.

"A constant failing of mine. Well?"

"No, of course not. It's, well, it seemed like a real imposition. You've taken care of me, wiped my butt, fixed my meals, everything. I was helpless for a while and it was very difficult for me to be in that kind of situation. But you didn't seem to mind. And you've been so kind and caring, and I think about you constantly, about making love to you, what you'd smell like and feel like and taste like and..." He paused while setting the pan in the sink. "It seemed very selfish on my part. You've sacrificed so much for me already, and then I go ask to make love to you and if you didn't want to, you might still do it and then I'd feel like a total jerk. Since I found you incredibly attractive, that made it that much more difficult to keep quiet."

"What about what I want?" she said.

He turned to her. "What *do* you want? Really?"

"You should know by now that I don't hide my feelings," she said, moving up against him.

He kissed her several times, holding on to her like she was his last lifeline.

"Let's finish breakfast, then go to bed," she said, turning toward the table, acting like the proposed action was the obvious, and only, solution.

• • • • • •

Finch sat in his underwear on the edge of the bed, thinking about how this would go. Nichelle was busy in the bathroom doing something. He heard noises but failed to connect them to any specific activity. Her shadow on the floor, enhanced by the light in the bathroom, disappeared as she turned off the switch. His pulse rose in anticipation.

She came into the bedroom wearing a loose robe and stood before him.

"We need to make sure things work between us. Physically," she said.

He detected a nervousness in her voice that he hadn't heard before. "Is there some reason it wouldn't?"

"I don't know. I want it to. But I'm worried."

He patted the top of his leg. "Come on, baby, sit down. We'll talk this through."

"Okay."

She sat on his lap and wound her arm around his neck while he rubbed her back.

"I want you to know that I expect to enjoy having sex with the man I love," she said, a tentative quiver in her voice.

"That's a good sign." He could see that her eyes were wet. "What's the matter?"

"I'm worried you won't like the way I look. Or we won't fit together right. Or. . ." Her voice trailed off as a tiny tear dribbled out of her eye. "I'm feeling really vulnerable right now, okay?"

"What happened to my always confident girl?"

"She's gone missing."

He undid the belt on her robe and slipped his hand around her waist, feeling her warm skin. "You know I love you, right?"

"Yes."

"You feel really special to me," he said, caressing her side. "What if I gave you a kiss? Think that would help?"

She nodded.

"Better?" he said after their lips parted.

"I could use a lot more of those," she said.

He kissed her again for a long time.

"I'm not using birth control right now," she said after they broke apart. "I could get pregnant."

"I can use a condom," he said. "Do you have any?"

She motioned toward the nightstand drawer. "I bought some the other day. In case."

"Then we're all set. If you're ready."

She nodded and opened up her robe. He saw she was naked underneath. "You're so beautiful," he said.

"Are you sure? You're not just saying that?"

"You know me. Always tell the truth." His hand moved up to her breast and caressed her. "How's that feel?"

"Wonderful."

She stood up and slipped her robe off. Finch rolled over onto the bed, making room for her beside him. As she lay down, he reached for her, his sun-darkened hands similar to the natural color of her skin, and started kissing her neck, then moved down to her breasts. Nichelle responded with soft moans.

"Is your back okay for this?" she said.

"I'll let you know if it isn't."

"I doubt you would. Maybe I better get on top."

He grinned. "Sure this isn't some kind of control thing?"

She laughed, a quiet chuckle. "Well, that could be part of it."

"Okay. Whatever you want, baby," he said, kissing her.

"You always say 'okay?'"

"I do with you. Besides, I want to try a few things I think you'll like," he said.

Nichelle closed her eyes as he moved down her stomach, kissing her as he went.

• • • •

When they finished making love an hour later, they both lay back in the bed, exhausted.

"Seems like that answered your question," Finch said, catching his breath as he pulled her leg across him. "About us being compatible."

"Sure did."

"I've fantasized about making love to you for a long time," he said. "It was better than I imagined. A lot better." He paused. "Would you like to get married?"

She pressed against him. "It's only important that I be with you. That's all that I really care about."

"I'd like to get married. If that's alright."

"You must promise me one thing."

"What's that?"

Nichelle propped up on her elbow. "Don't *ever* lie to me. I don't mean about the little stuff, like do I look great in my clothes or did you like what I fixed for dinner. Those things don't matter. I mean about the major events in our lives, the understanding and trust that will bind us together."

"I promise. Besides, you always look good in your clothes."

"I *mean* it, Finchie."

He stroked her side and kissed her. "You have my word."

She settled back to his side. "Then I'm fine if you want to get married."

"Nothing fancy, only a small service. With your parents and mine. I mean, my mom and dad practically think you're their daughter already. Also, I'd like to invite James and Jeanette. That's about it for me. Who else would you like there?"

"A couple of my good friends. Max and Ja'Neel."

"When?" he said.

"Call your parents and see what their schedule looks like. I'll call mine. Maybe we could arrange something in the next couple of weeks. Would that be too soon?"

"Not for me."

She kissed him again. "But I need to buy a new dress."

"Yeah, I should get some decent clothes, too." A troubled look crossed his face.

"What's the matter?" Nichelle said.

"I screwed up by not getting you an engagement ring. I wasn't thinking far enough ahead. Sorry."

"I only want a wedding band. That's all. Something simple."

He said, "And I want to adopt Davie. First thing, after we get married."

"I know he'd like that. I would too."

A bit later, she said, "I have another suggestion."

"What's that?" he said.

"I want to have another baby. Your baby. Is that alright with you?"

Pulling her against him, he stretched out and faced her, kissing her, taking his time. "I'd be incredibly honored if you wanted to have our baby. Davie could use a little brother or sister."

"Sure? Because if you need to think about it—"

"Yes, I'm sure," he said, interrupting her. Finch's fingers combed through her hair. "Looks like we're pretty good at agreeing on big issues."

"Looks like," she said. "You need to move into my bedroom. Davie's a sound sleeper. That will help if we want to make love at night."

"You can make a lot of noise," he said.

"It's because I enjoy having sex with you."

He moved his hand to caress her back. "I have a confession to make."

"What's that?"

"When I met you the first time, I thought you were the smartest, most beautiful woman I'd ever seen."

"Back when David and I first got married?"

"Yes. I was standing there, at the altar, with James and Max, thinking how special you were, and feeling like a total asshole for even imagining it."

Nichelle nodded. "Probably a good thing you didn't express your feelings back then. I thought you were a little creepy. Well, not creepy, exactly. Intense, I guess, is a better word. You hardly held me when we danced at the reception."

"I was afraid I'd get a hard-on with you up against me, so I acted like I wasn't interested. I still remember how you smelled, how you looked. You were so beautiful in that white dress." He stopped, thinking over her last remark. "I'd say that qualifies as creepy, right?"

She said, "Not anymore. I think I'm going to be very, very happy."

"I'm glad. I love you, Nichelle."

"I love you, too, Finchie. I was afraid when you left for Florida that we'd never see you again. Then James told me you were crazy about me and Davie. That gave me hope."

"And look how things turned out," he said.

"Yes," Nichelle said. "Look how things turned out."

"I guess we should get up and do something besides this," Finch said.

"Like what?"

"I don't know. I've never had the chance before to stay in bed with a woman I love. Seems odd, like I don't deserve it."

She said, "We have to pick up Davie from school this afternoon. We can tell him then that we're getting married. He'll be thrilled. That's all that's on my agenda. Maybe in a little while we could make love again, seeing as how the last time was pretty special."

"I'd like that. Very much."

Finch started kissing her again, luxuriating in the feel of her skin, the smell of sex on her, the absolute joy he had with finding out that this woman both loved him and wanted him. He never expected to have this kind of pleasure in his life. He felt guilty about the circumstances that had brought her to him, but promised himself that he would do everything possible to reward her for her faith in him. His wandering days were over.

37

David showed up early for the dinner invite and was most of the way through his first glass of wine when the other guest arrived. Max went to the door and David heard murmurs of thanks and welcome in the hall. Then the guest came into the living room where David and Ja'Neel were standing.

"David, this is our friend, Nichelle. Nichelle, David." Max said.

"Pleased to meet you," he said, extending his hand.

"You as well," the woman said. She was appraising him as they shook.

"Get you a glass of wine?" Max asked.

"Yes, please. Red, if you have it."

David looked the woman over as she turned to speak to Ja'Neel. Quite attractive, he decided, with a nice, broad smile. Almost his height with her medium heels on. The dark slacks and a long-sleeved blouse fit her form nicely. She was African-American, like Ja'Neel, something he noticed almost in passing. He thought back to when he was a lot younger, when those distinctions mattered so much more. They still did, even in today's society, at least to some people. But he was past that, evaluating people for who they were and not for what race they identified with.

Realizing he had been staring at the other guest, David turned to pretend to re-appraise the apartment that he knew so well and distract his thoughts regarding the new woman. Lots of people like him stumble through life, he thought, never sure of what is going to happen along the way, hoping that somehow you survived all the catastrophes. Michelle looked like those things didn't bother her. She displayed an assured confidence in herself and was, he guessed, about the same age as the rest of them. With a quick and easy manner, she seemed instantly at home, despite the intrusion of a man she had just met. He liked her immediately.

Turning to David as Ja'Neel headed for the kitchen, Nichelle said, "So, David, what do you do?"

"I'm a business consultant."

"Oh? What do you consult about?"

"Various projects. Basically, we evaluate businesses and determine how to improve them. Or maybe we do a study to decide if they should expand or get smaller, or if they're being sold, what they should be worth. It's part finance, part management."

"Sounds interesting," she said.

"I've been doing it for a while, so a lot of it's pretty routine now. How about you, Michelle?"

"Ni-chelle," she said, her tongue clicking down from the roof of her mouth with the first syllable. "With an 'N.'"

"Oh, sorry, I didn't hear that right. Nichelle. That's a nice name. Has a pretty sound to it."

"Thanks. I'm a PA, a physician's assistant. I work in a doctor's office."

"What kind?"

"Family practice. I take care of the routine things like colds, allergies, flu, sprained ankles. That sort of thing. The doctor handles the more complicated cases."

Max, having returned with Nichelle's wine, said, "She's being modest. She basically fixes everyone, and the doctor gets all the credit."

David noticed for the first time that Ja'Neel was drinking water. That surprised him. She always liked her evening wine.

"Thanks," Nichelle said when taking the glass. "What's new with you guys?"

Max gazed at Ja'Neel with a dreamy look and hooked her arm in his. "Well, we have news. Found out yesterday."

"Spill it," Nichelle said.

"We're going to have a baby," Ja'Neel said, and flinging a hand across her mouth to stifle a giggle.

"Congratulations," David said, thinking in a momentary flashback of how happy Iris had been when she found out she was pregnant. Iris. He wondered what she was doing right now, and what he would say to her if he could talk to her.

"Yes, ditto," Nichelle said, embracing Ja'Neel. "Planned, I assume, knowing you two."

"Yes, absolutely," Max said, then kissed his wife.

David gave them both a hug and kissed Ja'Neel on the cheek. He turned to Nichelle. "Understand, they've been this way toward each other ever since college."

Nichelle said, "I can believe that."

"I've tried my best to get her to leave him. Personally, I can't see the attraction she has for the tall guy."

Ja'Neel said to David, "Sorry, sweetie, but I'm still committed to what's-his-name."

Max laughed. He always enjoyed the kidding around with Ja'Neel and David, pretending there was a real rivalry for her affections.

Ja'Neel's frown betrayed a troubling thought. "David, about your and Iris' situation? I didn't mean to—"

"That's fine," David said, waving away the apology. "Our experience isn't typical."

Ja'Neel reached over and touched David's arm. "How's Iris doing?"

"I think she's okay. From what I hear. She's staying at her mother's for now. At least she's finally rid of me."

Nichelle watched the two of them as they talked, her intelligent, darting eyes showing that she was curious about the history of this conversation but was not the type to inquire about sensitive matters unless there was an invitation.

David turned to her. "I met my future wife here at one of their parties. After we got married, we lost a baby to a miscarriage. Iris had a really difficult time. Then we had other issues, which were my fault." He stopped, then said, "Our divorce was final today."

"Sorry," Nichelle said, looking at him over the top of her wineglass. "About one in eight pregnancies ends in a miscarriage. It can be a very emotional time. For both of members of the couple."

David shrugged. "Yeah, it was tough." He avoided saying anymore.

A shadow of dread crossed Ja'Neel's face. David could see that she had not considered the possibility of losing her baby. Nichelle's matter-of-fact statistics had vaguely unsettled her.

Breaking the awkward pause, Max patted David on the back. "Let's all go into the dining room. The pasta's calling out to us." Max adopted a high, squeaky voice. "Eat me, eat me."

38

The animated conversation caused David to realize he was thoroughly enjoying himself. He was quite glad he hadn't turned down the invitation to dinner. Despite his and Nichelle's offers to help, Max and Ja'Neel insisted on bringing everything to the table. By the time the meal was nearly over, everyone had eaten more than their fill. Ja'Neel, as usual, proved to be a superb cook.

She picked up the pasta bowl. "This will make great leftovers."

"Hey, you told me that's why I had to come tonight," David said. "To eat this all up."

"Really, David, I have no idea where you get your information," Ja'Neel said with a laugh.

"Never match wits with a clever woman," Max said. "Who wants more wine? Or dessert?"

"Dessert? Are you kidding?" David looked at Nichelle, whose shake of the head echoed his conclusion. "I don't know any way I could eat another—"

"Then you're going to miss out on my excellent homemade cannoli," Max said, interrupting their refusal. "The good news is I get both of yours for myself."

"No way then," David said. "Even if I have to take mine home in my pocket and it melts and runs out on the ground."

Nichelle chuckled at their exchange. "You two always like this?"

"Ever since I sat next to him in economics class in college," David said. "He was a terrible influence. It's a wonder I passed."

"Seems like I remember it was me who helped you make your grades," Max said. He rolled his eyes. "How memories fade in people with tiny brains."

Ja'Neel returned with the desserts.

"Honestly, I don't know how I can eat this," Nichelle said as her host scooped the cold cannoli onto her plate. "But it looks so delicious."

"Force yourself," David said. "I am. If only to torpedo Max's greedy intentions."

Initially reluctant, Nichelle started in. Once the first spoonful was in her mouth, her eyes closed in delight. "Oh, my God, I think I'm going to have an orgasm."

"That's why she makes them," David said, pointing to Ja'Neel. "It's the only way she could ever have one living with Max."

Ja'Neel moved over beside Max. "Sweetheart, is he making fun of you again?"

"Yes," he said. "David's such an awful shit. Let's never ask him over again. Nichelle, I like. She can come back."

"Thanks," Nichelle said, taking another bite. Her second reaction was the same as the first. "This is so, so good." Pointing her spoon at the cannoli, she said, "Would you make me one of these every week? That shouldn't be a lot of trouble."

"See?" Max said. "She's sitting too close to David. His manners are already rubbing off on her." He looked petulant. "Pretty soon she'll be making fun of me, too."

Bending down to kiss him, Ja'Neel said, "You just have to take your punishment, dear. I don't know what else to say."

"Next thing you know, the baby's going to chime in." Max sighed. "My lot in life, I guess."

Once they had all finished eating, Nichelle turned to David. "We'll clean up. You two take a break." Her chin jerked upward. "Come on."

"No, don't do that—" Ja'Neel started in.

David interrupted her protest. "Have a seat, Momma. Sorry you have to sit next to Max, but that's your punishment for marrying him." He stacked up their plates and headed for the kitchen, right behind Nichelle, who had her fingers clamped in the glasses. Ja'Neel moved her chair over next to Max and put her head on his shoulder. He put his arm around her and kissed her.

In the kitchen, Nichelle said, "They're so sweet together."

"They'll make excellent parents. That kid's going to be so spoiled. And so loved."

Nichelle rinsed the plates, then passed them to David, who loaded the dishwasher. She caught him staring at her.

"What?" she said.

"Your hair," he said. "I find it very interesting."

"Why?"

"Those braids are so complicated and then you tie it all up in a bun in back. How long is your hair?"

"Middle of my back." She eyed him with a half smile. "What is the deal with white guys and Black women's hair?"

David shrugged. "I don't know. I guess it's so different from what I'm used to."

"You want to touch it, don't you?"

"May I?"

As Nichelle turned her back to him, David's fingers hesitated, then barely squeezed her bun. "How long does that last? Until you have to redo it?"

"About six weeks."

"Fascinating," David said, dropping his hand. "What about you? Surely a woman as smart and attractive as you must have a significant other?"

"No, I'm a committed single."

"Ja'Neel told me that before, but now that I've met you, I can't believe it's accurate."

"Nice of you to say, but I like it that way."

"Well, regardless, it's true. What I said before. About you being smart and attractive."

"Are you coming on to me?" Nichelle said, having turned back to the sink and not looking at him. She held a plate under the clear stream pouring down from the faucet aerator.

"No, I mean I wasn't. . ." He stopped, seriously thinking over her question. "Maybe so. I apologize."

She laughed. "Don't waste your time. Besides, you just got out of an unsuccessful relationship, right?"

He pushed the heels of his hands against the edge of the counter and hung his head. "You're right. I should know better."

Nichelle reached out and touched his hand, even though her fingers were still wet. "Sorry. I have a bad habit of saying what I think."

"No, you're right. I should know better." He straightened up. "It was very nice to meet you."

"You too."

"I need to go."

"Don't leave on my account," she said. "I didn't mean to upset you. Really."

"No worries," he said as he carefully folded the dish towel and set it on the counter. "Time I headed out."

Nichelle watched as he thanked his hosts, telling them he needed to go home but how much he had enjoyed the evening. Ja'Neel gave him a kiss on the cheek, and Max responded with a bear hug.

An interesting man, Nichelle thought. Friendly, but also troubled. It struck her how honest he was about his previous marriage. Most people would have deflected, covered up what happened, or blamed the other party. Well, that chance encounter was over with. Likely, she would never see him again.

39

Randolph Wealth Advisors rented a small office in a strip shopping center. Nothing fancy, but the space came with a conference room plus another room with space for a few desks, records, filing cabinets, and a small closet housing their computer server. James and Madison agreed they needed to stay small for now and reduce the overhead. In most cases, they went to see their clients at their homes anyway, so having a fancy office didn't provide an advantage. James was very pleased by how quickly Madison completed the final round of her security licensing exams. She shared his passion for a new way to serve their clients, and the dedication it would take to carry that out. Aware that a woman had strengths that a man didn't, he believed their overlapping skills offered substantial advantages to their clients. Madison had the courage to leave Anderson-Markum for that very reason—the chance to make a difference in their industry.

She was sitting in front of his desk, discussing strategy, when the call came in.

"Randolph Wealth Advisors," James said.

"James, Michael here."

Surprised by a call from his old boss, he nodded at Madison and put the call on speakerphone. "Hello, Michael."

"Say, I hear your little boutique business may make it after all."

"We're holding our own with our limited number of clients. Enough to make ends meet for now."

"I suppose," Michael said. "Still, that flat fee structure of yours isn't exactly designed to maximize profits."

"That's the point," James said.

"Listen, I'd like to buy you lunch today. If you can tear yourself away."

"That's a kind offer, Michael, but we're pretty busy here."

"Just lunch. Say 11:30?" Michael named an expensive downtown restaurant.

"Well, alright. I'll be there." James hung up.

Madison frowned. "What's he up to?"

"Checking out the competition, I'm sure."

"Watch out for him," she said, and returned to her desk.

．　　．　　．　　．　　．

"So, I hear you sold your house," Anderson said, sipping on his second martini.

James said, "Yes. I had a long talk with Jeanette, and we decided it was time to downsize. Since our previous home was in a very desirable neighborhood, after we took the profit, we paid cash for our new house."

"In Jefferson Heights, right? Quite a comedown from The Parks, I would think."

James filed away the breezy slur. Exactly what he would have expected from Michael. "We like it there. Solid middle class, not a lot of pressure to keep up with the rich folks."

"What about your trust fund? Why not tap that?"

"I want to live on what I make from now on, save the rest for the future if I can."

Michael rolled his eyes. "And your kids? Don't they miss their old friends? Plus the private school?"

"They did, for a while, but they've adjusted. The public schools in our new neighborhood are really great. And as a family, we decided it was best to limit their extracurricular activities to two things that they liked the best. Turns out they were feeling really stressed with all the stuff they were into. Jeanette and I both think they're a lot happier now. We are as well."

"Well, that all sounds very nice," Anderson said.

"What is it you want, Michael?"

Anderson drained the last of his glass. As the server walked by, Anderson tapped the rim to alert the waiter that he needed another. "I have to admit you've done a good job rounding up some whales. I was beginning to think you didn't have it in you."

James didn't reply.

"Look, I see now that I was too hasty in firing you. I apologize. There, I've said it. You know me. I don't like to admit I was wrong."

"Alright," James said, still wondering what the man was up to.

"The fact is, Anderson-Markum would like to buy your firm and absorb it into our existing business."

"On what condition?"

"We'll give your shareholders fifty percent over their initial equity investment. And you'll receive a nice bonus, too, probably equal to a year's worth of your present earnings. Not bad for a few months' work. That way, you can go back to your previous lifestyle and stop pinching pennies. Nobody enjoys making do with less."

"What about Madison?"

Anderson dismissed James' concern. "Oh, we'd find something for her. If you insist."

James continued to press Anderson. "What happens to the accounts after they're absorbed?"

"We'll give the present fee structure another year, then we'll transition them over to our standard active management arrangement. Nobody really wants to settle for mediocrity, and that index idea of yours will eventually fall out of favor. Everyone wants to beat the market averages, so active management is the way to go."

"Michael, you know that statistically—"

Anderson dug in. "Let's not argue about this, James."

"The whole reason they're with me is that our business model is different and we're not layering on fees," James said. "Aren't you at all concerned that they'll leave?"

"You know people tend to stay with what they're used to, so I'm not that worried about a lot of defections, especially if they don't have an alternative like your present setup." Anderson forced a smile. "Be reasonable. You'll never get rich set up the way you currently are. It doesn't work. Remember in school when they taught you that the real purpose of a business was to maximize profits for the shareholders?"

"Yes, I remember, but I believe our concept is a worthwhile alternative."

Anderson accepted his third martini from the server. "Present this offer to your stockholders. You owe it to them to let them consider it. I think they'll be quite pleased with the quick return. And you will be, too, with a better job." Anderson took a long drink. "I'll have the offer sent over to you this afternoon. Really, this isn't a hard decision."

* * * * *

A week later, at a called stockholder meeting of Randolph Wealth Advisors, James and Madison presented the buyout offer. As soon as James finished, the comments started.

"You're saying we get a fifty percent profit on our original investment?" one man said.

"That's right."

"Pretty nice return for such a short time period."

"That's correct."

Richard Sinclair spoke next. "Then after the transition, we're back to the same model that most advisors use?"

"Yes, after the first year."

"Why would we want that?"

"The offer assumes you want to cash out now, and that you're less interested in the long term."

Sinclair frowned. "I think we discussed the long run before. We may be old, but we still care about the future. But what do you two think about the offer?"

Madison said, "Our responsibility is to present the offer to you, our investors, and see what you want to do. We think we've been fair about giving you the pros and cons of both options."

Sinclair hadn't finished with his questions. "But this move back to what we had before is not what we originally decided on."

"No, sir, it's not," James said.

"What do you get out of this, James?" a woman said. She was one of three female investors out of the original seven.

"I'm told I get a big bonus for bringing your accounts over."

"So that's what you recommend?" she said.

"No, I don't. I believe in our current plan. Wholeheartedly. I mean that. But I can't in good conscience refuse to present this opportunity. It would be a nice payday for all of you."

"Then you're willing to forego a chunk of money to keep things the way they are?" she said.

"Yes, ma'am. Madison and I agree that our recommendation is we don't want you to sell."

"But you both would be financially better off if we do, right? Isn't there a part of you that would like to fold your tent?" another man said.

"We both think that's not the real point. The entire thrust of this company is to offer unbiased advice that isn't dependent on the size of your portfolio." He paused. "The decision to sell or not is mainly yours, of course. Madison and I only have twenty-five percent of the voting rights, so whatever the rest of you decide on, we'll abide by."

The investors huddled together in a subdued exchange of opinions while James and Madison stood off to the side, nervously awaiting their decision. After a short time, the group came to a joint conclusion.

Sinclair approached James and Madison and shook their hands. "We believe in both of you. No deal."

James, visibly relieved, said, "Thank you, sir. We'll do our best not to disappoint our investors."

"I know you will," Sinclair said. "By the way, I've also been doing some scouting for our little endeavor. I think we have a couple more families with rather large portfolios that are ready to come on board." He smiled and placed a hand on both of their shoulders. "Adelle and I knew you two were different. Keep up the good work."

Once their investors left, James and Madison shared a high-five.

"I'm really glad it went our way. A little surprised, though," Madison said.

James nodded his agreement. "You never know how these things will go. Could've ended up completely different."

"You know, you had a lot more to lose than I did," she said.

James thought back on selling his remaining shares in Randolph Enterprises to Randall so he could fund his part of this new business. "Maybe, but I sincerely believe we're in this together."

She nodded. "I never liked Michael, anyway. When I started, he hinted he wanted to sleep with me." She jerked her shoulders in an involuntary shiver. "What a slimy old bastard."

"He came out and asked you to have sex with him?" James said, genuinely surprised.

"He was careful not to be too explicit, but I could tell what he wanted by the way he looked at me."

"Sorry. I wasn't aware sexual harassment was an issue there."

"A single woman starting in a traditional man's profession? A few token young women strung out in a formerly all-male office? Are you really shocked?"

He shrugged. "Not when you put it that way. Still, it was his place to set a standard, not come on to you."

"You do know he had an affair with his previous executive assistant, don't you?" she said.

"Yes, but. . ." James said, thinking over what she'd said. "I guess I should have been paying more attention."

"Michael's an old rich guy who enjoys his power over people. Besides, if a woman gets a reputation for filing harassment suits, she's done in this industry."

"It shouldn't be that way," James said. "That's really awful."

"Why do you think I came to work with you?"

He smiled. "I want you to know that you're as big a part of this business as I am."

Madison grinned. "How about we get back to work? The best way to kick Michael's ass is to take part of his business away from him."

40

David grabbed his robe and hurried into the adjacent room to pick up Charlotte. Her fussing had grown louder in the last few minutes, and he found he was more interested in the child's welfare than in sexually satisfying Jackie. Grumbling, Jackie got out of bed after him, headed into the bathroom, and slammed the door. Perfect, he thought. He needed a few moments alone with Charlotte.

He had to move fast. After taking out the sterile vials and swabs from the desk drawer, he stroked the inside of the crying child's cheek, then inserted the end of the stick into the liquid in the glass vial, snapped off the shaft at the break line, and put in the stopper. Hurriedly, he swabbed his own cheek and repeated the procedure. The package would go in the mail later today. The domestic lab guaranteed a turnaround in seven days, maybe less. By this time next week, he would know if Charlotte was really his.

Once he held her to him and kissed her, she stopped fussing and her light blue eyes widened as she looked up at him. She had Jackie's eyes, he decided, and what looked for now like his dark hair. Charlotte would be a heartbreaker when she grew up. As he stroked the side of her face with his finger, David knew, despite any paternity tests, that he loved this little girl. Even Jackie admitted Charlotte seemed happier in his arms than in hers. Charlotte had to be his, she just *had* to be. But what if she was? What was he going to do about it?

David was sitting on the living room couch, cooing to Charlotte with the fingers of one of her little hands wound around his thumb, when Jackie flounced in.

"You've decided that you like her more than me?" she said. "Figures."

"She was upset, but she's fine now. I love holding her, listening to the noises she makes."

Jackie reached down and abruptly took Charlotte from him. "Look, I have to go. Besides, you don't need to get too attached to her. Randall's her real father."

"Are you sure?" he said.

"Of course. Look, Randall and I are going on vacation next week. I can't see you for a while."

"What about Charlotte? Who's keeping her while you're gone?"

"The nanny, of course."

"Could I. . . Could I come by and see her?"

Disgust showed on Jackie's face. "Absolutely *not*." After placing the child in her carrier, Jackie headed for the front door. "We need to get a few things straight, David. If you care more about this baby than me, then it's time we ended our arrangement."

"I didn't mean that," he said. "Really."

"Good. From now on, I think I'll leave her at home. She's getting too big and too fussy to stay in that small crib."

"I can get a larger one. It's no trouble." He felt the anxiety rising in him.

Jackie looked him over with a sour expression on her face. "We'll talk about this later." With that, she opened the door. "I'll let you know when I'm coming back. And next time. . ." She didn't finish the sentence, but he knew what she meant.

"Enjoy your vacation," he said.

After Charlotte and Jackie rode the elevator down, David watched from the apartment window as Jackie walked to the curb and put the baby in her car seat. He ached to touch the baby again, to kiss and hold her. He realized, though, that if he acted too attached to Charlotte, Jackie would never let him near her again, and he didn't think he could bear the separation.

Watching them drive off, David knew Jackie remained pissed about not being sexually satisfied. She came to his apartment and fucked him for one reason only— her personal needs. Once he failed to satisfy her, he would never see her, or Charlotte, again. Jackie had no qualms about using Charlotte as a weapon against him. Iris had always been right about Jackie. She was a manipulative bitch, besotting him enough before that he could overlook all of her scheming, all of her faults. But now he felt a new stirring inside of him. Something had changed. Jackie, the woman he always desired, that he spent so many years constantly agonizing over, was becoming less important to him. A lot less. David smiled to himself. Perhaps for once in his life he was getting things under control.

41

David was sick. This was, he reluctantly concluded, likely the beginnings of the seasonal flu. In the past, during the few times he caught the virus, he toughed it out, expecting, as usual, that his symptoms wouldn't be that severe. This time, it hit him harder than expected. Worried that he was suffering more because he was getting older, David decided that this time he needed some professional help. He ended up getting an appointment at the family practice clinic near his apartment.

After waiting in the exam room, idly swinging his legs while sitting on the table, the door opened.

"Hello, David," Nichelle said as she walked in. She dressed in dark blue scrubs with the requisite stethoscope hanging around her neck.

"Nichelle? I didn't know you worked here."

"Would that have changed your mind about coming here?" she said, looking him over.

"No, but I'm glad to see you," he said, feeling silly about his initial comment.

"You think you have the flu?"

"Yes."

"Did you get a flu shot this year?"

"No."

"Do you usually get one?"

"No."

Nichelle gave him that frustrated medical person look. "You enjoy being sick?"

"Not especially. I don't like needles." Nichelle's professional mannerisms reminded him of her direct way of speaking and asking questions during the dinner at Max and Ja'Neel's.

"Let me take a look," she said.

After checking his temperature, blood pressure and pulse, then listening to his heart, she had him breathe in and out while she moved the stethoscope's diaphragm around from the front to the back of his chest.

"Hear any music in there?" he said.

"Hush."

She next examined his mouth and ears. Finished, she looked him over, sizing him up, but kept quiet about her conclusion. David stared back at her, intrigued.

While washing her hands, Nichelle said, "We'll do a test, but it looks like you have the standard flu. You also have a temperature. I can give you an antiviral prescription, but you need to stay home for several days until you're no longer contagious."

"What about an antibiotic?" he said.

"That only works on bacteria, David, not a virus."

"I've gotten them before for the flu."

"You only need that if you get a secondary infection that's not viral. I don't see any evidence of that."

"I bet you get tired of saying that, don't you?" he said.

"Yes."

"I've got projects to finish at the office. Can't you give me something that knocks it out by tomorrow?"

She sighed. "The medication will shorten the recovery period, but it won't eliminate it."

"I guess that was a stupid question."

"You need to stay home for a few days and get better. It would be helpful if you didn't go around infecting other people."

He nodded. "Okay. Sorry."

After he gave her his pharmacy location, she tapped the information into her tablet. "I've sent the prescription in. Start taking the medication immediately. And try not to breathe on anyone. You have a mask?"

"Yeah, maybe. At my apartment."

She reached into one of the upper cabinets and extracted a disposable surgical mask. "Wear this. Starting now."

"Thanks," he said, slipping it on.

"Need anything else?" she said.

"I still like your hair."

A hint of a smile played on her lips. "I better go check on the next patient. See the receptionist on the way out."

"Would you have dinner with me?"

She appraised him before replying. "Not while you're sick."

He chuckled. "Maybe in a couple of weeks?"

"I'll think about it. You need my number?"

• • • • • • •

Nichelle met David at the restaurant on a Saturday night. He arrived early to make sure he did not keep her waiting, but she was already there, sitting in the foyer, her legs crossed, checking her phone. She had on a short black dress that showed off her athletic legs. He thought she looked quite nice.

"Hey," he said, stopping in front of her.

She looked up. "Hey yourself."

"You look fantastic," he said

She stood and looped the purse strap over her shoulder. "Thanks. They said our table is ready, but I thought it would be best to wait out here for you."

"I appreciate that."

The same hint of a smile he had seen in the office appeared on her face. "You're welcome."

The hostess led them to their table as David followed Nichelle. He held the chair out while she sat down.

"You don't have to do that," she said. "I can get my chair."

"Sorry. I wanted to be a gentleman, impress my date."

After he sat down, Nichelle said, "I'm a direct person, David, in case you haven't noticed. I've been single for a long time, and I don't need a man thinking he has to take care of me."

"I wasn't patronizing you."

"I didn't say you were."

The server came and took their drink order.

"You seen Max and Ja'Neel lately?" he said.

"No. It's been a while. I've talked to Ja'Neel multiple times, though."

"Is her pregnancy going okay?" David said. "I haven't checked in this month since I've been so busy."

"Everything's fine. She's due in about five weeks."

David fiddled with his fork, then said, "Look, I didn't mean to piss you off or anything. About the chair. I'm not used to women who are so independent."

"What about your ex-wife?" Nichelle said, then shook her head. "Sorry, that was out of line. I shouldn't have asked."

David looked off. "She isn't like you. More fragile would be a good way of putting it. I should have been more supportive with her and less, umm. . ." He didn't finish his thought, letting the rest of it hang there in the air, helpless and unsupported without an ending.

The server reappeared with their drinks and took their food order.

"I'm paying for my half of the dinner," she said.

"I'd rather I paid for all of it," David said. "I asked you."

"Are we going to fight over the check?"

He sighed. This date wasn't going very well so far. "Whatever you want, Nichelle."

After considering his words, she softened her tone. "Maybe we should start over. I can be a bit of a bitch sometimes."

"You're not a bitch," he said. "Far from it."

"Don't you think I can be abrasive?"

"Maybe the word is determined."

After he made his comment, he thought of Jackie and their fight this afternoon. Recently back from her vacation, she wanted to come over and have sex with him, but had refused to bring Charlotte along. David told her she couldn't come if she didn't bring the baby. She was *his* baby; the DNA test had proven it. Jackie refused his conditions and yelled at him before hanging up, so they missed their rendezvous. Just as well, David decided, except he was desperate to see his daughter.

He said, "On second thought, I know one woman that the term 'bitch' fits exactly."

Nichelle smirked. "Don't we all."

"You're not her," he said.

"I hope not."

"Tell me how you got to be a P.A.," David said.

"Casual conversation starter?" she said.

"No, I really want to know."

She thought about his request. "I always loved biology, but my family didn't have the money at the time to send me to med school. So, it was the nursing route for my bachelor's. After working as an RN for several years, I got my Masters in P.A. Studies with an emphasis on family medicine. Later on, my dad changed careers and did quite well financially after that. They asked me then if I wanted to go back to med school, said they could pay for it now. But it seemed too late by then."

"Always wanted to be a doctor?" he said.

"Did. I'm not so sure anymore. I really enjoy what I do."

"Like telling dumbasses they need to take annual flu shots?"

She grinned. "Yes."

"I deserved it," he said. "I promise to do better next year. Can I come by and get you to hold my hand while I get a shot so I won't scream like a little girl?"

Her eyes twinkled. "Only if I can make sure it hurts."

"I'll bet you're the type that tries extra hard to make sure that it doesn't."

"Guilty."

"I'm really glad you agreed to have dinner with me," David said.

Nichelle waited a bit to reply, then said, "Yeah, me too."

42

Finch was already inside Perry's computer when the old man connected the external hard drive to download a set of new photos. Finch managed to log the password before Perry quickly disconnected the device. Though he didn't know physically where the device was located, Finch expected it was not at Perry's house, since Perry seldom did a backup, even after adding new material to the laptop. Finch wondered where the drive could be. Perhaps it was in a bank deposit vault and Perry went there periodically to update the drive, then returned it to storage.

Based on several months of eavesdropping, Finch became more and more certain of Perry's operation. The old man served as a clearinghouse for child pornography, basically operating as a broker for the disgusting material, taking his cut from moving the stuff between buyers and sellers. That meant he had access to lots of clients, and if Finch could determine their identities, he would ruin them all. Today, Perry had sold photos to a man in Toledo. After some social media snooping, David discovered the client's true identity. Most people, Finch knew, were not that careful with their on-line privacy settings. It was a simple matter of sending the local police department details on the purchase, a list of the photos he bought, and the price he paid. Apparently, the guy was, for now, a respected business executive whose wife was going to be very unhappy about the unexpected revelations. The man might try to turn in Perry as the source of the photos, but Finch expected that Perry had sufficiently covered his digital tracks to prevent that.

Finch had also recently confirmed that Perry kept most of his money in cryptocurrency. However, he had not yet entered the password for access. For now, he had enough funds in his modest checking account to cover his ordinary expenses, so had not bought or sold any coins lately. Without the digital password, the clandestine assets would be permanently inaccessible. One thing that Finch wanted most was to clean the old bastard out before turning him in. That money might be enough to fund Nichelle and Davie's modest lifestyle, allowing Nichelle to stay home with the boy, maybe until he graduated from high school. Finch had his own significant assets, carefully built up over years of saving and skimping, but Nichelle had been adamant that they both contribute equally to the cost of the household.

He heard Nichelle busying herself in the kitchen before lunch. It was two weeks past the wedding, and the house had settled into a comfortable routine. Finch thought back on the simple ceremony and how much he loved marrying Nichelle. Her father was an interesting character, suspicious of why his daughter would want to marry another white man, especially one partially disabled and without a current job. After an earnest discussion with Finch, her father seemed mollified, at least for now, but countered that he needed to wait for concrete results before changing his mind about the union. Instead, Nichelle's mother accepted her daughter's choice after hearing how much her offspring was in love with Finch, and how they seemed to fit together perfectly.

Finch closed the laptop and went into the kitchen, moving up behind Nichelle and putting his hands around her waist.

"Hi there," he said, kissing her shoulder.

"You finally decide to come see me?" she said with a laugh.

"Hey, I've been busy," he said.

"Doing what?"

"You probably don't want to know."

She turned to face him, a serious look on her face. "I'm not having another husband who keeps things from me, understand? One was enough."

"Alright. What do you want to know?"

"Everything."

"Let's go sit down. I'll tell you all of it."

•   •   •   •   •

When he finished the story about Perry, Nichelle was quiet for a while. She was sitting on Finch's lap with his arms around her.

He caressed her head, then kissed her. "Maybe I've told you too much. You know, plausible deniability would come in handy if I'm caught."

"No, I wanted to know. Promise me one thing."

"What?"

"That you'll destroy him."

"I'll do my best. I think I now understand his routine for backing up to the external drive. He does it once a month, usually on the same calendar day. My plan is to follow him on that day and find out where he goes."

"Good idea." She stood up and held out her hand. "Come on, let's have lunch."

•   •   •   •   •

"I'm going back to work," she said as they started in on their salads. "Maybe part time. I'll see what's available. I need to get some money coming in. We can trade off with Davie, getting him taken to and picked up from school."

"You don't have to. Go to work, that is. I've got a lot put back, at least for an itinerant contractor."

Nichelle shook her head. "I need to pay my own way. I feel strongly about that, Finchie. David insisted I give up my job after Davie was born, and since he had been recently promoted, we decided we could just make things work with his salary alone. But I missed earning my own money. And I missed my independence."

"Whatever you want is fine with me," Finch said.

She reached over and kissed him. "Thanks for not being the typical husband who tries to tell his wife what to do."

Finch chuckled. "Like that would work."

"How much do you have put back?"

He loved the way she asked direct questions, no bullshit, no devious means. Tell me the facts and we'll make it work.

After he told her the amount, she said, "I'm very impressed, Finchie. Really."

"I'll get you a list today of all my assets. Where everything is, how to get to it. What's mine is yours. Sorry I didn't give it to you sooner. I'm too used to being by myself."

She poked at her meal.

"Don't you want to know?" he said. "We're in this together, right?"

"I was thinking. About how different you are from David."

"In what way?"

"Just about every way."

"Look, I know he might not have told you everything, but he was a good man. He had his struggles, sure, but he was able to keep it all together. I'm not in the same class as him."

Nichelle reached over and squeezed his hand. "Shut up, Finchie."

"Why?"

"I loved David. But you're a better man than he ever could be." As Finch began a protest, she held up her hand. "*Stop* this. You're *not* him, and that's the way it should be. You're your own man. And I love that man. I truly do. So quit beating yourself up, thinking you're my second-class husband, because you're not."

He didn't reply at first, then said, "Thanks for saying that. It means a lot to me."

"It should."

He chuckled. "I've never met anyone quite like you."

"Hurry up with that salad," she said.

"Why?"

"I want to make love to you."

43

Jackie's expectation of a perfect life was not working out quite like she expected. In fact, it was in danger of failing in several important areas.

For one, her relationship with Randall had devolved into a quagmire of rituals. He got up, went to work every day, and except for the times when he visited the company's customers or suppliers, he was home at his regular time. They ate as a family and then he retired to his study to do additional work or to watch TV. She stayed in the main living room, by herself, unless Charlotte, who often played in her own room, infrequently joined her. Sex with Randall remained formulaic and had declined in frequency. She expected that as they grew older, the heat of making love would cool, but not this much, and not so soon. Now, they went weeks without having sex, and Jackie often privately reminisced about David and how intensely she responded to his brand of lovemaking.

David. He had fallen out of her life like a dropped shoe. He asked her to bring the baby each time she visited, but now Charlotte was too active to be expected to sleep while they had sex. Jackie insisted on leaving her at home after that, but David was adamant that she had to come with the baby. Expecting to get her way with David as always, Jackie refused, knowing that soon his burning desire for her would bring him crawling back. For some unknown reason, that approach backfired. Instead, he had not changed his mind, and they hadn't had sex since. She knew he adored Charlotte and wanted to see the baby more than he did Jackie. Well, the attraction was obvious, since he was the baby's father. She always denied it to David, but the result of their unprotected sex was obvious, since Randall had failed to produce another pregnancy in their last year of trying. Jackie figured it was high time she made up with David and got him to impregnate her again. She just needed to figure out the right angle.

Nichelle, the new woman in David's life, had thwarted that plan. Jackie didn't see the attraction at all. The one time she wanted to check the woman out, she faked a slight illness to visit the family practice clinic and insisted on seeing the PA. Jackie found Nichelle all business, and not the least bit deferential toward her. Besides, how David could fall for a Black woman was beyond Jackie's comprehension. She personally couldn't imagine marrying outside her race, and remained surprised and disappointed that David obviously failed to consider the issues surrounding a mixed-race marriage. Why make your life and your offspring's life more difficult? It was always best to accept the reality of the social order and get on with your life.

Lately, despite several discrete phone calls to David at work, Jackie failed to arouse enough interest to arrange a reunion. He remained committed to that new wife of his and was unwilling to repeat the affair. They could be more discrete this time, she told him. It wouldn't be like before, when their brief liaison destroyed his marriage to Iris. Still, he was steadfast in his refusal. The only weapon Jackie had left was Charlotte, but she hadn't yet formulated a solid plan on how to use his daughter against him. Give her time, though, and she would come up with one.

Charlotte. She was growing up fast and looked more like David every day. The child's attachment to both the nanny and Randall was strong, while she simultaneously remained indifferent towards Jackie. That result wasn't unexpected, considering how little time she actually spent with the child. Jackie wanted Charlotte as a social appendage—a well-behaved child to dress up and show off to her friends. The few times she took the baby to the country club, Charlotte became restless and cried, one time forcing Jackie to skip the rest of her lunch and take Charlotte home instead, an outcome she held against the baby for days. After that, Jackie resolved to leave Charlotte at home from now on. Having another child could give her an option of a more pliable second offspring, but that required David's help, something that, so far, he failed to seem interested in providing.

Sitting at her dressing table, Jackie examined herself in the mirror. Yes, she was still quite striking, but she could see the initial traces of future declines. Jackie had always counted on her looks and social standing to grease her way through life, and until now, that expectation had never failed. Randall provided the social lever and public support for the ideal husband myth, but she could see that in a few years she might need professional help to maintain her beauty. Expensive spa days and Botox treatments helped, but didn't provide permanent improvement. Taking her finger, Jackie grimaced and traced the small furrows on her forehead, the corners of her eyes, and down the sides of her face. Perhaps if she was happier, if her husband and lover and child were more compatible, more sympathetic to her, she wouldn't be pissed off so much and then could avoid further enhancing her frown lines. She picked up her phone and called David.

"David? Jackie. I wanted to see how you're doing."

His voice was cautious, remote. "I'm okay. How are you?"

"Fine. I wanted to know if we could have lunch. For old time's sake."

"Lunch?"

"Yes, that's what I said." His new, independent attitude grated on her.

"How's Charlotte?" he said.

"She's fine. What does that have to do with lunch?"

"I'd like to see her, is all. If you bring her, we can have lunch."

Jackie felt the anger rising within her. "And if not?"

"I think you know the answer to that."

"So, you think you have leverage over me now?" she said.

"I only want to see her. Is that too much to ask?"

"Well, alright. What about the club tomorrow?"

"Let's go somewhere else." He named an ordinary restaurant.

"Only if you insist."

"I'd like that much better."

They agreed on a time and location. Jackie hung up.

· · · · · ·

Jackie showed up ten minutes late, on purpose. David sat at a table near the back of the packed restaurant, waiting, nursing a glass of water. As Jackie breezed in, David looked up.

"Where's Charlotte?" he said, leaning back, his exasperation clear.

"She's feeling under the weather. I think she's developing a cold. I didn't want to get her out. Considering."

Skepticism and disappointment showed on his face.

"You think I deliberately left her at home?" Jackie said, looking angry as she sat down.

"It's possible," he said.

Of course, what he suspected was exactly what happened. This was a new, troubling David, she thought, one she couldn't manipulate like she used to.

"Look, Charlotte's not feeling well. That's the truth. You should be happy I left her at home and didn't expose her to. . ." Jackie turned back and surveyed the rest of the restaurant. "All the germs floating around in here."

"You don't like this place?" he said.

"Let's talk about something else," she said, reaching for the plastic-framed menu on the table. "What's decent here?"

"The sandwiches here are good. And they have salads, too."

"Sandwiches, ugh," she said, scanning the limited selection. "I'll have a chef salad, I guess." She closed the menu. "Do they have any waitresses in this place?"

David raised his hand and signaled a harried server trying her best to accommodate the large lunch crowd. "We're ready to order."

After the server took their order, Jackie tried a reset. "What's new in your life?"

"Nichelle's going to have a baby."

Stunned by his pronouncement, Jackie took her a second or two to recover. David was as potent as ever. This news had real implications.

"Well, congratulations. I hope this pregnancy turns out better than the first one."

He stared at her and didn't comment.

She said, "I mean, it's not like I expect that to happen again. I just know how damaging it was when Iris had that miscarriage."

"Damaging," he said. "That's one way to put it."

"How would you put it?" she said.

"I'd say our *affair* is what did the lasting damage. It ended things. For *good*."

Jackie leaned forward. "David, for God's sake, keep your voice down."

"Why?"

"No one can ever know we had a relationship."

"Even if it's over with now?"

She considered her options. "Is it really over with? Are you sure?"

He held her gaze. "Yes, I'm sure. No way I'm going to let you jeopardize another marriage of mine."

"You're being mean," she said, pouting. "I don't deserve that."

"Don't you?"

Jackie sat back, crossed her arms, and considered her next move. If he was serious, there was no reason for her to see David again. But David had been so handy, so pliable, before now. Plus, he was good in the sack, doing things to her that Randall wouldn't ever think of. Damn, this rendezvous was not working out the way she expected. Her intentions focused on trapping him again, making him remember how desperately he wanted her. His marriage to that Nichelle bitch must have screwed up his perspective.

The server arrived and set down her glass of water. Jackie swirled the ice cubes around, then took a sip. "I guess you're enjoying making me feel awful."

"That's not my intention."

"What do you want, then?"

"I want to see Charlotte."

"You need to get that idea out of your head," she said.

"I'm her father."

"No, you're not. Randall's her father. You're just a distraction."

David pulled a copy of the DNA test results out of his coat pocket and offered it to Jackie. "Here's the proof."

Jackie's lips pursed after she unfolded the paper and scanned the contents. "So?"

"So, I want to see my daughter."

"That's impossible."

"Would you like me to send a copy of that to Randall?"

"You wouldn't *dare*." Despite her impassive look, Jackie felt dread take hold of her. Was it possible? Would he even consider doing what he was threatening?

His tone softened. "I don't want to cause trouble, Jackie. Only to see Charlotte regularly. That's not too much to ask, considering."

"I have no idea how to arrange that."

"The same way we arranged to have sex. The official story before was that you were worried about me. We can see each other again, but without the entanglements."

She stared at him, waiting for his face to crumble, to accept the obvious—that he couldn't live without her. Instead, he remained serious, determined. Then a stunning realization hit her. David had outgrown his eternal infatuation with her. She no longer had an unshakeable hold over him. Time to change tactics.

"Does your new wife know about you and me?"

"No."

"Then how about I tell her?"

He fiddled with his silverware before answering. "Go ahead. I'll explain how you manipulated me into having sex with you. And that all of that happened before I met her."

Jackie was getting angry. "*Manipulated?* I seem to recall you're the one that was desperate to *fuck* me, *asshole.*"

"Keep your voice down," he said. It was his turn to look nervous. He twisted his head around to see if their altercation was attracting attention.

"Oh, so now you're worried about *me* making a scene?"

"Look," he said. "Let's be reasonable about this. The baby is what I'm interested in. When can I see Charlotte?"

Jackie pitched the printout back to him and slid out of the booth. "Don't call me, text me, or interfere in my life *ever again*. If you do, you'll regret it. I've got attorneys, David. Very good ones. And if you ever tell Randall..."

"Now who's threatening whom?" he said.

"*Good-bye,* David," she said, then hurried out of the restaurant.

When their food arrived, David said, "My guest had to leave early. Can I have the salad to go?"

He took his time eating his meal, thinking the whole time about Jackie and Charlotte. Jackie was vindictive and mean, a real bitch when she wanted to hurt someone. She would do whatever she could to punish him if she thought he was not appropriately responsive to her need for sex. The potential punishments included stopping him from ever seeing Charlotte. His fingers, closing around the imaginary form of his daughter, ached to touch and caress the real thing. He missed her desperately. But was he ready to capitulate to Jackie's demands, to risk another marriage to satisfy her? And Nichelle? Should he tell her about his past affair with Jackie? Or that Charlotte was his daughter? No, to all of those questions. That information would remain with the other things he kept from Nichelle, things already piling up, threatening one day to rupture the artificial dam he so assiduously worked on. One thing Nichelle insisted on was honesty, and he had already abused her trust in multiple ways.

Unsure of what he needed to do, David knew he would rely on an old standby. He would call Finchie and ask for advice. Finchie always had come through for him, no matter what he'd gotten himself into.

44

The divorce came as a complete shock to Jackie Weir. Sure, things between herself and Randall had not been that wonderful for a good while, but she never expected their mutual dissatisfaction to result in actual legal action. In their social class, once you got married you should *stay* married, regardless, just like her parents did. She suspected her own father had been unfaithful to her mother, but such a possibility was never discussed in the house, or even alluded to. Divorce signified failure, an acknowledgement that many worked hard to avoid. Okay, yes, a few people among their upper-crust friends actually *did* divorce back then, but they often kept the actual reasons for the split quiet to avoid upsetting the social fabric. That way, silence met any indiscrete questions, even if other, more private conversations had confirmed the worst. No public admission of aberrant behavior meant couples avoided the associated scandal and were then free to pursue other, more suitable partners.

Since David refused to continue their affair several years ago, Jackie had managed a few discrete flings with several other men, all taking place when Randall was out of town, of course, but nothing became serious, certainly not on the level of the intensity she experienced with David. To counter her frustration, Jackie re-dedicated herself to social causes, spending most of her time engaged in one event after another. Her crowded schedule left little time for interaction with Randall or Charlotte, which seemed to suit all the parties just fine. As expected, Randall's infertility remained an issue, though their sex life had trailed off the last year to almost nothing, meaning Jackie's original hope of 2.0 children, at least with Randall, was thwarted. Just as well, she thought. Having a child wasn't the life-changing experience she had expected. Yes, she felt a remote love for Charlotte, but Jackie had little interest in the daily distractions that arose from raising children. After all, that's what the nanny was for.

Randall planned this all ahead of time, unbeknownst to Jackie. He had already rented an apartment in the city, changed his personal mail to the new address, and moved much of his clothing there over a period of several months. Jackie, never engaged with laundry or cleaning, had not noticed that his separate closet gradually thinned out.

He told her about wanting a divorce late the night she returned from one of her numerous social outings, as usual without him. She noticed a suitcase standing in the back hall, but had dismissed it as some artifact of the maid's housework. Coming in from the garage, she found Randall sitting in the living room, sipping a drink.

"We need to talk, Jackie," he said.

"Can't it wait until tomorrow? I'm tired out, Randall."

"No, I don't think it can."

"Then how about you fix me one of those?" she said, pointing to his cocktail.

"With pleasure."

After handing her the drink, he said, "Jackie, we haven't been getting along for a long while."

"So?" she said, already thinking about her next event in two days. "Everybody has problems." She heard her own distracted voice. Why the hell would he bring this up now?

"I want a divorce."

It took a few seconds for his comment to register. "Be serious," she said.

"I am. I'm filing tomorrow."

Thoughts rushed through her head. Surely this was only a threat. He wasn't really going to go through with it. Not Randall. He didn't have the balls for it.

"You seem to forget who you're married to," she said.

"No, that's the whole problem."

Jackie stood to confront him. "How *dare* you think you can leave me?"

"I can and I will," he said, taking another sip. He was too calm, too matter-of-fact, for this to be an impulsive decision. "We can split things down the middle. That's the norm in this state. You can keep the house. And about Charlotte—"

"What *about* her?" Jackie said as her escalating blood pressure thudded in her temples. This couldn't actually be happening, she thought.

"I think she'd be better off with me. You don't seem that interested in her, anyway."

"I'm her *mother*, dammit." Jackie had to bite back the acid comment that Charlotte wasn't his biological daughter.

"You don't act like it."

Fuming, Jackie crossed one arm over her stomach, supporting the elbow of her other arm as she waved the drink glass around in frustration. "It'll be a cold day in *hell* before you take my daughter away from me," she said, thinking now more about receiving child support than actually caring for Charlotte.

"Guess we'll have to get our lawyers to sort things out." Randall stood up after setting his drink on the coffee table. "Time to go."

"Just like that? You *fucker*! You can't do this to *me*," she yelled. "Think you're so damn *smart*? When my father hears about this, you'll be out on your *ass!*"

He stared at her. "I don't think that's going to be a problem." He strode to the back door and picked up the suitcase. "You'll get the paperwork next week. Our lawyers will be in touch. Goodbye, Jackie."

Randall headed into the garage, Jackie in close pursuit.

"Where do you think you're going?" she said.

"I have an apartment in the city."

"Oh, yeah, for how long?"

He turned to her as he opened his car door. "Six months."

"Six *months*! You had this all planned for a while, didn't you, you *bastard*!"

Randall didn't reply while he placed the suitcase in the trunk, then eased into the front seat while Jackie continued to harangue him.

"What's going on? You have yourself a girlfriend?" she said.

"Yes, I do. One that's not a total bitch like you."

"How long, *damn you*, how long?"

Before he closed the door, he said, "Not like you don't have a few things to hide, either. I hired a private detective to check up on you, and I have the pictures to prove it. If you try to damage my reputation, then I'll return the favor."

Randall must know about at least a few of her casual affairs, a realization she hadn't expected. She quickly paged through the recent liaisons in her mind, wondering where she had been seen, or if perhaps he was bluffing instead. Regardless, the thing that pissed her off the most was that Randall didn't seem to have any remorse at leaving her. How was that possible? Jackie kicked the side of his big Mercedes, hard, before he backed out enough to clear her leg. She hoped it left a dent.

As the garage door closed, Jackie hurried back inside the house and checked on Charlotte. She was asleep in her room, so Randall must have put her to bed, since the nanny had taken the day off. Jackie was now stuck with looking after her daughter until in the morning. Shit. Maybe she wouldn't need anything until then.

Jackie called her parents' house in Florida to give them the news. Her mother answered the phone, despite it being quite late.

"Hello, Jackie." She sighed, exhaustion evident in her voice.

Jackie ignored her mother's obvious distress. "You won't *believe* this. Randall is *divorcing* me!"

There was a pause. "I see," her mother said.

"Well, what do you think about *that*?" Jackie said.

"I'm very sorry to hear that, dear."

"Is that *all* you have to say?"

"I'm not sure what else I can do."

Fuming, Jackie said, "I need to talk to Dad."

"I'm sorry, dear, but he isn't feeling well. . ."

"What's the matter?" she said. It wasn't like she kept close tabs on her parents. She was busy with her own life. Ensconced in a wealthy retirement community, her parents should be self-sufficient and not need any regular assistance from her. Being a good daughter, though, she checked on them anyway. Well, okay, maybe every other month her mother would call *her*. It had been a while since she talked to her dad, but he would back her up against Randall. That bastard would soon be out of a job.

"Well, the dementia has progressed rather quickly, Jackie. He's not himself."

"What are you talking about?" As she said this, Jackie realized it had been a good while since she had directly spoken with her father. Back then, he *had* seemed distracted, distant. She had dismissed any genuine concern because her mother soft-pedaled any hints of real trouble. That's the way she had always operated. Now, it sounded as if her father's deterioration was both significant and speeding up. Well, whatever. Fortunately, this was her mother's problem, not hers.

"I finally got him to bed tonight. Best not to disturb him now. I'm going to have to put him in a memory care facility, Jackie. I can't handle him by myself anymore."

"Mother, you didn't tell me things were this bad."

"I didn't want to worry you."

"At least I can count on your support."

"For what?" her mother said.

"To fire Randall. For what he's done to me. What do you *think* I'm talking about?"

"That may not be so easy."

"Why the hell not?"

She heard her mother take a deep breath. "Because of your father's condition, we transferred our assets to an irrevocable trust to save on taxes. Don't you remember, we discussed this beforehand, before your father got so sick? That transfer included the voting stock in Randall Enterprises. We sent you the paperwork months ago. You and James both signed it."

"Oh, I remember something like that," Jackie said, hedging. A vague recollection of the issue being discussed surfaced. Forms arrived in the mail from a new estate attorney with sticky tabs conveniently indicating the required signature locations. Once she saw it was all about her parents, she lost interest and stopped reading. These were things that other people took care of for her, so she wouldn't have to deal with the mundane issues of life. She dismissed its consequences at the time and hastily signed. She thought back, trying to remember where her own copy of the paperwork was. Probably lost somewhere in one of her desk drawers.

"What does all that mean?" Jackie said.

"The trustees will vote the company's shares as they see fit, honey. Their wishes may not, umm, line up with yours."

Jackie did some quick arithmetic in her head. She and James each owned ten percent of the company stock, and her parents controlled another forty. Ordinarily, that meant full control. But Randall had periodically bought into the company over the years, using bonuses and outright purchases to add to his personal ownership. She couldn't remember what he had told her, but she seemed to recall that his stake was now twenty percent or more. More than enough to block her if the trust went along with him in a proxy fight. Under Randall's leadership, the company had prospered, and it was unlikely the trust would oust him simply for divorcing the founder's daughter. Fuck.

"I have to go, mother. I need to find a lawyer."

"Alright, dear. Let us know how things go."

Stunned, Jackie clicked off the call. Her carefully constructed world was blowing up in her face.

45

Finch and James sat in the decrepit Subaru a half block away from Perry's house, waiting for the old man to come out. James had left Madison in charge of the office, only telling her he had some personal errands to run before lunch. Nichelle, instead, knew exactly what Finch was up to.

"You sure this wreck will start again?" James said, only half kidding.

"I keep telling you, it's in better shape mechanically that it looks," Finch said. "It's old but reliable."

"I hope to hell that's true."

They waited a while longer, with no appearance yet of their quarry.

"Sure this is Backup Day?" James said.

"If he follows his routine. Once a month, in the afternoon. I thought we might catch him, see where he goes. My money's on a bank."

"We should have taken my car."

Finch chuckled. "Not like he would notice a huge new Lincoln SUV following him."

"Well, at least the A/C would work."

Finch fiddled with the knob, but to no avail. It was hot outside, forcing them to roll the windows down to avoid suffocating. "I think the compressor's out," he said.

"Big surprise, cheap ass," James said. "Wait, here he comes."

Perry appeared at the front door with a laptop bag slung over his shoulder. The old man looked around, then locked the door and headed toward the nondescript Ford sedan parked in the driveway.

Putting on his seatbelt, James said, "Think there are cameras in his house? You remember seeing one on the front porch?"

"Who knows? Why?" Finch said as he buckled up.

"I was thinking maybe we should burn down his house while he's gone. That should remove any porno he keeps here."

"Unless the good stuff's in a storage building somewhere," Finch said.

James said, "In that case, how about we just go ask him could we please get rid of all his child porn for him?"

"I don't think he'd be receptive to giving us a straight answer," Finch said, listening to the Subaru grind before it started. He would need a new battery soon, but his frugal side wanted to wait.

Perry was backing out. Finch shifted the Outback into first.

"Why didn't you get this with an automatic?" James said.

"I enjoy shifting gears," Finch said as he eased off the clutch. The transmission engaged with a stuttering lurch.

"I think you could use a new clutch, too," James said.

Finch's eyebrow lifted. "Or a replacement vehicle."

"First thing you've said today that makes sense," James said, rolling his eyes.

"Hey, you wouldn't recognize me with a new car."

"That's no shit."

Without further conversation, they followed Perry at a discrete distance as he headed into the city.

•   •   •   •   •   •

Perry ended up downtown and parked on the street next to one of the large banks.

"Bingo," James said.

"Let's be certain," Finch said, getting out of the vehicle.

"Where you going?" James said.

"Heading inside. Behind him, see what he does. You stay put."

"Can you at least leave the keys so I can roll down the damn window and not die of heat stroke?"

Finch tossed them to James. "I'll be back soon, whiney-ass."

•   •   •   •

Pulling his ball cap down over his eyes, Finch entered the bank, far enough back that if Perry glanced around, Finch should have time to turn and duck over to a kiosk and pretend he was getting ready to deposit a check. But Perry didn't act suspicious. He moved like this was all routine and spoke to no one. Finch followed him all through the lobby, then watched as he headed down to the basement. A SAFE DEPOSIT sign, along with its indicating arrow, was mounted on the side of a marble-clad column adjacent to the stairs.

Finch followed, then halted on the stairs while appearing to check something in his pocket. Meanwhile, Perry presented his key and filled out the signature form. Finch slowed as he descended.

"Help you?" the woman at the other desk said.

Finch turned his back to Perry. "I wanted to check on getting a deposit box, see what the cost was. Could you show me the various sizes?"

About that time, the other attendant told Perry to follow her into the vault.

"Here's a rental sheet," the woman said, handing him a piece of paper. "If you'd like, we could go inside the vault. Then you can decide what size you want."

"That sounds good."

She picked at her keyboard, then used a sticky note to record a few numbers of boxes without present owners.

Finch glanced down the aisles of boxes as they crossed the threshold into the vault, not wanting Perry to see him. He could hear the old man talking to the other attendant two aisles over, telling him he needed to use one of the private rooms. Finch shifted into the aisle with the woman as the other attendant ushered Perry out of the vault, a long black storage box under his arms. Perry headed toward one of the small soundproofed rooms near the desk area and closed the door.

"Here is an example of our smallest box," the woman said, sliding one out of an opened door. You can see they're still pretty large."

"Maybe a bigger one," Finch said.

"Alright, we can open up another one." The woman closed the door and started hunting for the next box. The keys on the enormous ring jingled as she paged through them. "Let's see..."

"Tell you what," Finch said. "What sizes are in that aisle over there?" He pointed to the one Perry had left from.

"The box sizes are all mixed up," she said. "Each aisle has a variety. We can stay in this aisle—"

"I'm kind of superstitious," Finch said. "I don't like to be so near the door." He shrugged. "I know that sounds weird."

The woman smiled. "No problem. We can try over there."

As they rounded the end of Perry's aisle, Finch said, "How about this one?" and pointed to the partially opened door that Perry had extracted his box from. "It's about the right height off the floor. I wouldn't have to bend down."

"Sorry, that's taken. Mr. Jones has that one."

"Mr. Jones," Finch said, walking up to the door and memorizing the box number. "I think I may know him. Maybe I should say hello when he comes back. Is he in here often?"

"Once a month, like clockwork," she said.

"Look, I think he's coming back in," Finch said, pointing toward the entry door.

As the woman turned, Finch slid Perry's key out of the box.

The attendant scanned the front of the aisle, then turned back, a frown on her face. "I don't see anyone."

"Guess I was mistaken," Finch said. He fumbled a bit, then held up Perry's door key. "Are they all like this?"

"Sir, you can't do that," she said, reaching for the key. "That belongs to Mr. Jones."

He dropped it into her upturned palm. "Sorry, I was just looking at the size of the key."

"You can't take someone else's key out of their door. It's not allowed." She seemed upset as she fitted the key back into the door's lock.

"I'll remember next time. Don't want to get you in any trouble."

She softened. "That's fine, but we have specific rules that you have to follow. Now, what size box would you like?"

"Tell you what, let me think it over. I'll go home and check my documents, see how much space I really need. I have your rates." He stuck out his hand. "Thanks very much for your help."

"Sure, anytime. Consolidated would like to have all your business. Perhaps I could help you open a checking or savings account here as well?"

"That's a great idea," he said, smiling. "I'll get back to you. Could I maybe have your contact information so I can get in touch?"

The attendant returned to her desk and handed Finch her card. It contained her name, email address, and official position within the bank.

"Thanks." Glancing down, Finch added, "I see you've got a Fiji vacation brochure on your desk. Sounds wonderful. When do you leave?"

The woman reached for the colorful foldout and hastily shoved it into a desk drawer. "Only wishes," she said, acting a bit embarrassed. "Not like *I'll* ever get the chance."

"You never know," he said, giving her a cheerful smile.

• • • • •

Back in the car, Finch brought James up to date.

"She said he comes in once a month, like clockwork."

"So?"

"So we know his habits and where his safe deposit box is."

"And?" James said, not knowing where this discussion was headed.

"If we come in during an off period, we could pick up the hard drive without worrying he'd catch us."

"I thought you were going to erase it?"

"That was my plan, but if we can get our hands on it, we could give it to the police after I remove any evidence of David."

"But you need to be on the signature card, Finchie. And have the correct key."

He pulled out the woman's business card with her email address on it. "If I can spear-phish my way into the attendant's email account, I can get to the card and change it electronically, add another name. Maybe I'll use James Randolph."

"*My* name? What's wrong with yours?"

"They've seen me," Finch said. "And might remember me, too. I created a fuss about the box key."

"Don't they have security cameras in there? If I go steal his hard drive, he'll raise hell and they'll have a record of who went in there. Besides, you'll still need his key, which you don't have, in case you forgot."

Finch held up the wax impression of Perry's key. "Oh, you mean like this one?"

James shook his head and chortled. "You're a sneaky fucker, I'll give you that. Well done."

"Maybe Perry would keep quiet instead of making a public fuss."

"He'd claim the drive was legit. I'm sure it's all password protected, so not like the cops could see what was on it. Maybe you should just destroy the drive once you have it."

Finch thought through what James had said. "Maybe, but it gives us one more option. Let's go get Nichelle and Jeanette and have some lunch. You're buying."

"Figures," James said, a look of false resignation on his face. "Also, let's go in my car. I'd hate to get stranded in this piece of shit."

Finch patted the dashboard. "She heard that. Watch your language or you won't get the privilege of riding in her again."

46

Jackie's post-divorce expectations were unraveling, despite her best efforts to head off social stagnation. After months of wrangling, the separation from Randall was finally complete. Jackie got the house, along with its huge upkeep expenses. Randall received, as compensation, all their joint stock in Randolph Enterprises. Jackie scored a decent alimony payment plus added child support. Randall agreed, for now, that Jackie would have primary custody of Charlotte, provided he got his daughter every weekend, most of summer vacation, and several holidays. This was a perfect arrangement for Jackie—she kept the money and didn't have to deal with her daughter all the time. That left her plenty of opportunities to find a new, rich husband. Unfortunately, the dating routine within her social circle had failed so far to secure a marriage proposal.

Back when she grew up, Jackie's parents and their friends maintained a fortified socioeconomic barrier to outsiders. You were in the group or on the outside. If a couple ever broke up, they rearranged themselves with new spouses after the appropriate time period. This behavior might lead to awkward moments when the new couples emerged and confronted old spouses, but everyone understood the order of things. Grievances were to be left unspoken, at least in public.

Now, the rules had changed. Jackie had dated, flirted, and made herself available to a cadre of both recently divorced and single men of suitable standing. A few she'd even agreed to sleep with when it seemed they had to have her. However, these same men were now unwilling to commit to a permanent arrangement. Maybe part of the hesitation was that the first, or second, divorce of the previously married man had been too expensive. For whatever reason, the "best" people weren't getting remarried like they used to. Some couples lived together, while others led separate lives, only occasionally governed by joint appearances. Friends with benefits, they called it. Jackie hated the idea. She wanted a permanent arrangement or nothing. Most of the men near her age now seemed to prefer a younger model, something Jackie hadn't needed to consider when she was in her prime. Now in her late thirties, about to slam headfirst into forty, she realized her precarious position. The mileage was showing, if you knew where to look. And the women in her social circle all knew where to look. A small liposuction scar here, a discrete stitch line there, perhaps a patch of concealer imperfectly applied. Nothing escaped their critique. Jackie ought to know—she was often the ringleader of previous female appraisals.

Jackie considered, briefly, going to work, perhaps at some art gallery or other acceptable upper-class place where she could meet suitable male customers, but those few opportunities proved too constraining. Employers seemed to expect her to show up for work each day, and to stay there and get things done. It was all so boring and pedestrian. How could you arrange spa days and social activities when you were stifled by the grinding demands of a stupid job? Jackie concluded that work was too much of a bother, especially since none of the acceptable positions earned the requisite six-figure salary.

For years now, she spent not only the funds coming in from Randall's salary but also often raided her trust fund. After all, her monthly care and feeding *was* expensive, but leaving off some of the usual extravagances seemed like an insufferable demotion. Her father had recently died, portending a nice cash payout to his offspring, but Jackie was disappointed to learn that her mother inherited all the couple's remaining assets through the trust, and, to make matters worse, her mother was now dating a mature man from their Florida community. The likelihood of her mother passing away in the near term didn't look favorable, since the woman was unfortunately in great health. The possibility that her mother could split off part of Jackie's eventual inheritance onto an outsider sent Jackie into a deep funk.

She discussed all of this with James, who was plodding along in his new career. Frankly, Jackie couldn't see the attraction of going to work every day and facing people griping about their investment returns while he held their hands. James had reviewed her own portfolio and presented her with several potential solutions. None of them afforded her sufficient funds to pay for the appropriate care and feeding she required. The thought of doing with less chilled her.

Charlotte wasn't helping the situation, either. After Jackie fired the nanny, Charlotte had become even more sullen and defiant. The only time she perked up was when she went to stay with Randall and his girlfriend for the weekend. Well, Jackie figured, she had no choice but to get rid of the nanny after a shouting match over Jackie's lack of parental love and responsibility. No hired-hand bitch was going to tell her how to behave toward her own daughter. Charlotte had hung onto the woman as she left, then cried for days after the dismissal. Jackie insisted it was all for the best, Charlotte needing to get over her silly attachment to a lowly servant. But her daughter's mood had improved little since then, and Jackie was unsure how to handle her child. Maybe she would hire a new nanny, one without professed opinions of her employer's motherly instincts. After all, that was what Randall's child support was supposed to help pay for. God, it was all so much work. Every time she looked at Charlotte, she looked more and more like her real father, and Jackie's hatred of David, because of his rejection, grew with time.

One night, while she was fuming over recent events, Jackie hit on a new idea. She needed more money, and David wanted desperately to see Charlotte. Why not extract a monthly payment from him in return for visitation rights? She wasn't sure how she could square this with her daughter without revealing the reason for the arrangement. But the child was short of nine years old, meaning she had to do as her mother told her. Enough said.

Once she worked out the details of her story, Jackie called David. It was in the evening, and he was probably at home, but Jackie didn't care. She needed to get the funds rolling in.

"David? Jackie. We need to talk about Charlotte," she said, getting right to the point.

The hesitation in launching the conversation was delayed by him fleeing to the backyard where Nichelle couldn't hear him. Typical David, Jackie thought.

"Okay, what do you want, Jackie?" he said, his voice carrying over the sounds of a faint breeze and a bird singing in the background. "I was about to go to the store."

"It's more what *you* want, David. I expect you'd like to be involved with your daughter again, correct?"

"Yes," he said, the reply cautious, like he didn't trust her. Imagine.

"It's not like I didn't know about your little scheme before. Show up at the park on Friday afternoons with your kid when the nanny and Charlotte were also there."

"Well, I, uh. . ."

"Save it, David. I know all about your secret routine. But there's no nanny anymore, so no more park visits for Charlotte. How about I tell Nichelle? That you went there every week to see your real daughter? How do you think she'd like that?"

"Jesus, Jackie, that would be. . ."

When he didn't finish his thought, she knew she had him. "I have an opportunity for you. I can arrange for you to see Charlotte more frequently."

"That's *fantastic*!" he said, the enthusiasm in his voice bubbling up.

"There's one condition," she said.

"What's that?"

"You've had a free ride all this time regarding Charlotte. With me being divorced from Randall, I need additional income. It's time you owned up to your financial responsibility."

"What are you up to, Jackie?"

"You should've been paying your part all along," she said.

"You mean you've told Randall? That I'm the father?"

"Of course not. How stupid do you think I am?" God, was David this naïve about things?

"Alright, what is it you want?"

"Two thousand deposited into my checking account each month. That should take care of her clothes and ballet lessons, along with some reparations for her mother. Then we'll renegotiate the amount for next year."

"That's impossible. No way I can afford that. We don't have that kind of money."

"What about that bitchy wife of yours? Couldn't she go back to work at that clinic?"

"Are you serious?" he said.

"Look, I don't care how you get the money. The important thing is I need some added financial support."

"And if I don't agree?"

"Then I'll go to court and tell them what actually happened."

"What does that mean?" he said, caution rising in his voice.

She relished what she was about to say. "That when I asked you to come over that night, instead of helping me out, you raped me and got me pregnant. Threatened to tell Randall that I was unfaithful if I said anything. And I've stayed quiet all this time because of your repeated threats."

"That's a fucking *lie*!" he said.

The anger in his voice only partially masked the rising panic. Jackie knew David too well. She had been right about his vulnerability. Time to bring it all home.

"Oh, *is* it? And after I had the baby, you forced me to return, again and again, to your apartment, so you could brutalize me with that deviant type of sex you insist on. You kept saying you would tell my husband all about us and then blame me for initiating the affair. In court, I'll tell them what kind of sick fuck you are, about the horrible, degrading things you've made me do as you repeatedly raped me. That I had to put up with this to save my marriage. Oh, David, how could you have been so *cruel*?"

"It's insane that you're even *saying* this kind of shit. This is a complete and total lie you've fabricated. Besides, no way you could prove any of this."

"Watch me get up on the stand and tell the judge and jury, complete with lots of tears, how you abused and manipulated me. Maybe we'll call Iris, have her testify how she caught you feeling me up in your apartment, me helpless to stop you, and how you fucked me every weekend while you were separated from her. You'll lose your job, David, and go to prison if you don't do what I say. How do you think Nichelle will feel about you after that, huh? Or your son? And James? Wait 'til he finds out that his dear friend is really a low-life rapist bastard guilty of molesting his own sister. I think I know the answer to all of that. How about you?"

She could see his face in her mind, watching it twitch as he struggled to come up with an alternative plan. Jackie had thought all this through and didn't see any significant chinks in her defensive wall. Neither did David, or he would have voiced them.

After some silence, he said, "I can't believe you're doing this to me. You always said you'd never tell about us."

"So I changed my mind. Maybe if you hadn't spent all your life wanting to *screw* me, things would have turned out differently."

"Look, it was you that always wanted me." His retort was plaintive, insecure.

"Bullshit. I bet you spent every night in your room jacking off and thinking of fucking me. How'd you like to explain that under oath?"

"I need some time to, to think about this," he said.

"Don't take too long. One call to the D.A. and I'll ruin your life. The alternative is much better. You send me some cash each month and you get to see your daughter. Your family never finds out what a worthless *asshole* you are. It's a win-win."

"You're such a *cunt*," he said, the emotion in his voice rising. "Iris was right. You've the very *worst* type of woman."

"Your ex-wife hates me? That's all you got? If you think insulting me will get you out of this, think again."

He didn't reply.

"I'll give you a couple of days to agree to what I want. Otherwise. . .Well, I think you know how this will turn out."

She hung up and laughed to herself. What a stupid schmuck. His nuts were in a vise, and she was closing the jaws. He had to agree to this new arrangement. There really wasn't any alternative.

47

When David called Finch, he was almost berserk.

"Finchie, I'm in *trouble*, real *trouble*!" David said, panic rising in his voice.

"Whoa, hold on, buddy," Finch said. "What's happened?"

"It's Jackie. She's blackmailing me."

"About what?"

David related the previous conversation. After he finished, Finch remained silent. Impatient to get his friend's reaction, David demanded. "*Well?* What do you *think*?"

"She's an awful, awful person. That's what I think," Finch said.

"But what am I going to *do*? I'm at my wit's end."

"First, we're going to think this through, see what your real options are. Don't do anything right now, understand me? We've got time. We can work it out, you and me." He paused. "Have you told Nichelle?"

"No, of *course* not."

"She doesn't know there's a problem?"

David glanced through the sliding glass door into the house. Nichelle was standing inside, hands on her hips, arms akimbo, staring at him. She must have seen his initial reaction to Jackie's phone call. He wasn't sure how he had behaved, but he could not hide that he was extremely upset. She would ask him what was the matter, what he was up to, as soon as he went back into the house. And, once more, he would lie to her.

David turned his back to the door. "She's looking at me. Right now, through the glass."

"And?" Finch said.

"She knows I'm really upset."

"David, you're going to have to tell your wife what's happened. This has gone on way too long. She has a right to know the details of your history with Jackie. This involves her now."

"*No!*" he said, hearing his own hysterical voice. "She can *never* know. You *hear* me?" He paused and pushed a hand across his forehead. "Maybe if I hadn't given that thirty grand to my dad, I could buy more time to think about this. You know, pay her off for a while, see if that would work. Or I could raid our savings account, give Jackie a few months. . ."

"Look, David, giving in to Jackie's not the solution. She'll never be satisfied. She's running out of money and you're only a means to an end right now. Think about this. If she says the child is yours, that will screw up her child support from Randall."

"Yeah, and then it'd be me paying for Charlotte." He circled the yard, desperate, grabbing at whatever thoughts came into his head. "If I give her money, won't that be proof, wouldn't it, that she's blackmailing me?"

"She could just as easily claim you're paying *her* off. To keep her quiet."

David ran his fingers through his hair. He felt like he was losing his mind. All of his dirty secrets, the things he had kept from Nichelle so she would believe him to be a decent man, all that was about to be exposed. She would hate him for it. He knew that. Then he would lose her, and his son, too, just like he lost Iris. What the hell was he going to do?

"I've got to go think, think this through," David said.

Finch could hear the desperation cracking David's voice. "Look, stay calm, okay? I'll give this some thought. There's got to be a way through this. You don't have to do anything this minute."

"I don't see how," David said. "No way this is going to work. No *way*."

"Trust me. We'll come up with something."

"I don't think so. Not this time."

"There's always a solution, David," Finch said. "Always."

"I've got to go." With that, David hung up.

Within seconds, Finch rang him back, but David didn't answer the call.

The sliding glass door opened as Nichelle stepped outside onto the patio. "What was *that* all about?" she said.

"Nothing, *nothing*."

"*Bullshit* nothing. You're acting like a crazy person. Who called?"

"Doesn't matter."

"The hell it doesn't. Tell me, *dammit*."

"I need to go get milk," he said as he pushed past her.

She grabbed at the sleeve of his shirt. "Why won't you ever let me in? Why not? I'm your wife, for *God's sake*."

David shrugged her off. "I've got to go."

"*David!*"

He grabbed his keys as he headed out the front door.

•   •   •   •   •

Standing in front of the milk cooler, David wasn't looking at anything inside. His brain kept rerunning the two previous conversations. Yes, Finchie said he'd figure it out, and he always had come through before. But this latest fiasco was different, too serious to solve easily. There was no realistic way he could ask Nichelle to go back to work to pay off Jackie. It was his insistence, after he got that last raise, that she quit work and they live off of his income. She was angry because he didn't want to negotiate. Since he was adamant, she eventually gave in to mollify him. That made him happy, having his wife home full time, raising Davie. Best thing for their child.

Once they moved out of the apartment downtown, Nichelle had agreed to put some of her savings toward the down payment on a suburban house. The house wasn't fancy, not upscale like the apartment, but one side benefit was a mortgage with a reduced interest rate loan for first-time homeowners. The neighborhood had become more fashionable during the last few years, causing the resale prices of the nearby houses to increase significantly. Of course, the taxes rose right along with the valuations. They still made out okay, so far, on his income, but with little left over. He dreaded their constantly increasing expenses. The house needed work, sure, but one day he would get to it. They were building equity, he told Nichelle, not throwing their money away on rent, and that was what was important.

Now, his carefully constructed lie of a life was falling apart. Nichelle would rightly refuse to go to work to support Jackie Weir. He also understood Jackie well enough to know she could follow through on her threat. He would be arrested and lose his job. Jackie would be convincing on the witness stand. He could see her on the stand, crying about the false abuse, saying she was the victim of a rapist. The jury would agree. Interesting, he thought, to be convicted of a sex crime, considering his own history of abuse. He could just imagine his attorney, pleading for mercy, saying this man is so damaged from being abused as a child that you must give him a break. But he would still end up in prison. Nichelle and Davie would maybe come to see him a few times, then the visits would stop and he would receive the divorce papers, along with a restraining order keeping him from any future contact with his son. He would lose, as he always did, in the end. Everything he had worked for would be lost. How had he gotten himself into such a predicament? Well, one word. Jackie.

He lusted after Jackie for years, and their initial affair was more exciting than he had ever imagined. But when he found out that Charlotte was his daughter, everything changed. Jackie used that knowledge against him before and was still doing so. He knew he would never see his daughter again, even after he was released from incarceration. She would, of course, reject him. After all, he would be the man convicted of repeatedly raping her mother, and scum like him didn't deserve to live, let alone see their love child. Nichelle always said he was too pessimistic, but this fiasco would prove him correct. His life had always been based on lies and avoidance. Soon she would know for sure what a piece of shit she married.

David rubbed his forehead. He felt, for the third time in his life, that he was out of options.

Indistinct noises, then shouting voices came from the front of the store. David reached in and grabbed for a carton of milk. Probably someone was mad about the price of gas, or maybe a credit card had been declined. Minor problems, he thought. If only his own were that easy to solve. Best to get back home, tell his wife what a worthless bastard she had married, and prepare himself for the onslaught of Nichelle's recriminations. He would deserve everything she would say to him, and more.

David hugged the milk to his chest and headed toward the counter.

48

Finch and Nichelle worked out a simple routine for their lives together. They got up, dressed, shared a quick breakfast with Davie, then took him to school. After that, they came back home, got back into bed and spent a while talking and loving on each other. When that was over, they took a joint shower. Finch could not imagine a more ideal life, and was determined to relish each minute he was this happy.

This morning, they were in bed with Nichelle's back to Finch. He was caressing her front, taking his time, as she squirmed with complete enjoyment.

"This is too perfect," she said.

"Why's that?" he said.

"I never expected to be this happy."

"This won't last forever," he said. "I need to get a job. And you said you wanted to go back to work. But I've learned one thing from my wanderings. You need to enjoy the pleasant things when you get the opportunity." He kissed her several times on the shoulder. "This is my opportunity, and I want to make the most of it. You never know when it will end."

Turning back to face him, Nichelle said, "I hope you know how much I love you."

"All I want is to make you happy," he said. "I mean that."

"Thank you. For being such a good man." She started kissing him. "And for always being honest with me."

"Why wouldn't I be?"

Nichelle nuzzled against him. "I had another husband who wasn't."

"Maybe he thought he was shielding you from things that would hurt you. If you knew them."

"I'm a tough woman," she said. "I can handle a lot."

"Perhaps he wanted you to think more of him. Everyone likes to put a positive spin on themselves."

"You don't," she said. "You're the opposite."

"A habit I developed," he said. "Under-promise and over-deliver."

"Works for me," she said. "Make love to me."

He smiled. "If you insist."

●　　●　　●　　●　　●

After sex, they laid in bed a while longer, Nichelle acting like something was bothering her.

"What's the matter, baby?"

"How did David's first marriage break up?"

"Didn't he tell you?"

"He said Iris lost the baby, then they separated. After that, all he would say was that the actual rupture was his fault, but he wouldn't tell me anymore. Then after the funeral, Iris said Jackie broke them up, but when I asked James, he said it was an old infatuation David had from way back. Fill me in?"

"He had an affair."

"Who with?"

"Jackie Weir."

"Why am I not surprised?"

Finch told her all of it. How David grew up with Jackie, how they both wanted each other, how he fled to college to keep from getting involved, how they accidentally came back together.

"Was he sleeping with Jackie when he and Iris finally broke up?" she said.

"Well. . ."

"Tell me the truth, Finchie."

"Iris came home, unexpectedly, to see if they could reconcile. When she got in the house, she figured out he was still seeing Jackie. And that Jackie had a hold on David that he couldn't break. They divorced right after that."

"Did he continue to see Jackie?"

"For a while. But after he met you, he lost all interest in Jackie. She wasn't pleased, from what David said. I want you to know he said he never cheated on you."

"She seemed familiar when I saw her after the funeral, but. . ." Nichelle sat up in bed, realization dawning on her. "I've *met* her. Before. She came to the clinic for something minor. Asked for the PA. I didn't think she was really sick."

"Surprise," Finch said.

"She was checking me out, wasn't she? Seeing what her ex-lover was getting himself into?"

"Sounds like her."

Nichelle laid back and stared at the ceiling. "I guess this shouldn't surprise me. It makes a lot of things clearer." She turned and faced Finch again. "Did they. . ."

"What?" he said, but he knew what she was going to ask.

"Did she get pregnant by him? Did they have a child?"

Finch caressed her, trying to think of an easy way to break the news, but nothing came to him. "Yes. He got Jackie pregnant, unintentionally, but that was what she wanted. Her husband's infertile. The child's name is Charlotte."

"Did she let him see her?"

"At first, Jackie would bring her over when they had sex. I think that was the driving reason he stayed with her for a while. Then she refused to let him see the child again. After that, he broke it off."

"Does her husband know it's David's baby?"

"Ex-husband. Not to my knowledge."

Nichelle thought back. "There was a little girl at the house after the funeral. Maybe eight or so? I'm not sure, maybe a couple of years older than Davie. I suppose that was Charlotte."

"Yes," he said.

"I remember thinking she was a beautiful child. So. . .Davie has a half-sister?"

"That's right."

"She and Davie were playing together that day, in his room, acting like they got along fine. Guess that's the reason."

Finch thought over her comment. "There's more to it than that."

"What?"

He could see the look on her face, the recognition of another in a string of betrayals that she never imagined. "You should probably let this go."

"*Stop* taking up for him. I want to know *all* of it."

Finch took a deep breath before continuing. "David was crazy about the child, the same feelings he had for Davie. Jackie wasn't exactly an involved mother, always letting the nanny take care of her daughter while she worked on social events. Every Friday afternoon, the nanny would take Charlotte to the park in the afternoon and he—"

"*Fuck!*" Nichelle said, pounding her fists against her legs.

"What?"

"After his company started taking Friday afternoons off, he told me he wanted to take Davie to the park those days, make it special, just the two of them. I thought it was so sweet, but he was lying to me all the time."

"He wasn't lying, baby. Not exactly. He wanted to take Davie to the park. He found out which park the nanny took Charlotte to and made sure he was there at the same time. They became friends. They would sit together and discuss the children. That way, he got to be near his daughter, watch her grow. It became an obsession with him. We discussed it several times. Him not being a part of the child's life was eating him up inside."

Nichelle jumped out of bed, still naked, and headed for the office. She returned with David's smartphone. Holding the display out so he could see, she said, "Is this Charlotte?"

A photo of a smiling little girl standing next to Davie filled the screen.

"Yes."

"I caught him looking at this picture. Several times. He said it reminded him of the days at the park, no big deal. And then, after the funeral, she and Davie went into his room and I thought how familiar they seemed with each other and I remember thinking they both looked alike. . ."

Nichelle started crying. Finch pulled her to him, not saying anything. After a bit, she calmed down.

"It was like I was living with a stranger," she said. "This makes me so damn *angry*, all the things he kept from me."

"He wanted to protect you. That was his way of doing so."

"Well, he thought wrong."

"He did what he thought was right."

"I think," she said, "that you believe you always have to take up for him."

He considered her remark. "I felt a strong responsibility for him. I always have." He rubbed her shoulders. "But if you ask me a question, and I know what happened, I'll always tell you the truth," he said.

She kissed him. "Thank you. For being the husband I've always needed."

He grinned. "I expect you'll let me know when I screw up."

She moved up against him as he pulled the sheet over her. "You can bet on it."

He continued to rub her back, and soon she relaxed and went to sleep, her steady breathing comforting him and making him remember, one more time, why he loved her so much. Finch moved the hair off of the side of her face and gently kissed her cheek. He thought back to the last thing David had told him before he died. He expected there would never be a reason for Nichelle to question the official reason for David's death. This was good, because Finch intended to keep that last secret forever.

49

On her way home from the grocery store, Nichelle coasted to a stop in front of the elder Perry's house, thinking about the totality of terrible things that had taken place in there. On an impulse, she went to the front door and knocked.

"Mr. Perry?"

"What do you want?" the old man said, staring at her through the screen door.

"I'm David's wife, remember me? From the funeral? May I come in?"

"Who's with you?" Perry said, craning his neck to see around her.

"No one. Just me."

Perry glanced once more to each side, then opened the door. Nichelle stepped over the threshold, not knowing what to expect or what she would find. She had nothing but contempt for the old man, but she hid that. Of course, if Finch knew she was here, he would throw a fit. Her concealed intention was to case Perry's place, if she could, and get a general idea of the security in case Finch and James wanted to reconsider physical violence against the old man.

"Okay, now you're inside. What do you want?"

The way he spoke to her, the arrogant tone, made her want to put a fist in his face.

"Interesting place you have here," she said, gazing around the walls. The house was neater than she expected, except for some discarded boxes of takeout on the coffee table. She looked up in the corners of the room, trying to see if she could detect tiny red lights from security cameras.

"So?"

"I was wondering. Maybe we should get together, you and me and David Jr. David never wanted that, but now that he's dead. . . Well, it's an idea."

The man's scowl intensified. "He tell you why we didn't get along?"

"No, not really. He said you weren't close. That's all."

She stepped toward the back of the house, trying to take in everything she was seeing. "Nice house, Mr. Perry. You live here all by yourself?"

"What do you care?" he said, following her.

"Just wondered."

By then, she found an office near the back, filled with two filing cabinets and a desk with a laptop on it. The cabinets must be where he keeps the prints and his other records, she thought.

"Kinda nosey, aren't you?" Perry said, following her, then looking her up and down.

"Sorry. I like to look at people's houses. Hobby of mine. That's all." She turned and faced him. "Well, anyway, maybe we could work something out. Get together, I mean."

"You married to that man was a friend of David's?"

"Mr. Finch? Yes, I am."

"He's the one who took my boy. I'll get back at him one day for that." The old man's slitted eyes roamed over Nichelle. "Never figured why David took up with a colored woman." He grunted. "Guess now you've found yourself another white man to take care of you. You must really be something."

Nichelle bit back her comment. She found Perry disgusting and scary. He made her skin crawl. All she wanted to do was to break his head open. It was time she left.

"Anyway, think about it," she said, turning around and heading back to the front.

"How 'bout you send your kid over?" he said, grabbing for her arm. "Me and him could get to know each other, have ourselves a friendly visit."

She pulled her arm carefully from his grasp, trying to smother the revulsion. "I'll think about it, Mr. Perry. I've got to go. Groceries in the car."

As Nichelle drove off, a shiver went through her entire body. She felt like she needed to take a long shower to wash the slime off.

• • • • • • • • •

Nichelle came into the house and immediately headed for the kitchen sink, where she scrubbed her hands and forearms. Finch heard her washing up and walked into the room, watching her.

"Prepping for surgery?" he said.

"Not exactly."

"Why all the soap?" he said.

"I went by Perry's place."

"Why the *hell* did you do that?" he said as emotion filled his voice.

Nichelle was taken aback, since Finchie had never been angry with her before. "It wasn't planned, Finchie. I got this idea in my head, on the way home from the store, about finding out what the inside of his house looked like. I figured I had a better chance of getting in than you and James did."

Finch moved up behind her and put his hands on her shoulders. "Baby, I don't want you to do that ever again. Promise me you won't. If *anything* had happened to you. . ."

"I was careful."

"I know, but. . ."

She dried off, then turned toward him. "I promise I won't do it again. Trust me?"

He kissed her. "I always have."

Nichelle hugged his neck and wouldn't let go. He held her, giving her time.

"So what did you learn?" he said once she relaxed her grip.

She was all business after that. "I've got the layout of the house memorized. Plus, I didn't see any security cameras, but there may be little ones hidden where I couldn't see. His office is at the back, along with a desk with his laptop on it. There's two filing cabinets along the wall, which may hold the photos. I can draw you a plan."

"That would be helpful."

"He wanted me to leave Davie with him. Said he'd like to get to know him. Can you believe that?"

Finch's eyes glowed. "If he *ever* touches our son, I'd—"

"One other thing, Finchie. I smelled his breath. It's fruity. He's a diabetic, meaning he takes insulin. The vials should be in the refrigerator in the kitchen. If you and James go over there and can hold him down, I could give him an overdose. If he gets enough, he'll go into a diabetic coma. It'll kill him. If they do an autopsy, they'll assume he made a mistake, gave himself too much. In the meantime, you could go through the house, find whatever you needed to find."

"No way I'm going to involve you," Finch said, but he could see the determination in her eyes.

Her independent streak surfaced. "You think you can tell me what to do?"

He laughed. "I'd never think that. We'd need to talk about it first."

She pulled him against her. "All I'm saying is it's an option. We're in this together, right?"

He kissed the top of her head. "Alright. One option, but a very distant one. Remind me to never get on your bad side."

Nichelle murmured into his chest. "I'll always love you, Finchie. You're the best thing that's ever happened to me."

"I love you, too, sweetheart. Even if I am sleeping with a potential murderer."

She laughed, breaking the somber mood, but continued to hold on to him. "I know I can tell you anything, and that you'll always be honest with me. You know how special that is?"

He kissed her again. "I feel the same. Besides, I'm getting close to finishing this."

"I want to know something."

"What's that?" he said.

"Did something happen that prompted you to ask James' parents to take David in?"

"His dad threatened to give David injections. To slow down or block him from reaching puberty. Didn't want his cash cow to grow out of being useful. I felt like I had to take action right then."

Nichelle was silent for a while. Then she said, "I hope David understood what a great friend you were to him."

"He did."

"I asked you once before to destroy Perry. I want that even more now."

"You're not alone."

"I know you have a plan to ruin Perry. I want to hear an update."

"Alright. Let's go set down and we'll go over the details. You may have some improvements or suggestions that I haven't thought of."

50

Rounding the corner of the aisle, David saw what the commotion was. A robber was standing at the front counter, threatening the clerk with a handgun. Huddled against the wall was a woman and her young daughter.

"*Hurry up, motherfucker!*" the bandit said, the end of his pistol pointing at the clerk. He looked up and spied David. "You! Get your *ass* over here. *Now!* And get your fucking hands up!"

David did as he was told, stopping in front of the woman and her child. "Mind if I set the milk on the counter?"

"The fuck I care about your goddamn *milk?*" the man said, turning back to the clerk. "You take more'n thirty seconds to get that money out, I'll put a bullet in the middle of your stupid-ass head."

By this time, the clerk was on his knees in front of the safe, shaking with fear. "It's...it's a time lock safe. I can't open it for fifteen minutes after I put in the code." The clerk looked back, his eyes pleading for understanding.

"You're lying outta your *ass,*" the man said, his frustration rising. "I said *open up the fucking safe!*"

"Look, he's telling the truth," David said, still holding his hands up. "This type of store uses those safes. To stop robberies. I know because I work for a company that recommends them."

The thief's eyes thinned as he glanced at David. "You? You shut the *fuck* up, you *hear* me?"

"All I'm saying is—"

The man took a step closer and pushed the end of the pistol barrel against David's forehead. "How'd you like to start spitting gum outta a hole in your forehead, *asshole?*"

"I don't mean to upset you."

David worked to memorize the man's appearance. He would be called on later, after the police caught this idiot, to identify him. He knew that too many people were mis-identified by eyewitness testimony, and he didn't want to be one of those witnesses with vague, inaccurate recollections. Faded jeans, green camo jacket with a hood, gray sweatpants, some kind of t-shirt, with expensive tennis shoes unlaced. His pants were bagging down, so likely his jockeys were showing in the back, because periodically the man would hitch up his pants with his free hand, getting ready to run. David thought about a conversation he had with a cop one time, about how many robbers they caught because when they fled their pants fell down around their ankles. From the height measurement guide glued to the lock side of the entry door, he figured the man at five foot eight, maybe nine. Probably mid-twenties, needing a fix. David tried to memorize the features of the man's face, his scraggly beard, the wide eyes with dilated pupils. Either he's high or scared, David figured. Maybe both.

The clerk rose from the floor. He was still visibly shaking. "I can't open the safe. I'm telling the truth. I really can't." He stepped back and held up his hands. "*Please*, take the money from the register. All of it. Whatever else you want."

"Gimme some of them fucking lottery tickets."

The clerk hesitated. "Which ones you want?"

"The big winners, *goddammit*. I know you people know which ones are the good ones, not that shit you hand out all the time. Now hurry the fuck *up*."

David suppressed a laugh. The poor dumb bastard. They had to run the tickets through a scanner for them to be valid. Obviously, this guy wasn't a professional.

"The hell you laughing at, *fucker*?" the robber said, turning back to him. "How about I kill your stupid ass, see how you like *that*?"

"The tickets aren't good until they're scanned."

Turning to the clerk, the man said, "That right?"

The clerk barely nodded.

"You stupid *motherfucker*, you were going to give them to me, *anyway*?"

David could see a dark stain spreading in the clerk's crotch. He was pissing his pants.

"Well, *scan* them, dammit. Get *on* with it."

Trying to tear off the tickets from the roll, in his haste and nervousness the clerk kept dropping them or accidentally tearing them in two, further aggravating the robber. To emphasize his displeasure, the robber took aim at the security video monitor above the clerk's head and fired. The thin screen blew apart in a shimmer of glass.

"Still think I'm fuckin' *kiddin'*?" he said, repointing the weapon at the clerk.

By then, the potential victim was so upset that he could do nothing but shake and cry.

"How about you take the cash and take off?" David said, deliberately controlling his breathing. He had to act calm, try to reduce the robber's stress before he did something even more stupid. "Leave the lottery tickets for another day."

"Who told you to be my boss, *shithead*?" The man stared at David. "Give me your damn wallet."

David reached into his pocket and handed over his wallet.

"And that bitch behind you. I want her money, too."

Turning to the woman, David said, "It's best you give it to him. Let him be on his way. Get this over with."

Tears rolled down the woman's cheeks. In halting English, she said, "I no can do. Rent money. Must pay tomorrow."

"It's better than the alternative," David said. "Please."

"No can do," she said. "All I have."

"Listen, *bitch*, you either hand it over or you're fucking coming *with* me!"

The woman started screaming as the man stepped around David and reached for her purse.

"Please, don't do that!" David said, watching the situation spiral out of control.

"*Shut the fuck up!*" the robber said. Turning to the mother, he said, "Maybe I'll take your little girl instead, see how she likes spending time with a grown man. How you think she'd like that, *huh*?"

David looked down at the terrified child. She reminded him of Charlotte.

David said. "Take me instead. I'll cooperate. I promise."

"The *fuck* I want you for? Naw, the little girl will do just *fine*."

David thought through his options, trying to decide what to do. He couldn't, wouldn't, let the man take the child. The thought of her being abused by an adult man made his determination absolute. As the realization of his choice hit David, he had an epiphany. Why not let the man kill him instead? The Jackie problem would be solved, permanently. Nichelle would get the life insurance money, giving her time to decide what to do next. Likely, the robber would run as soon as he shot David, leaving the child behind. It would all be so simple. He glanced down at the gun near his chest. The man's finger was on the trigger, poised to pull it. He wasn't paying attention to David as he wrestled the mother for the child. Both were putting up a determined fight, with the child's arms strung out between them as she screamed out the intense, high pitch of a terrified child. One option was to struggle with the man and risk getting shot. The other was to take control of the situation and solve all of his problems. It was now or never.

David's hand reached out and grasped the barrel of the gun, jerking it toward the center of his chest. The blast so close to his face was shocking. He expected it to hurt more than it did as the bullet pierced his chest. Feeling left him as blood poured from the wound. He stumbled against the counter, hearing the woman start screaming again, even louder. There was confusion as the robber scooped up the money on the counter, spitting out curses. He heard the man's shoulder hit the door and the clerk pick up the store phone. Then things gradually went dark and his hearing deteriorated. He fell to the floor, hardly feeling the impact. The woman was on her knees beside him, trying to stop the bleeding. It was futile. He knew he was dying, really dying. The reality of that didn't seem to matter that much. A dark film fell over his eyes. His last thoughts were of Nichelle and Davie, and how he could finally protect them from all of his mistakes.

51

Nichelle checked her watch for maybe the tenth time. Would this day never end? The graveside services for David were finally over with, completed by the preacher's gentle message of salvation and lots of people coursing through the single file line. Nichelle stood and greeted each one, even those she didn't know, and listened to the platitudes, felt the often-insincere hugs, and wondered if her hand would ever be the same after too many men squeezed too hard. She appreciated the sentiment, she really did, but the entire process was becoming exhausting and all she wanted was for it to be over with. Being outgoing and revealing her feelings was not how she wanted to spend the day.

Now, family and friends were at her house. Max and Ja'Neel seemed to know everyone and acted as hosts, providing a grateful and unexpected buffer to Nichelle's drooping morale. She was glad they came. Finch's mother, whom Nichelle had just met, immediately took charge of the kitchen, after having insisted on bringing the snacks and desserts, and Nichelle was happy to oblige her as well. Nichelle had set up the water, punch, and iced tea beforehand, and only had to take them out of the refrigerator once she got home. Home, the house without David, she thought, a tightness coursing through her chest. She and Davie were on their own now, likely forever. They would need to adjust to that, go on with a new purpose, and bury their sorrow behind rueful smiles and shakes of the head.

Even though she hustled Davie back to the house as soon as she could, multiple cars filled with people idled in her driveway and on the street. Another chance to visit and say goodbye. Jesus, could they just give her a moment? No, she had to straighten up, get through this. People would judge her by how she behaved today, and eventually it would be over with. That's what she told herself as she struggled to hold it together, avoiding telling the guests to all get the hell out of her house and leave her alone. She was so weary that she thought about going into her bedroom, locking the door behind her, and not coming out until tomorrow.

Checking her watch again, Nichelle realized it has been less than five minutes since she last looked.

Fortunately, Finch's mother marshaled the circulating women into making new pots of coffee, setting out the food and cutting the cakes, and washing dishes as they went. It was what they could do to help, and Nichelle knew she owed them all a solid round of thanks. The rest of the bunch seemed like parasites to her, taking up space, consumed with idle conversation, eating up all the food. Even David's father was here, lounging on the couch and not talking to anyone. She closed her eyes, attempting to banish the selfish thoughts of ridding herself of her guests, but those tenacious thoughts clung to her brain. What a bitch I am, she thought. All they want to do is offer their condolences, and all you want is for them to all be gone.

Nichelle searched for Davie and found him in his room with a little girl. They were playing together on the floor, obviously happy to be out of the shadow of the adults' gloom. Davie said they were friends. Best to leave them alone, she thought, though the prospect of spending time with them was superior to interfacing with the adults. Oh, to be a child again, she thought, so easily distracted from the terribleness of life.

She left and headed back into the fray.

Nichelle's mother intercepted her and placed an arm around her daughter. Nichelle rolled her head onto her mother's shoulder, feeling love and comfort as they lingered in the hallway. Her parents had flown in two days ago and insisted on staying at a hotel, so as not to bother her, they said.

"If you and Davie want, you could come stay with us for a while," her mother said, giving Nichelle an affectionate squeeze. "Back in Philly."

"Thanks, but Davie needs to get back in school, Mom. They say reestablishing a routine is good for children after a big shock like this. Running away makes it that much harder to come back."

"What about you, sweetheart? How are you holding up?"

"Day by day. Just trying to make it through another one right now."

"Your father and I have talked. We want to help with the finances. We can afford it now, you know."

Nichelle's head popped up at the threat to her independence. "That won't be necessary. David had some life insurance. Not a lot, but it will help. I'll be okay. Promise." She hooked her arm into her mother's.

"Sure?" her mother said, taking in the worn furnishings as they entered the living room. "I thought you two were skimping to get by on David's salary."

"Not skimping. Being frugal," she said, but knew her mother was right.

"You want to go back to work?"

"I'll have to. At some point. Besides, I've always enjoyed working. David insisted I stay home with Davie. I think it helped, though, with Davie. Probably for the best."

A skeptical look crossed Nichelle's mother's face. "I'm surprised you gave up your career, sweetheart. You were always so committed to the things you wanted."

"It's what made David happy. We all have to make sacrifices in a marriage."

With that, she disengaged from her mother, saw the resigned look, and felt her mother's gaze on her back as she walked away. She needed to resume the role of hostess.

A small woman stood in the corner of the dining room by herself, arms folded, following Nichelle's movements with her eyes.

"You're Iris, aren't you?" Nichelle said, walking over and extending her hand.

Iris looked considerably different now than she did in the few pictures David kept of her. With her blonde hair in a pixie cut and a hardened look of despair covering her face, Nichelle hadn't recognized her at first. Iris was now the opposite of the happy, dark-haired woman in the old photos.

"Yes," Iris said in a faint voice. "I felt like I had to come, to see him off, even though. . ." She stopped and didn't finish her thought.

As Nichelle's eyes surveyed the broken woman, she felt an immediate kinship with her. Both of them immediately knew something about the other and what they had shared.

"Your marriage to him lasted," Iris said, tears forming. "Mine didn't."

"He wouldn't say much about yours," Nichelle said, taking the woman's hand in hers. "Just that it was all his fault."

Iris nodded. "Well, he was dead-on about that."

"What happened with you two?" Nichelle said, then regretted the question. "Sorry, that's none of my business."

Iris pointed to Jackie Weir, who was standing in the opposite end of the dining room talking to James. "She broke us up."

Startled, Nichelle said, "Broke you up? How?'

"She's bad news," Iris said, harsh emotion dripping off her words. "I hated her. Still do, the fucking *cunt*." Iris glanced back at a startled Nichelle. "Sorry. I shouldn't have said anything."

"What do you mean? What happened between them?"

Iris looked off. "David was difficult to live with. We both know that. He always had trouble escaping from his past. It formed the way he handled his problems, the lying, covering things up, never wanting anyone to know his darkest secrets. Except for James and Finch. He let them in on all of his awfulness, the whole damn history. But not me. He never told me the truth." Iris snorted, as if expelling a cruel memory. "I guess I'm not telling you anything new."

"What do you mean? About his history?" Nichelle said, confused. "He refused to talk about growing up, why he hated his father."

"You don't know?" Iris said, her eyes opening wide. "All the time you two were married, and he never *told* you. . ."

"No, *please*. You must tell me."

"Not my place. Besides, it doesn't matter now, does it?" Iris glanced around the room, looking desperate. "I thought I was over him, had put this all behind me, but I see. . ." She pushed her plastic cup into Nichelle's hands. "I've said too much. I have to go. Now. Sorry."

"Don't go, we need to talk."

Nichelle watched as the woman broke away from her and headed for the front door. Then she was gone.

James came over and gave Nichelle a hug. "Anything wrong?"

"That woman who was here? Iris? She said she thought I knew. About David's past." Nichelle looked up at James. "And she said your sister broke them up. What did she mean?"

James considered the question. "Hard to say, exactly. Jackie and David had a thing for each other, back when they were a lot younger and he lived with us. But that was a long time ago. She's probably blaming her own troubles on an old infatuation."

"I don't understand. Why would she still hold such a grudge?"

James shrugged. "Who knows? This one time, she and David invited us to a small get-together at their house. Everything was going fine, then suddenly Iris comes stalking in, looking like she's totally pissed, and tells everyone to leave immediately, that the party's over. That same night, she packed up and left David. That's the kind of thing I'm talking about. She had a hard time holding it together. Don't let her comments worry you, Nichelle. Iris was always a bit. . .unstable."

"Unstable?"

James motioned to Finch, who came over, acting like a six-year-old stuck in the wrong class at school and not knowing what to do about it.

"Finchie and I have been talking. He wants to help you out. Would that be okay?" James said.

"Help out with what?" Nichelle said, confused. She looked at Finch, whose face was turning red.

Finch said, "I, uh, wanted to know if I could help you around the house. Painting, fixing things up, that sort of stuff. From what he said before, I think David hated doing repairs. I'd be happy to take care of all that for you. If you wanted. I'm a contractor." He looked down at the floor after he quit speaking.

Nichelle stared at the weird man in front of her, wondering what his problem was. Why couldn't he summon the courage to ask her without James' help? What David had seen in this man, she would never know.

James said, "Finchie's a wonder with all kinds of construction, Nichelle. I think he could really help you and Davie out."

"If you want." Finch raised his head, an odd look on his face. "Say so if you don't."

She exhaled and found her voice. "That would be good of you, Finch."

"Okay. I'll hang around for a few more days."

"You staying with your parents?" Nichelle said.

"Probably not. My youngest sister's still there and the other bedroom they've converted. I'd have to sleep on the sofa. I'll get a room at a motel instead."

"That's silly," she said. "We have a spare bedroom. You can stay with us."

"For sure?" he said.

"Yes, of course. Makes sense if you're working around the house." As soon as the words were out of her mouth, she regretted her offer. But what else could she say? "Only for a few days, right?"

"Yes. Then I'll be moving on."

"David said you travel around a lot."

Finch nodded. "That's right. I don't like to stay in one place for long. Don't worry. You probably won't even know I'm here. I'll try to not bother you."

"No bother," she said, not meaning it.

"It's settled," James said, a smile crossing his face. He unwound his arm. "I think I'll check out your mother's cake, Finch. Looks delicious."

"Yeah," Finch said, sticking his hands in his pockets. "She's always been a wonderful cook."

"Come on," James said, nodding toward Finch. "We'll both get a piece. Then I have something important I want to discuss with you."

Nichelle watched them walk away and wondered for the thousandth time what those two knew that had cemented David's total loyalty.

52

Finch was working on the last phase of his plan to entrap and ruin David's father. He had spent all this time gaining the old man's confidence and hoped that this final round of messages would cement their relationship.

—*I'm ready to buy, but I want an exclusive.*

—*What does that mean?*

—*All the stuff on one individual. Not one shopped around after that. No one else can have it. Ever.*

—*That'll cost more. A lot more.*

—*I'll need a sample. One or two items to verify. Make sure I have the one I want.*

Finch had tightly bracketed his request to narrow it to photos that Perry might only have of David. Finch's intention was to buy all the images of his friend so he could permanently prevent their distribution elsewhere. The problem was whether he could trust Perry to deliver. Finch had no illusions that Perry might double-cross him. The key would be to make such a trick too painful for him to back out on.

—*Alright. Sample's headed your way.*

—*How many items do you have?*

—*A number. We'll talk later.*

Soon an image appeared in his folder. Finch waited to open it until he ran the photo through his customized scan for viruses and other malware. Satisfied that the image was clean, he opened it. It was a picture of David, maybe age eight or nine, taken from above, an adult man holding onto his hair and. . .

Finch closed the window and slammed the laptop cover shut. He thought he was going to throw up. Yes, he had always known, at least in general terms, what had happened to his friend. During confessions, he also heard a few of the gory details, but the reality of it hit Finch like a hard slap in the face. He put down his computer and went outside and sat in one of the lounge chairs on the patio.

Nichelle came out a while later.

"Hey, Finchie, what's up?" she said.

He didn't reply.

She circled around the front of the chair and saw the anguish etched into his face. "What's happened? Tell me."

"I got Perry to send me an image from a package of photos and videos I said I wanted to buy. It's David, about eight years old, and. . ." He didn't finish the sentence.

"Oh, God," she said, her hand moving to her mouth.

"It's so fucking horrible, baby. To think he put up with that for years."

"It's not your fault, Finchie."

Finch waved his hands around, helpless to find a use for them. "I should have done something earlier, saved him from some of that torture. I just feel so awful."

"You did what you could. Christ, you were twelve, remember?"

"I know, but. . ." He looked off, not finishing his thought.

Moving over to him, Nichelle sat in his lap and wound her arms around him. She could see the tears in his eyes. "Don't blame yourself. If it wasn't for you, who knows what would have happened to him?"

"I can't get that picture out of my head. And I know this one is probably mild compared to what else there is."

"Are you going to tell James?"

"Absolutely not. He'd go over there right now and try to kill Perry with his bare hands. James is a nice, calm guy almost all the time, but if he saw this. . . It's better he doesn't know."

"What's next?" she said.

"I'm trying to get exclusive rights to all of it. I don't know what it'll cost, but if I can, I'll pay it."

"What makes you think he won't sell those again? Especially if he believes now that they're even more valuable."

"I'm trying to think of a way. Nothing comes to mind just yet."

"You'll make it work," she said, settling against him. "I'm sorry you had to see that."

He kissed Nichelle while he rubbed her back. "Yeah, me too."

"I'm still up for the insulin overdose. In case you're interested."

"Thanks, but hopefully this other plan will work out instead,"

• • • • • •

Later that evening, Finch messaged Perry back.

—*Exactly what I was looking for. How many items?*

—*Three hundred. Give or take.*

Finch swallowed, feeling almost faint, but he continued on.

—*Still or video?*

—*Both.*

—*How much?*

—*Let's say twenty thousand for the set.*

—*Way too much. Besides, how can you guarantee exclusivity? I need reassurances.*

—*I'll think on it.*

—*And reconsider the price. Or maybe I need to consider another subject. Payment method?*

—*Bitcoin. Later.*

Finch closed the laptop. He could handle the full cost of purchasing the photos from his savings, but he didn't want to give Perry the impression he was desperate to get David's files. If he did, the price would surely go up.

• • • • • •

Perry replied to Finch the next day. Finch figured the old man wanted to make sure he was still interested.

—*Okay, for you, fifteen.*

—*I was thinking eight max.*

—*Be serious.*

—I am.

—Maybe we're in different leagues.

—I need a best and final.

As Finch waited, the reply came trickling back.

—Twelve. Take it or leave it.

—Way high, but that's what I want. I assume the quality is all there. Otherwise, I'll be disappointed, understand me? And I don't like being disappointed. Now, what about that exclusivity matter?

—I'll send instructions.

Finch watched his laptop's keylogger spyware carefully. Perry was accessing his cryptocurrency account to check on the balance. Apparently, he had moved his cold wallet into an exchange to facilitate the upcoming transfer. Now Finch had his crypto vault location and password. He would clean Perry's crypto account out as soon as the sale was complete. The question now would be if Perry went back to the bank and removed all of David's information from the external hard drive, or instead left it for a future sale. That would verify if he was serious about the exclusive. Time would tell.

Exhausted by what he had seen and learned today, Finch went to bed early. He kissed Nichelle goodnight and headed for the bedroom. Sleep, however, didn't come, as he internally debated differing possibilities and unexpected outcomes. She came to bed much later and was quickly asleep. Finch turned over and over, fighting various battles in his head, working through options. It was early morning before he settled down enough to doze off.

53

The morning after the funeral, Finch escorted Nichelle to the police station to talk to the detective investigating David's death. She wanted James to go with her, but he was committed to a client meeting, so Finch volunteered instead. Their trip to the station took place while exchanging only scraps of dialogue, Finch only replying to her when she asked random questions. In a way, that suited Nichelle fine. She wasn't sure what she thought of Finch, but he wasn't getting high marks for friendliness. She wondered, as she often had, what her dead husband had seen in this man of so few words.

Detective Mills met them in the lobby and escorted Finch and Nichelle back to his office. Mills was maybe fifty-five, slightly overweight and sporting a fringe of brown hair circling a tanned dome. His suit, Nichelle thought, looked like a mall special. She should know. That's the only kind David ever bought.

Once they took their seats, Mills shut the door.

"There isn't a lot left to take care of," he said, "but I wanted to bring you up to date. I know this has been difficult for you, Mrs. Perry. If you don't want to go over this now, please say so."

"I need to get this over with," she said, then signaled with her thumb. "This is Mr. Finch. He was David's best friend. He agreed to come with me today. I, um, I felt like I needed some support."

"Completely understand," the detective said. "Well, what happened is pretty straightforward. I think you know most of it. The man who robbed the store, a Maurice Johnson, had been in prison for robbery before and was out on parole."

"Don't they *care* about the people they release?" Nichelle said, instantly angry. "If he'd stayed where he belonged, my husband would be alive right now."

Mills held up a hand in defense. "Early release is up to the parole board. They never know for sure how people will behave once released, despite what the potential parolees say at their hearings. Johnson promised to go straight, but robbing was what he knew, so I guess he fell back on his old occupation. It happens. Our job is to catch the criminals. After that, it's out of our hands."

"Always someone else's problem," Nichelle said, folding her arms in disgust.

"What your husband did was brave, incredibly brave, Mrs. Perry. I want to say that everyone here at the station is a great admirer of his courage. Most people would never have intervened to save that little girl. Your husband's a hero, Mrs. Perry. I want you to understand that. The department's going to issue a commendation for him, at a public ceremony. I hope you can attend and accept."

"So he's a hero," she said, frustration building in her voice. "And now he's dead."

The detective glanced from Nichelle to Finch, who only raised an eyebrow.

"Anyway, as you know, Johnson fled the scene and was stopped for speeding several miles away. He resisted arrest, and after a verbal confrontation he pointed his weapon at the officers and fired. They responded and Johnson was killed in the exchange."

"Were any of the officers hurt?" Nichelle said.

"No, Johnson apparently wasn't a good shot."

"Except that he managed to kill my husband with a single bullet."

Mills took a deep breath. "It was close range, so. . ."

Finch spoke up. "You have statements from all the witnesses, correct?"

"Yes."

"May I see them?"

After rifling through his file, the detective produced several documents and handed them over. "Something in particular you're looking for?"

"No," Finch said. "Just wanted to clarify a few things."

Nichelle stood up. "If you'll excuse me, I don't think I need to hear anymore." Both of the men stood.

Finch said, "We can leave whenever you want."

She glared at him. "Take your time, Finch. I'll be waiting in the lobby." With that, she huffed out of the office and headed down the hall.

After she left, Finch said, "I was a better friend to David than to his wife."

Mills nodded. "Understood."

Finch speed-read the notes. Most of it seemed about the same as reported in the news. "Did Johnson say anything about what prompted him to shoot David? I know they were arguing over the man trying to take the girl for a hostage, but at what point did he pull the trigger?"

"Funny you should ask," Mills said. "When Johnson was stopped, he got out of the car with his hands up, still holding his pistol. He apparently thought they were stopping him for the robbery and not for speeding. He said right off that Mr. Perry grabbed his gun and pulled on it, that it went off accidentally. Said it wasn't his fault." Mills shook his head. "We went back and reviewed the convenience store footage. Mr. Perry's hand did touch the barrel of the gun, but he was obviously just trying to move it out of the way. That's when Johnson fired the shot." Another shake of Mills' head. "Typical criminal. Blame the victim."

"Do you have the officer's statements in the file?"

Mills dug some more and handed over the paperwork. The statements were brief but concise. Finch read through them several times.

Mills said, "Look, Johnson had a long record. The officers did society a favor by getting rid of a scumbag like that. I'm really sorry your friend had to be the one who didn't make it."

Handing the paperwork back, Finch said, "I know you see a lot of things that aren't fair."

"Curse of this job."

"Thanks for your time, Detective."

"Sure thing. Tell Mrs. Perry we're all sorry for her loss. If we had more people like her late husband, the world would be a lot better place. We'll be contacting her later on about the award ceremony."

"Will do."

Finch picked up Nichelle from the lobby.

She wasn't particularly friendly. "Find out what you wanted?" she said, her tone hostile.

"Sorry if I offended you. That wasn't my intention. I only wanted a better explanation of what happened."

"Not that it changes the outcome," she said as he held the front door open for her.

"No, it doesn't. You lost a husband, and I lost my best friend."

She softened after that and hooked her arm in Finch's as they headed for the car. "I'm sorry, Finch, I was only thinking of myself. I know you're hurting, too."

He reached over and touched her hand, unsurprised by his intense reaction to touching Nichelle, the woman he had always... Stop it, *stop* it, he told himself. You can't be thinking those thoughts.

"The detective said to tell you again how brave David was, and that if the world had more like him, it would be a much better place."

She said, "Maybe that's some consolation."

"Plus, he said again that they want you to attend the award ceremony. I'm sure Davie could come too. I don't know if that would help or hurt. Your choice."

"I'll think about it." With that remark, she let out a long sigh, her hurt rumbling out of her.

"I know we discussed this yesterday with James, but I want to make sure you're okay with me staying at the house and fixing things up. Is that still alright? If you don't want me to keep at it, please say so. I'll understand if you don't."

She thought about his concern as they neared her car. "Don't think I don't appreciate your offer. The house really needs some work."

"I'll try not to be any trouble," he said. "I promise to keep out of your way."

She mumbled her thanks as he opened the door and she slid in. It was clear she was distracted.

Once they were both in the car, he said, "I can only guess how awful this is for you."

Nichelle turned her head and looked out of the side window. "You know, David always had a troubled life. There were lots of things he wouldn't discuss with me. Things about his past, situations he found himself in. We fought about that. Often. Like the day he was killed. He got this phone call and went outside so I couldn't hear. It was obvious the call made him very upset. Then he called someone else. When he finally come back in, he had this wild look in his eyes. I'd never seen him like that. I insisted he tell me what was going on, but he refused. As he was leaving, I was angry and yelled at him. I'll never forgive myself for that."

"Don't beat yourself up. We all say things we regret. In any other circumstance, he would have come back home and you would have patched things up. There's no way you would have known that day would turn out any differently."

"Yes, but if I hadn't been such a bitch about it—"

"*Please* don't do this," he said. "David wouldn't want you to." As she turned to him, Finch could see the tears tracing rivulets down her cheeks. "Don't cry. Please."

Nichelle clinched her fists. "I'm so damn mad about all this, and yet I feel so guilty. I should have been a better wife, but I wasn't. Oh, Finch, what am I going to do?"

She seemed on the point of collapse, so he reached out for her and she fell into his arms. He held her tight, feeling her shake as she sobbed, the thrill of touching her subsumed by the guilt of wanting her. "We'll figure this out. You and me and James. We'll make it work. You'll see. There are better times ahead."

"How is that possible?" she said through her tears.

"Things change, Nichelle. They always do."

She pushed him away, abruptly sitting up and scrubbing away the wetness on her face. "I can't *do* this. I can't keep feeling sorry for myself. I have Davie to think of. I have to be strong for him."

"There's nothing wrong with feeling sad for what you've lost," he said.

She gave him an angry glance. "Oh, really? You haven't lost a spouse, have you? Don't tell me how I should feel."

"You're right. I haven't."

"Let's go home," she said, her determination resurfacing. "I've got things I need to do."

"Sure."

They drove home in silence.

Once inside the house, Finch said, "Give me a list of what I need to fix. I'll get started on it today."

"I'll do it later." She headed for her bedroom and shut the door.

Finch went to her door, his hand on the knob, trying to think of a way, words to say, to comfort her. He could hear her crying inside. Placing his forehead against the door, he knew he was helpless to ease her pain. Stepping back, he meandered down the hall.

Stopping by the kitchen sink for a drink of water, Finch looked out of the window. The house next door was like this one, with trim that needed painting. That was one thing he could do for Nichelle, he decided, before she produced an official list. He would go buy some paint and get started today. That would keep him outside, out of her hair, for several days. Davie was over at a friend's house now and would need picking up in half an hour. He could take care of that, too, but he would need to inform Nichelle first. She was in a surly mood, but it was understandable. The full impact of her husband's loss had hit her. In a few days, perhaps she might feel better. By then, it would be time for Finch to leave. He wondered if he would ever see Nichelle and her son again. If nothing else, he understood what had really happened to his friend. He knew David too well and sensed his intense desperation after he hung up from hearing the threats from Jackie. Finch was the only one who knew enough to piece together all the events. His conclusion, he knew, was something he would never reveal. To the public and his family. David died a hero.

As he continued to stare out of the window, Finch thought back on all of his efforts to help David. Despite everything he had tried, his friend was gone. Perhaps this was the way it was always going to end. Maybe all that effort did nothing but postpone the ultimate end. Why did bad things need to keep happening to good people? Finch didn't know the answer. Perhaps no one knew.

His thoughts turned back to Jackie Weir. What a conniving bitch. Though she hadn't wanted David dead, in which case her potential cash machine would be gone, she had no qualms squeezing him to support her lifestyle. It was her heedless self-absorption that created the chaos that cost David his life, which wouldn't have happened except for her attempt to manipulate him. Jackie had always been that way, needy and aloof, selfish, heedless of the consequences of her actions. If she wasn't James' sister, Finch would already be at work on a retribution plan for her as well.

The focus of his energies, though, was David's dad. Tomorrow, he and James were meeting to discuss exactly what to do to Perry. The opportunity to punish the old man for the ongoing ruination of his son's life gave Finch some solace. And Nichelle? It was clear he wouldn't have a future with her. Between her re-energized loyalty to David and her apparent indifference to Finch, no way that would ever work out. As time went on, her remembrance of David's virtues would likely increase as the recollection of her husband's faults simultaneously receded, and his final selfless act would become a salient part of the family lore. Finch sighed, accepting the inevitability, the unfairness, the cruelty of life. In a few days, it would be time for him to move on. By then, he'd be ready.

He left the house and headed to his Subaru. He had paint to buy.

54

Finch transferred twelve thousand dollars into a digital wallet account and stored his private alpha-numeric key, along with a backup, on a flash drive. He was ready to complete the transaction with Perry.

—*Okay, I have the funds available.*

—*Ready when you are.*

—*Still concerned over exclusivity.*

—*Guaranteed. You'll get a dropbox file location with a onetime key. Don't screw that up. It only works once. Instructions on transferring the funds will arrive first. Enjoy.*

—*Nice doing business with you.*

Finch received a message with Perry's crypto address, then transferred the funds. He hoped that the old man wasn't conning him, but figured that if Perry had been a clearinghouse for child porn for years, some honor among thieves was assumed. Sure enough, shortly afterward, Finch received his instructions and downloaded the digital files. After checking the size of them, he felt he had likely purchased the real thing. The only way to verify this was to look at the information he'd purchased.

Finch closed his laptop instead. He couldn't bear to open any of the files. He knew if he did, he would never forget what he saw. After transferring all the David files to a thumb drive, he went into the garage, found a hammer, and shattered the drive into tiny pieces.

Now it was time for the next part of his plan. He would watch Perry's laptop and hard drive access and see if the buy was really exclusive. For now, Perry removed the David files from the laptop. But would Perry access the external hard drive and make those same files available for sale again to another customer? Finch expected the betrayal, which would then trigger his private plan to terrify the old man.

Nichelle came into the dining room and asked what he was doing. He told her about what had happened, and how that made him feel.

"Let's go for a walk, okay? It'll help to get you out of the house."

Finch agreed. Walking helped his injured back while also gradually rebuilding his endurance. He still had twinges, and maybe always would, but he could see a future now where most of his activities, within reason, were unhindered.

As they strolled down the sidewalk, holding Nichelle's hand, Finch said, "This is the life I've always wanted."

"Yes," she said, giving him a quick kiss. "Me too."

•　•　•　•　•

After Perry's next trip to the bank, Finch again accessed the laptop. He wasn't surprised to find that the computer now contained the very files that Perry sold Finch and had promised to delete. That meant he had no qualms about taking the next step.

It took Nichelle a while, but after more than an hour's work, Finch's appearance completely changed. He now sported a full beard with his hair dyed almost black. She took his photo, then he donned the clothes they purchased at a thrift store. A bucket hat completed his outfit. The change in appearance was all Nichelle's idea. He was soon ready to visit the bank, carrying in his pocket the newly cut and number-stamped safe deposit key he had carefully crafted from a brass blank.

Nichelle parked the Subaru a block away to avoid any bank cameras. Finch got out and made his way slowly down the sidewalk, using a cane to exaggerate his disability. It wasn't difficult for Finch to remember how to do this, considering his painful recovery.

Once in the safe deposit area, he stopped at the desk of a different attendant, avoiding the woman he had talked with earlier. Even though he regretted exploiting her naivete, she had come in handy. After she clicked on a can't-miss exotic vacation sweepstakes offer, his spear-phishing program accessed her bank credentials. That allowed Finch to paste David's name, accompanied by Finch's signature, onto the safe deposit box's electronic card file. Immediately afterward, he removed the illicit program. Hopefully, no one would remember that a local man with the same name had died in an armed robbery. He knew that using David's name was a risk, but, somehow, what he had done seemed fitting.

"Looks like Mr. Jones was just in here the other day," the attendant said. "I see you have the same last name. Are you maybe his son?"

Finch said, "Yes. Dad forgot to get something while he was in here before, so he sent me."

"May I see some ID?"

Finch handed over David's still-current driver's license, now updated with Finch's new photo. His temporary hair color matched David's license description, while the rest of his own characteristics were close enough to David to pass ordinary scrutiny.

"Thank you," the attendant said as she handed back the ID. "Please sign here." After comparing signatures, she said, "This way please."

After Finch presented the key, the attendant opened the safe deposit box. Finch retrieved the hard drive and slipped it into the empty bag he carried. On the way out, he mumbled his thanks and avoided glancing up at the ceiling security camera. He spent parts of the previous days framing different scenarios in his mind, about being discovered, having to make a run for it, maybe someone dislodging his disguise. None of that came true. He simply walked out of the bank. It all went according to plan.

Once back inside the Subaru, Finch pulled off his disguise and started changing clothes while Nichelle took a route home through low-traffic residential streets peripheral to downtown. It took some time to shed his disguise, as contortions necessary for removing and putting on clothes in the front seat of a vehicle didn't square well with an injured back. Finally finished, he put the old garments into a bag they had brought and dropped the items into a homeless shelter donation box. They soon discarded the cane and beard in a trash bin behind a decrepit department store. Once home, Nichelle washed out the hair dye, letting his true light brown return.

"What are you going to do with the external drive?" she said.

"Give the case a good cleaning, inside and out, then send it to the cops. In the mail."

"Do we need to re-do your disguise? In case there's a security camera at the post office?"

"No, I'll pick an outside box without cameras."

"Then what?" she said.

"Mr. Perry and his clients will get a message they certainly won't care for."

"What about the money?"

"I'll clean out his account first, get back my previous 'investment.' You can have the rest. It will set you up for a very long time."

Nichelle frowned. "It's dirty money that came from a lot of suffering. Let's donate it to someplace that takes care of abused children."

"You sure?" he said.

"Aren't you?"

He smiled. "We think alike."

• • • • • •

Later that day, Perry's money disappeared from his crypto account. Finch returned his own funds plus established a new, separate account for the thirty grand that Perry had extorted from David. Next, he sent a notification, along with access information, of the availability of the rest of the money to the city's Center for Abused Children. Based on what he could see of their financials online, these funds would pay for a year or more of the center's entire operation.

Finch retrieved the list of Perry's clients he had stolen from the laptop and sent every one of them a common message.

—*To my many clients. I have recently had a personal epiphany. I deeply regret my past involvement in the abuse of children and the distribution of pornography. To atone for my sins, I will turn over all the child porn files that I have to the authorities. I will also include a detailed list of all my past and present clients and their purchases. I hope you will use this opportunity to turn yourselves into local law enforcement before this information becomes public. Toward that end, I am giving each of you four days before I take action.*

Finch knew that from now on, things would likely not go well for Perry. Next, he scanned Perry's laptop and permanently deleted the newly reinstalled folder that contained David's material. When that was complete, he sent Perry a secure message.

—*You lied to me. The images are not exclusive.*

—*Of course they are.*

—*I know better. You kept them to sell to others. I warned you. There will be consequences.*

Finch logged off, leaving Perry in the midst of typing a reply. Let him wonder about the retribution. Soon, Perry's many clients would start contacting him, demanding that he stop outing them. Finch relished the fear that the old pornographer would experience at getting caught. To try and keep Perry from closing up shop and running, Finch sent him an anonymous email:

—*We have verified that someone you contacted via email has hacked your account and sent your client list a spam announcement. Contact your clients and let them all know this is a false message used only to solicit future illicit payments. Signed, your cyber friends.*

Finch hoped that email would keep Perry busy dismissing Finch's threat of exposing the old man's clients. All he needed was a few days.

Later the same day, Finch stopped by an outdoor package drop without security cameras and left the hard drive, covered in brown paper wrapping and lots of stamps. The detailed instructions inside would make it simple for the Sexual Crimes Division to retrieve the images. He had also included an alphabetized list of Perry's clients and a confession. Finch made sure and put Perry's return address on the label.

Back home, Finch updated Nichelle. They speculated on whether or not Perry would rush to the safe deposit box to retrieve the hard drive. If so, Finch could only imagine the old man's dismay when he found it empty and was told that his own dead son had recently opened his box.

Finch placed a call to James. "James? Finchie here. I have news about our special friend."

"Good news?" James said.

"For us, not him. It's now a developing hurricane of shit headed toward our least favorite human being. Stay tuned."

Finch could hear the excitement rise in James' voice.

"Super. Can we have lunch later and discuss it? I'm headed out of town right now."

"Of course."

55

After the doorbell signaled a visitor, Finch headed to the front door and opened it. It was Detective Mills.

"Oh, Mr. Finch. I was expecting Mrs. Perry."

"We recently got married. She's Mrs. Finch now."

The detective raised an eyebrow. "Guess she changed her mind about you."

"Looks like. Come on in."

Finch led the detective to the kitchen. "Get you any coffee? I was thinking of making some for myself."

"Sure," Mills said. "That would be great."

Nichelle headed in from the back room, then abruptly stopped, startled to see the detective in her house.

"Mrs. Perry? I mean, Mrs. Finch. Sorry if I surprised you," Mills said.

"What's happened?" she said. "More news about David?"

"Not exactly. Another matter. I'd like to talk to you both, if you two have a minute."

Finch said, "Fine with me."

Nichelle nodded before sitting in one of the kitchen table's chairs. Mills dropped into the adjacent one.

"There have been some recent developments. Disturbing ones, I'm afraid," Mills said.

"Oh?" Finch said. "How does that affect us?"

Mills turned to Nichelle. "Your late husband's father was found dead in his house yesterday. What was left of him. He was murdered, then the house set on fire."

Nichelle and Finch looked at each other.

"That sounds awful. What happened?" she said. "We haven't heard about anything like that on the news."

"We've deliberately kept it quiet, out of the media, for now. The official story is that it was a kitchen fire. Later on, there will be an official announcement." He paused to glance at each of them. "Either of you close with Mr. Perry?"

Nichelle looked over at Finch, who was busying himself with the coffeepot. "No, not at all. David and his father were estranged. He wouldn't talk about why."

Finch spoke next. "I was his best friend, Detective. I knew he had issues with his dad. Back when we were kids, I suspected it was some kind of abuse, but he wasn't specific. Eventually, the family of another friend of ours took David in. He lived with them until he graduated from high school."

"When was that?" Mills said. "When he left Mr. Perry's house for good?"

"We were twelve. It was in middle school."

"I see."

"What does this have to do with David's father being murdered?" Nichelle said.

"We can discuss that in a minute. You said you weren't close, but did either of you ever contact Mr. Perry? Maybe go by and see him?"

Finch and Nichelle exchanged glances.

Finch said, "I went by once, with my friend James, after David's funeral. We wanted to come in and talk about his relationship with David, see what he had to say. He wouldn't let us in, though. Threatened us with a shotgun, matter of fact, if we didn't leave." Finch shrugged. "So we did."

"That squares," Mills said.

"With what?"

"There's a kid lives in the neighborhood. Rides his bike around a lot. Pretty sharp from what I can tell. We ended up interviewing him, along with his parents. He's the one who first saw the house fire."

"Fortunate," Finch said, relieved that his solo visit's outcome was corroborated. "I remember now talking to a boy on the sidewalk. Said his mother told him to stay away from Mr. Perry."

"Good advice," Mills said.

"Oh?" Nichelle said. "Tell us what happened."

"One other thing. Mrs. Finch, have you ever been inside his house?"

Nichelle caught Finch's slight nod to suggest she respond correctly. "One time. I was out getting groceries and stopped by on the way home. On a whim, I guess. I was curious about a man I'd seldom seen, and how he lived. After he let me in, I looked around his place, then said maybe we should all get together. That's all. He said he wanted me to send my son over, unchaperoned. I had a creepy feeling about that, so I left. I never went back."

"That squares too." he said.

"What do you mean?"

"Mr. Perry had a hidden surveillance system installed in his house. Lots of tiny cameras all over the place, which recorded video and audio. We discovered the system when we were searching the house after the fire was out. Then we tracked down who was storing the video files and got a court order to examine them. We only have the last thirty days. It included your visit, Mrs. Finch. Mr. Finch's was too far back."

"Can you tell us what happened now?" Finch said. He headed for the table with three empty cups. After setting them down, he stood behind Nichelle, his hand on her shoulder.

"Yes, of course, just tying up loose ends first. Mr. Perry was murdered, like I said before."

"You know who did it?" Finch said.

"It was early morning. Three men dressed in black entered the house and assaulted Mr. Perry. Professionals, based on what they did to him. We haven't identified the culprits yet, but we're working on that. The murder itself was, um, rather horrific. He was tortured and then. . . Well, I don't need to go into the details."

Finch and Nichelle exchanged glances.

"Do you know why he was killed?"

"Turns out he was a child pornographer."

"How do you know that?" Nichelle said, acting shocked.

"Fortunately, we've come into possession of detailed information recently sent to the police. The package included an external hard drive and a client list. We're not exactly sure of what to make of that situation. It seems quite out of character that Perry would suddenly incriminate himself like that, but a letter inside contained his written confession." Mills shrugged, then continued. "The murderers took his laptop and ransacked the office, apparently looking for incriminating evidence. Before they left, they opened the filing cabinet drawers and sprayed the office area with an accelerant, then set the fire. If it hadn't been for the neighborhood kid seeing the smoke, the house would have been a total loss."

The coffeepot had finished making, so Finch poured each of them a cup. "Need any cream or sugar?"

"Black is fine," Mills said. "Seems that he also sent out an email outing his clients and gave them several days to turn themselves in. Likely one of them apparently didn't appreciate the reveal, so they sent in a hit team."

Finch said, "How would these people know where Perry lived? I mean, if he was doing all this illegal stuff, wouldn't he have concealed his identity?"

"Our IT guys say the internet's a powerful search tool, if you know how to use it."

"But if these people knew Perry had already confessed and sent you the proof, why kill him if the information was already out there? Revenge?"

"Perry sent an email to all of 'clients,' saying they had four days to turn themselves in before he sent the information to the authorities. We figure one of his contacts got scared they were about to be outed, so they sent the killers to head it off and cover things up. Now, here's the part we can't figure. The postmark on the package was the same day the warning email was sent out. That means he'd already sent us the list. There was no four-day delay like the email promised."

Finch said, "Sounds odd, but maybe he was figuring in several days of delay before you got the package."

"Perhaps," Mills said, but his face remained skeptical. "Maybe he was toying with his clients. Anyway, with the list of names and what he'd sold to each of them, all we had to do was follow the trail. Perry's murder accomplished nothing."

"Seems odd," Nichelle said. "Him doing it that way."

Mills nodded. "Maybe he had a sudden attack of a guilty conscience. Hard to say, really. From what we've determined, Perry has been at this for years. Then, all of a sudden. . ." The detective stopped talking and took a drink from his cup. "Who really knows what motivates people? Say, this is good stuff. Thanks."

"So, this thing with Perry was a complete surprise to you guys?" Finch said.

"No, we've suspected him for a while. His ISP notified us he was using the Tor browser a lot."

"The what?" Finch said. "I'm sorry, you lost me there."

"It's a way to access the dark web, so people who use that software don't arouse suspicion."

"I see," Finch said, letting confusion show on his face.

Mill continued. "Our Sexual Crimes Unit has suspected him for a while, but we could never come up with any corroborating evidence. Our investigators contacted him several times, clandestinely, and offered to buy what he was selling, but he didn't bite. The old man was pretty careful." Mills took another drink before adding, "I guess not careful enough in the end."

"What happens now?" Finch said.

"It'll take a while to get all the paperwork done, but likely the city will demolish what's left of the house. Public nuisance kind of thing. If Perry didn't have a will, then your son will inherit, Mrs. Finch. If he doesn't want the lot, then I suspect the property will be sold off. Victim restitution kind of thing."

"That's fine," Nichelle said. "We don't want any part of that."

"Funny thing. The local center for abused kids received a big donation right about the same time. Reported it to us, since they weren't sure if they could keep it. It was a crypto transaction, you know, the type that criminals use to hide their funds."

"Who sent it?" Finch said.

"We don't know. The donor was anonymous and the transaction's untraceable. Anyway, the judge said they can keep the money, assuming no one turns up claiming it was stolen from them."

"You think it was Mr. Perry's money?" Nichelle said. "I mean, it seems like a coincidence. Time-wise."

"Probably, but we can't be sure. Well, I need to get going. Thought I'd stop by and bring you up to date." He took a last long drink of his coffee. "Wish the station had stuff this good."

"I'll get you some to take with you," Nichelle said, hopping up.

At the door, Mills, sipping from his paper cup, turned to Finch and Nichelle. "What is it you do for a living, Mr. Finch?"

"Construction work. At least I did. I had a back injury from a fall while I was working in Miami. Nichelle here nursed me back to health." He put his arm around her. "For some stupid reason, she eventually decided she loved me."

Nichelle beamed back at him.

"Nice to see you two are getting along. By the way, either of you dabble in computers?"

Finch said, "I can do the basics with office software. And I can play games. That's about it. Not much call for computer expertise when you're spending your days swinging a hammer."

"I'm not much better than a novice," Nichelle said.

"You going back to construction, Mr. Finch?"

"No. The doctor says my back wouldn't hold up if I did. I'll need to find another trade, since my workers' comp is about to run out."

Mills nodded. "Thanks again for the coffee. I need to be going."

• • • • • •

After the detective left, Finch and Nichelle sat down at the kitchen table, nursing the coffee remaining in their own cups.

"Think he suspects us?" Nichelle said.

Finch shook his head. "Not really. He needed to rule out relatives killing the old fuck. Good thing we told him the truth about the house visits."

"Yeah. Now what?"

"We go on with our lives."

"Do you feel bad? About what happened?"

Finch said, "I guess I should, but I think he got what was coming to him. We didn't do it ourselves, only set him up. How do *you* feel?"

"I've thought about this a lot. I know what I said I'd do before, about giving him an overdose of insulin, but if it came right down to it, I'm not sure if I could have done it." Her voice trailed off.

"It's fine, baby," he said. "It didn't come to that."

"Yes, thank God for your plan." Elbows propped up on the counter, Nichelle held her mug with both hands and considered her next question. "Can they trace the money you bought David's files with?"

"The transaction occurred in an old bank account I had several states over. I took twelve thousand out, then put twelve back in. A short-term use of money, that's all. The account's closed now. Give me some credit, babe. Also, I got back the thirty grand that he extorted from David. It's in a separate account, available whenever you need it."

"And Perry's laptop?"

"I put a facial recognition program on it. Unless the camera sees Perry's face, even if they have the password, it erases the hard drive when it boots up. It acts like it's taking a while to start while it's deleting all the files instead. They won't recover anything."

She got up and stood beside him, pointing her finger toward his legs. "I need some lap."

Finch scooted the chair out far enough for her to sit down. He put his arms around her waist while hers encircled his neck.

"You like sitting on my lap, don't you?" he said.

"Of course. I get my back rubbed, plus lots of kisses," she said.

"I like that too," he said as she put her head on his shoulder.

"Computers, huh?" she said. "Maybe you should look into that."

"Might be a good idea," he said before giving her a big kiss.

56

Finch and James picked a table near the corner of the restaurant's patio, a distance away from the remnants of the lunch crowd. The flowers in the encircling stonework were all in full bloom, a riot of yellow, red, and white crowding in against each other, their open faces searching for the warm summer sun. A slight breeze came up, softly caressing the petals as the wind moved past. Soon it would be fall and likely too cold to partake of the same experience, but today was glorious. Finch was bringing James up to date on the Perry situation.

"I'm impressed, Finchie," James said, reaching for his drink. "Very nice job. Still, I hated to miss caving his head in."

"Sorry about that, but the professionals apparently did a more thorough job making Perry's last few minutes on earth quite miserable. If we'd gone in and killed him like we talked about, or if Nichelle had gotten involved and given him an overdose and the cops had found the security cameras, we'd all be sitting in jail right now awaiting trial. Sometimes, you get lucky when you don't get what you want. I think we're pretty fortunate how things eventually turned out."

James said, "Yours was the best approach. Still, I wish he knew, before they killed him, that it was you who turned him in."

"The people who count know," Finch said. "Besides, imagine the terror of him realizing that someone was inside all of his shit, stealing his money, and ratting him out to his clients and the cops. I think my bogus email about this phantom security team discovering the hack of his account gave him a false sense of security, to convince him he didn't need to leave town immediately."

"If he'd left and gone into hiding, I imagine tracking him down would've been nearly impossible."

"Maybe. I'd have stayed after him, though. Besides, by then he would've been broke and a fugitive from the law. Anyway, it worked out. Things sometimes do, especially when you make your own luck." After a bit of silence, Finch said, "How's your business going?"

"Quite well, as a matter of fact. We've gotten several large accounts recently, which means we'll be filing with the SEC soon. It's required when we reach a hundred million in assets under management."

"Impressive."

"The good news is a few of those account transfers are from my old employer."

"That should piss him off."

"It has."

"I've been meaning to ask. Would your new firm be willing to take on our small account? Mine and Nichelle's? I know what we have isn't much compared to your typical investor, so. . ."

James thought for a moment. "No."

Finch nodded his acceptance of the rejection. It wasn't for him to dispute James' motives.

"You need a lot more assets than I think you both have for that fee structure to make any sense. But there's an alternative."

"What's that?"

"I take care of your investments by myself, personally. For free."

Finch said, "No way. That's not fair to you."

"That's the only way I would do it. You're my best friend, Finchie. I'd be honored to help you and your family."

Finch protested, causing James to hold up his hand. "Shut up, buddy. That's the deal. Take it or leave it."

"I believe you've made me an offer I can't refuse," Finch said.

"I hope so. Otherwise, I'll have to go see Nichelle, have her knock some sense into you."

Finch shook his head and chuckled. "I don't think that will be necessary."

"You know, you two make a perfect couple."

"What do you mean?"

James turned to his friend. "Don't get all modest on me. I've never seen you both any happier."

"That's true on my part. I hope Nichelle feels the same way."

"I ran into her the other day at the grocery store. We had a long discussion in the ice cream aisle."

"Sneaky," Finch said. "She didn't tell me."

"She practically glowed when she talked about you. For some crazy reason, she loves you, man. A lot. Personally, I can't see the attraction."

Finch fiddled with his drink. "Thanks, James, for telling me that. It means a lot, hearing that from you."

"You deserve it, buddy."

"Speaking of women, how's your sister, Jackie?"

"Not so good. She's having a lot of financial problems."

"That right?"

"She has this expectation of a lifestyle she believes she's entitled to. After her divorce from Randall, she didn't cut back and insisted on keeping the big house, which came with a lot of expenses. Jeanette and I were on the same track until we made the decision to change our lifestyle. As a family, we're a lot closer than before."

"So, she's short of money?" Finch expected as much. This confirmed Jackie's need to shake down David. He recalled his friend's desperate words of wondering how to cope with her demands, despairing of how he could ever make it work. If Jackie wasn't James' sister... Some things he knew he needed to let go. Jackie would eventually ruin herself.

"That's the picture I get. I told her she needed to sell the house, get something smaller, but she won't hear of it."

Finch nodded, thinking that sounded exactly like Jackie. "And your mom? She doing okay?"

"Remarried now, out in Florida, to a guy she met after Dad died. They travel a lot. She seems happy and content."

"Good for her," Finch said.

"You know, I told Jackie that Madison and I were going to expand our business, add another person. Asked if she might be interested in learning about investments, helping our clients." James grunted. "She said absolutely not, seeing as she had no interest in grubbing around in other people's money. Probably just as well. I don't think she and Madison would be very compatible. Jackie can't seem to get along with her own daughter, either."

"Oh?" Finch said. "Why not?"

"Hard to say. You can tell she's Randall's child because she really loves him. As far as Jackie, well, let's say the mother-daughter bond isn't very strong. I think as soon as Charlotte gets older and she and Randall think they can convince a judge, she'll be living with Randall instead. He's always wanted her full time. By the way, he got married to the woman he was seeing when he and Jackie broke up."

Finch thought about the certainty that Charlotte wasn't Randall's biological daughter. Even if Randall knew, Finch doubted it would make any difference in his attitude toward the girl. He knew he felt the same toward Davie. If Jackie brought that fact up during a custody battle, she would make a tactical error. He could see more downsides than up for revealing the affair with David, despite how she would frame the encounter. If Charlotte ended up with Randall, that would mean Jackie lost her child support. She would do everything she could to keep the cash coming in, regardless of how she felt about Charlotte. That confrontation should be interesting. He might even call Randall and offer to testify about what really happened. Likely the hint of an expose' would shut down Jackie's protests.

James continued. "I don't know what Jackie's going to do. She hasn't found a new man to latch onto. Maybe she needs to raise the age of prospective husbands."

"Think she'll do that?"

"Who knows?" James said. "I love her, but I know my sister. Jackie's always had a very high opinion of herself. When she was younger, her self-worth was wrapped up in how beautiful she was. Now she realizes she's not as attractive as she used to be. The last few years must've been hard for her."

"Something I need to tell you. David made me promise I'd never tell you this, but I think you need to know. He was afraid you'd hate him for it."

"What did he do?" James said.

"He and Jackie had an affair."

"No shit?" James thought over the revelation. "I suppose I'm not surprised. Who started it?"

"Jackie," Finch said.

"Not surprising. When did it start?"

Finch shifted in his chair. "How old is Charlotte?"

James' eyes widened. "You're shitting me."

"Nope."

"Charlotte's David's daughter?"

"Uh huh."

"Does Jackie know?"

Finch nodded. "David did a DNA test."

"How about Randall?"

"Not that I know of."

James stroked his chin. "How did David feel? About the affair? About Charlotte?"

"The affair broke up his marriage to Iris, but they kept it quiet. David believed Jackie began the affair so she could get pregnant. He was crazy about Charlotte, but Jackie withheld her on purpose, not letting him see her."

"That must have driven David insane."

"Yep," Finch said.

"I expect you know all the details?"

"Most of them, yes."

James considered asking the obvious, but then abandoned the idea. "I think I know enough. This is certainly a surprise."

"I wanted you to know. I hated keeping it from you."

"Jackie was hot for him in high school, but after he went to college, it cooled off. I remember, though, when David and Iris got married. She looked really pissed off at the wedding, even though she was married to Randall by then. Looking back, it all fits together."

Finch agreed. "I think she wanted them both, Randall and David, as long as it was convenient."

James paused, thinking over what he'd heard. "Shit. I remember I told Nichelle that Iris was unstable and then one day decided to divorce David. Now I realize she had a reason. A good reason."

Finch changed the subject. "Nichelle and I are trying to get pregnant. We both want a child."

James said, "I think that would be *fantastic*!"

"We'll see if it happens. Not for lack of trying."

"Be patient. Things will work out," James said. "Finch a daddy. I'll have to think on that. Maybe the universe will explode."

"I think the universe will continue to expand, regardless," Finch said. "Look, I better get going. Nichelle and I have to run some errands today. But it was great to see you."

"Sure. Any more info on the guys that whacked old man Perry?"

"No, but I hear there's a real shit show going on since someone mailed the cops a hard drive with all that porn on it. Along with names and addresses of all of Perry's clients."

James stroked his chin again. "Wonder who could have done that?"

"I'm sure I don't know," Finch said, then laughed. "I better hit the road."

•   •   •   •   •

In the parking lot, the men hugged before heading to their respective vehicles.

"Oh my God, you've washed your car," James said, pointing to Finch's Outback. "You ever going to get rid of that piece of shit?"

"If it makes you feel any better, that's where Nichelle and I are going. Shopping for a replacement. I'm sticking with Subarus, though. She wants a red one. I'm not sure if I can handle that color or not."

"She'll look great driving it," James said. "You, I'm not so sure. Fucking amazing how a good woman turns a man around, straightens him out."

"Isn't it?" Finch said, grinning.

57

Finch and Nichelle were lying in bed, doing their customary talk-through as the day wound down, discussing the things important to each of them. She cherished this time as a welcome compliment to the morning sex that had also become their routine. They reserved evenings for the more serious conversations, when each felt the soft glow of another day of being together. Nichelle knew that as they became more and more familiar with each other, the length and frequency of these conversations would decrease, but for now, it was a special pleasure.

"How's your back, baby?" she said. They'd extended the walking distance to two miles today, which was a serious effort for Finch.

"A little sore, but I'll get used to it. I know it helps in the long run." He put his hand behind his head. "I remember the days when a two-mile walk would have been nothing. Sorry you ended up stuck with a crippled guy."

"I'm not sorry," she said, edging toward him. "Without you getting hurt, Davie and I might never have had you with us."

Finch pulled her closer, kissing the top of her head. "Maybe so. Life's full of missed opportunities."

"I don't know if you would've ever admitted your feelings to me otherwise."

"Guess some things turn out alright."

"Some do. Others, not so much."

"You're different than you used to be," he said.

"It's the hair. You probably think you're sleeping with a different woman."

Yesterday, instead of her traditional braids, Nichelle had opted for a new style. She had her hair washed and cut and came home with it in long, lustrous curls that formed a triangle between her shoulders and the top of her head. Time for a change, she said. The difference in her appearance was striking.

"No, what's different is inside you," he said. "You're a lot nicer than you used to be."

She dug her fingernail into his side until he begged for a reprieve.

"You saying I wasn't nice before?" she said.

"You were what I'd call determined," he said, favoring the spot on his ribs with a quick hand massage.

"What about you? Before, you'd hardly speak to anyone if you didn't have to. Now I can't get you to shut up sometimes."

"Guilty," he said. "That's what happens when I'm this happy. It's all your fault."

He turned on his side and put his hand below her navel, sliding a couple of fingers into the top of her pajama bottoms. He held it there.

"Thinking about a baby again?" she said.

"Yes."

Placing her hand on his, she said, "We need to be patient, Finchie. I'm older now, so I may not ovulate every month, and my eggs aren't so fresh as they used to be. And if I do get pregnant, it would probably be the last baby I'll ever have."

"I know, but I can't help thinking how wonderful it would be for you to have our child."

"We can't do much more than we are. I'm practically swimming in semen every morning."

"I'm doing my best," he said, kissing her.

"And I really appreciate that," she said, kissing him back.

"Maybe we should have sex less often from now on. You know, let me get my sperm count up. How about that?"

"I'll let you know when I need less loving from you."

He rubbed her belly some more. "My parents never had much money, even though they've always worked hard. There were six of us crammed into that little house. Lots of arguing and fighting between us kids, all strong personalities struggling for dominance. Our parents somehow survived all that. What was important was we knew they loved and supported each of us individually. I think if you had my baby, it would be maybe the most wonderful thing that ever happened to me. Other than having you and Davie already."

"Sweetheart, we need to be patient, okay? There are lots of reasons a couple doesn't get pregnant."

"I understand. Since tomorrow's Saturday, Davie will probably come visit us early, so we may need to skip our morning ritual."

"I know," she said. "He loves cuddling in our bed when he's not in school. Do you mind?"

"No, I love having him with us."

Living with you is just so damn *easy*, Nichelle thought. "I need to go to the bathroom. I'll be right back."

"Okay."

She swept the sheet aside, got up, and opened a dresser drawer. Pulling out a long t-shirt, her favorite sleepwear, she slipped it over her head. The real reason she headed to the bathroom was to do a pregnancy test. She had an odd feeling the last few days and remembered the same reaction when she was first pregnant with Davie. It could be a coincidence, but she had learned from her P.A. days to trust people when they said they felt off. In most cases, there was something actually going on, not their imagination working overtime.

After peeing on the stick and waiting to see if HCG was present, she checked the result. She was pregnant. She felt her heart leap into her throat.

Grabbing the test, she rushed back into the bedroom to tell Finch. He was already asleep, his eyes shut tight, mouth slightly open, coupled to smooth, regular breathing. The walk this afternoon had worn him out. She smiled to herself and returned the test to a bathroom cabinet drawer. Carefully slipping in bed next to him, she lifted her shirt, pressing her breasts against his bare back, then dropped her hand over his front and caressed him.

He awoke and reached back, feeling for her bottom. "Hi, there," he said.

"Would you like me to rub your head?" she said.

Finch confided in her that his favorite memory of his mother was sitting in her lap and having her rub his head when he was a child. That comfort was what he looked forward to if he was injured or unhappy, the solace of a mother's loving arms and undivided attention. Once she heard this, Nichelle immediately called his mother and got instructions on the exact way Finch liked his head rubbed. His mother laughed at the question. Then, after revealing the secret, she told her daughter-in-law how pleased it made her that a woman would care that much about making her son happy.

"What did I do to deserve this?" he said.

"I want to make you happy, is all." After propping up on her pillow, Nichelle pulled down her shirt and made room for Finch at her side. He lay beside her as she started rubbing his head.

"That feels so good," he murmured. "Maybe I should suck my thumb."

"Men," she said, chiding him. "You're all little boys inside." She bent and kissed the top of his head.

"I suppose you're right." He dropped his arm across her, closed his eyes, and settled in. "You're too good to me."

"It's only because I love you so much. Hush and let me do my thing."

Maybe she should have told him right then that she was pregnant, but she had already decided she would wait until tomorrow. Reaching down with her free hand, she touched his belly, resting on the slight protrusion he was now so worried about. Years of physical labor allowed him to remain the same size, but the lack of constant activity recently caused a modest weight gain, which appalled him. Nichelle's opinion was that his pooch was charming and reflective of the new Finchie. As she caressed him, he moved slightly and mumbled something. How different it was now, she thought, from the first time they slept together. Back then, he was alert to anything that disturbed his sleep, even her touching him on the shoulder.

She kissed him again, thinking about how lucky she was to have a man like him. So different from David, so generous, so trusting and open with her. She was still amazed at how much she loved Finch, and how easy their relationship had become, like he had always been there. She often wondered, after he told her about David's early history, how different David's personality would have been without that early trauma he was always fleeing from. Likely a completely different man. Such a waste.

Deep down, Nichelle knew that her marriage to David would never have last for much longer than the seven years it did. Despite them loving each other, David was too withdrawn, too secretive, too evasive for her to be satisfied with their marriage. The tension between them had been building for a long while, and it was only a matter of time before it boiled over. Only his death had stopped the progression toward a certain separation.

Her thoughts drifted back to the last time she saw David, so upset and distraught, but still he refused to tell her what was going on. There were two phone calls, she remembered. But what had happened? David never got that upset over work-related matters, so it had to be a personal crisis, details of which he refused to divulge. Who, or what, could have made that kind of impact? History proved there was no medical crisis, no death outside of his, nothing that major. So it had to be some kind of threat, an apprehension of terrible things to come. Who in his life could have caused such consternation? She thought back on the brief conversation she had with Iris after the funeral. There was only one answer to David's psychological distress—Jackie Weir. But what had she held over him? Finch had already told her that David knew Charlotte was his daughter. Perhaps it was the threatened disclosure of the old affair. Or perhaps she was withholding Charlotte from him as punishment, or maybe for leverage.

She let herself wonder, for the first time, if Jackie's conversation had somehow prompted David to sacrifice himself, then immediately rejected that notion. No, David was determined to protect children from abuse, and the gunman's behavior had triggered an automatic response in him. Her husband's action in protecting the child were automatic, nothing he could have controlled. He *was* a genuine hero. Of that, she was certain.

The recipient of the second phone call was also obvious. David must have called Finch as soon as he hung up from Jackie. He always turned to Finch, instead of her, when he was in serious trouble. That fact had angered Nichelle over the years she was married to David. What kind of husband tells his most intimate secrets to another man and shuts his wife out? That resentment transferred to Finch, part of the reason she originally wanted him out of her house. But it wasn't Finch's fault. Finch was foremost loyal to David, and would take any punishment required to maintain that relationship. She knew he was going to be the same way toward her and Davie. Without Finch, God knows what further horrors David would have experienced. She thought back to her earlier indifference to and dismissal of her future husband. If she only knew then what she now realized. Finch was a good man, a great husband, kind and loyal. He had done the best he could with David's demands for secrecy.

By now, Finch was asleep. His mother said rubbing his head always worked, and tonight was no exception. Nichelle kissed his head again and held him, marveling at how close she was to this man. Soon her belly would swell and she would have trouble fitting the length of her front against his back, the way she often laid before going to sleep. With a second baby, she was likely to be bigger than before, creating an escalating difficulty in doing many of the normal things in life. But Finch would be there, supporting and loving her, thrilled at the prospect of his child inside of her. That comfort brought tears to her eyes. She reached down, feeling for his lower back, running her finger along the surgical scar. His rehabilitation had been long and especially difficult. Finch made amazing progress despite all the pain and discomfort, never wavering in his determination to get well. The doctor kept saying Finch was ahead of schedule, must be because he had special motivation. Nichelle knew that she and Davie were that special motivation, and that she loved this man for many reasons, including his strength of purpose. It had taken her time to reorganize her earlier feelings, to know for sure that she was in love with him. He had known long before and patiently waited for her to recognize it.

Finch's mother was no different. The day the Finches came over to celebrate his first steps out of bed, his mother brought a small cake for the celebration. She walked into the kitchen where Nichelle was scooping out the ice cream. Nichelle recalled the conversation as if it had just happened.

His mother said, as she set the cake down, "My son's in love with you."

"What?" Nichelle said, startled.

"My son's in love with you. It is obvious."

She dismissed the comment. "I'm his caregiver. Happens all the time."

"It is more than that. A mother knows. Look at me."

Nichelle remembered being startled by Mrs. Finch's fierceness.

"He loves you here," she said, touching Nichelle's forehead. She moved her hand down to Nichelle's breastbone. "And here."

"I think you're mistaken. He hasn't said a word."

"That is his way. He worries if he says something too soon, you will reject him. Know your own feelings so that when he does tell you, you will have the answer."

Nichelle set the scoop down, unsure of what to say next. "Has he told you he's in love with me?"

His mother went on. "No, but a mother knows. You also have strong feelings for him. I can see it in your face. You are too kind to him not to."

Nichelle thought about pleasuring him that afternoon, wanting to reward him, wanting. . . She realized then that she *was* more than a caregiver. Much more.

"It will happen between you two, if God wills it," his mother said.

"I'm Black and he's white," Nichelle said, getting to the point. "Does that concern you?"

His mother waved her hand through the air. "We are all God's children. What matters is love, what you hold in your heart." She put her hand on the side of Nichelle's face. "Oh, to have such a kind, beautiful daughter. And your sweet boy as a new grandson. It would truly be a blessing."

Nichelle remembered covering Finch's mother's hand with hers. Then they embraced, her feeling unquestioned love and comfort in the older woman's arms.

"Come," his mother said, finally breaking away, all business now. She wiped away Nichelle's tears and gave her a kiss on the cheek. "We must go. The ice cream." Without further comment, she picked up the cake, along with plates and forks, and headed for Finch's bedroom. Nichelle followed with the brimming bowls.

She could still see the three of them sitting there at the card table, laughing, kidding Finch about his slow recovery, then celebrating how hard he had worked. She caught herself staring at him sitting up in the hospital bed with his silly party hat on, him laughing as she felt her feelings for him surge inside of her.

Nichelle disentangled herself from her husband and eased him over to his side. He didn't even wake up. She kissed his shoulder and said, "Goodnight, Daddy." She fixed her pillow, then rolled over and put her back against him. He shifted slightly, then was still.

If she asked him, Finch would tell her about that last conversation with David, what Jackie had threatened him with, and Finch's counter. But the new knowledge wouldn't alter the outcome. David, along with all of his troubles, was gone. Nothing could change that. With every question she asked Finch about David's secrets, the more lies and concealment she discovered, the more hurt she felt at not knowing the real David at all. She was ready for all of those revelations to end. For the first time, she realized she didn't really want to know what fiasco the last phone call concerned.

Nichelle's thoughts turned to how to let her husband know tomorrow that she was pregnant. Maybe she would tell him and Davie simultaneously, in the morning, when everyone was in bed. Or afterward, during their shower, holding his hand over her tummy. Maybe she should wrap up the pregnancy test and give it to him as a gift. Perhaps later in the day, when they often sat on the couch and read books, she would look up and say, casually, I almost forgot, you're going to be a father, then return to reading. Or maybe she would set an extra plate at the dinner table, saying that it was for the next member of their family.

Regardless of how she told Finchie, she knew how thrilled he was going to be, the gush of love and kisses, the concern immediately following, asking how she was feeling and what he could do for her. Her medical knowledge raised a healthy concern for the success of her pregnancy, but she felt that knowing was always better. They would discuss the pros and cons of her going back to work now, or if it made sense for her to stay home until after the baby came, what they needed to budget for the cost of the new arrival, where the money would come from. The funds that Finch recovered from Perry made the options easier to manage. Regardless of her ultimate choice, she knew she could count on her husband's full support.

Nichelle got so excited from the prospect of telling Finch about the baby that she couldn't go to sleep. Each scenario she replayed over in her head, making slight changes each time, imagining her husband's enthusiastic response. Sleep stayed away. She reached back, touching him again, an affirmation that wasn't necessary but wanted. She needed to settle down, get some rest, quit fretting, and take extra-good care of herself for the next nine months.

After over an hour of tossing in bed, she calmed down enough to doze off.

Nichelle dreamed of them all sitting on a blanket in the backyard on a late fall day, cool and cloudy with the prospect of rain later on. She helped the baby sit up while Davie went on about how cute it was. In her mind, it would be a girl, but maybe another boy, instead, would be best, giving Davie a little brother to help raise and torture at the same time. Or a little sister to spoil and torment. In her dream, she bent down to see the baby, but its face was indistinct. She asked Finch why she couldn't tell, and he told her she had to wait, be patient.

They laid back on the blanket, the baby between them, Nichelle's fingers intertwined with Finch's as they looked up at the sky for answers. The clouds just laughed at her. They're making fun of me now, she told Finch, her mouth cinched up in a pensive pout. No, they're only marveling at how silly people are. Don't worry, baby, he said, this will all work out. She rolled over on her side, put her hand gently on the baby's stomach, and gave it the slightest tickle. The baby cooed its appreciation and kicked its feet. Finch, watching the show, smiled and stroked Nichelle's arm in the loving way he always did, making her anxiety fade away. Yes, she thought to herself, I believe he's right. Everything will work out. Like you said, I just need to be patient.

The clouds laughed and smiled and spun tales of all the things they had seen and heard. Reforming with the wind, they headed off, away to see other silly people in far-off places, each of them different, but also all so similar.

ABOUT THE AUTHOR

Parman Reynolds has enjoyed a diverse career path, which includes working as a utility engineer, a consulting engineer, and a university instructor of finance and economics. His previous novel, *All For Summer*, was published in 2021. Mr Reynolds' outside interests include service on various volunteer boards and as a long-term supporter of the arts. He lives in Austin, Texas, along with his wife.

For more information, please visit:
parmanreynolds.com

NOTE FROM THE AUTHOR

Word-of-mouth is crucial for any author to succeed. If you enjoyed *The Boys*, please leave a review online—anywhere you are able. Even if it's just a sentence or two. It would make all the difference and would be very much appreciated.

Thanks!
Parman Reynolds

We hope you enjoyed reading this title from:

BLACK ❀ ROSE
writing™

www.blackrosewriting.com

Subscribe to our mailing list – *The Rosevine* – and receive **FREE** books, daily deals, and stay current with news about upcoming releases and our hottest authors.
Scan the QR code below to sign up.

Already a subscriber? Please accept a sincere thank you for being a fan of Black Rose Writing authors.

View other Black Rose Writing titles at www.blackrosewriting.com/books and use promo code **PRINT** to receive a **20% discount** when purchasing.

www.ingramcontent.com/pod-product-compliance
Lightning Source LLC
Chambersburg PA
CBHW010515100726
47903CB00009B/2754